THE
Pilgrims

TOR BOOKS BY WILL ELLIOTT

The Pilgrims
Shadow

THE Pilgrims

WILL ELLIOTT

TOR®

A Tom Doherty Associates Book

New York

THE PILGRIMS

Copyright © 2010 by Will Elliott

Map by Will Elliott

A Tor Book
Published by Tom Doherty Associates, LLC
175 Fifth Avenue
New York, NY 10010

www.tor-forge.com

Tor® is a registered trademark of Tom Doherty Associates, LLC.

The Library of Congress has cataloged the hardcover edition as follows:

Elliott, Will, 1979–
    The pilgrims / Will Elliott.—First U.S. edition.
        p. cm.
"A Tom Doherty Associates book."
ISBN 978-0-7653-3188-5 (hardcover)
ISBN 978-1-4299-4493-9 (e-book)
1. Slackers—Fiction.   2. London (England)—Fiction.   I. Title.
PR9619.4.E45 P54 2014
823'.92—dc23

                                            2013029756

ISBN 978-0-7653-8106-4 (trade paperback)

Tor books may be purchased for educational, business, or promotional use. For information on bulk purchases, please contact the Macmillan Corporate and Premium Sales Department at 1-800-221-7945, extension 5442, or write to specialmarkets@macmillan.com.

First published in Great Britain by Jo Fletcher Books, an imprint of Quercus

First U.S. Edition: March 2014
First Trade Paperback Edition: February 2015

Printed in the United States of America

0   9   8   7   6   5   4   3   2   1

For Christine

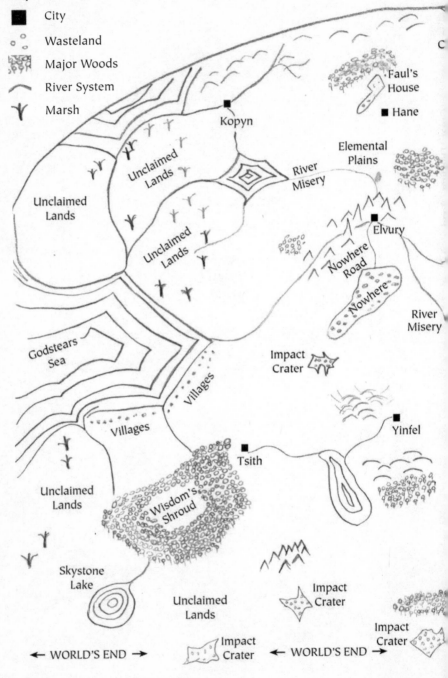

Levaal North

Key:

- ■ City
- ⚬ Wasteland
- ▦ Major Woods
- ∿ River System
- ⋎ Marsh

Kopyn

Faul's House

Hane

Elemental Plains

Unclaimed Lands

Unclaimed Lands

Unclaimed Lands

River Misery

Elvury

Nowhere Road

Nowhere

River Misery

Godstears Sea

Impact Crater

Villages

Villages

Yinfel

Unclaimed Lands

Tsith

Wisdom's Shroud

Skystone Lake

Unclaimed Lands

Impact Crater

← WORLD'S END →

Impact Crater

← WORLD'S END →

Impact Crater

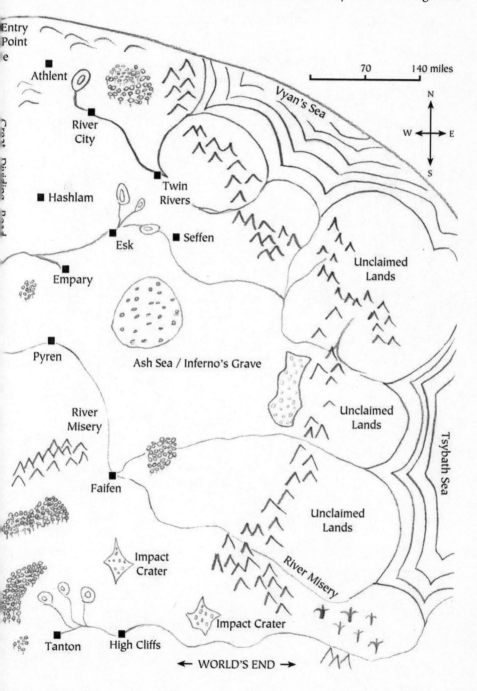

East/West: 945 miles across World's End.
North/South: 500 miles by Great Dividing Road.

Entry
Point
e

Athlent

Great Dividing Road

River
City

Hashlam

Twin
Rivers

Esk

Seffen

Empary

Vyan's Sea

70   140 miles

N
W ←→ E
S

Unclaimed
Lands

Pyren

Ash Sea / Inferno's Grave

River
Misery

Unclaimed
Lands

Faifen

Tsybath Sea

Unclaimed
Lands

Impact
Crater

River Misery

Impact Crater

Tanton   High Cliffs

← WORLD'S END →

Elvury City

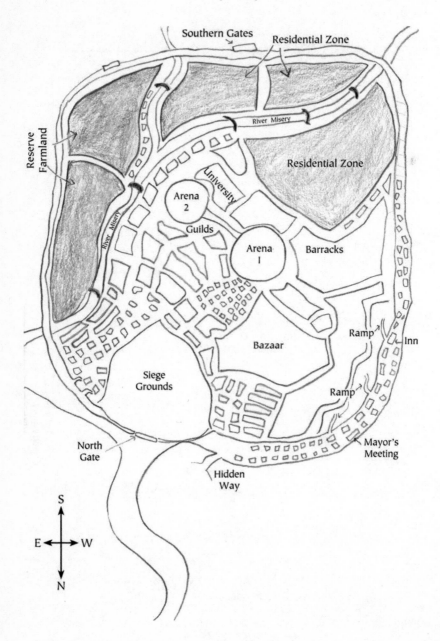

DRAMATIS PERSONAE

Eric Albright: a journalist who discovered the door
Stuart Casey, AKA Case: a homeless drunk

Mayors' Command:
Anfen: former First Captain of the castle's army
Doon: a half-giant in Anfen's band
Far Gaze: a powerful folk-magician
Faul: Doon's aunt
Kiown: one of Anfen's band
Loup: one of Anfen's band, also a folk-magician
Lalie: an Inferno cultist
Lut: Faul's husband
Sharfy: one of Anfen's band
Siel: one of Anfen's band, a low-level happenstance mage

Castle:
Aziel: Vous's daughter, imprisoned in the castle, heir to rule, in theory
Arch Mage: Vous's advisor, confidant, and overseer of 'the Project'
Ghost: a conglomerate of five personalities housed in Vous's mirror (and other glass surfaces)
Vous: the Aligned world's Friend and Lord

Council of Free Cities:
Erkairn: Spokesman of the Scattered Peoples
Ilgresi the Blind: Mayor of Elvury
Izven: Mayor of Yinfel
Liha: Mayor of Faifen
Ousan: Mayor of High Cliffs
Tauk the Strong: Mayor of Tanton
Wioutin: Advisor to the Mayor of Tsith

Gods/Great Spirits:
Nightmare: young god
Valour: young god
Wisdom: young god
Inferno: old god
Mountain: old god
Tempest: old god

Dragon-youth:
Ksyn: one of the eight major personalities
Vyin: one of the eight major personalities

1

The Arch Mage and four Strategists stand grim-faced and silent in the dark hall, watching. The most powerful men in the world, they are here, in the vast castle's innermost chambers, reduced to spectators. It is an ugly feeling. Vous, their Friend and Lord, stands on a small balcony with his back to them. Light shines from his rigid body in thin, shifting beams, which run over the walls like small searchlights, and over the watchers' skin with a touch that is icy cold.

The balcony is carved from blood-red stone and Vous's hands, tensely gripping its rail, look white as bone. Below him is a deep square room once used for lecturing apprentice magicians, though it is now for all intents and purposes a pit. In it a few hundred people crowd and jostle, peering up, trying to stay on their feet in the press of bodies. They are packed in tight. The stuffy ozone-scented air here is rife with strange magic, so most of them hardly remember being marched in by guards from the castle gates, where they'd trekked from starving cities to seek work. They were fed, ordered to bathe, then brought naked to this room where it was too dark to see the person next to them. The lights playing about the room's walls did nothing to relieve the darkness, and looked as though they shimmered on the surface of water, rather than on slabs of polished tile.

Now these lights fall on the people below, and a strange feeling comes over them, as though their being here, their jostling and shoving and trying to stay upright, are thrusts and heaves in a slightly sickening, yet potently sexual act between them and their Lord. Minutes ago, the door they had come through clanged noisily and inescapably shut.

It's a surprise, of course, to find Vous himself here above them, a figure almost of myth, seeming to have stepped out from the history books. Many gaze up at him with awe. Here is a being they are instructed to swear to, to pray to, as though he is a god. Some of them have heard old men in taverns curse his name with hot, angry tears, seldom daring to explain their grievances aloud. And now, well within a stone's throw, there he stands: someone who changed the world with the very same bone-white hands now resting on the balcony rail. With the very same voice soon to speak to them.

Though it's dark, Vous himself is well lit, his silk gown exposing one flank from hip to shoulder, his young-looking face frozen in glaring intensity. So slight and slender he seems to the Strategists standing behind his glowing body; but his short stature is totally warped now in the eyes of those below. They can see no higher than his balcony, for the chamber's tall ceiling is concealed in the gloom; but an occasional beam of light, sweeping high on the tile walls, hints at hidden shapes up there.

This 'speech' has the Arch Mage curious, the Strategists uneasy. They have acquiesced, of course; even though, while he is their Lord, Vous is not so much obeyed these days as *handled*. The Arch Mage alone does not look at him — he cannot. The many wards and charms about Vous's neck and on his fingers reduce him to a painful red blur in the Arch Mage's sight. Vous insists on wearing them, fearful of a magical attack which has never, in reality, been contemplated. But the Arch Mage *can* see the light playing about the hall, and feel its cold touch. He knows Vous is not a user of magic; he is rather a *force* of magic. Nor is he any longer wholly human, though he still looks it. It is a century's progress on display. When he will actually become a Great Spirit, no one knows. Years, another century, or days? Or — and the Arch Mage's heart quickens — this very hour?

'Friend and Lord,' Vous murmurs at last, seemingly to himself. 'Their Friend and Lord. I am their Friend and Lord.' His eyes clench shut. Some below are surprised to see tears run down his face. 'You have come,' he says to them, and says no more for nine long minutes. From above, the jostling hundreds are little more than the gleam of their eyes peering up.

At last Vous continues: 'You have come. You are here, as I willed. I, who brought you here, with but a few muttered instructions. You are here.'

Someone beneath coughs.

'You will think, perhaps, that you have angered me somehow.' Tears still flow down his cheeks, and his voice chokes up. 'You will perhaps think ... it is some quirk of the Project, some mistake. But you should know the truth. I do this to you ... *knowingly*. I do this to you with *foreknowledge*. I do this to you with, even this passing second, the power in my hand, easily, to stop it being done. And choosing, instead, to do it. Further, I do this to you, gaining no pleasure, but also with no real *purpose*, with nothing at all accomplished from the ... the deed. The deed to be done. To you.'

A murmur ripples through the room like a breeze, then others say, 'Shh, shh,' and the breeze is gone.

Their Friend and Lord's body shakes with grief and he clutches the rail like someone about to collapse. 'When I was a younger man,' he says, 'I had dreams filled with beautiful things, beautiful places. I had meant, one day, to capture this beauty, freeze it in time, so it could not die, so it lived forever against the natural pull of rot. Before that could be done, I had to wade through much pain, blood, war and murder, of which a sea still lies before me. And now, though I need not venture sideways, or backwards, or even pause in the drowning depths ... and though jewels and flowers are at last in reach like flotsam on the waves ... I *still* look onwards, bravely, towards that time of which I dreamed. Yet here, in *this* moment, I choose to craft something else. Something that is *not* beauty.'

More tears stream down his face and fall on those directly below the balcony, catching light which makes them look like gleaming gems. Above Vous's head a shape in the darkness moves, and another anxious murmur sweeps through those below. Their Friend and Lord raises a hand for quiet, and receives it. He begins to sing: '*Last sight, last sight. Last sound, last sound. My face, my voice. My face, my voice. Shadow, Shadow. You are, Shadow.*'

A scream erupts and is chorused by all those below as light suddenly blooms upwards and reveals the shapes on the ceiling. Malformed beastly faces are lined all across it: large, rust-coloured and reptilian, wide jaws open, with long sharp teeth. They seem at first little more than horrid decorations, sculptures perhaps or painted statues, too hideous to be real. Then the wide, flat eyes all open at once, and the mouths all gnash with a furious sound of clashing teeth: *clack, clickety-clack, clickety-clack* ...

Though he sings quietly, Vous's voice can somehow still be heard through all this, and through the panicking screams. '*Shadow, Shadow. Watch me, Shadow. Shadow, Shadow* ...'

One of the heads suddenly descends on a long, rubbery stretch of flesh, falling clumsily amongst the group. Whether it is a machine or actually alive is hard to tell. Its jaws slam shut. It pulls quickly back up to the ceiling with the others. A spray of blood flies in an arc from the lump dropping out of its mind-lessly snapping jaws.

Closer to the balcony, another of the snapping heads descends and bites, and the crowd tries to push away. Another drops heavily from the ceiling's middle. Then two at the sides fall at once. Steadily as thrown punches, the lethal jaws fall into the cringing, screaming mob; arms, heads, sometimes whole torsos drop from the retracting mouths and fall back into it. There is an impotent push for the door. Soon they are all wet with show-ering blood, slipping and stumbling over each other for a few more seconds of life.

The Arch Mage alone can see with clarity the strange ripples spiralling and building in the room from all the death in these unstable magic airs. It is not structured enough to be a prac-tised, deliberately created *spell*, as such, and that is truly alarming, for there yet seems a deliberate intent in the patterns at work. He also senses the direction towards which these ripples are already being drawn: back behind the castle, to the long high valley near the entry point to Otherworld. What this may imply fills him with terror, but he keeps it well cloaked and his voice calm. '*Some* measure of instability is a good thing, don't forget,' he says quietly. 'It means the Project is succeeding.' The Strategists do not reply.

It goes on for a long time. Vous sings, and weeps.

2

Eric did not believe in ghosts, and was therefore quite surprised to wake from a vivid nightmare — people were in a pit, being killed by he wasn't sure what — to find one standing in the middle of his bedroom. It seemed to be a man draped in white silk, to Eric's eye not unlike a Roman emperor. It flickered like an image cast by an old projector. A white glow filled the room about it.

For a few long seconds Eric and this stranger eyed each other. Then the ghost's arms rose as though to embrace him, its mouth opened, and words came out despite the lips not moving to form them. '*Last sight, last sound, last sight, last sound* ...' it sang in a voice thin and high-pitched: just about the most frightening sound Eric had ever heard.

He sat up, part of him as fascinated as the other part was afraid. 'What does that mean?' he said. 'Who are you?'

'Shadow, you are called,' the ghost said.

Eric rubbed his eyes and then the ghost wasn't there. There was only the shard of street light spearing through the window to fall on the *Captain America* comic book he'd spent three-quarters of an hour desperately trying to find earlier that night.

He flipped on the bedside lamp, grabbed the comic and had trouble reading it at first for the shaking of his hands. By morning, he'd actually managed to convince himself it was a dream. And just maybe it was.

3

Though it goes by another name there, the game of chess came into Levaal with one early group of human Pilgrims from Otherworld. They brought other things with them too — the way days and hours are measured, systems of numbers, measurements and more, all gladly adopted (for some reason) by the cities and temples. They brought seeds of plant and vegetable, which have grown here and thrived. Also species of bird and beast, including the very useful horses and dogs. Weapons too: bows and arrows, plate and chain mail, kinds of blades until then unknown here. And chess, chequers and backgammon, as well as other fine games.

The Arch Mage sits in his tower; light comes thinly through the high window and falls upon his half-melted face. Magic is not kind to those who use it, and it is hard to tell, looking at the Arch Mage, how gently he has been treated considering the vast amount of power that has gone through his ancient, ruined body. About his study are parchments on stands, with ink scrawled across them in writings nearly incomprehensible, even to him. These are composed spells in progress. Most are far too ambitious to ever be cast or attempted: a mere hobby, the way an alchemist might play with poisons. A homesick drake scratches about at the floor of its cage, the deep red shine completely gone from its scales, the flame dead in its throat as it waits to see what use its captor has for it, other than the pleasure of possessing such a rare creature — and the occasional extraction of its blood. There are jars filled with what appear to be smoky curls of coloured mist, which are rare power types found only here, in the castle's inner airs: purified and concentrated thus, they are priceless. If destruction were to come to this room, it would be these jars the Arch Mage would run to, out of all his charms and treasures, to clutch to his chest as he fled.

Not that he wouldn't mourn the loss of the old tomes lining the shelves in their hundreds. Possession of these books was once the cause of feuds and almost outright wars between the old schools of magic. Even the Arch Mage battles to comprehend some of the grave secrets written therein. He is occasionally saddened it was necessary to kill off the world's major magicians . . . it would be nice to ask their thoughts. Then again, it was nice to pluck each tome from the smashed safe or chest of its ruined temple.

The Arch Mage views through the window glass the world he knows: Levaal, which is his chess board. He beholds its pieces, many of which are still stubbornly arrayed against him. Other pieces move indifferently, ignoring the human opponents facing off, trampling as they like across the squares while all others duck aside, waiting for them to pass.

Many old, mighty pieces — the five schools of magic, the half-giants, and more — have long been knocked off the board, for they were great threats to the Project. Their removal was difficult, perhaps the Arch Mage's greatest accomplishment.

The Great Spirits are a different matter. *They* simply have limited interest in the games and affairs of humans, or so history claims. Which is not to say their presence doesn't make the Arch Mage nervous, and take up large portions of his thought;

the Project after all is about *creating* a Great Spirit from a man and perhaps, one day, facing off against the others. That will be a new game altogether.

Still, the Arch Mage has almost won the game in progress, the game of *human* rule and control. The six remaining Free Cities are his opponents, and they are in a very bad position — worse, it seems, than they themselves know. They do not yet know of Tormentors from beyond World's End, but they soon shall. In months, another of the Free Cities may well fall and become Aligned with the castle. The rest will follow. To speed the process up would be pleasing.

The drake gives up its scratching on the cage floor and falls asleep. With a sigh, the Arch Mage reflects on the day's events, and realises Vous no longer plays the same game as he does. No longer pondering moves by his side, now Vous is a piece *on* the board, a piece moving in its own directions, with no care where he, the Arch Mage, wishes to place it.

The Strategists, after today, have realised it too. What distresses them is not what happened to the peasants, of course; they themselves, like the Arch Mage, have given orders resulting in far more deaths than today's, and they shed no more tears for peasants than they would for culled livestock or felled trees. Rather, what disquiets is the fire of their Lord's personality spreading too wide, too quickly. Being close to it, they are perhaps right to worry.

The Arch Mage wonders how a more gentle, timid man would have fared in Vous's place at this stage of the Project. And he begins to wish he had such a man on the throne now.

In the far distance, he sees the spiralling, winding thread of disturbed magic going skywards like a wavy line drawn in pencil across the white sky, indicating a powerful spell has been cast that way. A war mage, most likely; he does not concern himself with it. More troubling to him is the speck flying towards the clouds, then gone. It is an Invia, surely off to visit the dragon-youth in their sky prisons. They are pieces on the board he doesn't know well.

Other Invia have lingered in the air behind the castle for some days now. What interests them here? A possibility disturbs his thoughts and demands to be examined, however unlikely: when people come through into Levaal from Otherworld, the entry point is behind the castle.

The thought is new, and troubling, and connects immediately with another: one of the Strategists claims that Vous was in that valley himself some days ago, walking with his head bowed, hands clasped behind his back. That Vous has left the upper floors at all, much less the castle, is very strange. And the Arch Mage has felt himself the pull from those strange rippling effects, like blind groping tentacles reaching for that spot, for the entry point . . .

Otherworld. People from that mysterious place are not wanted on the Arch Mage's board, where already there are too many free and mighty pieces beyond his hand. From the Hall of Windows he has glimpsed their world and what he has seen disturbs him. They command no traditional magic, it appears, but much machinery that *looks* magical. He has seen weaponry that left him sleepless for days with fear and desire. He has seen pillars of flame beneath enormous clouds shaped like mushrooms, and wondered if he were dreaming.

To open the gap between worlds is high, high magic; a human would not survive even a failed attempt at it. But Vous is not human any more. The Arch Mage pictures him lurking near the entry point in that high green valley. It is likely that Vous doesn't even *have* a reason for being there; he is under the influence of much more than his scattered human brain. The Arch Mage thinks: Not a user of magic, a *force* of magic, and his worry grows.

In chess, you cannot take your own pieces off the board, only invite your opponent to do so. *His* opponents — the Free Cities — have not wits or will left among them to take Vous away, and leave room for a new, more suitable replacement. The Arch Mage himself dares not try it. The only way it can be done is by Vous's own choosing.

The sky's lightstones begin to fade. The Arch Mage thinks long into the night, but just two things keep seizing his thoughts. He summons a war mage, sends it to guard the high valley behind the castle and orders it to kill everything that comes through, for *the entry point* is one thing his thoughts linger on. The other, about which he has less certainty, is the word 'shadow'.

4

The working day ahead loomed like one of three big unwelcome hills between Eric Albright and the weekend. The saving grace of the modern age was that it was socially acceptable to spend that weekend playing computer games in your underwear, inhaling pizza, with or without a sixpack open on the desk beside you, at age twenty-five and beyond. The extended adolescence, some called it. He called it therapy.

For now Eric played grown-up and dressed in business shirt, slacks, tie and polished black shoes. Following the career path of Clark Kent, he was a journalist for *NSx*, a 'cool' newspaper geared to twenty- to thirty-year-olds, distributed free throughout the city (and slowly going broke). That Eric had held his job so long was a mystery just recently and unpleasantly solved. He'd become aware that he was a sort of cult attraction for the paper's readers, as his fifty-word entries for lost dogs or the odd sports report and restaurant review (when a real food critic couldn't be found) were always far too emotional and involved. Fan mail had been sent to the editor, something they'd tried to keep hidden from him. It was both novel and deeply worrying: in the trade he'd staked his dreams on, writing, it was his inability, not his ability, that had kept him employed while heads rolled all around him.

It had not been deliberate: the people calling to report lost dogs had actually made him sad. He cringed with embarrassment, thinking back to what they'd published in his name: *Our dear friend Rexie, part Scottish Terrier, part cattle dog. Last seen Brickworks Ave. We're lost without your simple little joys. Furious wagging tail to welcome us home. Even the bad: barking, holes in the yard. Don't be afraid. You will chase your ball again. Help us! Rexie, come back.*

The fan mail described him as 'hilarious' and 'a trip'. How then were his novels going to fare? The printed pages were scattered across his bedroom floor where they'd been flung in despair. One was a murder mystery, with ghost story parts thrown in (the ghost did it). The others were about superheroes he'd invented. One was named Death Row, a former convict who'd escaped and seen the light, and now fought crime via magic powers resembling methods of execution: lethal injection, electric chair, hangman's rope, so on. Perhaps it was all uproariously funny . . .

He hesitated before locking the flat's front door behind him, very tempted to call in sick. How was he supposed to submit articles knowing they were being read by people trying not to laugh until he'd left the room? Worse, how was he supposed to be funny on *purpose*, now he knew that was what they wanted?

His polished shoes beat down on the old concrete regular as clockwork, *tap tap tap*, carrying him towards an air-conditioned room in a tall building in the city's inner peaks. More pleasant-looking than handsome, he was slim with straight blond hair falling in a cropped wave, bright eyes and a soft mouth with a slight overbite. Seeing himself stride across the glass of store windows, he did not think a stranger's eye would pick him out from the street's background of normality; but if it did, its owner would be unable to imagine him as anything other than *office worker*. Nor, to his horror, could *he*. He wore not a suit, but himself, and suddenly knew he could never take it off. If he slipped into a phone booth, he'd leave it buck naked, to jeers and pointing fingers.

He hadn't realised how badly this business at the paper had affected him. The very concrete underfoot seemed to slip and shake. It was as if he'd caught a mirror's reflection from an angle never seen before, and was now unable to look away.

The street dipped and curved. At its end was a bridge, with a bike path underneath running through a wide shadowy tunnel, opened like a yawning mouth. The bridge overhead clattered with the ungodly sound of a train, howling its way across with another load of Erics and Ms Erics, young and old, towards their own air-conditioned rooms in tall buildings, where, like the Eric passing below them, they did this or that with paper, computers, calculators, pens, phones, headsets, coffee cups, and all the rest. He fancied he saw their faces in the passing windows, each one identical to his own.

Beyond the bridge was a seedy old park you didn't want to walk through at night, where slept a seedy old drunk Eric occasionally played chess with.

Below the bridge the mostly brick wall was thick with colourful graffiti slapped on with deft skill, almost pleasing to the eye but not quite, thanks to the tangled black scrawl across it saying *MINE* in street code. In the part of the wall that seemed always to be in shadow, there was something Eric's peripheries sometimes caught on, something he felt (without ever really reflecting on it) to be an odd addition to the paintwork. It was a small red door made of little wooden planks. Black spray-painted tags had made their way like cracks across the boards.

What he hadn't noticed until now was that the wood was *real*. The door was real. Not a painting, as he had always assumed; no, someone had built it into the wall, or stuck it on somehow. Why?

The *tap tap tap* of his footsteps paused as he looked more closely. This red door — about the height of his shoulder and just a bit wider than him — had been so much part of the background that it was a bit of a jolt to see it right here before him now, despite its having been there all the while. It *had* been there the whole time, he assumed . . .

He reached out and flicked the wood with his fingernail, just to make sure his eyes had got it right. They had. It was . . . well, it was a door. It had a keyhole, and a small handle — more a copper groove for the fingers to fit under, to pull. An odd decoration for the wall, but surely nothing more; nothing on the other side but the old bricks of the train bridge, cool to the touch.

Surely nothing more . . .

So he kept walking, and could not later have said just what made him pause, turn and look back. But when he did, he sucked in a sharp breath and dropped his briefcase. It opened as it fell, spreading papers over his feet. His lunch orange rolled sideways along the ground into a puddle of filth. Just for a moment there'd been a glimpse of movement, a glimmer of light at the keyhole.

He crouched before the door, then shrieked and fell back. Looking back through the keyhole for just a second was an *eye*. That glimmer of light? It had been like daylight, when the owner of the eye shifted away.

Now the keyhole was as it had been before: dark, nothing but brick behind it. He scrambled back to his briefcase, hands shaking a little as he put it back together. The orange he left in the gutter. And, though shaken, he kept walking, and the day panned out just as he'd dreaded it would, till it was time to go home, and things — for good or ill — began to change.

*

'Here's young Eric Albright, late home from work.' Whoever spoke was lost in the shadows under the train bridge. The cleaners' vacuums had woken Eric at his desk around nine. The voice was of course familiar.

'Well, if it isn't Stuart Casey,' said Eric.

Casey, or Case, moved into that wedge of the path revealed by the street light. He might as well have stepped out of a costume shop having just dressed in its most convincingly generic-old-drunken-man garb: battered hat, fingerless gloves, ragged shirt and mismatched jacket and trousers sitting loosely. Case's unsteady footsteps sprayed little stones across the concrete path, indicating he'd put away at least one bottle since noon.

'You're looking well,' said Eric. Case laughed uproariously, and Eric joined in. They both knew he looked like shit.

'How're you looking, then?' said Case. 'Eh? Saw you this morning, checking out my wall. You dropped your briefcase all over the place. Something scared you pretty good, eh? What was it, a ghost? Maybe a naked woman with wings?'

'Naked woman with wings!' said Eric, pretending not to be unnerved by the mention of ghosts. 'Where'd you get that?'

'I seen one myself. No lie. She flew right through from under here, night before last. Pretty as a diamond, she was. Glittered like one too. I'd put a few away, but I saw her all right.' Eric was surprised by how straight-faced and earnest Case sounded. The old man sighed a long breath reeking of cask wine. 'How bout a game?' he said.

The cheap plastic chess board was already set up not far from the door. Eric had played him on maybe a dozen occasions, often when Case was too drunk to stand up, and had never once beaten the old guy. He had twice forced a draw, but that was all. 'Nah, not tonight.'

'Why not? Still scared of the wall? The door?'

Eric didn't like the glint in Case's eye. 'What about the door?' he said.

'You tell me,' said Case. 'What about it? What'd you see?'

'Why do you want to know?'

'Why don't you want to tell?'

This would go on for some time, Eric realised. He shrugged and kept on along the path.

'You think I'm joking about that woman, don't you?' Case called after him. 'Does this look like I'm joking?' He dug around in his pants and held up a black pistol.

'What the hell are you doing with that?' said Eric. 'Where'd you get it?'

'Never you mind where I got it. I'm here keeping watch. That door — something's going on, and you know it. You saw something. Well, so did I. I heard something too. It's making noises down here at night. Has done for a week or two.'

'Noises? Like what?'

'You tell me, I'll tell you.'

'Fine,' said Eric. 'An eye. OK? I thought I saw an eye at the keyhole.'

Case made a strangled noise. He staggered forwards and grabbed Eric's sleeve. 'You wait here with me tonight. OK? We'll stand guard, you and me. Something's gonna happen, I can feel it. It's your chance to see something no one else ever has, you bet. We'll keep watch. OK?'

This was possibly a very elaborate scheme via which a lonely old man hoped to garner a little companionship. It was so ambitious Eric almost felt duty-bound to oblige him, at least for half an hour or so. He sighed and crouched with his back to the graffiti-clad wall. 'Fine, let's play.'

And just as they finished their third game, and Eric began to say his goodbyes, white light bloomed into the tunnel of the train bridge, beaming through the keyhole of the door.

5

They ran, abandoning game and briefcase, out of the tunnel towards the park and dropped onto the footpath's smooth concrete. It was cold on their legs and arms. 'What's the plan?' Eric said.

'Just listen,' Case whispered. A sound came from the tunnel: *rick rick rick*, like long fingernails being drawn across old wood. It abruptly stopped, and the light dimmed to nothing. A cold breeze swept over them from the park, stirring up some litter on the nearby road. Case quietly laughed. 'Lots of secrets in the world, eh? Just when you thought you had the place figured out. Damn, but it's quiet around here too, isn't it? This little spot manages to shoo people away when it wants to act up. But you and me are here, aren't we? Why us, eh? What do we matter?'

'Um; you know, to me, it's kind of still just a train bridge. And that light — there has to be an explanation.'

Case laughed again. 'Bet there is. And you think there's an explanation for that woman too?'

'With the wings, Case?'

'You think I'm joking about her.' Case sounded affronted.

'No, man. I think you were whacked out of your head on some pretty good stuff.'

'Pfft. Wait and see. You might just — wait. Look, it's starting up again!'

A line of light threaded along the door's bottom edge, moving slowly up the left side first, then the right. Another point began to glow from the keyhole, beaming out like a searchlight. 'Quick, you get up the other end of the tunnel. And take this.' Case handed him the gun.

'Why am *I* taking this?' Eric said.

'Cos I'm too drunk to shoot straight.'

Shoot at what? Eric thought. Martians? But he took the gun and sprinted through the tunnel past the glowing door. Then he tripped over the chess board and briefcase and went down, pieces scattering across the path. His mobile phone and gun both clattered to the ground. He scrambled to get them, but then a human voice called out from behind the door. Empty-handed, he charged through to the far end of the tunnel and crouched there, panting. Smooth moves, man, he thought. Cool under pressure. Resourceful too. Batman you ain't.

For a time the tunnel's light dimmed till it had almost faded completely, when there was a loud bang. With a jolt and rattle of wooden boards, the door slammed open. Light flooded the tunnel like day pouring in. A gusty wind sprayed dust and pebbles across the ground, knocking chess pieces from the path and rolling them on the dirt.

He felt strangely, eerily calm as a shape appeared in the doorway. A face, a *human* face, he thought. It was a man of middle age, ugly and scarred, with coarse curly hair. Behind him there was a sky, dim, white instead of blue, with thin grey cloud crawling across it. The invader seemed to be climbing up as though from a stepladder below the door's other side. With a grunt, he was through, standing a little bow-legged, looking left and right up the tunnel, hands at his sides as though to draw a weapon, and indeed long knives were in sheaths on his belt. In the distance was a huge shape, sparkling bright as a gem. A tower? Some kind of building ...

But Eric had only a glimpse before another shape in the doorway obscured the sight. The man who had climbed through reached down and helped up a young woman wearing a grey cloak with a hood obscuring her face. Slung around her back was a longbow on one side, a quiver on the other. A long curved dagger was displayed, hanging from her belt. A third face appeared in the door. The other two helped up a man whose black leather covered his whole body to the neck. His red hair was piled up in a bizarre pointed cone. He was much taller than the others. He peered around the tunnel and laughed, perhaps in nervous excitement, high-pitched and penetrating. 'Hello, Otherworld!' he cried.

A fourth figure was at the door: a bald head, huge face, bulging white eyes. He peered around, looking startled, and tried to lunge forwards through the entrance, but the door frame was too narrow. An enormous meaty forearm, glistening with sweat, flopped through the door, the fat hand grasping for purchase. There was no way the huge man would fit; he was too big, even, to *be* a man. His efforts sent the redhead into gales of squealing laughter.

The first to come through shouted, 'Get back,' but the huge man in the doorway kept trying to squeeze in, eyes pleading with the others. The redhead laughed hysterically, raised a boot, and with it gently pushed the massive face back down. He slammed the door shut and peered around the tunnel with a grin. Light from the door's outline dimmed till it only just illuminated the invaders with flickering white. The noise of wind died down to a quiet that was startling, leaving the sound of the invaders' feet shuffling and scuffing on the concrete.

The redhead's insane laughter continued in more muted bursts. 'Now let's get busy,' he said.

The woman spotted the briefcase. She crouched before it, her long curved knife in hand, and poked it.

'What's that?' the redhead demanded, coming over.

'An object,' she replied. 'Though that is just a guess.'

The first man — who kept glancing up the tunnel towards Case's outline — grabbed the briefcase and shook it, listening.

'Careful . . .' said the woman.

'Just a box,' he said. 'Open it.'

With a touch that seemed delicate she drew the curved blade across the top of the briefcase, then spilled out its contents through the gash in the leather. The other picked up the mobile phone and looked uncomprehendingly at it. He fiddled with it until it switched on, glowing, then dropped it with a yelp.

The redhead's laughter screeched without shame. 'Don't play with magic, you silly man,' he said, and kicked the phone away.

The shorter man picked up the gun, sniffed it, and tossed it aside. He was more interested in Eric's newspaper and payslips. He gently put them in a little knapsack he held. 'They'll like that,' he said.

'Paper? Why'll they like paper?' said the redhead.

'Not the paper, fool. Otherworld *writing*. They love new languages. What's this?' He picked up what must have been one of Case's old bourbon bottles, and sniffed it. 'Strong smell. Think it held drink.' He closely examined the bourbon's label, stroked it, then put the bottle in his bag too. 'Let's go back. The mage won't be gone long.'

'We're not leaving yet,' said the redhead. 'Get more stuff. They'll close this off soon,' he gestured to the door.

'Not safe—'

'Too bad, you little sack of fright! This is a one-off. If they figure out how to shut it, this door will *not* open again. Plunder, bastard. Plunder.' He ran towards the newsagency and the other two followed.

'I'm not scared,' the shorter man said. 'Just smarter than you.'

'Then there's been some mistake. Because *I* am leading the raid!' He cackled like someone possessed as they ran right past Eric. The woman's steps were light and her gown rippled, the streetlight seeming to fall away from it like water. She threw back her hood and gaped with sheer amazement at the starry sky. The redhead turned on his heel at the street corner, surveying his surrounds. He saw Eric and jumped, startled, the cone of red hair swaying.

Eric swallowed, his heart beating hard. He wondered what to say and could only come up with: 'Hi.'

The other two spotted him. The shorter man immediately had two long knives drawn, with a little smoke running off the blades as though they were very cold. With very fast hands the woman had an arrow nocked in her bow and pointed at the ground ahead of her. She licked her lips.

The redhead held an arm up. 'Uh-ah! No you don't. You don't just kill people because they're from the other world. It's not his fault. He's going to *help* us. Aren't you?'

'Absolutely,' said Eric.

'Is this a tavern?'

'No, that's a newsagency.'

'Hmm!' The redhead spun about, examined the closed glass door, dark within. 'And what sort of thing is that? A store?'

'Yes. Can I ask something? How is it you speak English?'

'Speak what? Your tongue? We don't!'

'I ... see.'

'Now then. Is that wall made of glass?'

Eric nodded.

'Protected by a spell?' said the redhead.

'Far out, you're for real.'

'Hmmm?'

'No spell,' said Eric. 'Not to my knowledge.'

The redhead skipped closer to him, lowering his voice to confidential pitch. 'You'd *tell* me if it was, wouldn't you?'

'Sure! We have no spells here.'

'Oh? How odd. Your mages must be useless. And very bored. A final question. Are *you* the store master?'

'No time for this crap,' the shorter one snarled.

'Shoosh, you!' said the redhead. 'So, are you?'

'No,' said Eric. 'Help yourselves. And ... welcome, I guess!'

'Thanks!' The redhead bowed low then ran straight for the large sliding glass doors, the cone of red hair flopping behind him. Shoulder first, he threw himself into it. A big part of it shattered with a cacophony of falling shards. The other two ran in after him, stepping carefully over the broken pieces.

The noise of their rummaging through the dark newsagency seemed to carry a long way. They'd certainly have triggered a silent alarm, which Eric hoped couldn't be interpreted as a spell. Before long all three emerged with their arms full of blocks of printing paper, newspapers, pens, pencils, rulers, magazines. The redhead's forehead was cut, but he didn't seem to care about the blood sheening down his face.

'Was this junk worth the risks we took?' said the woman.

'Hush, you. I don't need two critics,' said the redhead. 'No one knew what we'd find. Could've been anything. We got something to trade the groundies, at least. But they're not getting this.' He tried to examine a *Penthouse*, in the process dropping a load of plundered stuff which clattered to the bitumen. Eyes glued on the unfolding pin-up, he didn't seem to notice. 'Wow,' he said.

A train passed over the bridge. All three of them screamed in alarm and scattered away from the tunnel entrance, dropping most of their wares.

'Wait, relax,' said Eric. 'It's not going to hurt you.'

'No spells, you fucking pirate!' roared the redhead, drawing a sword from his belt and charging up the embankment towards the tracks. The shorter man gaped as though dumbstruck by the huge metal demon. The female had an arrow nocked and pointed at Eric's heart, then evidently decided the train was the more immediate threat. Her shot sailed in a fast arc and skimmed off the metal panel with a flash of sparks. Then the train passed, receding towards the city.

'Just a train,' Eric said. 'Harmless.'

The shorter man nodded sagely as though he'd known that all along.

'Oh. How embarrassing,' said the redhead, sliding his sword back into its leather scabbard. While the other two picked up the goods littering the path, he pranced towards Eric. He crouched down low, peering at Eric's feet with a critical eye, and said, 'Mmm. I like your shoes. Now, bye bye.'

'Wait! Don't go yet,' said Eric. 'Spells! Can you guys really cast spells?'

But back into the tunnel they went. The door's outline was still faintly glowing. The shorter man kicked the wood twice. It bounced back open. They tossed their goods through, then leaped down one at a time, the woman last. The door swung gently shut behind them. The light outlining it faded to nothing. The tunnel was quiet again.

Case staggered towards him from the other end of the tunnel. 'They *spoke* to you,' he said in disbelief.

'Tell you all about it at my place.' Eric laughed. 'Did you see what they did to the newsagency? They stole *stationery*! Pens, paper, magazines!'

A police siren sounded, not far away. A trail of stationery led from the broken window right to their feet. 'Crap! Run.'

So they ran.

6

In the morning, it was the strangest thing to see a day unfolding through his bedroom window, normal as always. He watched the world outside for a while to assure himself it was really still there. Case was already awake and helping himself to various delicacies from the pantry. There were biscuit packets and empty herring tins, licked clean, scattered over the coffee table. 'Morning,' he said, offering Eric a cracker.

They went back to the bridge but found nothing more than footprints, which could have been anyone's, by the door. They searched fruitlessly for the arrow the woman had fired at the train.

Back at the flat, Case gave him a lesson in handling the gun. 'If you have to shoot it, hold it tight. Works better if you don't drop it in fright. Makes a hell of a racket, this thing, but shoots straight enough.'

'What make is it?'

'Glock. Nine shots left in that clip, ten in the other.'

That night they went back to the bridge, pausing on the way to get Case some liquor. Then they set up the chess board. 'I notice we're not enlisting any help with all this,' said Eric. 'Why not?'

Case took his first mouthful of bourbon. 'Don't know your reasons, but I kind of feel like it's my secret. I wanna talk to em, ask em some questions.'

'Like what?'

'Like, what the hell d'you want?'

'So, you're our planet's ambassador. Stuart Casey, of no fixed address.'

'Sure am. You're only here cos you're paying for the drinks.'

'Anything for my planet. Know any knock-knock jokes?'

'Nope. Rack em up again, if you're game.'

So they waited and the night crept by. Soon it had crept by completely, and nothing at all had happened other than the sun rising on a cold winter morning.

The next day, they came back; the next night, too. Not once did the door make a sound. There was no hint anything strange had ever happened. When a week had passed, Case and Eric both began to doubt their sanity, and the point of further vigil at the bridge. A few phone calls revealed, meanwhile, that Eric was no longer employed. One of his imitators had been given his own bi-weekly column, which they had named 'Whacked Out'.

Another week went by, and another. What had seemed the most unlikely thing of all soon occurred: life returned, more or less, to normal. Soon Eric found himself dressing up in a business shirt and tie, slacks and polished shoes, getting out of the flat early to go find a job. Case was asleep on the couch that cold Monday morning, snoring loud. It was getting a little weird hiding him in the bedroom when friends dropped around ...

Tap tap tap went his footsteps, his breath white puffs in the air. The bridge appeared around the bend. And there amongst the graffiti was the door, barely worth turning one's head to look at. 'You strange little decoration,' he said.

He'd meant to simply walk past like normal, but found he hadn't. He picked up a rock and threw it; it ricocheted off the wooden panels. 'Hey!' he yelled. 'Hey you! Knock knock.'

Nothing.

'You don't fool me, shithead.' He beat on the panels, then took a stick and poked it in the keyhole, jammed it through till it broke against the brick behind. He kicked the door the way the invaders had.

Nothing.

'So, now what?' Eric yelled into the keyhole. 'Hey! There's another *world* in there. I know it, all right? Why are you hiding?'

He kicked the door as hard as he could, and sent himself sprawling backwards onto the concrete path. He charged it with his shoulder. He pulled on the copper notch with all his weight, yanked it until he was panting and sweating. The wood creaked, but that was all.

A slow train rumbled overhead. Eric caught himself. His clothes were now dirty and ruffled. He was in no state for job-hunting. A customer exiting the newsagency stared at him, then hurried away, as though he were dangerous. 'Great,' he muttered, heading back home to change. 'Just great.'

Then a voice cried: 'Help!'

A woman's voice. He stopped; had he really heard it? The train's noise obscured it.

'Help!' From the door. It was real! He ran back, crouched before the red wooden panels and cupped his hands over the keyhole. 'Hello?'

'Help meeeeee ...'

'How?' Eric yelled. 'What do I do?'

'*Help* meeeee!'

'How?' Eric shouted through the keyhole. There was no answer. He beat the door with his fists, kicked the wall beside it. 'Hello? Is that the woman with the bow and arrow? I want to help you, but how?'

He dug his fingers in the copper groove above the keyhole and gave it a huge, desperate wrench, then fell on his backside, blinking stupidly at an ivory-white sky. Light poured through the open door into the train tunnel's shadows. The air was full of an electric humming sound and that whistling wind ...

Shaking, he got to his knees and peered through. It was as though he crouched on the ledge of an open window, metres above a grassy floor. Stretching out ahead was a wide lane of lush green cut into a sheer valley of smooth white stone. At the end, in the distance, was that tower he'd glimpsed before. He could see only part of it; the rest was obscured by the rise of the ground. It was far away, but still loomed huge. The stuff of storybooks. They have magic in there! Magic, real magic ...

'Help me, please!' Clearer now. Eric looked quickly around but didn't see her, though he saw someone lying down there, motionless in the grass. He swallowed, thought of Case. He grabbed the broken stick and frantically gouged at the dirt nearby:

Case I opened it went in

He glanced through the door, one last moment's doubt, but there was that ivory sky again, that beautiful ivory sky. Beautiful because it was different, it was there, it was *real*. The door swung, as though in a light breeze. Eric tried to think what else he should write, fearful it would slam shut for good.

May not be back

No time for more. Whoever had called for help had stopped calling. He took one deep breath, held his briefcase to his chest, and hesitated. This could be his last second on Earth, his last words spoken here. 'I'm Batman!' he cried. He rushed at the open door, then his feet caught and he tilted and flipped. He heard the sound of it slamming shut, right before the *crunch* of his own body hitting the ground on the other side, his back taking most of the impact, but his head getting a nice thump too. He saw stars and, for a moment, or an hour, or a day, knew nothing more.

Hours later, Case nervously headed out. It was approaching 9pm. Eric's note on the kitchen bench had said he'd be back no later than three in the afternoon.

Case had looked around for the gun before he set out. It had to be in Eric's new briefcase, stuffed into its holster, for they'd taken it to the door each time they kept watch there.

There was the park with its rustling grass, the bridge with the secrets it suddenly refused to share, its tunnel like a gaping toothless mouth. Funny how this place had become familiar enough for him to miss it, if he were to leave for good. 'Eric? You here?'

Cursed dark! He should've brought a torch. And a drink, come to mention it. How in hell had he forgotten to bring a drink? He laughed at himself. Well, it was a short walk back.

Nearly half an hour later he returned with the bottle of cheap scotch Eric had bought for him. The lid seal cracked, a nice sound, and he sniffed it, sipped it. *Ahhh* ... His eyes roamed from the door to the path, where he hoped to see the young man strolling by after another late night. He thought of sharking Eric in chess that first night, and chuckled to himself. He set the bottle down gently after another sip, and shone the torch light on the ground beside the bike path.

There were footprints near the door, in that reddish-looking dirt, but they could have been anyone's. And — just a moment — writing, right there, writing! It was addressed to him! Parts of the message had been covered by wind-blown dust, which he carefully wiped away. *Went in!* his mind screamed. He went in! What? *How?*

Case staggered back to the bottle, took a deep pull of the stuff to clear his head. You couldn't just *open* the door! Could you? He bit a knuckle, tucked the bottle into the crook of his elbow, grabbed the torch. He already knew what he was going to do. Or try, anyway. What the hell, I've lived long enough, he thought.

He dug his fingers into the door's copper groove and pulled. He leaned with what force he could, one foot planted on the wall, groaning with effort, until it felt like his shoulder was about to pop out. His startled cry rang through the tunnel as light wormed up the edges of the door as though in answer to his efforts. There was not a soul in sight at either end of the path to witness it. His own words came back to him: *Funny how this spot chases everyone away when it wants to act up* . . .

He gritted his teeth, breathed deep, and gave another big pull with shaking arms. The door opened and he fell on his backside, scrambled to his feet again, and looked inside. It was a fair way down, but the turf looked soft. Carefully holding the bottle, he shut his eyes and dropped. He landed with a grunt and not without pain, but at least, unlike Eric some hours before, his feet hit the ground first.

7

At first he knew only the dim ache of his fall. Thin light of either an ending or beginning day lit the blackness of his closed eyes. The soft, thick, shin-high grass made a comfortable bed to lie on. It smelled fresh and pleasant, bringing him childhood memories of afternoons at the park, when bad things like death and suffering were worlds away.

Everything came back slowly. His mind recounted the first wild dream, then the old drunk accosting him with cryptic words, then his feet catching as he went through the door.

Hold on a second: as he went through the door?

Of all the stupid, stupid, STUPID things I could've done . . .

There was nothing but air above him, nothing to indicate the door he'd fallen through. That ivory sky was a touch brighter now, he fancied, which made it morning. No moon, sun or stars could be seen, only cloud like threads of cotton being slowly pulled along. To the left was a sheerly cut wall of stone, with thin grooves and bands of colour weaving through strata of clean white rock. It was very tall, stretching up out of sight until its whiteness was lost against the sky's. A similar wall opposite was more or less parallel and together they fenced in a green valley that widened ahead over rising and falling ground. Behind him, the sheer walls curved around in a dead end. In

the distance was the tower that had held his eye so command-
ingly, but which, right now, lacked the same power. For there
were stranger things to see, much closer.

Other shapes lay in the grass, some nearby, some further away,
perhaps a dozen of them between the two valley walls. Like him,
they were bodies, and they lay still ... unlike him it seemed
they didn't have the option of moving again. Some were face-
down, some sprawled on their backs or sides. Some were just
dead; others were messily dead. The neat, groomed corpse at
Uncle Craig's funeral had not looked like this.

Eric got up on his elbows. He fumbled for the briefcase and
drew it closer, comforted by the feel of it pressed to his side,
its familiar clean leathery smell. Further away, he glimpsed glistening red on a shape in a large billowy dress. He shut his eyes,
shuddered, and angled himself away from it. The cries for help
echoed in his ears. Had it been her crying out? And he'd been
thinking Lancelot, maidens in distress, fairy tales as he leaped
in. His guts swirled, mouth dry. Quietly as he could, he retched
in the grass.

A flash of light, distant, over near the sheer rock face to the
right. It was like the sparkle of a small fireworks display, little
red beads of light blooming slowly through the air. A figure
crouched down in the sparks, too distant to make out other
than as an outline. Its head tilted back and a fearful cry swept
down the valley, echoing between the sheer rock walls, inhuman
and piercing. It stood, waved its arms and hopped in some prim-
itive dance. It seemed to shimmer, then vanished. A wave of
hot air rushed through the grass as it reappeared a good deal
closer, feet slamming down as though landing from a high drop.

What had looked like a helmet in the distance Eric saw now
were thick curved horns like a goat's, curling from the side of
its head down past its cheekbones. Its hair was a thick tangle

of shaggy ropes, as was the beard hanging heavy from its face. It wore a stiff, ugly gown made from something's skin woven into stiff square patches. Unnaturally long fingers clutched a thin notched staff with a diamond-shaped metal tip. Heat emanated from the creature, just perceptible from where Eric lay, some way behind it. Its feet were long claws like a bird's, but made with human flesh, and scuffed and kicked at the ground, slicing up patches of grass.

Its head swept left and right, though if it noticed the new shape in the grass clutching a briefcase, it gave no sign of it. In a very deep voice it muttered incomprehensible babble, then crouched down, not moving. Waiting. Seeming to listen for something.

Eric swallowed, lay motionless, hardly dared draw breath. His hand slowly, slowly worked its way around the front of his brief-case, to the clips that opened it. The gun. I *think* it's in there. Please, let it be in there ...

His hand found the latch buttons, but they'd make a sound if he pressed. What's more, if the gun was there, they hadn't kept it loaded — he'd need time for that, too. He wished the cursed apparition would leave, just go a little further away. But for a torturously long time it didn't budge, other than the slow sweeping movements of its head side to side, and soon he hated it more than he feared it.

Slowly, slowly, his other hand went to the briefcase's second button. A hissing noise came from the thing's throat. His blood froze; but it wasn't watching him, its head was tilted *up*. Above where it crouched, a thin line of light was being drawn in the air, horizontal, then vertical, forming a rectangle. It stood, hands shaking around the wooden staff, knuckles white, it gripped so hard.

Those lines of light — was that the inside of the door Eric

had come through? Is that what the door looked like from this side? If so, it was off to the right, too far away, he'd have thought, to be the same door he'd fallen from ...

A face suddenly appeared in mid-air, inside the rectangle lines. A young Asian man — Korean? — poked his head through the gap, mouth open with wonder. Another door, Eric thought. There must be others all over the world. But on this side, they all open here ...

The hissing sound was loud in the thing's throat now, rising with rage and threat. It stood, as again that horrible high-pitched scream shot out and echoed between the sheer valley walls. A call for help? A warning? The face in the door looked down, the young man too overcome with wonder to understand his danger. While the man-beast was distracted, Eric clicked open the briefcase.

The thing turned its head at the sound and looked directly at him, its mouth hanging loose. Its eyes gleamed like a cat's.

Oh shit. Oh shit ...

It turned back to the open door and made chopping motions with its staff, body convulsing like it was about to be sick. Then there was a *crack!* Something flew through the air: it looked like a shooting wave of heat, the kind that shimmers on a hot road. A sickening fleshy thud. The man fell from the gap in the sky, half his face pressed in and broken. He thumped to the ground and didn't move. The door in the sky swung shut and the outline of light began to fade back to empty space.

There it is, Eric thought, numb and despairing. There's the magic you wanted to see. There's the magic you threw your life away for. Pretty, huh? Was it worth it?

The thing crouched down, shoulders hunched over, sucking in deep breaths, its eyes closed. Little coils of white smoke trailed like ribbons from the tips of its horns, the ends of which were now black as charcoal, as though the spell it cast had burned them.

'I guess I'm next,' Eric said.

It regarded him with eyes that seemed an animal's. 'You're Shadow,' it rasped.

Eric heard: *your shadow*. 'I don't understand.'

'Your shadow,' it repeated. Its voice was so deep it could have been a machine's.

Eric looked down at his shadow, trying to understand. It was cast just faintly in a few different directions on the grass, in the fashion of being under stadium lights. He said, 'I don't know what you mean. But I'm not here to hurt you or fight you. I just . . . fell in. Didn't know it wasn't allowed. I'll go back. Gladly.' His hand went to the briefcase and quickly clicked open its other clip.

The creature cocked its head at his movements, raised a finger in warning. So ended his bid to get the gun. The little curls of smoke puffing skywards from its horns were thinning. 'Your shadow,' it said. It clutched at something in the air he couldn't see, as if trying to grab a thread of hair. 'Do you see? Lord's thought a groping hand, winding and reaching this way, a tendril broken off the swirling mass. Do you not . . . feel it? It is unsure of its *own designs*. Conflicts with Master's, perhaps stirs the pot of its own poison broth, but I shall not rebel.' The creature bared its broken teeth as though in the grip of inner turmoil. 'Two winds push here, I lean with the stronger. Depart now. Flee with haste, if flee you will. For his moods change.'

Eric, dismayed at its cryptic speech, tried to sift through for meaning. *Flee with haste* was all he could comprehend. Unless he knew better . . . 'Are you saying I'm free to go?'

The creature waved a stiff hand around at the corpses and

hissed like a snake. Eric took that for a very welcome *yes*. He grabbed his briefcase and ran, hardly daring to believe his luck.

Over his shoulder, he was sickened to see the creature stamping on the newly dead man, tearing up the corpse with its clawed feet. It crouched low to the ground, head down, and came up with blood on its chin. Eric had read horror novels and seen horror films in which all manner of gruesome death was served up as titillation. Yet now he froze. He literally felt a stiffening coldness spread through him and lock up his limbs as the creature's yellow eyes met his, for, even from a distance, he saw it was eating the body.

The tower. Eric sprinted for it as fast as he could, glanced over his shoulder once to see if the thing pursued. Not yet, but now it got slowly to its feet. It threw back its head and another high-pitched scream rent the air. From far away, there came either an echo or an answering cry.

'In here,' a coarse voice called. Below him, a face! A small gap in the grassy turf. A hand reaching out. Right away he knew that face. It was the invader who'd come through the door first that night. Eric threw himself flat, crawled head-first towards the man. Rough hands closed on his arms and pulled him into a darker space. His legs gave from under him and he sank gladly to the ground, sucking dusty air.

8

The Otherworlder caught his breath in gasping heaves. Encasing him were the smooth, cool walls of a dark cavern. Sharfy marvelled at the young man's luck on several counts, not least because he'd run just past the mouth of this groundman hole. Sharfy's charity would not have stretched as far as going above-ground to wave him over if he'd sprinted off at a different angle. Even from a distance he'd recognised the young man from their brief excursion through the entry point.

Anfen and the others would be intrigued to have an Otherworlder brought back alive ... what was the word Loup had used for them? Pilgrims. Whatever *that* meant. Them mages and their secrets and lore they didn't share, just cos they didn't think you'd understand it.

On tiptoe Sharfy observed the war mage, whose cries and rasps still echoed off the valley walls. How lucky of the young man to get past it. Suspiciously lucky. 'Do you even know what that was?' Sharfy asked him.

The young man shook his head.

'War mage,' said Sharfy, smiling. His smile was not pretty, he knew — he had a face full of scars and old pocks, a head like a bruised and dented apple. It invited people to recoil from him, to distrust him. No matter. If the young man was around long enough, he'd find Sharfy kept his word when he gave it. 'Don't have war mages in Otherworld, do you? No spells, you said. It should've killed you. Like it killed everything else that come through. Even a bird that flew in, it killed. It speak to you? They speak strange.'

The young man swallowed, still a little shaken. He was no warrior, that was certain. Too young for a magician, surely. 'It spoke,' he said. 'I didn't understand, but it told me to run.'

Sure, sure it did. He thinks I'll believe that, eh? Fine, I'll act like I do. But something happened, all right ... 'Stay there for now, get your breath. But no noise. There's stuff in these tunnels we don't want to hear us. Got it?'

'Sure. Thanks.'

'Don't thank me, thank your dumb luck,' said Sharfy. But he could not keep up the pretence. 'Come on, how'd you get past it? You carrying a charm?'

'No.'

'Sure about that? I won't steal it. You can tell me. I'm ugly but I keep my word.'

'No charm. We don't have spells, don't have charms.'

Sharfy scoffed. 'What *do* you have?'

'Newsagencies and dumb luck, I guess.' Eyeing off possible escape, the young man peered down where the tunnel curved off to the left, narrow at first but wider at the end. It was thinly lit by little glowing lightstones embedded in the walls, gleaming like pretty eyes. Then he jumped in alarm as an answering shriek to the war mage's call came from off towards the castle.

'Damn it,' Sharfy muttered, looking back through the tunnel's mouth. 'I'm not gonna get it now.'

'*Get* it?' The Otherworlder laughed grimly. 'Were you going to attack that thing?'

'Sure. It's about to cook itself. It casts a couple more spells, it'll almost melt. They don't get like this, mostly. One or two spells and the fight's over. But it's been busy out there. Most of the killing, it's had to do in the last hour. That's why it kept calling for a friend to come help it. Hear that sound? Knows it's in trouble. Great time to go out and cut its throat, while it's stumbling around, blind with heat.' Or let it cook itself, which it would do without a thought for its own life. Then go and take the staff from its harmless corpse. They were worth a fortune. Could cut off its horns too, sell them for a few scales each, or more. But the answering cry sounded again, closer . . .

The young man bent over and retched. Nothing came out but a string of saliva and some unpleasant noise. 'What's the matter?' said Sharfy.

'It was eating one of the bodies.'

'Eh! So?'

'*So* excuse me for mentioning it. Maybe it's what you guys do here instead of go get a hamburger, but I don't see that sort of thing very often.'

'Keep your voice down. If you think that's bad, things I seen would turn your hair white. They'll eat anything. Helps em cool off inside. Twigs, grass, seen em eat rocks.' The twigs and grass part was true enough; it was theoretically possible that a war mage *might* eat rocks, which to Sharfy was just as good as being true. 'Relax,' he said. 'Don't think about it.'

Some time passed in silence as Sharfy watched outside, though his ears were carefully tuned behind him for sudden movements (if the skinny young man thought he'd get the jump on *Sharfy*, he was making a big mistake). No more people fell through the gaps between worlds. And those two Invia up on the rock wall hadn't moved once. The newly arrived war mage came and sat beside the first. They seemed to hold a conversation made of clawing gestures and hopping dances.

'Can I ask something?' said the Otherworlder.

'You don't need permission to speak. I'm not your Lord.'

'Why is it you speak my language?'

Sharfy grinned. 'Ha! I don't. Something happens when you cross through. Loup told us it might happen but we didn't believe him. Nor would you, if you knew *him*.' Sharfy laughed very hard at this witticism and slapped his knee. 'You're still thinking in your own tongue, but speaking in ours. At least that's what it sounds like to me. Some words you say don't make sense, that's all. Like *hum burg uh*.'

'How does that work exactly?'

Sharfy didn't like questions he didn't have a good answer to. 'Something on the barrier between here and there, Loup says. Says there's a reason for it, but wouldn't say what. Dragon's will.' He waved the subject away irritably.

'Can you still speak English?'

This guy and his questions, jeez. Sharfy tapped his head. 'All gone. Unless I go back.' He scowled, thinking of the peculiar diamond-studded sky, and the howling metal demon rocking side to side as it careered past with living people in its belly. 'Which I *won't*. Didn't like the place.'

'You didn't see much of it. Try the seafood, next time.'

'Eh? No! Not going back. Why'd you come through anyway?'

The Otherworlder laughed. 'It's either a very long story or a very short one. Not sure which.' He was relaxed, off guard at last. Now was a good time to disarm him. Sharfy had his knife out quickly. The thin white smoke wafting from its enchantment felt cold. The young man backed against the wall but didn't reach for a weapon. 'Have to check,' said Sharfy, 'since I don't know you yet. Weapons?'

'No. I could've attacked you when your back was turned if that's what I wanted.'

'And your guts'd be spilled on the ground.'

The young man emptied his pockets. Sharfy went through his confusing leather pouch with great care, taking out some small pieces of paper and some metal coins, which he examined for some time with growing excitement. What would some of those Engineers in Tanton or Elvury pay for these? Or those rich snobby collectors at the Bazaar? Voice casual, he said, 'What city these from?'

'No city you've heard of.'

'Aw c'mon, just tell me.'

'Gotham City. Those are genuine Gotham City coins. Keep it all. It's not worth much.'

'Not to *you*.' He handed back the soft leather pouch, pocketing the coins and glad the young man's gift had spared him a moral dilemma: to rob or not to rob? It would've been a tough one. 'What about that box?' he said, pointing at the square leather case.

'Just a briefcase. Here.' The young man clicked it open. Sharfy excitedly rifled through it, grabbing out sheets of paper. 'That's my résumé. That's my bus schedule. Enjoy them. Rare and precious things, they are.'

Sharfy nodded agreement. 'Good for trade or for paying tolls. Groundmen love the strange writing. Those paper blocks we took, all blank. Quality, though. Would sell decent if we got it to a city, but Anfen said too much bag room to carry.'

'I could write on the printing paper, if that's valuable to you.'

'Too late, we used it for fire. What else you got here? What's this?' He held a cold metal object, encased in what almost seemed a small leather scabbard with shoulder straps. He'd seen one of these when they'd gone through the entry point.

The Otherworlder hesitated. 'It's nothing. All these boxes have them.'

'I knew *that*. But what's it do? Weapon?'

'I'll show you . . .' The young man held a hand out for it.

Watchful, Sharfy gave it back, with faith enough in his enchanted knives and the speed in his arm, if it came to that.

'It makes light,' said the young man. 'But this one's broken. It's a cheap one. See?' He pulled the trigger: *click, click*. 'Light's supposed to come out of this end. Must have been the fall that broke it.'

'Won't matter,' said Sharfy, mollified. '*I* know these tunnels. Better than anyone.'

'Still, maybe I can find someone to fix it. Do you want to keep it, or should I?'

'Not much room in my pockets,' Sharfy grunted. 'You take it. And these?' Sharfy held up two smooth black objects that felt cool in his hand.

'Those are computer parts, called clips . . .'

'What's a . . . *com pu hor*?'

'It's . . . well, a device for computing, I guess. Working out numbers, that sort of thing. Kind of difficult to explain. Mind if I hang on to them?' But Sharfy smelled something up . . . perhaps *these* were the Otherworlder's weapons. He hadn't got past that war mage from the goodness of its heart, after all . . .

Sharfy pocketed the 'clips' and noted the Otherworlder's jaw clench with frustration. 'Your name?'

'Eric.'

'Sharfy. Not my name, but 'swhat they call me. Let's get out of here. I'm not waiting for both those mages to cook. Enough death and killing. Turns my guts.'

Eric groaned. 'Shit! Case might come through there. I left him a message by the door.'

'A friend? He might be all right. *You* got through.'

'I can't risk it. What can we do?'

'*We* do nothing,' Sharfy said. 'I took enough risk with you down here. It probably saw where you went.' This was a new and startling thought. 'We have to move! Get up.' The Otherworlder began to protest until the knife reappeared in his hand.

9

Some hours later, as Case dropped, he glimpsed that there were other people lying in the grass nearby, but that was all. It wasn't until he'd landed on his backside and rolled a little way, stood up painfully and dusted off the black slacks Eric had loaned him, that it seemed strange to him so many people would be asleep out here in the open. The truth wasn't long in coming.

He set his hat back in place and looked around the field of corpses, spread between the sheer white cliff faces. In some spots five or six were piled in groups. Elsewhere they lay more sparsely, as though some had made a run for it before being killed. 'Eric?' he called. Silence answered him. Not a body stirred, only a breeze swept through the grass.

Was there a point in being sad? Their lives weren't so important in the grand scheme. The young man wouldn't be bothered by anything, now. He'd never hurt or be lonely again, that was certain. Soon Case would be in the same boat, and they'd be on the other side of yet another door, maybe in a better place altogether.

But looking among the corpses he couldn't see Eric's, unless something had killed him so badly there wasn't anything left to recognise. No point being sad, perhaps, but tears welled up in his eyes anyway. He called his friend's name again before taking a long, careless pull of the scotch.

A rasping, guttural sound from behind, to the right. He turned.

The war mage squatted down, its staff across its knees. Its horns were now almost entirely black and thick smoke poured from them. Its face was covered in what looked like soot. Smoke also puffed from its thick tangled beard. Only its eyes, yellow and gleaming, could be seen clearly through the mess. It rasped, muttered and babbled, pointing a long crooked finger at Case.

Case knew he was looking at death, maybe Death himself, right here in the skin and bones. Did everyone who was about to die see this same scorched face? Did the fellow Case had shot, all those years ago, see it too? Somehow, before Case had seen it, it had been a lot more frightening. What could it do now but put him to sleep, into a state where nothing mattered?

Strange, though, that it seemed to be trying to talk to him. 'Can't follow you, friend,' Case answered it.

It listened, head cocked like a bird's, then babbled some more. What a horrible voice, unnatural as a robot's. Only one or two words stood out, the rest was like an animal growling. Case looked where the man-beast pointed. There was another just like it, lying dead as all the other bodies. It was charred to a crisp — two curved horns were charcoal. The lower half, where its legs were supposed to be, was a pile of ash being slowly scattered in the light breeze. Smoke drifted off it gently.

Case turned back to the one still living. 'You won a fight, that's what you're telling me? With something as foul-looking as you? You're a pretty mean customer. But why'd you have to kill my friend?' With those words, Case was startled to find anger boiling over in him, sudden and powerful. 'Huh?' he yelled, 'Why'd you kill my friend? Ugly bastard!'

The thing gibbered, grunted. It sounded like its breathing was difficult.

'You going to keep making noises like a dog? Speak up! Tell me what you done to him!' Case threw the bottle of scotch. It spun end over end, falling well short of the war mage and landing in the soft grass. Any regrets? Case thought to himself. Yes, one ...

The war mage didn't react, as though it were too sick to care. 'You. I've a question,' it said, voice deep and rasping. 'Tell me of a large beast in your world. The beast's name.'

That Case understood it perfectly was a shock that left him off balance, as though an animal had stood on hind legs and spoken. He swallowed. 'A beast?'

'The name of a large, mighty beast,' it said. 'An animal. I've a question. I expect myself to answer. Yet I wish to be under-stood.'

Case recovered a little from his shock. 'Death wants to chat, eh? Elephant, then. Elephant's a big animal. You mind if I go pick up that bottle? I could use another taste before you get me.'

The yellow gleaming eyes sparkled. 'My question. An elephant runs through a wall of stone, and makes a house collapse. An elephant beats to the ground a castle old as Time. An elephant slays a mighty elephant, exactly big as it is itself. It is tall as the sky, feet big as mountains. But what can it *not* do?'

'I don't know,' said Case, tears brimming in his eyes. How he hated that voice, which made him feel so small and weak. 'I don't know. I just want a drink.'

'Insects crawl behind its ear. They give it a frightful itch. They near drive it mad. It cannot kill the insects behind its ear. That is what it cannot do.' The war mage laughed, a sound like rustling leaves.

Case nodded. 'Thanks. Thanks a whole freaking lot. Now can I get that bottle?'

It looked at him, sickened and exhausted, almost dead itself, if Case judged right. The scotch lay in the grass a little way before it. He headed for it slowly, palms open to show he meant no harm. He just wanted a drink, a goddamn drink, more than he ever had.

'It now needs other insects. To do the killing *for* it,' the war mage said, its eyes following Case's movements closely. 'But what of when the killing's done? Are they to kill themselves? Or do they *nest*?'

'You're nuts. But if you let me get that bottle, I'd really appreciate it.'

It hissed a warning as he took another step closer.

'You go ahead and kill me,' said Case, anger rising in him again. 'Just like you killed all these other poor people. But I'm going to get that bottle.' He jogged right over, leaned down and grabbed the bottle by the neck. He was within spitting distance of the thing now, near enough to get the foul stink of burned hair and its own flesh cooking in heat Case could feel. It showed its teeth as a dog would, a growl loud in its throat.

Case backed away quickly, hands shaking as he undid the bottle's lid, took a swig and allowed himself to close his eyes, here, on the brink of death, and savour the scotch. 'Now, you seem busy,' he said, buoyed, 'and I have to find my friend. I'm gonna take a punt and guess he's not dead here with these poor souls. So I'm gonna leave you to it. So long.' Case tipped his hat and began to walk away.

The war mage had seemed undecided, but now it stood, shoulders hunched like someone frail and sick, murmuring words too low to hear. Its arms were stiff, its skin scorched and cracking as its staff made chopping motions in the air. Case felt heat rising.

'You some kind of wizard?' he called. He spread his arms, offering himself as a target. 'Go on ahead, put on a show, let's see what you got.'

The thing pointed a long claw-tipped finger at him, swayed, then hunched forwards, a strangled painful cry in its throat. Such a pitiful sound compared with its rasping deathly voice. Hot air rippled outwards from it, and the space around it shimmered, but then its staff fell sideways in the grass, and its stiff gown of skin was swarmed in worming flames. It fell to its knees, slumped sideways and lay still, burning like a campfire.

'Some wizard,' Case said, laughing. 'I could've done that with a box of matches. What's your next trick? Encore!' He took a long pull from the bottle and whooped. 'Still alive!' he yelled. 'Let's see what else you folks've got around here, besides dead people and wizards dumb as a box of hammers. Eric, you here? Eric?'

10

They'd walked for about a minute but the cries of the war mages could still be faintly heard. 'Step quieter,' said Sharfy. 'Your shoes are loud.'

'Surely they can't hear us from here.'

'Groundmen will. Their tunnels, all these secret ones are. Castle don't even know em yet. We're trespassing right now. You are, anyway. I paid a toll.' Sharfy's voice became thoughtful. 'Other things might hear, too. Never really know what might be down here.'

Bright little points embedded inches deep in the rock sparkled all around them, giving the air a ghostly light. The coins jingled in Sharfy's pockets with each step and Eric felt the frost from his knife when it got close. He was entirely conscious of that smoking sheath of metal every step they took. 'Here's an idea,' he said. 'You could tell me where we're headed. That way it might feel a little less like I'm walking to a shallow grave somewhere.'

'I won't kill you,' said Sharfy, sounding surprised. 'If the castle wants your kind dead, means the Mayors will want you alive. Why's not for me to say. But if you come at me I'll cut some of your guts out.' He laughed. 'That was a joke.'

'Nice one.'

At first, Eric kept an eye out for the chance to catch him off guard, maybe drive an elbow into his jaw, take the clips, load the gun ... But this was not a comic book: action would not happen in still frames, and he was well aware a man with as many scars and dents as Sharfy would know a thing or two about fighting.

In a stretch where the lightstones were dim and sparse, they came to a large round opening in the rock wall. Sharfy paused to examine it, troubled. A horrible and very strange smell wafted from it, conjuring sickly colours in the mind. 'This is new,' Sharfy whispered, nervously tapping the opening's edge with his knife. There was, just faintly, a distant creaking sound, perhaps in response. Sharfy peered in, but it was pitch black, with no lightstones in the gloom ahead, no way to know if the tunnel led straight, up or down. 'Something bad in there. Don't know what. Keep real quiet for a while. Take those shoes off.'

They walked on through passages that mostly descended, the downwards plunge sometimes so steep they had to slide several metres on their backsides. Once in a while a draught swept through, cold and stale, and vibrations from the surface could be felt now and then when touching the walls. The caverns seldom opened up enough to ease the sense of claustrophobia but for a few places where, without warning, to either side would appear a sheer drop down into absolute nothingness for just a few paces, before the walls closed in on the path again.

Eric tried not to worry about Case. He noticed Sharfy had put away his knife. Sharfy saw him noticing. 'Groundmen see me armed, they might spring traps, no warning. Never know if they're watching or not. I'm good hand to hand, so don't try it.'

'I had the feeling you'd be good hand to hand.'

'Very good!' said Sharfy, pleased. Indeed ... their conversation had revealed that Sharfy was good at many things, and that what he wasn't good at, wasn't really worth doing. He hesitated a moment, then said, 'Should've been there when those third-rank spearmen tried me.'

'Do tell.'

So Sharfy did just that for several minutes. 'I was at a pub in Yinfel, drunker than pissed ale. Six of the bastards came up to me at closing time ...' In Sharfy's tale, he was wrongfully slighted but laid waste to many foes.

'Pretty impressive,' Eric said when it was finally done.

'That was nothing. Should've seen the time in Esk ...' There followed a story in which Sharfy left a trail of carnage over many deserving wrongdoers. There were pauses to demonstrate some combat manoeuvres, one of which nearly broke Eric's wrist. 'It's where I got this scar,' said Sharfy, pointing at something on the back of his neck. 'You tell one.'

'Why not?' Which edition, which edition ...? 'So, it was a dark and stormy night in Gotham City. I had finished repairing the damage to my Batmobile when Robin — my associate — brought grim news ...' Before long, Sharfy was a fan of *Batman* comics, and almost as enthusiastic about Eric's stories as his own.

In some tunnels, the plain white lightstones gave way to mosaics of vivid glittering colour, filling the space around them with shafts of light probing the gloom like angelic fingers. The coloured stones themselves did not form clear pictures, but on the walls opposite, light beams cast from them projected shimmering visions almost clear as portraits, more beautiful than any work of paint. Though he'd complained at their slow pace, Sharfy paused to examine any of these they came across. 'Groundmen art,' he said with a hint of contempt.

The shimmering picture showed what seemed a gang of giants,

whips and swords in hand, terrorising small people who were labouring in chains. There was even blood on the giants' swords, which, with a slight flickering of the red light, seemed to drip and flow. Sharfy laughed. 'Those big mean people, guess who that is? You and me. The small people in chains is *them*. That's what they think of us.'

Staring at the picture, at the profound sadness on the small people's faces, Eric could not help sharing the artwork's sentiment. 'Back in Otherworld, we don't oppress ground-dwelling creatures,' he said. 'That is not our way. Did you guys actually enslave them?'

'Not me! Someone must've, somewhere back. The castle still does. But they make slaves out of anyone.'

'I'm detecting a pattern here. If something bad happens, the castle did it. Which means people who live there, I assume. Not the actual building.'

'It's them all right. Always them.' Sharfy's voice became thoughtful again; he sounded a different man when he spoke this way. 'Each person's a blade of grass, to them. Trample on whichever they need to, grow some when and where it suits. And not with love or care even then. No matter when some has to be cut or the turf left bare. No matter at all.'

'Don't worry. I'll fix it.'

Sharfy looked at him. 'Eh? How?'

'I know how these things work. Someone from my world comes into another, they end up a hero of great renown. Well, that's me, apparently. Someone here's going to teach me magic, you're going to teach me how to use a sword, and I'll be the greatest hero you people ever had. I know the script, man. Believe me. I'm Batman. Did I tell you?'

Sharfy looked lost for a reply. He shrugged. 'Good, then. That's good.'

'You got it,' Eric muttered, suddenly buoyed to realise he meant it. 'I'm fucking Batman.'

Batman was, however, tiring of this stroll in the dark. Every so often Sharfy paused to examine the cavern's roof, running a finger over little crisscrossed scratches in the rock. 'We're right under the castle,' he said. He pointed at a squiggly line, no different to Eric's eye from all the other squiggly lines they'd stopped to read. 'Can almost feel it up there, eh? All that weight pressing down. All them high-ups, right up there.' Sharfy shook his head in wonder. 'If you could go far enough straight up, you'd be face to face with Vous. Face to face.'

'How much longer are we going to walk? I may be a hero, but I'm a bit out of shape.'

'Break now,' said Sharfy. He took from his pocket a strip of dried meat, cut off a piece and tossed it to Eric. It was so stiff his teeth could hardly bend it till it had soaked in his mouth for a while. His head buzzed lightly with good cheer and the muscles in his legs suddenly craved work.

'They feed you that in the army,' said Sharfy, wrapping the rest in some kind of leaf and pocketing it. 'Keep you going a long time, one little cut. It's good stuff. Too much though, you drop dead on the spot. Heart just quits. Seen it many a time.'

Sharfy stood, stretching his arms, then frowned at something on the left wall. He bent close to examine it, again looking troubled. 'Look. See these?' There were gouge marks in the rock, deeper than the marks he'd claimed were writing of some kind. 'Pit devils have been here. Not long ago.'

'I take it that's bad. But how can you tell they're recent tracks?'

'Here.' There was a little powdered rock on his fingertips. 'Means they're new. Claws gouge right into the stone. Think what they'd do to *us*.'

'It's pretty soft stone ...'

'We got pretty soft bodies.' Sharfy looked back the way they'd come. In both directions they had a long view of the tunnel's gradual slope, and were suddenly aware of all the peculiar little noises that had been background until now — *tap ... grind ... scrape, tap* — all so quiet it was possible to think the ear had been tricked into hearing something not really there. Their whispering voices now seemed very loud.

'Are you trying to freak me out here, Sharfy?'

Sharfy shook his head. He nervously eyed the path ahead and behind them. 'We have to move.' There was a muffled noise close by, not at first easily recognisable as speech. Sharfy grabbed him and signalled *shh!* so frantically he looked like a distressed chimp. The sound came close enough that whatever made it could only be on the other side of the wall. Nor could the wall be very thick, for even the shuffle of passing feet could be heard through it. Soon it faded. 'They're gone,' whispered Sharfy. 'But stay quiet. I'm allowed here, paid a toll. You didn't.'

He examined the scratched markings on the roof. 'Left way's quicker,' he muttered, 'but goes across the grain route. If a shipment's in, guards'll see us. We don't want that.'

At that moment something bounded out of the left tunnel. It was tall, long-limbed, and made a horrible shrieking noise. Its face was red-skinned, and it had two thin spiked horns through its crown. A flapping large jaw hung loose, lined with knots of sharp bone.

Sharfy screamed and fell backwards, hitting his shoulder on the rock wall. His hands fumbled for the knives at his belt, but he was so startled he struggled to free them. The monster didn't bear down on him; it stood there with its arms raised — its human arms — and kept screeching at him, until its screeches dissolved into laughter. Unmistakeable laughter, which Eric had last heard when the invaders came through the door under the bridge. The beast had a cone of red hair.

The redhead took off the mask and gasped for breath. Sharfy's eyes widened in rage. He got one of his curved knives free and lunged with a snarl, pinning the redhead by the throat with one forearm, the knife drawn back to strike.

'No no no no,' the redhead gasped, desperately trying to stop laughing, palms up. 'Wait, wait, mighty warrior, wait . . .'

Sharfy sputtered, lost for words, then pushed him hard into the wall and turned away. Tears streamed down the redhead's face. He curled on the cavern floor helplessly laughing, long after the joke would've ceased to amuse any normal person. He seemed to see Eric for the first time. Some of the cheer drained out of him. 'Oh . . .' he said, standing again. He looked Eric up and down, fascinated. 'It's the chap from Otherworld, from near the paper store! He got through!' The redhead crouched low. 'Different shoes? The last ones were white.'

'Yes. Well, these are socks. Here.' Eric opened the briefcase and held his polished black shoes up for the redhead's inspection.

He examined them from several angles, put a hand inside each, then gave them back. 'I like those, too. Not *as* much. But, pretty good!' He turned to Sharfy. 'Calmed down? Good. They sent me to find you. Anfen and the rest got chased to the surface! There was a miscommunication. We said "buy", the groundmen heard "rent". Or they just changed their minds. Either way, they wanted more rent. There shall be no underground base of operations below the castle. We have wasted three weeks.'

'We agreed a price, gave what they asked,' said Sharfy.

'Mmmm. I am very much with you on this. Not very nice *at all*. Now what's with our new friend?'

Sharfy explained what had happened, though according to

his recollection, there'd been four or five war mages, and he had bravely run out in the open and dragged Eric down the tunnel, right as a deadly spell blasted their way. He seemed to earnestly believe it. 'Saw a couple of Invia too,' he added, voice lowered. 'Up high on the cliff face. Just watching.'

'Wait, wait. War mages sent to guard the door,' said the redhead, rubbing his chin. 'Sharfy said five, so I'm guessing one, *maybe* two. They let one Otherworlder through, but killed a whole lot of others. Is that much true, or is it a Sharfy special?'

'It's true,' said Eric. 'It told me to run, so I ran.'

The redhead looked dubiously at them both, but shrugged. 'And the Invia just watched it all? All the poor helpless Otherworlders getting slain, not a bat of their wings?'

'Just watched,' said Sharfy.

'I'm not sure what he means by Invia,' said Eric. 'If there was something else there, I didn't see it.'

The newcomer nodded, his cone of hair swaying. 'Mmmm. And just because Sharfy saw it, doesn't mean it was *there*. Anyway, I believe you about the pit devils. Their tracks are all over the place. Most odd, and we just may bump into some. It is why I wore this. But I only brought two.' He held up the mask he'd worn by its horns. 'They aren't bright critters. Wear one of their skinned faces stuck to some hide, and some scent, and you can walk right past them, I'm told.'

'You've never actually tried this?' said Eric.

'Of course not. Far too risky. Even if they think you're one of them, they still often enough attack *each other*.' He leaned close and whispered: 'There's an *excellent* chance we're going to be mauled. *To death*.'

They let Sharfy take the lead. The redhead introduced himself as Kiown. He looked Eric up and down as they went, quizzing him about his garments. The tie in particular fascinated him. 'Just a decoration,' Eric explained. 'You wear it on formal occasions.'

'Mmm! Are you nobility, back there?'

He was about to deny it, but then ... what if such an illusion was useful? 'Well, yes,' he said, affecting slight embarrassment. 'Not a king or a prince, but connected to the ruling family, you could say. It's nothing, really.' Kiown whistled, impressed, his imagination clearly filling in many blanks. 'Here.' Eric undid the tie's knot, slid it free, then handed it over. Kiown held it, stroked it, then gave it back. 'No, you keep it.'

'Really?' Delighted, Kiown experimentally draped it over his shoulder, then wrapped it around his wrist. 'Can it be worn like this?'

'Sure.' Eric reflected he wouldn't need a tie for a while. Maybe never again. And how did he feel about that? Not too bad, whatever the dangers ... not too bad.

11

From her perch on the sheer cliff's face, the Invia watched the green valley, here at the world's highest and northernmost point. She had done so since the doors began to open, her sister on the cliff face opposite. They had watched the castle's Lord walk through here too, and seen what he had done. Opening the gap between worlds had *looked* like an accident ... if so, it was an accident the Invia had seen coming. The dragons had predicted it, down to the very hour and, as a rare treat, shared their knowledge.

It took a moment for recognition of the old man to dawn: on her brief excursion to Otherworld she'd seen him for just a moment, she was sure, lying under the bridge asleep and knowing no more of her than the passing wind as she flew by, invisible. She had barely picked him out from the background of that strange, strange place, with its air so stale, foul-smelling and empty of power, its sights and sounds so alien, and its incredible big ball of fire in the sky.

Old but sturdy enough, he seemed, though his footsteps were unsteady. Not lacking in courage, unless he was just too stupid to understand the risk he'd taken, approaching a war mage, even one on the brink of its own death. About the old man, the aura light was an unhealthy smoky grey. So many of better stock had died on the grass. Though she could have, she had not been tempted to save him from his danger, nor any of the others. Yet: he lived. Perhaps he carried a charm.

Nor did she know why the war mage had spared the Otherworlder first through that particular door, but she meant to find out.

She whistled across to her sister on the opposite canyon wall, a sound human ears would not hear: *This one! Here is our spy.*

Her sister whistled back in acknowledgement, wry humour in the sound, then flew straight up before angling south, presumably off to tell the others that things had transpired as mighty Vyin of the dragon-youth had said: *two* had indeed passed safely through the gap between worlds, not just one.

The airborne Invia flew till she was a disappearing dot passing through a band of cloud, soon hidden even from the remaining one's far-seeing eyes.

And now the old man, if his luck held, would hear the hidden words of Vous, of the Arch Mage, and understand them, the same way she herself had understood the voices of men, of dogs, even of the rustling wind, when she'd ventured into Otherworld. (Not that any of those had had much of interest to say!) For decades, none beyond the castle's heavily enchanted walls had heard the private words and plans spoken within. One could only watch their actions below like pieces moving in an almost comprehensible game: the armies marching about; war mages flocking here or there like carrion birds; the new cities being built close to the castle, despite the old cities further away having already too few people.

Watch as they might, the Invia never knew much more than one trying to discern the intentions of whoever had left old footprints in the sand. The young dragons, if they knew, kept their secrets; they could not descend in body to act in the world below, nor disturb events through servants or spells, as the Dragon-god willed. Nor could they so much as crane their necks out through the doors of their prisons to gaze with *their* eyes, which saw so far and clearly. No: they simply conversed amongst themselves, dropping morsels of careful thought like crumbs from a meal, an act perilously close to, if not actually, breaking the natural laws. And it happened that the Invia might be outside their sky prison holds, to catch them.

Likewise, the Invia conversed amongst *themselves*. Messengers, news bearers? No! For none would break the Dragon's laws and risk waking It from slumber, in wrath. At least, not *blatantly*. As luck had it, their talk outside the dragon-youth's holds was sometimes overheard . . .

And when it came to interference in the world below, the Invia followed no orders. But they had a touch more discretion than the imprisoned dragon-youth . . .

The charm wrapped around her wrist had been made in the presence of Ksyn, just before the eight major personalities were banished. Was it possible he had even foreseen its use, uncounted centuries away? Time had surely dulled its power. It was hard to know how much: she and her sisters could only feel magic force ebb and flow through the air, not clearly see it in the way of mages. If enough power held, the charm would keep the old man hidden, even as he wandered the castle's halls. If it had weakened too much, he would need some more of his luck. A very good deal more.

But no more of his kind would come through, not this time. More war mages would be back to guard the entry point, and soon the castle's rulers would find a way to stabilise the accidentally fractured barrier, if that was their wish. When the entry point opened, it had been like a blow to an eggshell, making cracks in many places at once. And this had about it the beginnings of something greater than surrounding events suggested. Perhaps.

It was hard to know, looking at the feeble figure shuffling along below, with his sickly grey aura like a coat unable to keep out the cold; but huge floods start with raindrops, like her sister had said. As the Dragon wills.

The old man was peering at the distant tower, realising, it seemed, there was really nowhere else for him to go. He headed towards it. Good. She dived from the wall, plummeting fast, then spread her wings.

Case twisted the bottle's lid back on, wanting to make the scotch last until the next goat-horned sonofabitch managed to set fire to *him* instead of itself. He walked in a staggered line. Careless cheer bloomed through him, to know the end was close, that soon he'd catch up with Eric, and Shelly bless her heart, and others he'd known and missed. It was really all about to be done and dusted! Why the fuck not? He'd spent a lifetime dreading his own death, at times certain actual Hellfire awaited, but now he felt light as a feather. If he was to burn, what could he do to change it at this late hour? Why worry? He sang a drunken song whose words he forgot, filling it instead with profanity.

The tall white cliff faces opened out and far below, the flat horizon spread as far as sight. That tower now stretching above him seemed part of some larger castle made of gleaming white marble, green in places with moss and lichen. A closer look showed veins of colour running through the white stone in webs.

The castle itself, if castle was even the right word, was so huge he saw only part of it, nesting among mountains of a similar stone, as though it had been chiselled down from them into its present shape, layer by layer. A mass of windows — round ones, square ones, some glass-covered, others not — dotted the colossal stone slabs of its flank.

Though the castle partly obscured the view of the land spread beyond, he could see that it was like a tabletop model of rolling hills: large plains of white or green, clusters of woodland. Other distant structures curved skywards, maybe lookout towers, maybe geographic features, bone-white like the land's protruding sun-bleached ribs. A patch of the far horizon shimmered and gleamed like a sea. A vast paved road ran dead straight into the distance, dividing the landscape left and right almost perfectly into halves. Small as insects, things moved along it.

Just visible at the very end of sight were the high walls of a city, within it a cluster of red rooftops. But the castle kept commanding his attention back whenever he looked away. He squinted at the windows, fancying he could see people on the other side, but it was hard to be sure . . . perhaps a trick of the light. He felt very visible himself; surely from those windows someone could see him, if they looked his way.

Drunk as he was, grief and sadness burbling below his false cheer, Case had to stop and take in the dizzying sights, and admit to himself this would be a fitting last thing to see before clocking off to the next life, if this wasn't the next life already. The castle itself, well, he could still only see part of it, even from his vantage point above and behind it. How it must look from ground level! You'd damn near fall to your knees and pray to it.

So he stood and gazed, and inside sighed deeply with relief; though he wasn't sure how this sight, this other world spread out as real as the shoes on his feet, had eased some burden on his heart and mind which he hadn't been aware of until now, despite having heaved it around all his long life. Was it the secret fear that the world he knew was all there was, in all its good and bad, banalities and miracles?

He didn't know. He just gazed, and savoured the taste of every gulping breath, and said, 'How about that, then. How about that.'

He didn't know how long he stood and gazed, but the act was broken by the sound of beating wings, and air buffeting him. For a crazy second Case thought he was being swooped by a butcher bird, and he ducked to the ground, hands shielding his head, an instinct recalled from decades before: a boy doing a paper route, crying as birds swooped down at him from the power lines, to go home with streaks of tears on his cheeks and a beating from a father who needed his son tougher than that, and probably never got his wish.

Now, when he thought of how he'd marched right up close to that deathly beast to get his bottle, and that here he was ducking in terror from a potential *bird*, he burst out laughing, helpless with it, rolling around in tears on the soft grass.

Then he opened his eyes and saw her, one of the creatures that had appeared in his dreams. His heart leaped. She was here! She was real! And oh yes, she was beautiful, far more than the glimpses he'd caught of her in his sleep had shown. Her body was a naked woman's, young and sleek, with an hourglass figure. Silky black hair blew and tossed about on her shoulders with the wind. Her eyes gleamed and flashed with colour. 'You're real,' said Case with wonder, though he knew nothing of her, whether she were as dangerous as the thing with horns or not. In his dreams they had flown like flocks of birds, high up, now and then dropping down to peer at him with curiosity, speaking words he could not understand, then darting back to the sky so fast they left streaks of blurred motion behind them.

Two white feathery wings spread out behind her, soft-looking, and he wanted to run his hands over them like he'd wanted nothing else. He said, 'You're real, and you're beautiful.' Ah you old fool, he thought, don't say things like that.

She did not smile, nor did she blink. She stared at him with hands on her hips, bright red lips slightly parted, her expression completely foreign to him. Was she displeased? Angry?

'I am real,' she said back, voice stilted as though she did not often use it. 'You are real. Your friend is real. He lives.'

If Case had been spellbound, that broke him free. 'Eric? Eric's alive?'

'Yes. He and you are the ones who lived. I heard you call him, but there's no use. He is far away.'

'Where? Now where is he? I need to find him!'

'I have a task for you first, then I will take you to him. You understand my speech?'

'Of course. I'm talking to you, aren't I? But I don't see why you can't just tell me where Eric is. You better tell me.'

'Quiet, listen. I am speaking the tongue of the Invia. Not your tongue. Yet you understand me, as I understand you. Pilgrims to and fro always have such magic about them, as It wills. You may understand their speech too.' She pointed at the castle looming behind and below. 'Enchantments protect their words in the upper halls, for they fear to be overheard by the great ones I speak to. It may be you are immune to this disguise. We are not.'

'Now, damn you, if you know where my friend is and you don't tell me, I swear I'll choke the breath out of you!' He took some shambling steps towards her, the bottle raised like a club.

She stepped lightly up and out of his reach without even beating her wings, though she extended them now, gracefully flexing and angling them flat. The look on her face hadn't changed; it expressed nothing. She just watched him from above, nothing more.

Case sat down hard on the ground, body shaking with sobs. 'Too much for me to understand,' he said. 'I don't get it any more. Don't know where I am or what it all means. Thought I was about to die, back there, and I would've let it kill me, because I dragged my friend into this in the first place. All those people, deader than shit. And you're just looking at me like that. Damn it, tell me where he is.' He cried harder, wiped his eyes, and when he looked up she wasn't there.

Lying in the grass beside him was a long necklace of dull silver beads. He hesitated then grabbed it. The beads stuck against each other a little, like they were faintly magnetic. He cast his eye around, trying to find the woman with wings, but she was nowhere to be seen.

Wait — over there, by the castle. She floated in the air above the nearest tower, distance making her seem hardly bigger than a bird. She waved. *Come.* Case stood, wiped the tears from his cheeks, and grabbed the bottle, muttering curses.

The strip of valley ended just a little further ahead, where it curved steeply down to the castle's back edge, nestled in the sheer cliff base. It was a long drop, but there was some semblance of a path zigzagging down through a few trees, shrubs and boulders of white stone. I'm too old for this, he thought, already puffing from the first steps of his descent.

And he was too drunk for it. His foot slipped and down he went. As much as he'd been casual about the prospect of dying a few minutes before, now the moment had come, perfectly involuntary panic bloomed through him like an explosion, and he clutched desperately at the ground as he slipped over the edge into air.

But hands caught him under his armpits. He felt a steady

lurch as the Invia's wings beat. He grabbed hold of her arms as hard as he could, too alarmed by the sight of the world far below his feet to worry whether he was hurting her. Her grip was strong and painful; her breasts pressed into his back firm as fists. He looked down at the forearms he held onto and was startled to see thin little scales covering her skin, clear as glass.

Between his feet was the round marble-white roof of a lower part of the great structure, which seemed a grouping of fat dome-shaped temples, while other parts led off and trailed in giant branches curving away from the main mass. The whole thing had some huge deliberate *shape* to it, like an enormous sculpture, nothing like any actual castle that Case had ever seen. There were courtyards way down there where dot-sized people scurried about. Case's head spun, guts spun, and he tried not to reflect on the odds of her letting go if he puked on her forearms. 'Don't drop me,' he said. 'I'll do what you want. Don't drop me.'

'Hush! You are annoying.'

Each beat of her wings brought them closer to a tall tower, its upper half coloured gold. Case thought it was about to smack them head on until she parked on the wide ledge outside a window two-thirds of the way up. She set him down and stepped backwards onto the air as though standing on an invisible plat-form, angling her wings so they held her still. She said, 'Now it becomes difficult. You must go inside when the prisoner opens her window. She will not see you, as long as you wear the charm. No one will see you. Do not take it off! And do not speak. You are a fool, I think. I hope you listen.'

'No argument from me. What'm I supposed to do here?'

'Find a man named Vous. Stay near him, and listen to what he says. The charm you wear does many things. It will preserve what you hear, so that I may listen later.'

'Are you coming with me?'

'No!'

'Well, then what? Once I'm in there, how do I get out again? And where'll I go? And you better tell me about Eric after this, I swear.'

But she'd vanished. And Case had only just realised that at some point he'd dropped the bottle.

12

They hadn't gone much further before something approached, making the chittering noise they'd heard through the walls earlier. They began to double back, but the sound came from behind too. Gleaming yellow lights appeared at both ends of the tunnel, bright as candle flames. The lights were eyes and the groundmen who approached were no higher than their waists. They looked human enough — bald little heads, pointy noses and ears — but their stocky bodies were covered in mats of brown or grey fur. Four came from ahead, three from behind, all nattering angrily.

'Hail, tunnel masters,' said Sharfy, bending low to kiss the floor. He gestured urgently for Eric to do likewise. Kiown did the same, making his kiss far more passionate and drawn out than was perhaps necessary. The groundmen watched this carefully as though to ensure the large people were suitably humiliated, then stared at Eric silently, the gleaming candles snuffing out for a moment when they blinked. Their small faces were bunched in shock and anger. 'Toll?' Sharfy sighed, nodding at Eric. 'Pay?'

'Toll!' one of them snapped back in its high voice. 'Pay!'

Sharfy dug in his pockets, coming out with Eric's bus schedule.

He handed it over. 'Otherworld writing,' he said as extravagantly as a game-show host. 'Otherworld language. Real, very rare. Hard to get.'

They took it, pawing the pages, grappling with each other for the chance to get close enough for a look. For a long while they muttered and whispered. The language wasn't the same they'd been speaking to Sharfy, but Eric caught words here and there:

'Messages! See? Numbers.'

'That line. See? Like map mark.'

'My turn! My turn!'

'Different paper. Shiny, green!'

'My turn! Give!'

'Careful! You rip!'

'We share. Lots time. Shut up.'

'Enough? Let pass?'

'They have more. Perhaps. Ask?'

'Ask!'

Their apparent leader — one with thick dark eyebrows that made him look furious — reverted to the normal tongue. 'More! Not enough. Pay more.'

'We pay more later,' said Sharfy. 'When we get through the tunnels safe.'

'Pay *more!*'

'No more,' said Sharfy. 'Don't be *greedy*. We gave you lots. Then you kicked my friends out of the cavern you sold us. You don't keep bargain, no one bargain with you again. No more toll for you.'

The groundmen conferred amongst themselves. 'Leave it be,' said one in its own tongue. 'Tallest has sword. Ugliest has knives, enchanted. Send them down left tunnel. Traps there to kill them. Steal from bodies.'

'Don't send! Traps broke. Devils came through. Set off traps. No good.'

Sharfy and Kiown watched the groundmen, their faces indicating they didn't understand a word. Eric tried to catch their eye, but they didn't look at him.

'Send *other* way,' the groundman leader said. 'Devils still there. Right passage. Wide cavern. Lots devils. Close off this way. No escape.'

'Yes! Good!' A burble of chittering noise broke out; it seemed to be laughter.

'Toll enough,' one of them said in the common tongue. 'We go. You pass right tunnel. Left trapped. Middle blocked off. Go right. Only way through.'

The groundmen scurried back up the tunnel. Several little kicks hit all three of their shins as the pack of them passed. Soon they heard the sound of stone sliding on stone. Behind them the way was now blocked off. 'Little bastards,' muttered Kiown. 'Ever tried groundman, Sharfy? Tastes rather like puke but at least you know one of the little fuckers died to make it.'

'They can't tell us which way we have to go,' said Sharfy, nervously fingering the scar on his lip. 'Can't shut us off, either. If we pay a toll, we're free. How it's always been.'

'Didn't you guys understand what they were saying?' Eric whispered. 'They said they're going to send us to devils.'

'*What?*'

'That's what they said. I could tell you didn't understand them, but I didn't want them to know *I* could. So I kept quiet, let them talk.'

'You couldn't understand them,' said Sharfy. 'No one does. They have about a hundred languages. Most of it's code inside other codes. Not even the castle people can speak it. No one can. Why you think they want Otherworld language so much?'

'I'm telling you, I heard some of what they were saying.'

'I don't believe you,' said Sharfy, crossing his arms.

Kiown looked from one to the other. 'Mmm! Ironic. Sharfy won't have a word of it. Sharfy's bagged himself a genuine *exaggerator*! Fine, fine work. What else did they say?'

Eric thought back. 'Something about the left tunnel being trapped. But that devils set the traps off, and they're no good now.'

Kiown rubbed his chin. 'If there're traps, it's worse than devils. If even one trap is still set? Whoever gets it will be waist-deep in the floor, stuck tight. Below, they'll poke your butt and legs with spears until you drain dry. *Most* unfriendly. So, we go the way the groundies wanted us to. They didn't see our pit devil masks! Sharfy, do I speak sense?'

'If you do, speak it quieter,' Sharfy answered sullenly. 'They might be listening.'

Kiown tossed Eric the mask he'd worn, and got the other out of the knapsack.

'Now hold on a minute. There is no *way* he understood what they were saying,' Sharfy insisted. 'Do you know how many have tried to learn groundmen tongue?'

'Someone's not very bright,' said Kiown, a hint of anger changing his long, lean face dramatically with just a few twists and lines. 'When we went through the door, we spoke their tongue. Or at least, it sounded like it to *them*. I bet we could understand all speech in Otherworld, just like Loup said. Now Eric creeps into Levaal — for reasons he certainly isn't *volunteering*, one notices — and gets past the war mages in circumstances *most* mysterious and peculiar. Guess what? He speaks every tongue! If not *speaks* it, at least understands it.' Kiown turned to Eric almost menacingly. 'You can probably converse with elementals on the Misery Flats. Chat with hounds and

horses, with trees and birds and buzzing flies. Bzzzz!' Kiown
paced around him, peering at him as if he were a prized farm
animal. 'I bet he could even understand castle speech, that the
high-ups use, hidden by magic and all. Hmm! Do you know
what this means, Eric?'

'I'm sure you'll tell me.'

Kiown did, pointing an accusing finger: 'You are now property of Anfen's band, which is us. And you are a very valuable
trinket! Which is good *and* bad for you. As a valued trinket, you
will have food to eat and people to protect you.'

He knew where this was headed. 'But you can't let anyone
steal me, either?'

'Correct! So. If you wanted to go back to your own world, I'm
afraid not. Discussion over.'

Eric shrugged. 'You seem to forget that I was sent here. I'm
not meant to return yet.'

'*Sent* here?' Kiown looked at him, and a flicker of doubt went
across his face.

'Don't tell him,' said Sharfy. 'Kiown's not in charge. Save it
for Anfen.'

'Well and true,' Kiown said. He produced a little jar half filled
with paste, which he rubbed on his clothes, neck, legs and arms,
then passed it around. It smelled musky and unpleasant. 'Put
on that mask,' said Kiown. 'This could prove a good little test
of things. If you heard the groundmen right, we shall have to
sneak past some devils. Then we'll know Eric was right, and
Sharfy was wrong. None shall be surprised.'

'Coincidence,' Sharfy said sourly. 'We already seen the tracks.'

Kiown grinned. 'One day you're going to be telling the story
of how you lost nearly a hundred arguments, with a thousand
people who were all way, way smarter than you. As in, so much
smarter you wouldn't *believe—*'

'Fuck you.' Sharfy's hand went to his knife.

'Oh hush.' Kiown stood on tiptoe, examining the marks on the roof. 'Hmm. Not far from the grain-wagon tunnels, this way. If there *are* devils in this tunnel, I will be puzzled. We're smack bang under the castle. They should not be here at all. Now listen: we are in disguise. If we see devils, we will crawl on hands and knees to be extra safe. Do *not* speak, or they shall know that you are not in fact a pit devil, and be truly pissed. They shall proceed to savagely maul you. And maybe everything else in sight, including each other. They're like that. A bit unbalanced in the head, like Sharfy. Maybe they, like him, have heads stuffed with traumatic memories. And foul secrets. Who can say?'

Sharfy looked at Kiown darkly, and suddenly looked more like doing him harm than he had earlier with his knife drawn. Seemingly oblivious, Kiown said, 'Eric, do you understand?'

'I hope so.'

'Mmmm. So do I. Because if you don't,' he cackled nervously, 'we're all going to die.'

The musky stink of their pit devil scent was dizzying, and soon pushed all other observations to the background. When the walls widened out they came to a spectacular mosaic, spread over a large area of the wall and linking up with another, set some way distant, its blooming light beams crossing the first's, to form a huge three-dimensional portrait on the opposing wall. A lush garden was depicted, a scene of feasting and joy, the groundmen looking far nobler in this artwork than they'd been in person. Eric only just spotted the dead 'evil giant' in the grass amidst this splendour, the corpse seemingly a decoration like the flowers and jewels. He had to hand it to the little people, they knew a thing or two about holding a grudge.

As yet there'd been few of those slitted tracks in the stone.

Then they came to a part of the tunnel where the lightstones were sparse. Ahead, something moved which Eric's eye had marked as just an outcrop of rock on the cavern's side wall, some way off the path. It might have been a large dog's silhouette, but for the two pointed horns atop its skull, visible against a distant slab of lightstone. The others had missed it. He tapped Kiown's shoulder and pointed.

Kiown pulled the mask down over his face and got on hands and knees. Sharfy straddled his back, hiding his head under the much taller man's shirt. Eric gingerly slid his own mask on, and kneeled down too. Perhaps the thing heard them, for its head turned their way and it made an inquisitive sound.

They began their crawl. Beyond the first pit devil, another raised its head their way, and another, all little more than black shapes in the gloom. Rounding a bend where the light was better, they suddenly found dozens climbing over the cavern's walls and floor. Little clicking sounds came from their claws across the stone; now and then there were faint inquisitive growls. Kiown balked to see so many, and looked nervously back the way they'd come. So quietly Eric could barely be sure he heard it, the redhead whispered: 'We ... are ... dead.'

By the path now were scattered piles of small, broken bones. To their left, the nearest pit devil stood perfectly still. Its head slowly turned to watch them crawl by. Its eyes were blank pits. A ridge of naked white bone above its nose, dividing left and right, curled up as twin lumps in the brow, and seemed to pierce the forehead like a weapon driven through it. That aside, strangely, it did not look too far from human. But its eyes expressed nothing at all: no intelligence, emotion or even hunger. They were perfectly dead, and its lethal mouth hung wide open like something with broken hinges.

When they were safely past the first, there was a scuffling, grinding sound. It was trailing them, mindless as a sheep just following the herd. Kiown halted, subtly gestured for Eric to do the same. The pit devil made a sound in its throat then slowly loped past them on all fours, its shoulder brushing against Eric with intense warmth. It continued ahead, movements lithe and seeming to defy gravity slightly. Its clawed feet and hands left gouged slits in the rock floor like knives through wet clay.

To their left and right, yet more of the creatures watched them with distinct interest. Some were high up on the walls, even hanging from the cavern's roof by their claws. As Eric began to wonder if the path through these fiendish things would ever end, he was amazed to discover he *understood* the gargling, snarling sounds they made.

'*Hunger. Builds.*'

'*Shape. Moves. Comes.*'

'*Scent. Good.*'

'*Pack. Need . . .*'

'*Teeth. Bone. Horns.*'

'*Scent. Natural.*'

'*Climb. Dark.*'

'*Seek. Hunt.*'

He shuddered.

13

Outside the high tower window she waited, hidden as the Invia could hide even in plain light, as long as she stayed stiller than a statue. His charm she would faintly perceive even through the enchanted walls, and thus follow his progress inside. But she would not save the old man's life from danger, for there was an extremely powerful mage walking the halls nearby. She felt his presence, and surely her presence disturbed *him*; maybe like a background noise he'd hardly notice, or maybe he knew exactly what she was, where she was, but was just too busy to bother with her. Yet.

The old man fidgeted nervously on the window ledge, speaking to himself and trying not to look down. She waited ready to catch him if he fell or jumped, and the time passed slowly.

At last, Vous's daughter began her daily routine. Sometimes, even from high in the clouds, the Invia had heard the girl scream in this way and wondered why. Her curiosity was what had made her choose this window to set down the spy.

The girl opened the latch now, pushed open the glass and cleared her throat. The old man saw his chance and slipped past her. He was inside! Good.

Case had never seen such sadness in all his life, not at funerals, not even worn by those posh grieved parents walking away from gaol after visiting a son who they never thought would be in such a place, face newly busted up and all. This girl topped it all, in her long black gown with her long flaxen hair tied back in a ponytail. How old — seventeen? Twenty? She had one of those slightly heart-shaped faces, with eyes and mouth that drooped a little, and a soft undefined chin. Pretty, but her slow movements and bowed head were grief itself, with — if he wasn't mistaken — something almost *ritual* about it. His heart went out to her and for a second he forgot he was meant to sneak into her room.

He quietly ducked past her while she rested her hands on the sill, sad eyes staring unfocused into the distance. If she noticed his feet touching down on her floor she gave no sign.

The room was neat and filled with pretty things: ornaments made of crystal, dolls of all sizes, weavings, knitting balls and needles, and a large plush bed Case felt he could sleep for a week in. There was a ticking device on the wall — a clock? Hard to tell, with those funny symbols on it, and the odd crisscrossing hands at weird angles. The girl watched it, waiting for (if Case judged right) the hour hand to tick over.

A mirror on a stand in the corner showed his reflection as no more than a dim outline, with the insides invisible; what the hell ... ? Then the beads around his neck clicked just a little when they bumped together, and he remembered the charm. So, it worked. Well, of course it did, you old twit, he thought, the girl didn't see you, and you went right past her.

Why was she so sad, anyway? It wasn't for lack of possessions, nor lack of a view. Outside that window, you could see a big portion of the castle down below and, beyond that, the glorious spread of the landscape. Looking out there every day, you'd feel like you owned the whole lot, and for all Case knew, she did. He went to the door, tried the handle as quietly as he could, and found it was locked tight. So, she couldn't leave. Maybe that explains it, he thought, some of it, anyway . . .

That was when the girl began to wail. The sound made him jump. She leaned far out over the balcony, head angled up as though she wanted the sound to carry to a higher window, and screamed. No words, as far as he could tell, just the saddest voice he'd ever heard, and it nearly broke his heart.

Case nervously fingered the beads around his neck. He wanted to tell her it was all right, could be worse, she could be an old drunken fool like him who didn't even have the sense to stay in his own *world*. He imagined himself saying that to her, and her smiling, maybe a little laugh. Putting his arm around her — no, not like *that*, just to make her feel better. But she kept on wailing, louder and louder, her voice sometimes breaking.

Peering through the locked door's keyhole, he saw the backs of people walking past. They had to be able to hear this, but no one even turned to look twice, let alone come comfort the girl. Her cries were edged with anguish now, like she physically hurt. Case squirmed. He couldn't take much more of this — it was worse than a baby's crying. The woman with wings had told him not to take off the charm, but by hell she could come here and do something herself, if she wanted to!

Case pulled the chain from over his head. As he did, his reflection solidified in the mirror like normal. 'Hey, hey now, listen—' he began.

The girl whipped around, eyes boggling like they were about to pop out of her head. She saw him, gasped, and ran to the door, hitting it with her palms. 'Help!' she screamed. 'Help!'

Running footsteps approached from up the corridor.

'No, no, wait,' said Case, backing into the corner. 'Look, I just wanted to cheer you up, is all. I'm not going to hurt you. What're you so sad about, crying like that?'

She watched him as though he might turn into a snake or maybe already had, but at least she'd stopped yelling for help. Too late: there was the sound of keys clanking in the lock. Guess I'm screwed now, he thought, before it occurred to him to put the charm back around his neck.

He did it just as the door knob twisted and a dumpy older woman stood in the doorway, wearing an apron and what looked like a plain nurse's outfit beneath. Her face was mean, Case could tell, the kind of mean that hides behind big insincere smiles.

'Aziel?' said the woman in the doorway. 'You've stopped your wailing. Now why do a thing like that?' She looked at the clock. 'Not even halfway through! You know he'll have shut his window already!'

'Someone . . .' the girl began, but she looked from the woman to where Case had been and back again, and seemed to doubt that she should speak.

'Someone? Yes, someone's for it, all right. And now I'll have a mess to clean up next door. You've been so good for so long, Aziel, doing your wailing every day like your father loves. Too late now! Without *pause*. Those are the rules.'

Something seemed to have occurred to the girl, Aziel, and she forgot all about Case. 'No. Oh no, please, don't! Don't let them, nanny!'

The woman's smile was sympathetic but her eyes were cold, and sucking up the girl's distress, every bit of it. 'Don't *let* them?' she cried. 'Well! What am I supposed to do? Pick up a sword and start cutting off heads? *You* were the one who could have stopped them. Think about that, when you hear it all. It's been too long since you did, I'd say.'

The nanny began to close the door. Case didn't know if he should stay or go, but the closing door was, for all he knew, his last chance to slip out. He did so just as the nanny paused to take another hungry look in at Aziel's distress. 'So sorry for yourself!' the woman said. 'Spare a thought for *me*. When they're done, *I'll* be in there with mop and bucket, not you.' She shut the door and turned a key in the lock, then held her ear to the door, that hungry look still on her face.

Case stood behind her in a wide, curved hallway. Staff in robes of bland grey, male and female, walked past in a slow shuffling gait. They didn't look twice as two burly guards dragged a naked man, bound and gagged, down the hallway towards Aziel's room.

'He's a big one,' said the nanny, turning away from Aziel's door. 'Going to be a bleeder, isn't he?'

The guards didn't respond to her at all. They carried the man into the room next to Aziel's. There was a large stone bench in there; that was all Case saw before the door slammed shut.

'They're about to begin!' the nanny called through Aziel's keyhole.

Aziel's voice could be heard, screaming out her window: 'Father, *don't*! Stop them! Don't do it! *Don't!*'

'You did it,' the nanny called through the door. 'Your wailing, girl. You know how he loves it. You've been so good for so long, and your voice is *so* lovely.'

Case didn't quite know what was going on here, but he knew that right then he wanted to put his foot to that woman's rear end more than he'd ever wanted a drink in his life, and only his utter bewilderment stopped him.

When the prisoner dragged into the room next door began screaming, Case thought at last he understood what was happening. He knew that for the rest of his days he'd never understand *why*, not even if someone told him. Some things, he guessed, you simply couldn't know, and it would ever afterwards

throw his mind sideways to think back on it and try to comprehend it.

He ran from Aziel's door to get the sound of the slowly dying
man out of his ears, and that poor girl's wailing as she heard
it happen, and the woman telling her through the door to listen
close, because she'd done it all herself. By the time he was out
of reach of those awful sounds, the whole thing seemed *too*
strange to be real, even in another world, and he seriously began
to doubt he'd witnessed anything of the kind at all.

14

Finally, blessedly, the cavern narrowed and there were no more creatures either side of the path. To be safe they kept on their hands and knees for some distance beyond. Kiown stood and Sharfy slipped to the ground, wiping off sweat. 'What took so fucking long?' he demanded.

Kiown and Eric rubbed their tortured knees. 'Perhaps I enjoyed the pleasure of your body pressed against mine?' Kiown snarled back. 'Your weight on my ribs? Do you know how *many* there were? I was expecting four or five! There was a whole *horde*.' Kiown was pale and shaken. 'If I'd known there were that many, I would've chanced the traps.'

'We seemed safe enough,' said Eric.

'Oh no we were *not*! Try to appreciate our luck. They sometimes work as a pack, but more than a few in one place and it's time to scrap for turf. As newcomers, we would've been prime targets.' Kiown paced anxiously, the cone of red hair flopping side to side. 'I can only guess they had other natural enemies nearby, recent contact, so were teamed up. Why *here*? Any more riddles today and I will be quite full.'

Sharfy said, 'Here's one, then. Hope it makes your filthy guts bust open. There was a cavern, not far from the door. Newly tunnelled. No lightstones in it. Smelled rotten. Worse than rotten. Something in there. Not devils, but something.'

Kiown shrugged. 'There's a saying: "Consider the source." Of information.'

Sharfy didn't pick up on the insult; he looked troubled. 'Something's wrong down here. Shouldn't be one pit devil, not this far north. They're here for a reason.' Sharfy lapsed into thoughtful silence.

Eric wondered if he should say it. 'I could hear the devils talk, you know. They must have their own language too. Did you know that?'

Kiown looked at him, startled. 'What were they saying?'

'Nothing that made much sense. Only what you might expect animals to say.'

'You are a most intriguing little trinket,' said Kiown. 'Believe him yet, Sharfy? Or is he still a liar?'

Sharfy muttered to himself and walked off ahead. They followed him. Eric said, 'Is he as good a swordsman as he says he is?'

Kiown laughed. 'Nooo! Not a soul who ever wielded blade possibly could be. Still, you'd have him with you in a fight. Knows some tricks, throws a good knife.' Kiown considered. 'And it *is* true you can trust him. He just doesn't look like it. Me, on the other hand? Who knows. And it's time we plunged onwards.'

The draught suddenly picked up. They became aware of a distant rumbling sound, becoming more defined as they neared it. Then light poured through their tunnel, which opened out to the side of a vast paved road, with a huge cavernous roof overhead and sheer walls. Big slabs of lightstone in the walls and roof made it better lit than the ways they'd come through, helped by brands and braziers of orange fire along the roadside.

At walking pace down below passed truck-sized metal containers on wheels, stretching in both directions as far as sight, filled to the brim with grain, livestock and mined ore. Men in grey robes rode small platforms jutting from the vehicles' sides. A cart passed, full of shaggy cattle-sized animals, some of which stood on two legs. The sight of the alien beasts made Eric forget, momentarily, his tiredness. Another world, he marvelled. And yet there passed other carts with familiar sights: horses, cows, and poultry in cages.

'These are going to the castle,' said Kiown for Eric's benefit. 'See? That's the ramp up, where the road starts to rise. All this came from farms down south. The castle takes it, counts it, then sends it back to Aligned cities. Or not, if they deem people need to be starved. A citizen in Aligned cities is advised to behave himself, and not do silly things like organise resistance, because dinner is nice. In any case food often rots before it gets to places further away.'

Stationed by the roadside were soldiers in metal breastplates with swords at their sides. The two directly beneath them sat playing a game with round pieces on a striped board. Sharfy's eyes gleamed. 'We used to raid these carts. Can't, now. Those guards, down there? Because of us.' He sounded like a proud father. 'Kiown, look! Dirt cart from the mines! Ah, those were the days. Used to make a fortune, raiding dirt carts.'

'We can still raid them,' said Kiown. 'You just need a little help.' With that, he dashed back up the tunnel, leaving Sharfy confused behind him. A minute or two later, Kiown's squealing voice reached them: '*Yoooo hoooooo! Pit devils! I have a surprise for youuuuuuuu! HEY! HEYYYYY!*'

Sharfy looked stricken. 'Get down, now! Down to the road-side. If we stay here he'll get us killed.'

It was a steep drop down the embankment and they had to slide most of the way. The guards below had their board game sprayed with rubble. They stood and drew their blades as Kiown made it back through the tunnel at a mad sprint, whooping. He plunged right down the drop towards Eric and Sharfy. 'Here they come!' he screamed. 'I threw rocks! They're coming! Raid! Plunder! Go go!'

The guards jogged over, yelling orders lost in the rumbling of the goods train. 'Forget us,' Kiown told them, pointing overhead. 'Look up there. I suggest you panic.'

Five of the red-skinned pit devils loped out, jaws open wide as they went heedlessly down the drop, two overbalancing and sprawling to the roadside with a thud. The surprised guards screamed for help. The men in grey robes shrieked and leaped from the carts' platforms. More guards rushed over, no longer interested in the bandits. 'Go! Loot!' Kiown yelled, hopping up on the side of a passing cart.

Behind them, the guards tried to stand in formation while the devils frenzied. They had loped along slowly, but their long thin limbs now thrashed like striking snakes, claws slicing through armour. The guards fell screaming, with breastplates cracked open, arms sliced off still clutching swords. Their frenzy mounting, the pit devils swarmed over grain carts, chewing and swiping at the carts themselves.

Up on the side of the 'dirt cart', Sharfy and Kiown stuffed their pockets with what appeared to be hard lumps of black soil. Urgent to make room, Sharfy took the gun's clips from his pocket and tossed them clattering to the ground. Eric rushed to pick them up, unnoticed by the others.

'Take some!' Sharfy called to him and tossed a few pieces down, one of which broke apart. Gleaming gems scattered left and right. Only they weren't gems — they were flat as coins.

Kiown dropped down beside him, still panting from his sprint. Eric hesitated, not yet quite knowing his place among these bandits. Would a hero just go along with this? he thought, and said, 'Whatever these things are, these scales, are they worth killing people for?'

Kiown blinked at him, baffled. '*Killing* people, you say?' he laughed. 'Poor little innocents? Those guards, they work for the castle.' Kiown suddenly loomed over him, a hint of anger behind his mocking face and voice. 'Did you think the war mages were little innocents, too? I hear they killed your people dead without a thought. Know who the war mages work for?'

'The castle,' said Sharfy, hopping down with his pockets bulging.

'How does one treat enemies in Otherworld?' Kiown went on, spittle flying from his lips. 'Does one *politely discuss*?'

'Enough!' Sharfy said, standing between them. He pointed at the clumps of black dirt at Eric's feet. 'Grab some, quick. Then run.'

Eric did as told, and they ducked through the gap between two grain carts, up the far embankment, along a ledge where more small passageways opened up. No guards chased, not when they saw the entire horde of pit devils belatedly pouring through the hole on the other side like a red nightmare, swarming down the embankment. 'Anfen says hello!' Kiown yelled, waving to one guard who paused, looking up at them. The guard stared, but made no move to pursue them as they fled.

15

Through the wide hallways Case went. Bright and busy the place seemed, well ordered as a hospital. The human traffic was heavy enough that his footsteps need not be silent, but he was careful to sidestep the men and women in their bland robes, with their bland faces showing not much, saying nothing. When they did speak, it was seldom loud enough to be overheard, seldom more than a word or two. Some had paper scrolls in hand, or little notebooks slung about their shoulders. Many ducked in or out of the doorways on either side, all steadily going about some incomprehensible business like ants in a stump. There seemed something very wrong with them which Case couldn't quite pinpoint: something was missing. Maybe it was the way their mouths hung open a little, the dullness of their eyes. Maybe it was the place's quiet despite so many going back and forth, with only the *tap shuffle tap* of footsteps on the stone floor.

Sometimes the doors on either side of the wide hallways were open. Case paused to look in, once finding a store room full of plain-looking objects: cups, plates, tools, simple jewellery like the silver beads around his neck. It was all valuable, since there were serious-looking men with swords sitting inside, silently watching over it all.

In other rooms, seated around tables, were people who by

their manner discussed matters of grave importance. Something separated these people from the rest of these castle dwellers. They were dressed differently, but that wasn't it ... there was clearly some 'on' switch that had been flicked in them, or maybe the others had been switched off. Case passed several such meetings before he stopped in a doorway to listen, thinking that in here might be the man he was supposed to find:

'... if I may, to me, this is ... I won't say paranoid, but I have not ever detected a scrap of further ambition in that general than the next course of dinner.'

The others at the table exchanged looks of grave alarm. Said one very slowly, 'Perhaps others have better foresight than we.'

The first speaker, stricken: 'Yes, of course. I did not mean to say I was questioning—'

'You already have questioned. Already questioned.' He grinned like someone who was very much looking forward to a drink of the other's blood.

Case listened a while longer then left the worried-looking bunch to their troubles and secrets. Further along, an open door blasted freezing air and mist into the hall. Inside was a spacious chamber, and placed over its floor were many large lumps of blue ice. Shapes were frozen within each block and, if he didn't know better — yes, there were people in the ice blocks, horned men, identical to that monster that had set itself on fire, back near the door. The chamber was full of them, all frozen solid, their eyes open. Were they alive or dead? He couldn't tell.

A block of ice nearest the door had water running from it in little rivulets, slowly thawing. The war mage inside had its eyes pointed right at the doorway where Case stood. He shuddered then hurried away, soon as thoroughly lost as could be.

It was endless, this maze of hallways and arches and doors

to secret chambers. When one passage branched off, winding upwards, Case followed its plush red carpet, recalling that Aziel had seemed to direct her mournful cries to a higher window. The top of the steps was guarded by sentries, heavily armed with shields and spears, but they didn't react in the slightest as Case very carefully crept past them.

He found himself in a lofty hallway without the background sound of shuffling steps to shield his own. Tall glass windows double a man's height were embedded at intervals down either side. Before each of these sat people taking careful notes on paper scrolls with pencils. The windows looked out, but Case assumed they were televisions or something similar, for they didn't show the sky, nor the landscape he'd expect to see from this high up. The one nearest seemed to give the view from in the midst of a town; there were buildings in the background, and what might have been a pub. In the next window along, women in rags walked by a marketplace carting a wagon full of hay, which kept spilling out, and which a young boy kept trying to put back in.

Some of the windows showed grassy fields where nothing seemed to be happening at all, besides a little breeze. But the window-watchers stared at these just as avidly, taking as many notes as those monitoring the others. Case looked over their shoulders but couldn't decipher anything . . . if he spoke their language now, he sure as shit couldn't read it.

In another window was what looked like a big looming wall of glassy ice, its top too far above to see. In fact, many windows — Case counted thirty as he strolled along — viewed this looming wall, which seemed to stretch to the sky itself. It was either vastly long, or there were several of its kind, for some windows watched it from grassy plains, others from between the trees of a woodland, others from fields of dust and rubble. Before some of these were huge grey statues with round featureless faces, tall as buildings.

The views were so clear it looked as though one could step through the windows and go to wherever each place was. Every so often one of the note-takers touched a slab of rust-coloured stone set on tables before them, and the view of the window shifted left, right, or spun right around. Then they'd watch closely and take more notes.

The windows stretched as far ahead down the long hallway as Case could see. He didn't bother to look closely at most of them — they all showed the same kind of stuff, seemingly random views of random places. Until, that was, he saw a window showing a busy road, with cars going past. He did a double take and went back. Cars? Trucks? And they weren't alien cars either — that was a Ford! This was a city, a *real* city.

Over at the next window, there was a similar view. The same place, or a different city? There was a bridge that looked familiar, some well-known foreign landmark, but he couldn't place it. A whole bunch of these windows were looking out at places in the real world. The window-watchers here were excited, as though each sight was a rare one, and they crowded three or four per window.

Case nearly took off his necklace again, just to ask one of these people what the hell they thought they were doing. It felt like he'd found someone trespassing in his yard. So they know about us, he thought, but we don't know about them. That can't be real good.

He also noticed that the view from these windows was blurry, and often quickly faded to darkness, like eyes closing now and then. A minute or so later, all the Earth-watching windows suddenly blinked out. The note-takers didn't seem surprised, but sighed in disappointment, set down their pens, and waited for the windows to open again.

Something caught his eye — the strange woman, standing right there in the hallway, her wings spread wide, completely naked but for beads, similar to his, around her neck. She looked the way Case's reflection had in the sad girl's mirror: an outline, mostly transparent inside it. No one else looked her way, and two of those robe-wearing zombies walked right past her.

Her face hadn't changed its expression: watching. She waved an arm, *this way*. Finally, a little help. But a second later she'd vanished completely.

When he passed where she'd been, her voice said quietly, 'Do not speak. You are taking so long! Follow the wall as it curves around to the right. There is a large chamber, with swords crossed atop the door. Go in there. Do not remove your charm again. Try not to touch it at all. I cannot help further. A mage comes. I flee.' There was a feeling of rushing air, something moving past very quickly. A few heads by the windows turned, disturbed, then went back to their notes. Then a nightmare stepped into the hall.

As the war mages had horns, so did this, but this thing's were thicker, longer, and curled down to its shoulders. But it was otherwise unlike them. Its head was far too large for the rest of its body, and hung forwards, a heavy weight on its neck. A third horn came from atop its burn-scarred scalp, spiralling back behind its neck. One side of its face had a horribly *melted* look, as if it had been gouged from cooling wax. Set in that eye socket was a square, gleaming gem, which swivelled around as the thing surveyed the hall.

If it was a man, Case could not imagine an uglier one. Not even mangling the 'normal' half of its face would make it much worse. One hand held a tall forked staff of dull silver. The other hand, of the same side as the melted face, looked incapable of holding much at all — like the corresponding leg, it was blackened and shrivelled, withered to a thin claw, twitching and shaking. It was a wonder the knotted bone-thin leg held the beast's weight as it limped down the hall.

It went right past Case, who flattened himself against the wall. *Clack, clack,* its forked silver staff banged into the ground, helping it along when it had to step on that withered, burned leg. A long mane of feathers dragged behind its head, trailing like a cape on the floor behind it.

Its head turned to look at the windows it passed. The robed servants did not look at it, nor did they tremble as it reached them the way Case would if such a thing could see him. They just kept taking their notes, watching their windows.

When the mage was some way down the hall, it stopped and turned back. Its human eye swept past the line of robed people, past the doorway, and lingered for just a second, or so Case thought, on the very spot where he stood. From such a monster as this came the civil voice of a learned, wise man: 'Tell me. Who among you carries a charm?'

The row of window-watchers ceased taking notes and turned their heads. 'Not I, Arch Mage.'

'Nor I.'

'Nor I, Arch Mage.'

Each of them denied it. The Arch Mage's lips gave a twitch on the more human side of his face. He waited patiently until each window-watcher had spoken, which took several minutes, then said, 'No one? No one here carries a charm?'

There was no answer. The window-watchers turned like robots back to their task. The Arch Mage's gem-eye gleamed with light and turned in its socket, wrinkling the flesh around it as his huge head swept about, gazing up and down the hall.

'No matter,' he said at last, drumming his fingers on his staff. 'Many functions, such things have. Many uses.' It was hard to translate the expression of such a face, but the Arch Mage seemed lost in thought and troubled. Abruptly he turned and limped away, more hurriedly than he'd moved before, and no longer interested in the windows to either side.

Case shut his eyes, breathed deep, then decided he'd had enough of this place and these people. He wanted out of here right now, to go find a tavern somewhere and beg for a sample of the local ale. After all this, he'd dance and sing for it if need be.

He turned his walk to a jog, no longer mindful of the robed people he passed, knocking several of them aside and leaving a trail of them perplexed behind him. The Hall of Windows ended at last, turning into yet another corridor, much narrower. 'Where's Vous?' Case yelled, grabbing the only grey-robe in sight by the scruff of the neck. 'Your king or president or whatever the fuck he is. Where is he?'

The young man squinted ahead. 'Is that you, Arch Mage?'

'Sure. Whatever you like,' said Case.

'I cannot see you, Arch Mage.'

'Of course not, I got powers.'

'Mighty powers, Arch Mage. Is this a test, Arch Mage?'

'Where's this Vous?'

'Our Friend and Lord is in his chambers. His meal has been served. None have since disturbed him, Arch Mage.'

'Where's that, you spud-faced bastard?'

The young man placidly raised an arm behind him. There stood the door the winged woman had described, with swords mounted above the door frame. It was open. Case marched to it, then held himself in check. OK, this is what she wanted. Get in, get the job done, then we'll ask her for a drink and she can tell me what happened with Eric. Spent too long on this sordid business to blow it now. Get it right, Stuart Casey, for once in your life.

Through the door was a huge room with heavy bookshelves on one side and a thick carpet down the middle, rich with woven patterns of threaded gold. Pronged stands held gleaming candles, lending the room a soft golden light. A window at the far wall had its curtain drawn.

There was no one in the chamber, no guards or servants. The man seated on a throne by the far wall, not moving, Case had taken at first for a statue: one knee raised, an elbow resting upon it. He wore some kind of ceremonial gown of loose, shining silk.

Case took a deep breath and went inside.

Vous's head was tilted forwards at an angle, and his eyes — glassy, pure blue, encased in slanted lids — didn't blink once. He was slim, maybe Eric's age, but somehow not young *seeming*. Short golden hair was cropped neatly over a head that seemed to slightly bulge. He was handsome in a sense, with features well defined, but also delicate-looking, as though one hard blow would smash his face like glass.

Case went closer, very careful to keep his steps silent. Jewellery hung over Vous's neck, thick lengths of chain not unlike the charm Case wore, though much newer and fancier. Rings gleamed on his fingers. A small table was set some way before the throne; it held a plate of food and a goblet of wine. Case's eye lingered on the wine and he felt a powerful urge to go ahead and swallow it down, whatever might happen to him.

Vous stirred at last: his head tilted Case's way, listening for something. 'She did not wail long, this morning,' he said quietly. Case's blood froze. 'She did not wail for me. Perhaps, at last, she's learning.' Vous fell quiet. The hand resting on the throne's arm was very tense, knuckles white, and its fingernails picked at the gold. Vous looked down at his hand, pale and stiff, scratching, and he blinked, seeming surprised by what it was doing.

Case couldn't be certain Vous was talking to him. Looking around the room, he saw a tall, thin mirror mounted on the wall and approached it, just to double-check his reflection was still invisible. When he stood before the glass, he nearly cried out — there was no reflection, just a smoky swirl of light, and ghostly faces within it. Five of them. One was a woman's, her hair flowing as though she lay in water. Another had sharp teeth and beast's eyes, and seemed barely human. They were asleep but for one, its face almost featureless as a skull, with wide, dark eye sockets. That one's mouth opened and it gasped in alarm. 'Friend!' it called. 'Vous! Friend! Beware. I hear something. I hear steps—'

'*Shut up!*' the scream from the throne lashed out like a whip. Case jumped at the sound of it. Vous's teeth were bared like an animal's. The skull in the mirror whimpered and went quiet. All the others opened their eyes. They whispered quietly amongst themselves, then separated fast as fish darting away in different directions when water's disturbed.

The smoky light faded when they'd gone, revealing Case's reflection, almost invisible. He sighed, relieved, and tried to calm his heart before all these frights made it quit altogether. Boy, did he want a sip of that wine now.

He went back to the throne. Vous's head was still turned towards the mirror, but his face had gone back to its previous expression, eyes still unblinking. 'You're here now, aren't you?' he whispered. 'You're here right now. Watching me again. Watching me.'

Case swallowed, and he tried to breathe without any sound

at all. His mouth was very dry and the wine was calling to him, positively singing. He could almost taste it, sweet and strong.

'Watching me,' said Vous. 'But, ah! You never speak. You . . . never . . . *speak*.'

And then he was up, prowling around his throne as though to catch someone hiding behind it. He looked suspiciously at the far doorway, through which Case had come, then turned to the curtained window and approached it like he was stalking prey.

Case knew he would not get a better chance. He grabbed the wine goblet, and he'd have sworn on his life afterwards that he only intended a *quick* little sip, just to wet his parched tongue. But when he tasted it — so very sweet, fizzing across his tongue, unlike any wine he'd sipped before — he was startled to find the goblet seemed to have drained itself down his throat. Panicked, he set it back, and very nearly ran away. But oh, his head spun so pleasantly, almost coaxing away the fear of what he'd just done.

Vous stepped away from the window. He'd been catlike and tense a moment ago, but now his head slumped forwards and a tear crept down his cheek. 'Watch,' he whispered. 'Watch, if you must.' He slumped back on the throne, chin on his chest, glassy blue eyes staring at nothing.

It took a minute for him to see the empty wine goblet. When he did, he stared at it hard for a long while, not moving, not saying a thing. Slowly, he nodded. 'Yes! You *are* here.' He laughed bitterly. 'I *knew* you were here. But I grow so tired . . . so tired.' Vous shut his eyes as more tears rolled down his face. 'Why, Shadow? What more can I give you? You have seen all my forms, splayed and bare. To the pits of pain with your hideous judging eyes! Shadow! What more can I give . . .?' He choked up, a knuckle in his mouth, then stood, grabbed the plate and with an echoing scream of rage threw it hard at the far wall, where it shattered.

He took the wine goblet and did the same. Then he stalked towards the door, his gown rippling. Case followed. Only now, as Vous passed the candles and the light of the open doorway, did Case notice something peculiar: Vous's body cast no shadow on the thick red carpet.

Back out in the hall the drab grey-robes shuffled on their way, though a few heads turned to watch Vous pass. He stopped in their midst, seeming undecided. 'You,' he said, pointing to an older man. The man came forwards, head inclined. 'Take that girl's clothes off. Rip them off.'

The older man inclined his head further, and did as he was asked, clumsily pulling at a young woman's grey robe. It took a while before her slender pale body was exposed. She watched Vous, waiting without expression.

'Fuck her,' said Vous. 'Now.'

The older man shoved the woman over and began removing his own clothes. The other grey-robes didn't react, just waited patiently in case they too were called upon.

'Hurt her,' said Vous distractedly, his lip curled in a look of distaste.

The man clumsily struggled to do as he was asked, with little slaps or half-hearted tugs at the woman's hair.

'Harder. Make her cry out, whimper.'

Soon Vous turned away, seemingly bored by it all. He stalked up the hall the way he'd been going before. Behind him, both servants stood and began fixing their clothes, without a word to each other, without any apparent effect at all. A passing grey-robe paused to help them, businesslike and impersonal, like they were bits of equipment to be put back in place.

Vous stopped again, some way further up the passage. He ordered two male servants to do the same thing, and watched this performance a while longer, before walking off in boredom after instructing them to continue for the rest of the day.

'Shadow!' cried Vous, suddenly pausing, arms raised high. He peered around with flinty eyes. 'I still . . . *feel* you. More tokens, for you to collect. Are you pleased? There shall be others. For I still . . . *feel* you.' Behind him, the two naked men clambered over one another. Passing servants calmly stepped around them.

The longer Case trailed the obviously insane ruler, the more he could have sworn 'Shadow' was he himself, that his footsteps had given him away. But he kept following, and Vous ranted about 'Shadow' every few minutes, in between ordering more staff to do more humiliating things: sex acts, often as not, or beatings. He seemed especially intent on seeing the older men do sexual things and asking the women to fight. He ordered one female grey-robe sent away to be lashed, muttering he thought she'd scream beautifully, and that he envied those who would hear it.

Whatever the Invia had wanted Case to overhear, he somehow doubted he'd heard it yet. And although this whole business made him feel ill, Case had to wonder if these were really people at all, suffering this abuse, for it was like watching a sadistic child play games with dolls who could not actually be hurt. He wondered: *should* he feel sorry for them? The more he saw them endure, mutely and obediently, the more he doubted it. And he had just decided that he'd seen and heard enough, and had begun to turn on his heel to find a way out, when up the other end of the hall, there again was the Arch Mage.

Case ducked behind Vous, fearful that the Arch Mage could see through his charm's spell of invisibility. A long silence stretched out as Vous watched the Arch Mage without a word. When he strode fast towards the Arch Mage, the latter backed away. 'What is it?' demanded Vous. 'Why do you cower?'

'Your charms. Anki Kala especially. It burns me.'

Vous paused, absentmindedly removed a bracelet from his wrist and put it in a pocket of his gown. 'Come closer,' he said.

The Arch Mage approached slowly, his large head bowed as if he were a dog afraid of its owner. He groped the air before him. 'Vous. Could you be so kind as to remove Tapishuk also?'

'Why?' Vous said quietly.

'It blinds me, Friend and Lord. As you well know.'

Vous's lip curled back in a silent snarl, but his voice remained quiet. 'We are talking. You have ears and tongue. What need have you for sight?'

'Please, Vous. I perceived a charm in the Hall of Windows. I would like to keep my senses free. Even without those two wardens I am withered to nothing. You are well guarded by the others, which I do not beg you to remove.'

Vous watched him for at least a full minute with no reaction. The Arch Mage groped his way ahead, then stood gasping for breath. 'I must sit, Vous. Your wardens drain me so.'

'What kind of charm?' Vous said. He took a ring from his finger and put it in the same pocket as the bracelet, but kept his hand in that pocket.

The Arch Mage blinked, rubbing his human eye, which watered. 'Do not be worried. I think a stray one escaped storage. But it is best to be careful, for I did not see its wearer, and he or she did not step forwards when asked. It will be dealt with. Vous, if I may? Have you been troubled by ... by your suspicions again?'

Something in Vous seemed to soften, a touch. 'He ... he has been here again.'

The Arch Mage nodded. 'Shadow, Vous? Or another?'

A long pause. 'I have felt him all morning.'

'Do you feel him now?'

'Yes.' His head hung forwards forlornly.

'Would it help, Vous, if I removed the enchantment banishing *your* shadow?'

'No!'

'Do consider it, Friend and Lord. Are you sure?'

Tears ran down the lord's face. 'I don't need it . . . catching my *eye* every time I walk past a *light* . . . No! There are times in the day, where I have peace now. Before, it was . . . relentless. It was cruel. So cruel.'

'If you are sure, Lord. But please. Call on me if you wish. Not just as a subject, but as a friend.'

Vous eyed the Arch Mage, his face ambiguous and still as a carving. A long silence stretched out. 'Your business?'

'A plot has emerged, Vous, and I am concerned.'

Vous scoffed. 'A plot on my life? They may have it.'

'You mean to shock me, Lord, and you do succeed. But I will tell you what I know. Someone seeks to break down the Wall.'

'Which wall?'

'*The* Wall, Vous. The barrier at World's End.'

Vous laughed. The Arch Mage said nothing. 'That cannot be done,' said Vous.

'There are ways. The Mayors are resourceful and becoming desperate. They may try.'

Vous began pacing. 'What about Glint?'

The Arch Mage shrugged, showing perhaps as much irritation as he dared. 'We have discussed him. I feel that particular general remains loyal but I watch him closely.'

Vous laughed bitterly. 'A wolf snarling at another that the meat is his.'

The Arch Mage's hideous face looked up, his voice gentle with concern. 'I do not aspire to your place, Friend and Lord, though of course my assurance will ring hollow. Your fear is a natural consequence of power. All history's lords and rulers would agree.

For your health, I advise you: let your suspicion sit in you easier.'

Vous shut his eyes like someone very tired. 'Who else?'

The Arch Mage gave more names until Vous snarled, 'Enough of this!' and put back on the ring he'd removed. Case saw nothing happen, but the Arch Mage cringed away, hand over his human eye. Vous crouched beside him, his expression venomous. 'You have never mentioned World's End before *this* moment. Never as it relates to the Project, as a threat or otherwise, in *all* the miserable years. Not from our earliest days planning coups in darkened rooms with wax-eared brats watching the doors. You have never raised the possibility of its being destroyed, by anyone or anything, enemy of ours or not. Why *now*?'

The Arch Mage seemed to fight to keep his voice even under immense strain. 'It is more a potential combination of forces, Friend and Lord. It has worn on my mind for a time, but only as a distant chance. You laugh when I mention it — so did I, until I learned of the plot. Then I gave it some thought and grew afraid. It is not likely, but *possible*, with a determined, resourceful enemy. We will always have enemies until the Project succeeds and they no longer matter. Until then, I am forever nervous of them, Friend and Lord. As is my duty.'

Vous licked his lips and leaned very close to the Arch Mage, watching him writhe and squirm. Then as though convinced of his vulnerability the lord's face softened and he stood. 'I am sorry. I . . . I am sorry.'

'It is fine, Vous. It is fine.'

The lord hastily walked away, his knuckle between his teeth and tears in his eyes. Panting for breath, the Arch Mage watched him go, then struggled to his feet, sweating and shaken. No emotion was translatable from that face.

And that's quite enough for me, Case thought, backing quietly away.

16

As time dragged on, Eric only wanted to stop and rest. But onwards, onwards, onwards they walked, till it all became a blur. The tunnels rose steadily, and Kiown said they were headed for the surface soon, always just a little further, just a bit more . . .

His head began to spin. I'm a valuable trinket to them, he thought, so maybe they can carry me. He stopped fighting the dizziness and let his legs collapse. Kiown rushed to stop his head striking the rock floor. 'Get his legs,' he told Sharfy.

Eric felt himself being lifted, and wondered whether the gun was secure enough not to fall out. Did it matter? Did anything matter apart from the chance to shut his eyes?

When they set him down he smelled the sweetness of fresh air. One eye opened. It was night, but there were no stars. They seemed high up on a hilltop. There were distant lights. There was the smell of campfire smoke.

I can't believe I'm here, seeing this, living this. There really is another world, and I've found it. I can't believe what I've seen . . . The thoughts should have left him awestruck, or terrified, but he was so tired his mind hurt like a strained muscle to think them. Reality jet lag, he thought.

'Others aren't far.' Sharfy's voice. Eric quickly shut his eyes, feigning sleep.

'Is he ill?' said Kiown.

'Keep him here, let him rest. Anfen'll want him.'

'I'm going back to camp.'

'Tell em not to bother us yet. I'll mind him.' Footsteps padded away. Eric lay on flat, smooth rock that seemed as comfortable as any bed he'd known. He thought of his comfortable, soft mattress back home, with its creaking springs, right now still unmade.

Sharfy draped a blanket over him and put something soft beneath his head. *You can trust him*, Kiown had said. *He just doesn't look like it.*

Who cared either way? Sleep. Deep sleep, this time not troubled by wild dreams. Those, he supposed upon waking, were now for the daytime.

17

When he was out of the Arch Mage's earshot, Case ran. Heads turned in the Hall of Windows as his footsteps scuffed on the floor.

The way wound downwards, until he was sure he'd gone well beneath the floor on which was Aziel's bedroom. Soon he was out of the tower altogether, and into a larger part of the castle's body. Some long passages here were completely abandoned, others packed with busy staff. Every so often he found a window and stuck his head out, calling urgently for the winged woman, but she didn't answer him. He began to think he'd been swindled, that she had never meant to keep her side of the bargain — which, he realised with a sinking feeling, might mean Eric wasn't alive after all.

The lower he went, the fewer vacant-faced grey-robes there were. Soon, it seemed the people were normal people, and were in a fashion just like people anywhere else, doing their jobs behind benches or at tables, though those jobs were mostly pre-industrial. He passed smiths making things of metal, women weaving straw and fabric, courtyards where teenagers lined up to be taught how to use weapons or tools. He saw so many things, some normal-seeming and some peculiar, that his mind began to shut it all out, and to long just for it to be over, for a bed, even just a soft field of grass to rest in, naked sky above, cool breeze to breathe in.

Sometimes he came to mess halls where workers sat for meals. More than once, Case helped himself to someone's plate or cup, not caring about the startled reaction of its owner. The goblets of wine were far inferior to Vous's upstairs, but they kept him going.

At last, at long last, he came to what felt like the ground floor. More chambers, more hallways, until a cavernous space opened before him, bigger than an aircraft hangar, clattering with the sound of busy people and machinery. Hundreds, maybe thousands of people bustled around large metal wagons, which drove in from an underground passage. Across from this was the outside world, a view of the horizon from ground level, and that big flat road Case had seen from the sky, dividing the horizon in two.

Bundles of hay and straw, crates of fruit, livestock with its animal smell, and all manner of other things were being unpacked from the underground wagon train and loaded onto smaller carts; the smaller carts were wheeled off through side passages and out of sight. Case sat to rest for a spell, watching it all. If he hadn't been so tired, he'd have been glad to see the semblance of normality here, of real people doing real things, whatever insanity happened on the floors high above them, which he knew they themselves were probably forbidden from knowing. Foremen shouted orders, strong men did heavy lifting with grunts and curses. One or two grey-robes roamed about, scrolls and pencils in hand, seeming to supervise it all, not half as dead-headed as those upstairs had appeared. Here, they gave orders and were hastily obeyed.

Then, as though Case's very relishing of normality had given the signal, some kind of commotion broke out near the entrance to that underground passage. Shouts and cries broke out. 'Why's that wagon unattended?' a passing grey-robe demanded of no one in particular.

A large wagon lurched up the passage and onto the floorspace, where rails ran along the floor. Blood was spattered thick over its side. Shrieks and cries spread around the large space and people began to scatter.

That was when the pit devils leaped from the wagon. Four, five of them. Then more poured out of the tunnel in a scurrying pack, dozens of them loose among the workers, jaws open wide, teeth gnashing as their heads whipped around on unnaturally flexible necks, mauling anything that moved.

Case shrugged and calmly walked towards the exits, not having to try hard to shut out the chaos that ensued, the screams, human and inhuman, the blood and the death. He'd had enough of it all. He didn't even bother worrying about whether the evil-looking monsters could see through the charm's disguise or not. At any rate they left him alone.

On a patch of soft grass outside, some distance off the long flat road, he collapsed, exhausted. He slept right there, shutting out the background noise and not caring a damn about anything just then: not the castle, the winged woman, not the real world nor this one, nor even Eric. Sleep was what mattered, sleep in the soft trampled grass and, as he'd wished, the cool breeze blowing over him.

Meanwhile the Invia just watched, just watched, as the powerful mage paced around her frozen and trapped body. She had known the danger of coming within the home of one such as this; even a war mage would have been dangerous for her where there were walls and roof to prevent an easy escape if the fight went ill. Her chances against *this* mage, much greater than they, had been poor. She had barely even realised she was cornered and must fight before he snared her, blind and deaf, in an invisible web that held her still. She had been dragged to this small dark place and left here to wait.

The Arch Mage now regarded her as if she were a puzzle piece that didn't belong. His blazing aura filled the room, shocking waves of multicoloured plumes radiating power. She'd have been impressed and scared, had she not beheld the dragon-youth, whose auras could be seen long before they themselves were in sight, beaming through the rock layers of their prisons. *That* power was real greatness, a blazing inferno. This was a campfire . . . yet, she had put her hand in it, and been burned.

He had asked many questions, of the dragon-youth mostly, demanding news of the eight major personalities (and of some of the minor ones, whose business she did not know or care about). She had answered truly to save pain, time, and trouble. It did not matter what words of the dragon-youth this man now knew, for they would have foreseen *this*, probably, her very imprisonment, and chosen their words with care. Yet she wished to get back — there was much to tell her sisters, even without retrieving the old man's charm.

She also knew the mage's dilemma: to kill her was easiest, but if he did, he would be Marked, and the skies here were often travelled by her kind. Should twenty of them descend upon him, he would not fare as easily.

'I will keep you caged here for a time,' he said at last. 'You have entered my home without leave, and deserve to be punished. But listen. You have not acted for the dragons, only for your own curiosity. Had you acted for them, it would have been a breach of the natural law, and they would risk doom. I know this. Do not think fear of them is what stays my hand, only your utility. Yesterday's enemy is today's friend, if he is of use to me, and to the Project. Can you be of use to me?'

She would not serve him, and thought him insane to ask, but why say so? 'Yes.'

He studied her. 'Very well. I must consider in what way you can serve. *I* will allow you to live, in my service.' For a full day he left her there alone, before there was a sound of keys in the lock, and a guard came in with a sword in hand, which he lifted high, smiling down at her. 'Pretty,' he said.

He would be Marked, no doubt sent out on the rooftops right away, where her sisters could find him with ease and tear him apart — that would be the matter's end. The mage was smart. He must have communicated his order with as subtle a signal as he could; or, perhaps, he'd long ago made provisions for what should happen, if an Invia needed to be slain. If the mage had been careful enough, and if this servant were bound and gagged, her sisters would not know the mage's real part in her death, and he would go where he wished without fear. Not so, *this* ignorant man . . .

She did not care either way, even as he ceased leering and the sword descended. Her purpose had been fulfilled. Others like her remained, others would be made. Had her life been important, the dragons would have warned her.

The cry of her death, as the cries of a dying Invia always did, swept across every corner of Levaal, from the castle to World's End, through the fishing villages by the Godstears Sea, across the hot smouldering ash of Inferno's Grave, through the icy peaks of Nightmare's Crown, heard by all who had hearing. Those asleep had fleeting, grief-filled nightmares of beautiful things being broken; those awake had shivers down their backs. Not many knew what it was they heard.

18

Case opened his eyes, bleary with the light of a sun he couldn't see in the ivory-white sky. If he'd had dreams, he'd forgotten them. His legs and back thanked him for all the recent walking by making it feel as though he'd spent the night being drawn and quartered. His knees were especially polite in their thanks.

He looked around for the sun, but it hid from sight, if it was even up there at all. He'd been entertaining some notion that this world was right next door to the old one, like two balloons stuck together, and that it had to physically *exist* under the same sun, even if for whatever reason no one back home had seen this place. But ah, that familiar smell of grass on waking! (This was not the first time it had been his bed, not by a long shot.)

The burbling sound of a nearby crowd was what had woken him. There ahead was the exit he'd stumbled through, before collapsing on the lawns outside the huge white castle, and — Christ on a crutch, look at the size of it! It made him feel like he was a little speck of sand. He'd seen from the sky in the winged woman's arms that the castle was sculpted into some sort of deliberate shape. It was still too close here to see what the shape was, but Case had an inkling that before him was a gaping open mouth, which alone must stretch for half a mile in either direction, or more.

People milled about on the lawns. Despite a sprinkling of bald heads and greying hair, they seemed mostly university-aged, their clothes of plain make. Some were European-looking and light-skinned, blondes and redheads; some were darker, with faces distantly Oriental. But to Case's eye, there were no clear distinctions between types, and the crowd could, he judged, be of one ethnicity. Almost all were unhealthily thin, and all eagerly jostled towards the open part of the gate through which Case had exited the castle. A bunch of guards with spears angled downwards stood on the platform near the steps, barring the way in.

He sat up, stretched, his head a little seedy.

'Hello there,' a voice said behind him.

Case wheeled around, startled. A young woman sat on the grass, legs crossed, hands in her lap, watching him. She had short blonde hair and wore a long green dress that seemed medieval in style, tight on her body but loose around her arms. Her face was friendly, plain and pleasant; he'd found as he got older that young women all looked amazing to him, like a whole new species entirely more beautiful than they'd been when he too was young ... but he did not desire them in the way he had in his youth, any more than you'd want to screw a beautiful sunset. How long had she been there, watching him sleep? And what in God's name was the appeal in the sight?

'Morning,' Case said. He pondered the problem at hand, and could think of no classy way to say it. 'I don't mean to offend, but, if there's some kind of bathroom around here ...'

The woman laughed. 'You need to relieve yourself?'

Case nodded, feeling his cheeks redden. 'Normally not in public, you understand. I don't normally sleep in front of castles either.'

'I shall look the other way, be assured.'

'Thank you.' Case worried that some of the crowd would look over as he pissed in the grass, but they seemed too busy trying to get up those steps, pleading with the guards, who ignored them. Then he remembered the charm still around his neck — they wouldn't see him.

And yet, the woman had . . .

Case turned. 'You can see me?' he said. 'How's that, then? You know about this?' He shook the beads around his neck.

'I know about your charm,' she replied. 'That is, I know you wear one. Not how you came across it.'

'Is it broken?'

'Its spell won't work on *me*. Those people can't see you. A few who've wandered past turned their heads at the sound of snoring coming from some invisible source. It was loud. I thought you had swallowed a large, angry hound.'

Case hesitated then sat back down near her. 'Why can you see through it? You a witch or something?'

She laughed. 'I'm a friend.'

'Friend?'

'Yes. Shall I prove it? Here.' In her hand now was a goblet of wine. He hadn't seen her pour it and saw no bottle nearby. She offered it to him. He liked the look of her accompanying smile very much: intelligent and sweet. And Case would have taken the drink had she snarled like a dog. Yet . . .

'Pardon me. Last thing I'd want is to offend you. But we have a saying where I come from. If something's too good to be true, it usually is. And to me, the best thing I could think of right now is a nice-looking young lady with a free cup of wine in her hand.'

She laughed again, and the laugh — aside from making him feel exceptionally witty, which he knew he wasn't — gave her face a sparkle that made Case ashamed to have doubted her.

She said, 'That is a very wise saying. We have a saying here, too. If you see an Otherworlder asleep on the castle's lawns with a very powerful charm around his neck, pour him a drink!'

Case considered. 'Cheers to that.' He sipped and found the wine as delicious as if not better than the cup he'd skolled last night in Vous's chamber. If it's poisoned, what the hell. It tastes good enough, he thought. And she's not a bad last sight to have. He took the luxury of draining the cup more slowly this time.

'I suspected you would enjoy that vintage,' said the woman with another smile.

Case frowned; did something in her smile suggest that she *knew* what he'd done last night, stealing the lord's drink? If so, she didn't seem to mind. He wiped his mouth. 'So that's what you call us? Otherworlders? I'd figured *this* was the "other" world, and ours was the real one.'

'That is probably to be expected.'

'You know, some people from here came into ours first. That's why me and Eric came in. Well, *he* came in, and I followed him. Long story.'

This seemed to interest her. 'Oh? How many from our world entered yours?'

'Hard to say, miss, I wasn't watching the door the whole time. Three or four I know of. They robbed a newsagent. That's a kind of store we have, back home. Took a whole bunch of paper, then jumped right back.'

'Paper! Is that all? Gold or magic or scales I could fathom. Why such trouble for paper? Or was there writing on the paper? That must be it. Trade for the groundmen, I assume? Not the paper, of course, but the language on it. To them, such would be priceless.'

'Wouldn't know, miss. And I never heard of groundmen.'

'Of course, of course. Do you know how many from your world are roaming through this one?'

Case sipped the delicious cold wine and felt in a relaxed, conversational mood. 'Me and my friend that I know of. Some others tried to get in, but didn't make it far.' Case shut his eyes at the memory of those bodies, for he too easily pictured this young woman lying dead among them. 'Rather not say more on that, if you'll excuse me, miss. You got a name, or should I keep calling you *miss*?'

She smiled. 'In fact, I don't have a name. I seldom have need for one. Call me Stranger, if you like. Does that suit?'

'Well sure. I'm Stuart Casey. Case for short.'

She inclined her head. 'I have no name, you have two! Is that a custom of your people?'

'Most have three names, first, last and middle,' he said, then delivered a brief lecture on the practice, which she listened to politely. At its end, he asked, 'What're all those hungry-looking people doing over there?'

The woman looked over and shrugged as though the milling crowd was of no importance. 'They're here from the cities, seeking work. The Aligned cities send their sons and daughters, since wealth is hard to find back home. The castle takes some, but most are turned away. They keep coming back, though, every day. Case, I notice you often look skywards. May I ask why?'

'Well, there's this — may sound strange to you — but this woman with wings. She's the one who gave me this.' He rattled the necklace's silver beads. 'She was gonna come get it, then tell me where to find Eric.'

This seemed to interest Stranger a great deal. 'Woman with wings! So, you have seen one of the Invia?'

'If that's what you call em, yes I have.'

Her look said she was impressed. 'Do you know many regard Invia as creatures of myth?'

'Not surprised. But she was real, all right.'

'What did she want of you?' said Stranger, eagerly leaning forwards. Case hesitated. She smiled. 'Ah, I've hardly told you aught of myself, and here I am, asking all your secrets. But perhaps *I* can help you find your friend. If, that is, you wish to remain in Levaal, and not go back to your own world again.'

'Levaal? What's that?'

She smiled. 'That's what this world is named. Another word for its meaning is *link*.'

Case frowned thoughtfully. 'Link. Like in a chain?'

'Yes. Have you a word for a chain-link which also acts as a protector of something?'

'Suppose not.' Case shrugged. 'If you help me find my friend, I'll be in your debt, for what that's worth. Another glass of wine'd hit the spot, too.' Case had intended this as a self-deprecating joke, and he was surprised to find his cup had filled. 'How'd you do that?'

'It is a small trick I learned, but it taxes me a little, so your pardon for leaving your cup alone once you are finished. I also have some ability to see the future. Not far, just a short way, and never beyond what happenstance magicians call *event junctions*. Or forks in the road, if you will. But you have stepped beyond the last junction and the next one is ahead of you. So I *am* able to help you, Case.'

He hesitated. She reminded him of a hippie girl who seems to look at all people like they're fine in her book, even old drunken ones who piss right in front of her. But those hippie girls had a kind of starry-eyed *not-there* vibe about them. This one didn't — she was switched on all right, with her bright green eyes so attentive, and he got the sense she was here talking to him for a reason she was unlikely to share. 'Now, why would you want to help me out like that, Stranger? Are you just a terribly nice lass, or is there more to it?'

'That saying of yours again! I assure you, had I evil intent, you'd have told me more than enough by now to suit my designs, and told me in a deal less comfort. But you need not worry. It may be I find the act of helping another very good for me, perhaps to right past wrongs. Or it may be that my own interests are aligned with yours, in ways difficult to explain: that I too benefit from bringing you and — Eric, is it? — together again. It may be that to tell you too much of myself would endanger you, or me, or others. Who knows?'

'Miss, when you smile like that, I don't much care either way. If you can help me out, please do.' It was true: it was hard not to trust her, and he even felt a bit silly for his doubt. But she hadn't quite come clean with him, he noticed . . .

She said, 'Very well. Listen, Case. Something happened earlier, in there.' She pointed to the opening in the castle, just beyond which was the large space where wagons from the underground passage were unloaded. 'An attack, of sorts, from what little news I heard. There are beings called pit devils. Just pests, but dangerous ones. Many swarmed inside from an underground wagon train. It seems they were herded deliberately.'

'I think I know what you're talking about,' said Case. 'Saw it myself. Quite a mess, it was.'

'Yes. Many died, many goods were spoiled, and this is displeasing enough, to them. But more than that, it is a symbolic gesture, an act of open war. It has angered the castle a great deal, signs indicate, and they feel they know who did it. They have sent out patrols this morning already. You may have heard them marching past.'

'Can't say I have. I slept pretty deep.'

'No matter. The next patrol to pass down this very road — it should be within the hour — will head south-west. They will succeed in finding the bandits who did this. They may or may not apprehend them — I am not a great seer, I'm afraid, and that is beyond the event junction. But I can see this much: if you follow that group, you will find your way to Eric. Be careful, of course, to keep your charm on at all times.'

Case digested all this. 'Well, if this is all true, I'll thank you kindly. Is it far to walk? I can't see myself keeping pace with a marching army.'

'Half a day's march, more or less. You may be able to ride a supplies cart, if they have one. And, some advice. That charm is very valuable, very old, and very powerful. It is valuable enough that anyone would prize it, especially those with any magic ability. Would you believe the dragon-youth themselves made it, or at least blessed it? I can't tell which personality. But their touch is still visible upon it, if you've eyes like mine. How it glares! Few such things are left in the world. Keep it to yourself until you find someone you trust. We may meet again before long, perhaps when you next need help. Keep an eye out for me.'

Case sensed she was about to leave. 'Miss? Stranger? One question before you go? That castle there, it's supposed to be something, isn't it? To look like something, some big, huge animal. What kind?'

She laughed. 'A dragon, of course. *The* Dragon.'

Case turned to try and see it. 'Hmm. Well, that might be its mouth right there. What's that long part, over yonder? A tail, or a hand or what?'

But she didn't answer, for she was no longer there. Case laughed, surprised and delighted. He held up the cup. 'To your health, miss.' He sipped the wine, just a taste, so it would last until he had to move. Guess at least not everyone here's the kind you wouldn't piss on, if they were on fire. He thought of the war mage, engulfing itself, and winced. And there you go, I even had the chance to choose.

19

The grey stone hilltop plateau was flat as a plate. Their campfire was off to one edge, near the shoulder-height ridge of stone
that acted as a shelter, usefully hiding them from the seldom-
used road directly below. This hill and the tall cliff across formed
a gate for the long mountain pass the band had to travel through
to gain access to the roads south and west, and which they
should have travelled through last night, had not Sharfy, Kiown
and the Pilgrim been too exhausted for it. The rest of the band
was awake on the platform further down, cleaning their clothes
and themselves as best they could, while the Otherworlder still
slept, curled by the fire. It was a cold, dim morning. Thin streaks
of cloud spread over the sky like slowly uncurling fingers.

The man sitting across from the Pilgrim on a piece of log by
the campfire looked young and careworn at once, with a powerful
athlete's build, and — though his skin was light — something
more acutely Oriental about his face than most others in Levaal.
His hands dug into the hair by his temples and pulled it enough,
surely, to hurt. He was not even aware he did this; in truth he
was savouring the quiet and felt as at peace as he could while
on the road in enemy country. Before descending into his own
black thoughts, Anfen had watched the Otherworlder for a while,
wondering what marvels of knowledge he had brought with

him. Another hour's sleep was the most that could be spared, for the hornet's nest had been kicked, and they were still too close to it. This little shelter was probably as safe as they'd get until well south of here and out of Aligned country altogether. And there was no knowing what spots their windows viewed at any one moment.

Anfen says hello. Very funny. If Kiown had known how *perilously* close Anfen had been to whipping his head clean off when he heard about that, he would probably have turned and fled, not sulked and made excuses. Kiown thought he'd been hard done by when his troop leader drove an elbow into his cheek and knocked him out cold, the *crack!* of it still echoing in Anfen's mind with a morsel of satisfaction. To yell at the guard had been impulsiveness rather than treachery, Anfen had hesitantly bet; but a saboteur could not have done much better. His hand squeezed around the blade of the sword that rested across his lap, and only when the edge bit into his skin did he know quite how angry he still was. He glanced abstractedly at the line cut across his fingers and wiped off the blood on his pants, hardly even noticing it.

Had the Otherworlder just stirred? He examined Eric's face closely, then had to look away, for Eric's face was now covered in blood and half smashed apart, its pieces like a broken plate held together by stretching, loose skin. Anfen was not alarmed or surprised by the sight; it was nothing new to him. He had, earlier, seen the young man decapitated, as clearly as if it were real. He had, whilst hearing Sharfy's account of Kiown's stupidity, seen the battered soldier's jaw break off and drop to the ground. A blink later, it was merely Sharfy's ugly, trustworthy face before him. He wondered if they had a name for this curse, or illness: whatever it was that caused the years of bloodshed and violence he'd been part of to flash before his eyes. It came and went, sometimes for weeks, and most commonly with newly met people.

Eric's face was normal again. Nobility, Kiown had claimed, as though this made up for what he'd done. Anfen wondered. The young man was well fed, had no visible scars, had good teeth and grooming. His clothes seemed formal and well made. It was possible.

Anfen checked the sky again but saw no sign of any Invia. How long would his luck hold? He was Marked, and they'd see him from a long way away. He picked up the deadstone, rubbing it across his sword's face: *scrape, scrape, scrape*. He could have had the sword enchanted with some useful effect, but preferred deadstone's ability to bother and distract mages. Having to rub it on the blade every day, however, was a pain.

The sound made the Otherworlder stir. Anfen saw his eyes open a crack, then close, feigning more sleep. 'Good morning,' said Anfen. 'There's stew in the pot. Loup blessed it. It tastes better than it smells and looks.'

Eric yawned and sat up. He took in his surrounds, looking behind them at the cave cut into the hillside, through which Kiown and Sharfy had carried him. He said, 'Are you going to cut my head off with that sword, or are you just sharpening it?'

Anfen tried to soften his manner, for he knew he looked flinty-eyed and that each battle and kill had changed his appearance, however minutely, so that by now death hung about him like a veil. So it felt. 'Your head is safe enough. Nor am I sharpening this. Eskian blades don't need much sharpening. They hold their edges. They'd want to, for the price.'

Eric stumbled to the fireside and took some stew from the pot. Anfen saw him hesitate, possibly unsure of the etiquette: how much should he take? 'Have it all, if you've room for it. A hard road lies ahead. Worse than the one you came here by, no doubt. I know your name already. I'm Anfen.'

Eric ate ravenously, pausing once to feel the bulge in his pockets, checking that something was still there. Anfen saw a bloody mess in one of the young man's eye sockets, an eye recently gouged out, the face black with bruises. He saw one arm broken in two places and lying inert and useless, still clutching the wooden bowl half full of stew. He shut his eyes and things had become normal again when he opened them. 'You're nobility, I'm told,' he said.

Eric glanced up at him. 'Sort of.'

'Sort of? How do you mean? What exactly is your title?'

Eric's mouth was too full to speak. He chewed for a while, which conveniently gave him time to ponder an answer. He said, 'We have a custom, where I come from, not to give details of our families and how they're connected. I am not the highest placed, or even especially highly placed.'

'But your absence would be noticed?'

'Yes. It will be.'

So, he was not sent or ordered to come. Did he wish me to think so? 'Do they know where you went?'

'I left word of it. I don't think the door itself is something widely known. Yet.'

'They will close the entry point soon,' said Anfen, setting his blade back in its scabbard, for the Otherworlder's eyes kept nervously returning to it. 'What are the likely consequences, do you think, of your absence? An expedition here?'

The young man pondered that for a while. 'I'd say if my world — Earth, we call it — found out about this one, they would make a very big fuss. They'd probably send in some explorers and the like first. If those were attacked, they might send armies. What would result from that I couldn't tell you.'

Eric frowned. 'Your fire,' he said. 'There's no smoke. I smell it but can't see it.'

'We are on a hilltop in enemy country,' said Anfen with a shrug. 'Why wouldn't we have treated the wood? We have a magician with us.'

For some reason Eric laughed. 'Right you are. Silly me.' He attacked his food for a while, then said, 'I just remembered something. Kiown said you own me now. Is that how you'd put it too?'

'We don't *own* you. You're free to go at any time, if you wish.' A lie, of course; why not first try things the easy way? 'My advice is that you come with us back to the Council of Free Cities in Elvury, the nearest Free City. It is the safest thing for you. This is Aligned country. Wild things and Inferno cultists infest the rural parts. In Aligned cities, you'll be enslaved or killed. Even if you find some place to dwell and hide out, you'll likely starve. They are short on food these days, except when the citizens decide to eat each other. You will be safe and fed with us, at least.'

Eric set aside his empty bowl. It seemed he could spot a lie when he saw one. 'So, I'm really free to just up and walk away.'

'You are as free to do that as you are to jump from this hilltop right now and bounce your skull on the road below. The results would be similar. A waste.'

The Otherworlder sighed. 'A friend of mine may have come through the door after me. Your friend Sharfy stopped me from going back to save him from that thing, that war mage. I won't tell you I'm happy about that.'

'And just how would you have *saved* him, Eric?'

Eric winced. Ah yes, there is a secret or two here, thought Anfen. What is it? A weapon? A power of some kind? Not enough to overwhelm Sharfy's knife, obviously, but enough to flummox a mage? Enough to get past a mage in the first place — some kind of disguise?

The Otherworlder quickly said, 'I don't know how I would have saved him. I don't know why it spared me. You're right. Maybe the second time around, it wouldn't have.'

'Then perhaps you owe Sharfy some thanks.'

'Maybe so. And you're right about all the rest. If you'll have me, I'll come. But . . . you don't want me just from the kindness of your heart, do you?'

Anfen smiled. 'No. What your presence means to the Mayors I can't say. They delight in confounding my predictions and advice. But they would prize you.'

Eric weighed this up, too. 'Why do I understand things the rest of you can't? Sharfy said it was some magic in the door itself. Or something.'

Anfen pondered, staring into the distance. He was glad to look away from Eric's face, which had now peeled and shrivelled as though it were long dead. 'The question is deeper than you may think,' he said. 'There were scholars and mages who studied Pilgrims like you, and the entry point, and Levaal's very creation itself. But their work has been destroyed or seized. I was high-ranked in their armies; I did some of the seizing.' I co-ordinated it, ordered it, kicked down doors with my own boots, killed with my own hands, ordered ditches dug by roadsides and in the woods, filled them with corpses by the dozen. And I was very, very good at it all. 'Then I began to read some of the books instead of burning them. And I decided to stop taking the castle's orders. Far too late, of course.' Because it's nice to be promoted and made a hero, isn't it, and be told sweet noble words about the foul things you've done? He sighed heavily. 'All I can tell you is that all things here, people, events and forces, are like little numbers in a puzzle being solved by a great mind.'

A log popped on the fire with a shower of sparks. 'Whose mind?'

'The Dragon's. Don't confuse It with those lesser ones you may hear of, the dragon-youth, imprisoned in the sky. I refer to that which *made* this world, or at least decided its natural laws. Perhaps the Dragon meant for people to travel between worlds, and wanted knowledge to be exchanged, or stolen. More little numbers gathered for the solving of that enormous puzzle. That may be why It laid such a condition at the boundary. You may be an ordained Pilgrim, long ago predicted. Who knows? The easiest way to put it is a phrase you may have heard by now: as the Dragon wills.'

Eric looked both impressed and sceptical. 'This Dragon. Is it real? I mean, are you giving me a religious explanation? An actual history? Do you worship it?'

What strange questions, Anfen thought, especially that last one. He frowned. 'It's real, though none have seen It in the flesh. We have only seen signs of its passing, from times It roamed the land, huge and awake. Footprints hammered into the world's crust, shed scales buried deep. We suspect It sleeps underground, near the castle, for there's heavy magic in those parts, and the gods do not go near it. No one swears to It, that I know of. Why would they? If you found a great sea or mountain, would you worship it, just because it is greater than you? We do not, unless it may have bearing on us, hear our prayers and answer them. Sometimes the Great Spirits do. The Dragon does not, unless in ways we can't see or measure. And if It *does* have a hand in our fate, It must mean us ill, for things have gone badly. I hope I answered you well enough.'

Anfen glanced at the sky again, and for a moment his heart raced — a shape moved up there. A bird, probably. He'd soon know if it wasn't, that much was sure.

Eric said, 'You've answered well, but I have to tell you, this is all totally weird to me. Why was I brought here? Why *me*? If you could understand how insignificant I was back there—' he cut himself short.

'Insignificant amongst the other nobility, you mean?'

'Well, yes. You know, there are court jesters more important than me. I wasn't all that high on the ladder, really.'

The Otherworlder's limbs had all been hacked off. Blood pooled about him, stumps of white bone glistened. Anfen shut his eyes. 'You may or may not have been summoned. I can only say what I know. For some reason the entry point opened up. Loup, our folk magician, foresaw it. He was adamant we seek it out, adamant in a way I've never seen him, though he wouldn't say why it mattered. And still won't. As we were already nearby on other business, I relented. And here you are.'

'Where is this castle? I only saw a glimpse of it before.'

'Behind us. Stand atop that rock there.'

Eric did, peering over the top of the plateau's shelf to see what had been obscured before. A huge white shape in the far distance gleamed like a piece of fallen sky. It looked like a long, fat dragon lying asleep, its head resting chin first on the ground, front paws to either side, a tail curling behind the bulging round mass of its middle.

Anfen tried to imagine how the sight would affect him, with eyes new to it, but could only think of the orders that came from its upper halls, and the beings who gave them, and he felt only hate, dark and bitter, so strong it almost numbed itself from being felt.

Eric however looked almost dizzy at the sight. 'Wow,' he said, and laughed.

'You were underneath that, some hours ago. The entry point through which you came is above and behind it. An impenetrable cliff runs around like a fence behind: no doubt you saw it. It is said Otherworld is differently built, that you may walk in one direction forever, eventually passing the point you started. Is that so?'

It seemed a cool breeze blew from the castle's direction, ruffling their hair like a friendly hand. 'Technically, yes. Who built it?'

'It was here before we were. Only the dragon-youth or the Great Spirits could properly answer you. And they keep their secrets. Mages of the old schools hollowed it out with chambers, halls and stairways. Then they gave it to the cities, which were *all* Free Cities, back then. To make a long story very short, Vous and his cohorts stole the castle, then began stealing the cities. They are still busy with that task today, among others. And they will succeed. It is a question of when. Are you good with a sword, Eric?'

'Not yet. But I'm going to learn.'

'Is that so?'

'Yes.'

Anfen sat by the fire. There was much to think about. 'Any magical talent, Eric?'

'Not yet. But again, I'll learn.'

'I'm afraid if you can't already see magic in the air, you'll never be able to wield it. Magic is a perilous trade. Why would you want to learn it?'

'I'm here for a reason,' Eric said. 'Since no one's told me what it is, I'll decide. I'm going to be the greatest hero you've ever heard of.'

Sharfy already is, Anfen thought with amusement. The young man could have been joking or not, it was hard to tell. Perhaps he'd been driven insane by his trip into a new world. It was certainly a stupid thing to say, if he meant it. Anfen saw blood gushing out Eric's slashed windpipe and looked away. 'Welcome, then,' he said.

20

No smoke came from the campfires spread out on the lower platform, which was a quiet bustle of activity as people ate or tended to clothes hung on makeshift lines. Most wore leather, furs and skins, and there was no shortage of swords and knives lying about. The camp had clearly been here for some time.

Eric counted four women, six men, all of them giving the impression beds and hot baths would be quite welcome. One of the men was easily double a normal man's size. His face tugged somehow at Eric's memory: those big, dumb, startled eyes, the bald head ... the door! This was the huge being he'd seen struggling to fit through, before Kiown's boot was planted on his face to push him back.

The woman who'd fired an arrow at the train held a small razor and tended to the giant's moustache, trimming off a little at the sides with a very careful hand. Eric's eye lingered on her. Her skin was darker than that of anyone else he'd seen in this world. She had big almond eyes and jet black hair in two thick braids that hung down to her hips. She'd stepped from the set of a film about Native Americans, he was sure; even the tanned skins and tunic she wore would have seemed at home. She softly sang as she brushed little wisps of hair from the giant's naked chest, and said, 'All done!'

The giant peered at her, puffing air with his cheeks. When she saw Eric making his way down, she watched him intently and a change came to her face, no longer carefree and smiling; there was an intensity there now he could not interpret. If he had to guess, he'd say her look meant she wanted to kill him.

Eric spotted Sharfy and Kiown seated close to the path, embroiled in a heated argument with voices they strained to keep low. The others seemed to be listening with amusement they politely kept as hidden as possible. Kiown had a piece of dressing on his cheek and an impressive black eye. His face was totally rearranged by anger, leaving no trace at all of the practical joker he'd seemed at first, his voice an angry hiss: 'And what of your part in it all? Was *that* disclosed? You scuttled over that dirt cart like lice on my balls. You stuffed your pockets.'

Sharfy sat back placidly, watching the veins bulge in Kiown's neck, the flying spittle. 'You finished yet?' he said.

'No! Traitorous shit! After I brought you the masks and all. You made it sound like I *want* us to get caught and killed.'

'Guess I'm the one whose face he should've smashed. I done you wrong.' Sharfy laughed his loud ugly laugh, then spat. Eric had seldom seen a meaner-looking face in his life than Sharfy's gnarled, scarred and dented one. 'Guess you won't be leading any more missions any time soon,' he said.

'Aha! *Now* it comes out,' Kiown said, looking triumphant and newly enraged all at once, the cone of red hair swaying wildly. He stood and walked away, his long lean body convulsing with anger, jerking him as if puppet strings pulled from above. Eric sat in his vacated place by the fire, glad of its warmth.

On the ground before Sharfy was a pile of that brackish dirt. Next to it were about a dozen flat, sparkling pieces that they'd dug out and rubbed clean. 'You're awake,' said Sharfy. 'Anfen doesn't let me sleep that long. Not in Aligned country. You and your luck. Got that dirt I threw to you?'

Eric felt his pockets. 'Yeah, but there's not much.'

'Your loss, your fault. You had a chance to grab plenty.'

Careful not to reveal the gun's clips, Eric pulled out two handfuls of hard dirt from his pockets. Sharfy examined them. 'Not much at all,' he said. 'Be lucky if there's one or two scales here. Probably none. You're crazy. Don't get many chances at a dirt cart these days.'

Sharfy picked through the dirt pieces with his knife. Kiown, who'd angrily paced up the path, came back, unable to resist watching what Eric's share would bring. Sharfy dug out what looked like sea shells buried in the dirt. 'One, two … four, in this little clod? Ha! You and your luck.' He spat on a rag and polished them one by one. Three of them gleamed brightly, two red, one blue, but one remained dull.

Kiown made a strangling noise. 'He's got a black scale!'

'Nah, it's just dirty,' said Sharfy, rubbing it harder. The scale did not get any brighter. 'Wait. It *is* black! Wish your luck'd start spreading around.'

Kiown made a noise like he was going to be sick. He looked at Eric in accusing disbelief. 'You know how many black ones I've seen in my life? One! *That* one!'

Eric thought he was about to be struck by Kiown's accusing, pointing arms. 'It's about the only thing in this world that I own,' he said. 'Does that make you feel any better? And can someone tell me what these are exactly?'

'Scales,' said Sharfy with a gleam in his eye. 'Dragon scales.'

Eric looked closely at one of his other three. It gleamed a beautiful deep ruby red. 'From *the* Dragon?'

'No, from the mighty god-chicken, whose beak can peck at Time Itself,' said Kiown in disgust. He stormed off, wringing his hands.

'Ignore him,' said Sharfy. 'Lots of scales buried, over at World's End, in the ground.' He unfolded a small map, showing an oval shape, and pointed at a line running dead down the middle. 'That's World's End. That line there's the Wall, runs all across. Scales buried near it, mostly in the middle part, deep in the ground. Shallow ones all got dug out back when they started to use em for trading. Mad rush for scales. Now, only way they get new ones is in the mines, dirt from way down deep.'

'Why so many, over in that spot?'

Sharfy waved away this clearly unworthy question, which Eric had learned meant he didn't have the foggiest idea of its answer.

'Professor Sharfy!' Kiown called mockingly from up the pathway. 'Say, Professor? Why are some men born short and ugly?'

'How's your eye, precious?' Sharfy replied. 'Aw, did you hurt yourself?'

'Stop your squabbling,' yelled an old shirtless man from one of the other fires. Apparently to himself, he said, 'We been on this hilltop too long, like I told him. Past the point of being safe, by now. Is a tight squeeze now, oh aye.'

'Ignore him too,' Sharfy muttered.

'What makes these things valuable?' said Eric, putting the scales in his pockets.

'Rare, pretty. Plus you can crush em up for visions. Not many people do that. Show you why.' He took Eric's black scale, laid it on the rocky floor, then tried to smash it with the handle of his knife, many times. The scale didn't break or crack. The underside of Sharfy's knife handle had some new slits cut into it. 'See? Got magic in em. Hard to crush up — that's why no one knows about the visions. Good thing, too. Visions sometimes show you too much.'

In that moment, Eric resolved to do a vision as a matter of priority. 'So how would I crush it up, if I wanted to?'

'Shh!' Sharfy's lopsided eyes bulged with alarm. 'Against Anfen's rules. He won't have it, not while we're on the road. But if you wanted to, that's who you talk to.' He pointed at the grisly old man, who now lay flat on his back, snoring.

'What the hell is he supposed to be, anyway?'

'Him? That's Loup. He's our magician.'

The magician in question farted loud enough to turn heads all across the platform his way.

'Not quite Merlin,' Eric murmured. 'Not quite Gandalf. Live and learn, I guess.'

Anfen's voice called from the upper platform. 'Pack up camp. We ride soon.'

21

The women changed their dress out in the open, unconcerned if they were seen naked. Likewise the men. Eric found he was seeking out the one who'd shot an arrow at the train, hoping for a look at her changing garments, but when he saw her, she was watching *him*.

She stood and approached, the long braided plaits of hair swaying against a hide tunic which hung stiff over her, showing little of her figure. She stood close to him, chocolate-dark skin accentuating the whites of her eyes. Her tongue ran across her lips and, later, looking back, it was *that* one moment he'd look back on, as though it were a seed planted, or perhaps a bomb set. 'My name is Siel. Come with me,' she said, unsmiling.

Eric shot a questioning look at Sharfy, who seemed to be very carefully examining a stray thread in his sleeve and was totally absorbed in the task. A few heads turned to watch as Eric followed her further along the winding path, his heart beating fast. One of two things, he knew, was probably about to happen. The curved knife she'd used to cut up his briefcase hung from her belt, and he envisioned her hand moving it across his skin, opening it with the same gentle ease, spilling its contents. Her bow was still slung across her. His hand went to the gun at his side.

They came to a point on the rock path where the encampment was no longer visible behind them, nor could its noise be heard. She stopped and moved a little away from him. To their right, the rock shelf dropped off, giving a view of a paved road winding below, visible a short distance away till hidden by the hillsides through which it wound.

He wanted to gently run a finger along the bumps of her braids, see her skin below her tanned animal hide. Just that — if he could just *see* it, he would need nothing more.

For some reason she paced as though wrestling with a private decision. 'You are a prince?' she said, turning to look at him again.

Not a hard question, he found. 'Yes.'

She bit her bottom lip, seemed to silently curse, none of which he could make the least sense of. She resumed pacing. 'I must watch here to ensure the road is clear when we depart. Go some way further, look to your left. You've seen war mages. You can now see the stoneshaper mages, down below.' Seeing the look on his face, she said, 'Don't fear, they aren't aware of us and don't care. They are far too busy building things. Watch them.'

'Why do you want me to?'

'You are new to Levaal. You have little time to learn about it before you will need the knowledge.' She unslung her bow, set it down and sat with her back against a boulder, one knee raised, an arm resting on it. He did not avert his gaze from the part of her skirt that fell away and showed a smooth muscled column of thigh; in fact briefly he *couldn't* avert it. Her other hand rested between her legs as though to protect modesty, though she remained in that pose, watching as he pulled his gaze away with some effort and headed up the path.

The area beneath was like a huge flat bowl scooped out of

the basaltic hillside, in which taller shafts of rock had been raised and placed like buildings in a street. Milling around these were twenty or more men in drab robes. They had horns on their heads similar to those the war mages wore, but straighter, and pointing outwards rather than curling down. They looked decidedly more human, though all appeared to be tired, old men, so similar that each could've been the twin of any other. They shuffled around like sleepwalkers.

A group of them coalesced around a short pillar of rock. They stood murmuring for some time, then all moved their arms skywards. The rock piece jolted, and a crumbling sound carried up the canyon. With perfect synchronicity, the mages lowered and raised their arms, each time making the rock pillar rise further. At its base the rock seemed to flow like liquid. Soon they had its top level with the tallest around it, then they dispersed and shuffled away to a new location, to begin the process again. Some crouched down to rest, smoke trailing from the tips of their horns.

'They are building a new city here.' Siel's voice made him jump. He'd not heard her approach, yet she was right behind him. 'It's all they do. They are nearly machines. Later they will hollow out the insides of the pillars, make buildings of them. In a year it will be ready for people to move in. It will be filled with those who swear to Vous, and it will be a place where life is easy, at first. Others will learn to worship him, so they too may live this way. It is why most Aligned cities accept starvation. People cling to their old ways so stubbornly.'

There were more of the stoneshaper mages below than he'd first seen. Many groups clustered further away, moving in and out of visibility between the raised pillars. 'Are you sure we're safe here?'

'You were scared by the war mages, weren't you?' Her voice

came from very close. 'They won't come here. War mages fear stoneshapers.' Her hands slipped around his belly, under his shirt, and rubbed up his chest, cold to the touch. One began to seek its way below his belt line. He felt himself stir, but reached to halt her hand before it went further. She sighed, lips so close he felt her breath on his ear. 'I'm not fit for a prince?'

'You are more than fit for me. Whether I was a prince or not.'

'Then it's something else. What? Do you live forever, in your world?'

'No.'

'We could die before the day is out. In moments of rest, I like to remember I am alive.'

He turned to look at her, lower lip thrust out and eyes turned down, a pose of vulnerability he could scarcely believe; he knew she was a warrior, she looked like one, moved like one. She had probably killed people in battle. He felt a pang of guilt for his lie; was that the only reason she wanted him? He laughed. 'To be honest, I was more concerned that I haven't washed for a long time. I probably stink.'

'Welcome to the road,' she said with a shrug. 'Is that all it is?' Her eyes were still wide and doubtful, looking deep into his. He didn't even decide to touch her — his fingertip just ran gently down the long knotted braid the way he'd wanted it to earlier, as though his hand had decided for itself. She didn't smile, but the doubt was gone from her face as she quickly undid the thin knots of strapping about her shoulders and waist. The gown fell away in two parts, leaving her only in her boots, her breasts larger than shown by the flatness of the tunic, the nipples fat, wide and erect in the cold. Little goose bumps were across her skin. There was a wild nest of untamed hair between her legs. And he'd been wrong: a look wasn't enough.

She tugged at his pants, examined what was beneath them

with open curiosity, as though seeing if Otherworld men were built differently from those she knew. He took the holster off his hip, not caring suddenly whether she saw the gun or not. Her hand was clumsier on his cock than it had been on her bow, but that hardly mattered. She lay on her robe and opened her legs, pulling him down into the warm wet nest between them.

To him, it seemed at first like the act of animals in the wild, scratching an itch without emotion, and he realised this was because he hadn't kissed her. He tried but for some reason she turned her head away; he tried again, and she denied him again, and a sudden burst of possessive anger flared in him. He held her face still and pressed his lips down on hers. Passively she opened her mouth for him to do as he liked. In that irrational moment, it was her fault he'd lied and was left to doubt himself. He squeezed hard on the underside of her thigh. It was firm and cool in his hand. He flung aside one of the woven braids from where it lay across her moving breasts and clutched her arms as though to pin them. Then when he came and lay panting on her, her eyes closed, he felt almost sick with shame.

The stoneshaper mages continued their work below, and occasionally came the grinding sound of rock being moulded. She didn't say a word as she stood and dressed, her face still unreadable. He wanted some assurance he hadn't hurt her or used her. He realised, suddenly, he had wanted that very thing in those fevered seconds: to hurt her. Why? He had never in his life wanted such a thing before. 'I'm sorry,' he said.

She looked at him as though he'd said something totally incomprehensible. 'What?'

'I'm just a long way from home ...' he said, and shrugged helplessly.

'Why are you sorry? Aren't princes supposed to, with nobodies?' She fixed her clothes more properly in place.

Nobodies. If I'm not a prince, am I a nobody? 'No, it's not that ... I don't know what it is. I wanted to hurt you, that's all. And I don't know why. I wish I hadn't ... hadn't wanted that.'

'You didn't hurt me, whatever you really wanted.' She turned away and reached for her bow. Then, hearing something Eric hadn't, she rushed to the platform's edge, overlooking the path, and gazed out over the stone ridge, her slender body as taut and tense as the bowstring she drew back, an arrow in place. 'I told you death was close. If not here for us, here for them.' She gave a nervous little laugh.

Eric went to look, but she waved him away. 'Go back,' she said. 'Run. Tell Anfen that castle swordsmen are below, some in heavy armour. Too many to fight. Now the pass is blocked. We've camped here too long.'

22

It had been a long, bumpy ride for Case and he was losing hope
Eric would be at the end of it. He needed badly to piss. The
march had been going on for hours — how many, he couldn't
tell. To keep track he'd begun counting the trudging sound of
metal boots like a second hand on a clock, before it occurred
to him just how pointless that was.

The supplies cart rocked under him, its wheels squeaking.
Two mules dragged it along at a slower pace than the soldiers
nearby wanted. They had remarked the cart was a touch heavier
than it should be and couldn't work out why; early in the march,
the whole patrol had stopped while they examined its wheels
and axles. Case sat between stacked pouches of water, whose
sloshing sound didn't help him one little bit as the miles ticked
by. He would've lain down to sleep, but every so often had to
dodge hands that shot in as thirsty soldiers gobbed a mouthful.

The march had been far more formal and disciplined near
the castle. As they moved away, the commander loosened the
leash, and the troops ignored fancy formations and keeping
their steps in time. Their helms came off; the march became a
stroll through the countryside, with laughing and gossip. The
scenery hadn't been much to look at, in Case's opinion. He
didn't mind *that*. He'd seen enough fancy wondrous things to

last him his remaining years, or days more likely. A sand-coloured paved road, the *clop* of donkey hooves, the *clank-clank* of boots with rattling mail, pleasant meadows and rolling, hilly fields either side. That was fine by him.

Every so often at forks in the road, local villagers with solemn faces had approached the patrol carrying wooden trays loaded with home-made delicacies. The soldiers — against their orders, as conversation revealed — took what they were offered, thanked the locals, then joked about how ugly their women were once out of earshot. The locals had seemed terrified of them.

There'd been no such people lately. The ground had been moving upwards into less populous terrain, the road cutting through hillsides of dark grey stone. Hideous birds of a type Case didn't know watched them pass with hostile eyes from the bone-like branches of lone grey trees.

Case didn't much like spying, but there hadn't been anything to do but eavesdrop. The men had spent no time discussing their present mission, whatever it was. Instead they'd talked about some business with 'Free Cities', and much about Vous; it sounded like they knew a hell of a lot less about him than Case felt *he* did. There'd been plenty of talk — some quite heated — about which cities made the best swords, the best armour, or produced the best horses. Case had heard enough on these subjects to reliably form his own opinion, he felt, and longed for them to talk about something else.

At last, at long last, the commander called: 'Drinks! All halt.'

Tall outcrops loomed on their right and left. There had to be a quarry nearby, for there was the sound of rocks being shifted somewhere out of sight. The soldiers gathered around the supplies cart. Case dropped to the ground just in time, wincing as his bad knee flared up, and sneaked off behind a stone outcrop, leaving it much damper than it had been before.

The soldiers took biscuits and what looked like meat jerky of some kind, sitting in twos and threes some way off the road. Two sat near the supplies cart when Case returned to it. He carefully climbed aboard and gazed up at the shoulders of stone, longing for a nap, only half-listening to the soldiers' conversation. 'They got a name yet for that city?' said one, nodding his head to whatever was making the quarry-like noise on the other side of the rock wall.

'Not that I heard.'

'How long till it's finished?'

'Less than a year. Those mages work fast. Applying?'

'Already have. Better hurry, things are heating up. If we're killed tomorrow, family gets pushed to the back of the queue.'

'Well I've no family, just girlfriends. Going to keep it that way.'

'Adopt them. Make it a family.'

The soldier laughed. He lowered his voice and leaned closer to the other. 'Looking forward to Vous's temple?'

The other scoffed again. 'A joke. I'm not fussed. It means breaking bread and toasting his name at meals? I can do that, if it's worth a good home. If it's worth *having* bread to break.'

'Did you read the whole law? They're allowed in your home any time to see that you "worship in earnest". It also means you can't make rituals for the other Spirits. Who's your preference?'

'Inferno.' They both laughed at this apparent joke. 'Tempest, mainly. I was raised on a farm, we needed the rain. You're a Valour man, I take it?'

'I don't bother with any of them.'

'That's fair. My wife swears to Wisdom, of course.'

'Not for long, if you mean to go through with this.' The other's voice lowered further. 'You worried about ... what it might mean, long term?'

'Nahh! I don't believe it. You can't just make someone a Great Spirit by building him a temple, praying to him, teaching him some magic, or whatever it is they do. They might think otherwise but they're wrong. He's a good enough lord anyway.'

The other lowered his voice. 'Half the cities are starving.'

'We aren't. I didn't say *great*. But good enough. People accept the new ways and they'd be fine.' The other soldier said nothing to this. 'He can be a little crazy if he wants,' continued the first. 'Food in the belly.' This was a common saying Case had heard, along with 'as the Dragon wills'.

The commander stood and cleared his throat. 'Let's get going,' he said. 'Up we get.'

'*Up we get?*' muttered one of the soldiers disbelievingly. 'We're back in the nursery.' They tossed their half-empty skins back on the supplies cart. One bounced off Case's chest and fell to the ground. The soldier frowned at the cart. 'Now wait, that's the second time I've seen that happen.'

'I didn't see anything. Forget it.'

'Drink skin bounces in mid-air? There's something funny about that cart, I'm telling you.'

But they lined up behind the other soldiers, and Case's heart slowed a little.

Until, that was, he saw the shape in the rocks above, to the left. It wasn't the same Invia who'd given him the charm and set him loose in the castle; this one had long flowing hair as white as her wings, and her limbs were long and gangly. She crouched on a jutting outcrop like a cat about to jump. None of the soldiers seemed to have seen her. She watched something atop the rock wall opposite, then stared right down at Case.

His hand crept to the charm around his neck. 'You want this

back, don't you?' he whispered. And he could tell she was about
to come and take it.

Verily, she was.

She did not know all the secret business of her newly dead
sister, but she knew the charm down below bore Ksyn's touch,
and did not belong around this old Otherworlder's neck. She
would take him back with her, too, to see what the others made
of it all — peacefully, if he would come that way.

It had not been the charm that drew her here; it was the
Marked one, rather, who had temerity indeed to travel so openly,
this far north, let alone to make camp on a high place, where
his Mark could be seen from a long way. On sight of it, anger
was not what she'd felt; in fact, she felt very little. It was just
a fact he must be killed, that was all. Marks were rare, yet this
blazed on him with a huge red glare, its noise painful in her
ears. But she didn't yet see *him,* hidden behind the rock wall
opposite. Was he enormous, with fangs and claws? An elemental?
A mage perhaps?

It was not he who had killed her newly dead sister, she knew
that. *That* Marked one, tied to the castle roof with tongue cut
out by his elders, had been dealt with, that matter resolved,
the birds pecking at what was left.

And now she realised this one bore not one Mark, but three.
Rare! To have slain three Invia! In one attack, or did he hunt
them down over time? No wonder the aura flared so bright and
huge. Had there ever been such, in all the world?

He first, or to collect the charm? The soldiers appeared to be
guarding the old man who carried it, since he sat so comfort-
ably in their midst. She looked from one to the other, undecided.
Either fight could be a risk — many men below, swords, halberds,
short-bows with fast little arrows. The Marked one had allies

nearby — would they help him? If the Marked one had killed three sisters, he too was very, very dangerous, maybe more than all the others combined. What mistakes had her sisters made? She would be cautious of him when making the kill.

The glare of those Marks was so bright! The ringing in her ears so painful. Best to shut that sound out first. She jumped from her place on the wall.

23

The whole band crouched in a line along the ridge with weapons drawn, except Eric, whose mind even now was back with Siel, back with himself tossing one of her long braids away so he could better see the movements of her breasts, as if she were a toy he played with. The rest watched the soldiers below, whose conversation and laughter drifted up.

No one saw the Invia come until the air around them pounded with the sound of her beating wings. An arrow flew from further up the path where Siel kept watch. It gracefully sailed very close to the Invia with a sound of sliced sky. But the creature moved like a dancer in mid-air, white hair streaming behind her. The arrow skidded across the ground.

Anfen rolled to his feet, sword in hand, knowing he was the one she wanted. Siel now too, probably. Stupid girl. His wrists swung the blade two-handed, cutting overhead in a very fast figure-eight for such a big weapon. The Invia jerked backwards through the air as though pulled hard by invisible hands, and watched him with a face oddly expressionless. Someone threw a rock but again she dodged it with ease.

The others rushed over, weapons ready, despite Anfen yelling: 'Hold!' While he was distracted she darted forwards with incredible speed, just a blur of the white of her wings. She came up like a bird that had swooped, in her hands Anfen's sword. He now lay on the ground, dazed, his face cut. It had to be the sword handle hitting him as it came free from his grasp ... the Invia's hands would not have struck him so lightly.

Slowly the Invia flexed her arms and with some effort — that much at least the sword's maker could be proud of — broke the blade in two, examining then dropping the pieces. She watched Anfen to see what he would do. He did about all he could think of: lie on his back in a daze and think his last thoughts.

Sharfy leaped up, a knife biting through the air, but he didn't get close enough. The creature didn't seem to notice him. Kiown likewise sprang through the air, a mindless open-mouthed look on his face that was almost comical, but he slashed upwards with a long blade that came within a hair of striking the Invia. She spun away from his cut, moved out of his reach and gave him a quick look which, though expressionless, said loud and clear enough: *you, sir, are next.*

Eric, fascinated by this creature, felt about half a minute behind actual time. Only now did he sluggishly think: the gun. Hey now there's a plan. Get the Glock out. Shoot that thing. Save the day. Batman would do it.

His hand had reached his pocket when from below came a shouted order. A dozen arrows shot up and fell across the platform with a fast drum roll of stone being struck. No one was hit — the arrows arced too far from the sheltering ridge — but one of them passed through the Invia's wing. A burst of light flashed through the punctured gap; feathers puffed in the air. She spun, eyeing off the castle soldiers with still no expression troubling her face, then she swooped down fast.

Anfen got to his feet, feeling his face, where the cut had left a smear of blood down his cheek. 'How many *times* do I have to tell you,' he snarled, 'do *not* attack them? No matter what.'

'Get in the cave,' said Sharfy, tossing Anfen another sword.

Anfen had already begun heading back to the tunnel mouth cut into the hilltop. 'Watch below, tell me what happens,' he called over his shoulder. 'If they don't kill it, we chance the groundmen's traps. You should hope they don't or you're probably Marked.'

'You're welcome, boss,' murmured Kiown.

The Invia was less cautious of these men than she'd been of the Marked one. Most humans knew better than to shoot arrows at her — these ones would learn their mistake sure enough.

She flashed through them, her swiping arms too fast to see, breaking bones and cracking open their hard plate armour. Ah, they would stop spears and arrows, those pretty polished shells, but not her hands if she hit with all her strength.

Little nicks from swords cut her as the panicking soldiers slashed at the blurred force in their midst. Others fired more arrows, foolish so close to their own men. Sure enough two fell back with arrows in them. Ten were dead or near enough after just a few seconds. For fun, she broke some of their swords without removing them from their owners' hands.

Then her arm caught behind the hole of a breastplate, which she had punched through up to her forearm. It was enough pause for one of them to hack down with a halberd and cut her badly down the side. She shrieked. Newly strong with pain, she yanked free her arm with a spray of gore, then swatted off the attacker's head and sent it flying like a punted ball. Light burst from the wound he'd inflicted and blood gushed down her side. Their blades hurt!

No more cuts. Later, later, she'd return. First she'd heal. The charm was old and would wait a little more. She might never find these men again — to wound her was not enough to be

Marked, unless she soon died — but enough of them had already paid for firing upon her. She launched herself skywards, flying awkwardly and painfully, a dozen corpses below her, the rest of the unit scattering in panic, some holding badly broken arms, swords and armour in pieces on the ground like broken toys.

Case hardly even knew what happened. One minute, he'd jogged away from the supply cart, thinking he'd seen Stranger, the young lass, standing up on the rocky pathway that led up like a steep ramp on the right side, the quarry side. Just a glimpse of her, less than a blink of her green dress, and he couldn't even be certain he'd seen it.

When he'd jogged off that way, the soldiers had been arguing. The furious commander had demanded to know who'd given an order to fire, because he sure hadn't, he reckoned. The others had said yes, he bloody well had. Case had heard the commander's voice too, but it had almost sounded like it came from some distance away from him.

Next time Case looked back, most of them were knocked over like ninepins, and the woman was flying skywards with slow lurches of her wings, dark blood dribbling down one side and over her foot as the army unit scattered.

He'd heard *something* going on — shouts, clashes of metal, and an unearthly shrieking that had been like a stabbing pin to all his senses. But she couldn't have done all that damage herself, not in so little time. Surely. 'Stranger?' he called. 'You here, miss?'

'Case?' called a surprised, familiar voice above.

'Eric?'

'Case! You're kidding me. Is that you?'

'*Stay down*,' growled a less familiar voice. A head popped over the edge of the rock wall nonetheless and had time to glance around before someone up there yanked its owner back down. Case waved, then remembered that no one could see him.

He ran panting up the steep pathway, pausing for breath at the top. He passed the woman with the bow and arrow — he'd seen her fire, and the soldiers had seen her arrow sailing across. Now she turned at the sound of his steps and reached for her knife, crouching low like a hunter, but he was quickly up the path.

Out onto the open platform and there he was, crouched down at its far end with a bunch of others, all armed. 'Eric!' Case called. 'Don't worry, I think the fight down there's all over. They got a piece of that winged woman, too. What in Christ she did to them I'd like to know, but she's hurt. She flew away.'

Eric turned and stared about, as did a few others. 'Case?'

'They won't see me. I got this weird necklace on, keeps me hidden. Magic, I guess. Safe here? These guys OK?'

'Yeah, they're OK. Are you?'

'Need a drink and a bed. Back rub too if anyone's granting wishes. You sure it's safe? I see a lot of swords in their hands ...'

'Your friend?' said Sharfy to Eric.

'That's his voice at least.'

'I'm gonna take off the necklace,' said Case. 'Eric, you aren't gonna believe the things I seen.'

Eric laughed. 'Try me!'

Below, only two live soldiers remained. One had unhitched a mule from the supplies wagon, stuck a wounded friend on its back and slapped its rump. The mule didn't move until the soldier started dragging it. They left behind the supply cart, with the second mule. 'Weapons away,' said Sharfy. 'Fight's over.'

'Are you in charge now that Anfen got a face cut?' said Kiown, who did not sheathe his sword.

'Put it *away*,' snapped Sharfy. 'Anfen! Safe out here. They scared it off and it scared them off. Guess we won. And we got a visitor who can't be seen.'

Case took off the necklace. Eric spotted him, laughed and ran over. They embraced as the bandits murmured amongst themselves. Siel jogged up the path and stared at Case, her knife still in hand.

Anfen emerged from the cave and gazed at Case, his Oriental-looking face a neutral mask, the sword Sharfy had thrown him held at the ready. He seemed about to speak, but let the pair have their moment, instead turning to the wreckage below. To the others: 'Get down there, grab that supply cart. Don't dawdle. They'll send more out here now. We won't get another chance through the pass.' To Sharfy, 'Stay with the Pilgrims.' Anfen paused as he saw the necklace hanging in Case's hand. 'By Nightmare! And what might *that* be?'

Case quickly stuffed it in his pocket and backed away, cursing himself for a fool: had Stranger not warned him to keep it hidden?

'You're safe from *me*,' said Anfen impatiently. 'Time's pressing; we'll deal with it later. But keep that thing hidden.'

'You folks see a young woman in a green dress up here?' said Case.

No one had.

Embarrassed, Case wiped tears from his eyes. 'I thought they'd got you, is all.'

'What about me? Thought I'd killed you with a message in the dirt. Case, I hope you didn't come here to rescue me or bring me back. I'm not going, not yet anyway. This is a new start.'

'Hadn't thought that far ahead, to be honest.' They followed the rest of the bandits who hustled along the ridge and down the steep pathway. Sharfy walked with them, listening. 'Who opened the door anyway?' said Case.

'Not these guys. They just saw it was going to happen, and ducked in to get the morning paper.' Eric lowered his voice. 'So I'm told.'

'You're told true,' said Sharfy.

'Eric, you really won't believe what I seen. They had me inside this big huge castle. I saw this guy, this sick bastard they call "friend and lord". I stole his drink! Believe that? It was a good drop too, let me tell you. He's their king or something, and I stole his wine!'

Sharfy made a strangled noise, and was suddenly so agitated he hopped from foot to foot. 'What? You saw Vous? How? Invisible! How close you get? Could've put a sword in his guts! Why didn't you? No! Don't speak of it. Wait for Anfen. Hush about that. Hush!'

'You got it, I'll hush,' said Case, giving Eric a look that said: *what a nut . . .*

Down by the roadside's carnage someone had already beheaded the remaining mule. Eric paused, transfixed by the sight of Siel carving from its flank with her curved knife, her forearms covered in blood. It was that which tipped him over the edge in his gorge's battle to cope with the bodies scattered over the road. He bent over and retched.

Others went through the soldiers' pockets, taking coins and such small tokens. Anfen crouched beside a survivor and asked questions, but didn't get much response. 'Valour men,' he sighed, giving up. To Eric, 'There's a myth. The last-second reprieve on the battlefield for the dying, if they have fought well enough. Talking to the enemy wouldn't help him get it. He'll take his chances on a Great Spirit no one's seen in a lifetime or so. If ever.'

Sharfy added so the dying man would hear, 'A Great Spirit

he hopes came to watch combat that lasted a few seconds. If you call *that* combat. More like men under an avalanche.'

But the man lay in pain keeping his silence, and they gave up on him. The others drank what water was left on the cart. They bagged and pocketed the meat strips and biscuits. 'Same as what I gave you in the tunnels,' said Sharfy, tossing a leaf-wrapped piece to Eric. 'Keep it for later.' He went through the discarded weapons. 'All standard issue junk,' he said. 'All shit. Not even city-made. Castle-made. Cheap and nasty.'

'Halberds are city-made,' said someone else. 'They're quality.'

'Too heavy for us,' said Sharfy, 'we're in a hurry now.' He looked pointedly at Kiown then picked up two swords, held one in each hand. 'All the same weight!' He laughed. To Eric and Case, 'Pick one out, you two. Get a scabbard for it too, dagger if you want. Take a bow if you can shoot. What the shit, steal their dicks if you see one you like.' Sharfy laughed. He patted Eric on the back and whispered in his ear: 'You want to be a hero, you're going to see a lot of this. Heroes kill the bad people, they don't sneak past them. How many men you killed?'

Eric swallowed. 'Only seven.'

'Must've done it pretty clean,' said Sharfy, smiling. 'You're white as bone, seeing all this blood.'

'I'm fine.'

'You sure? You look dizzy. How are your eyes? Fading in and out? Here, how many fingers am I holding up?' In Sharfy's hand were three fingers which had been cut off in the mêlée, perhaps from a stray swing while the Invia charged through the soldiers. He wiggled them in Eric's face. Eric retched again and Sharfy brayed laughter like a barking hound.

Siel wiped the mule's blood from her hands with a soldier's tunic. She had not spared Eric a look since he'd fled up the path, but now she did, and it indicated nothing to him at all.

Something had clearly changed but he didn't know what it was.

Anfen took Case aside. 'Friend, I think we should talk.'

Case sighed and pulled the necklace charm from his pocket, its beads clicking together. 'I was getting to like having it, but I'll part with it,' he said, handing it over.

'Something like this no one ever really owns,' said Anfen, holding the necklace away from himself as though it were dangerous. 'I may return it to you, once I know more about it. I may not. Loup!'

The magician jogged over to them, grinning. Loup wore no shirt, evidently proud of a torso still hard with gristly muscle, peppered with white hairs or not. Anfen handed him the charm. Loup's eyebrows raised, and a toothless smile widened through his beard. 'An oldie!' he said, twisting it around his leathery fingers. 'She's an oldie, all right. Still got some kick in her, too! My word, she has got some kick.'

Case said, 'Someone told me dragons touched it, or made it. That probably means more to you than it does to me.'

Loup nodded as though very impressed, and fingered its beads. 'How long've I got her?' he said to Anfen.

'Learn what you can, sooner the better. But we must move.'

'I'll try. Oldie like this, won't tell her secrets in a hurry! Need t'be coaxed, she will. Give her time, she'll come good.' He seemed to be muttering this to himself as he walked off, tenderly stroking the charm like an adored pet. 'She'll come mighty good, this one will, oh aye. Lots to tell, she has. Lots to tell.'

Not far from the scene of the Invia's carnage, on a flat, smooth piece of stone on the cliff face, the word 'Shadow' had been written in letters that looked like they'd been burned on with great heat, like a brand across the skin of cattle. There the word waited patiently to be seen by the next passing patrol.

24

The day's march was at a hard pace, first a tense stretch through the mountain pass, locked in on both sides by dark grey cliff faces sheer and lifeless. Once through they cut across hilly terrain, the country green and picturesque with no visible threat of danger, nor people in the scoured and abandoned villages. There was only a silence eerily complete but for the wind. Even the birds there just watched without a sound, seeming to wait for something, perhaps more remains to pick over.

Case had done his best not to complain at all this exertion, but he lagged at the back of the group until Anfen ordered the giant, Doon, to carry the old man on one shoulder. Loup, the folk magician, occupied the other shoulder. The giant frequently grunted in a way Loup understood to mean *scratch, please*. Loup's gnarled fingers somehow knew which spot to scratch each time. Occasionally he'd say, 'Not there, not for me! Find yourself a lady giant!' and laugh as though it were the first time he'd made the joke.

Doon was part of the reason Anfen had apparently considered chancing their arm against thirty armed and armoured castle soldiers, before the Invia had cleaned up that mess for them. 'Swords and arrows won't bother Doon,' Sharfy told Eric. 'Not unless he gets caught in a whirlwind of em. I seen Doon take eight spears in the back before he even slowed down. Trampled down the men who threw em *and* their horses, all wearing heavy plate mail. A week later, was like it never happened.'

Kiown sidled up to him and whispered: 'You will soon be fluent in Sharfy. Translation: three spears, three men, wearing maybe hard leather or light chain mail. The horses got away just fine. I was there. Still, pretty impressive.'

Eric had tried walking with Siel, and talking with her, but she'd been too busy scouting the group's right flank, with her bow at the ready, and he got the sense she was faintly annoyed by him being around. It was as though he'd said or done something to give away his lie: he was no prince, and perhaps now she knew . . .

He'd walked behind her, watching her hips sway beneath the tanned leather, but quickly felt like a stalker and made an effort to stay away. Always, though, he found his eyes returning to her, no matter what else was going on around them. He longed for another chance alone with her, to do more gently what he'd already done, to get up and put his clothes back on without a sense of guilt and shame.

As night approached the group went off road and split into two camps. Loup, Sharfy, Anfen, Eric and Case sat around a small fire. Outraged at his exclusion, Kiown sulked amongst the others some way further into the scrub, but Eric had seen the way Anfen tensed at the mere sound of Kiown's voice, and was not surprised. Some of that group were already dozing on their unrolled mats, barely an hour after nightfall. Birds, silent in daylight, now cooed gently as though singing lullabies. Eric saw Kiown and Siel get under the same blanket, and it felt like the ground beneath him had opened up, swallowed him, and sent him plunging through some abyss with howling winds. He lay down on his unrolled mat and tried desperately to think of anything else, anything at all.

The rest of Eric and Case's group relished their campfire as the night grew cold, using wood Loup had spent some time blessing. From a distance it had looked like he was simply talking to the wood and slapping it gently. The resulting fire's light and smell would carry no more than a dozen metres, allowing them to camp close enough to the road to hear the boots of passing patrols. Anfen had not actually expected them to range this way, but one came not long after they'd camped, marching fast and in formation. 'Half an hour longer on the roads and we'd have run right into them,' he said with a sigh. 'Eric's luck is catching.'

'They've heard what happened to their mates,' said Sharfy.

Anfen nodded. 'Question is whether they're looking for us or the Invia. Who do they blame for that little party?'

'Who would you rather they blamed?' Eric asked.

Anfen's smile was grim. 'Not us. I don't want to be feared by them. Doon's people were feared by them. There aren't many half-giants left. They'll get us all in the end. Those low on the list have a chance to fit in a full lifetime, perhaps.' He lay back by the fire and closed his eyes. 'Though I somehow doubt they're sending foot-soldiers after a creature that lives in the sky.'

They ate gathered herbs and stewed mule, which Loup blessed, making it taste like shreds of the finest juicy rump steak in a dozen subtle spices. When it was swallowed however the belly was not so easily fooled, and Eric felt queasy as soon as his plate was finished.

'If they haven't sent mages our way, they can't be too worried about us,' said Sharfy, whose face in the campfire light looked like a Hallowe'en mask.

'Did you notice it took some while for their mages to come

and guard the door?' Anfen replied. 'They're probably busy trying to find whatever it is that wiped out an entire company of the castle's soldiers and left no trace of itself but holes in the ground.'

'What did *that*? And when?'

'The same thing that's been attacking travellers and wagon trains in the far south. A small patrol of our own was wiped out too, out in the middle of nowhere. We thought it was the castle's doing. Then last month an entire mining station was slain near World's End. And those were the castle's assets. Probably the very cart you three robbed underground came from there.'

'Ah, enough of that talk,' Loup suddenly interjected. He rattled the charm's dull silver beads and grinned, the firelight casting ghastly shadows on his face, making him look like he regularly dined on human flesh. 'I figured her out a little, just a little, now that you stopped pestering me to make your dinner taste better, and the firewood blessed and all.'

'Stop whining and tell us what you know, you old poser,' said Sharfy.

'Poser nothing! I saw you gobble that soup. And that mule we just ate was prettier than you, alive or dead or digested!' They both laughed, but Sharfy's rang a touch false, as though a nerve had been struck. 'This kind of charm,' said Loup, 'oh aye, ten charms in one. All pretty handy on their own, mind! She's a nice old girl.' He lovingly stroked the necklace and grinned his toothless grin. It made him look none too wise at all. The others patiently waited. 'Been alive longer than most of the cities. She's an old darling, she is.'

'We've established that she's a nice old girl,' said Anfen sleepily. 'What else can you tell us?'

Loup flashed his gums, clearly enjoying centre stage. 'See these little beads? Each one's a charm by itself. Some of em are active, some aren't. You can switch em on or off, *if* you know how. I don't. Could learn, maybe . . . problem is, we don't know what we'd switch on! Maybe some aren't friendly at all! Best to leave her rest a little, she may want her sleep. Right now there's three of em working. This one . . .' he picked out a bead no visibly different from the others '. . . keeps the wearer from being seen. Just like that! Handy trick? Oh, aye. Powerful, too! Wager it'll keep you hidden in bright light, in a room full of people. I can't ever do that, nor most mages I knew. Hiding out in the wild, see that's different. Half *that* spell's done by the trees and scrub.' Loup gave a friendly wink to no one in particular, then picked out another bead.

'This one here, see, this does something else. There's power flowing *into* it, not out from it or around it like a whirlpool. Can't be sure, and I'm nervous to toy with it, but I'd guess something from the wearer goes *into* the charm. What does? Well, hey now, that's your guess much as mine. Right now it's almost full. Real weak stream going in, just a trickle. Maybe I can get out again whatever's inside. Maybe it's something to do with this third switched-on bead, right here.' He pointed at the dull silver knob. 'This one I can't seem to figure out at all. Strange old patterns she makes in the air about it. So let's hear a little from the lucky gent who got to court this old darling.'

Case had to be woken, and was not pleased about it, but he cleared his throat and told everything he could remember, in as good an order as he could, not even sure what he was leaving out nor what his memory had distorted. He didn't recall much of the conversation between Vous and the Arch Mage. Sharfy and Loup were most intrigued by descriptions of Vous's chambers, and by the story of his daughter. 'Don't know, I think my head was playing tricks,' said Case. 'Wouldn't be the first time in my life I saw things that weren't really there.'

'She's real,' said Loup, grinning. 'That's young Aziel, like a bird in a cage. Talk is, Vous planted seed in one of them lady servants, in their silly grey robes, whether or not she wished it, no surprise at all. A hobby of his from way back. The Arch Mage talked Vous out of killing the mother, so the talk goes. He sees far ahead, that one. But only with a man's eyes, mind, and so not in all directions at once!'

'That Arch Mage didn't look like the type to save anyone, to me,' said Case. 'Looked worse than those horned things near the door.'

'Oh aye, he is,' said Loup earnestly. 'Worse cos he's greater than them, but worse yet cos he's *saner* than them. Enough magic's poured through *him* as would cook any honest mage's brain, but his brain's still raw as fish! And rightly said, didn't save *anyone's* life from the goodness of his heart, that one. They got grand plans at that castle, and Aziel may have her part.'

To Case's surprise, the part Anfen seemed most alarmed by was the mention of Stranger. He questioned Case about her many times — what she wore, how she spoke — but Case didn't have much more to tell.

'I felt her all right,' said Loup in a lowered voice. 'She's never far away. Been on us since the fight. Sometimes far back, sometimes a stone's throw.'

'Who and what is she?' Anfen demanded, sitting up and looking quietly furious.

'Hard to say, but she's a handy mage,' said Loup. 'Making a cup of wine taste better? Well, *I* can do that kind of thing. I did it to the stew tonight! *Creating* a cup of wine right there on the spot? See, I never heard of *that*. Only summoning I ever saw took three mages and nearly a full day's work, mind you that's without all the old books and such to guide em. But she's game enough to do her trick right in front of the castle, too?' Loup whistled. 'Can look after herself, I'd reckon. We'd be worried if she meant us harm!'

'Wouldn't we?' said Anfen. He rubbed the bridge of his nose and seemed suddenly to have aged another year or two.

'If she did, she's had her chances to get us,' said Loup.

'She seemed nice enough to me,' said Case, a little rankled.

'Sure she did.' Loup flashed his gums. 'Nice of her not to take this old necklace, too. She'd have known it was a good one! Maybe she knows what the other beads do, and doesn't want to touch it. Maybe she wants to get it as far away's she can, and is watching to make sure we get rid of it. Nice old girl, but maybe one with a bad temper! Your Stranger must know a thing or two about it.'

'Is she nearby, now?' Anfen demanded.

'Nope,' said Loup. 'But she came and had a look at where we set up camp.'

'*Why* didn't you tell me about her?'

'Oh, I'm watching out for her,' said Loup, unperturbed by his anger. 'She never got too close yet. I told Siel to keep an eye out. I don't care what tricks our Stranger knows, a goodly aimed arrow'll put a stop to her, if we need to, 'less her skin's made of rock. I don't reckon she means us ill. Plenty of patrols she could've steered our way. Wouldn't surprise me if she had a hand in the scrap back at the hilltop, somehow. A few strange turns in that scrap and we come out the other side just fine. She's handy enough, believe *that*.'

Anfen lay back down and sighed deeply. 'If she sees through a spell the Arch Mage of the castle didn't, handy is an understatement.'

Loup gave his *beg to differ* smile. 'No mage is great at everything. It's why they had five different schools, back in the old days! Doing some kinds of magic don't let you do the others, though you can get away with *some* mishmash. Some mages kill good. Some do things with the dead. Some, great with charms, making and using em. That ugly bastard isn't, by the sound. No matter, a lot else he's good at. Plenty of dead people to tell you that.'

For another half hour Anfen, Sharfy and Loup asked Case various details of his trip inside the castle. The more Anfen heard, the more troubled he seemed, though he wouldn't say what bothered him.

Eventually Case's composure slipped: 'I told you all I know! Enough questions. And yes, I probably forgot big parts that are important. I can't remember every word I heard in there, I'm not a tape recorder.' At their puzzled looks, he sighed. 'It's a device, back home ... look, forget it.'

'No matter.' Loup grinned and held up the charm necklace. 'Our nice old girl might know some things too. We'll have to ask her, polite as can be.'

'Where to, tomorrow?' said Sharfy as the folk magician laid a blanket across the flames.

'We stay off road,' said Anfen. 'We're going to have to head towards Faul's house until things settle. There is more going on here than we know, that's all I'm sure of.'

'We're not going through *those* woods?' said Sharfy, incredulous.

Anfen smiled. 'It's our safest bet. You know who to thank that the roads aren't safe.'

'What's the matter?' Eric whispered to Sharfy, surprised at the rare display of fear.

'Woods're haunted,' Sharfy answered. 'No one who gets in gets out, unless you can speak to the dead.'

'Loup can,' Anfen murmured drowsily. 'So relax.'

25

Eric drifted in and out of sleep, his dreams full of Siel or a woman just like her, running about him fast and ethereal as a ghost, her bright echoing laugh all around him. She was laughing at some private joke at his expense, then fled as a great shadow stretched out before him, while the old-young lord towered behind.

Twice in the night, some of the camp woke to the distant sound of chain mail clinking and heavy boots stomping past in a fast march. Now and then Eric woke and wondered dazedly where the hell he was. Silhouettes of the sleeping band were comforting around him, strangers or not. He remembered being a boy on camp with the Cub Scouts, learning knots, fistfights: memories from a world ago, a world away, suddenly hardly seeming real. That whole time, this place had been *here*, its own travails and problems just as serious as those of the world next to it. How long had this world really called to him? No memory he could find gave any hint that he would one day spend a night under a completely different sky.

Case slept next to him, but Eric didn't stir when the old guy got up to empty his bladder. It was still dark, though the night was old. Some way closer to the road was the silhouette of whoever kept watch — one of the women, it appeared. Mindful of the crack of twigs underfoot, hugely loud as they seemed in this gloom, Case went as far to the edge of the group as he dared. Then a glimpse of green caught his eye between trees further into the scrub. Her.

His heart raced, though not with fear. 'Miss?' he whispered. 'Stranger?'

There wasn't an answer, and he strained his eyes into the darkness ahead. She hadn't been far away. Then something ripped the air nearby, *whoosh! Thock!* An arrow striking a tree trunk. Siel was just behind him, her bow in hand, another arrow already nocked and drawn, its string creaking. 'Go back,' she said.

'You shot at her?' whispered Case, outraged. 'You shot at my friend?'

'Your friend should introduce herself. By day.'

'She introduced herself to *me*.'

Siel's mouth hung open and she stared at him, amazed to be chastising someone old enough to be her grandfather. 'You are not an honoured *guest* here! You are a newborn again. There's much to learn. Go back to sleep. Don't wake the others.'

Case was equally amazed to be chastised by someone young enough to be his granddaughter, so fiercely at that. He was lost for words, so he spluttered for a moment then did what she said.

They had buried the fires' remains well before the sun began to rise. Except of course there *was* no sun. The sky lit itself slowly and evenly, the eastern part no brighter than the rest.

Now they walked deeper into a forest with a floor of brittle grass, the thin light showing no more than a few metres ahead. Undergrowth crunched beneath their boots.

Anfen's mood was far brighter than it had been the night before, and at their first rest break it became clear why: he was about to part company with Kiown. He called the group together. 'We separate here. Sharfy, Loup, Siel, the Pilgrims, myself. The rest of you stay with our contacts by the Godstears Sea until you're sent for. Enjoy the fish, don't be noticed. Doon, we are visiting your aunt; I will send your greetings. But you need to be with this group to protect them. Kiown knows the roads best, and for that reason he leads you, wisely I hope. Be well.'

The group departed, though it was clear most of them weren't pleased with the orders. 'Watch out for magpies,' Kiown called to Anfen, referring to the Invia. 'I won't be here to save you next time.' Anfen did not indicate he'd heard. Kiown turned to Eric. 'You! I will make you a good deal for that scale. *Don't* crush it up for visions. And be careful of Sharfy. Among his collection of dirty secrets is a ... shall we say *fondness* for scale visions. Can't help himself, you wait and see.' He leaned close and lowered his voice. 'I see how you look at her. I see how you look at me now. You don't approve of my sleeping arrangements last night. Probably you plain don't like me at all. I understand! But it went no further than sharing a blanket. Never bedded her proper and never would. Be careful, you smitten thing. She's a killer. Don't be fooled by her age.'

Eric frowned. 'Her age ... wait a second, how old is she?'

'Fourteen. Thanks for the "tie". Be safe!'

As those remaining prepared to leave, Loup took Anfen aside and they had a long, quiet chat. After it, Anfen seemed very pleased. He clapped Case on the shoulder. 'Loup has uncovered some of your charm's secrets! You, my friend, have collected a mine full of treasures. This could be a pivotal moment in history.

Well done.' But he said no more about it, and the group resumed their march through the trees in waxing light.

'Glad he's happy,' Case muttered.

Eric was still on the brink of throwing up, in a dizzy, reeling world of remorse. He snapped, 'What's wrong with you?'

'I don't trust these people, Eric. What I saw at the castle was pretty bad, but I haven't seen anything from *this* lot yet to convince me they're the good guys.'

'Good guys? Case, is this a movie or are we trying to survive here?'

'I don't know, but the only ones here who showed me any goodness at all was Stranger and that wings woman, whatever they call em.'

'Didn't the Invia put you in harm's way? She put you inside the castle and made you see all those bad things.'

'She had her reasons.'

'Oh, come on.'

'She also gave me that necklace and saved me from falling down a cliff. You should see em up close, Eric. They're beautiful. And last night, that Stranger lass, she came to visit, just beyond the camp there. Well, that woman who never smiles or talks shot an arrow at her.'

'Not *woman*, Case. Girl.'

'No warnings, nothing, just *whoosh*! They tried to kill Stranger, Eric, after she helped me out and all, sent me back here to you.'

'They don't know who she is yet. Did you hear them? They were nervous because she can do serious magic. Why *doesn't* she come and introduce herself?'

'Maybe she tried last night. And by the way, are they keeping us captive or do they plan to let us go if we find a town or something?'

Eric felt reluctant to admit it in Case's present mood, and he wondered how much the old guy was just in need of a drink. Yet . . . 'We are . . . I think not quite captives, but not quite free, either.'

'There!' said Case, triumphant. 'I want out of here, Eric. I want my charm back and I want to go.'

Eric laughed. 'Case! Where are you going to *go*? You don't have a map, don't know anything about this place.'

'I don't care. I had a long enough innings already. If something gets me, well and good. I'm done with this shady bunch. They never tell us outright who they are or what they're doing. You stay with em and keep the gun. Just don't tell them what I'm doing.'

'Maybe I should, before you get yourself killed.'

'Oh no you *don't*. I get myself killed that's my business, I don't give a shit. You got years ahead of you, I got weeks or days, I'll spend em how I want. Wouldn't be here at all' – Case bit off the words which Eric thought were likely to be: *if you hadn't jumped through the door like a lemming off a cliff.*

'Case, I would dearly love this conversation to be over, because I have hard work to do glossing over something I feel extremely guilty about. But let me ask you something. And don't get mad, OK? This Stranger woman. Did she really come last night just to see you? Do you think she's going to follow you around and keep you safe, if you leave the group?' *And maybe conjure you another drink or two? And, maybe in your heart of hearts, give you a little kiss . . .?*

That touched a nerve, perhaps what he hadn't said as much as what he had. Case stormed away from him, not before turning and whispering fiercely, 'I tell you what, I'm gonna wait for my chance. And don't you tell them. You owe me that much.'

'I guess if you don't measure what's owed or not in a *material* way, you're right,' said Eric, thinking of the money he'd spent on this geezer's alcohol alone.

Case frowned. 'What's that supposed to mean?'

'Nothing, forget it. OK, Case. You got it. My lips are zipped.'

It was several hours before Eric discovered Kiown had been joking about Siel's age. She was really nineteen. When Sharfy told him this, he suddenly shared every violent wish Anfen may or may not have had for the lanky redhead, although the relief he felt was like a gift from the heavens.

Meanwhile the ground bore no path for them across its sloping turf; the bush was thick in parts, then thinning away to bare fields of stiff grass; and the trees were mainly kinds not dissimilar to pine and eucalyptus, some hugely tall with thick, strong branches, others skeletally thin. There was small game to hunt: creatures that seemed cousins of deer and rabbit. They were easily caught, full of good meat, and seemed to live for little purpose other than to feed travellers. Eric tried to think of what bothered him on sight of the creatures, why they seemed less real than they should. He thought, sketched by a different nature. Each looks pretty much the same as every other of its kind. But it's not like that with people, or with the animals you see of our world, like crows and horses ...

As days and nights of marching took them deeper into the woods, mist which never lifted covered the ground in a white shroud. It was so thick in parts that they lost sight of each other, and the march became a blind stagger with arms extended to stop head-on collisions with trees. There was no sign yet of the ghosts Sharfy had feared, unless the peculiar echoing calls of birds they never saw, seeming to report their progress, came from the throats of ghosts.

Occasional clearings held the corpses of old villages: long-neglected huts of log and stone. They stopped to explore these, finding in them no recent signs of life, human or animal — just abandoned stone water wells and the trees keeping silent vigil.

Their feet began kicking up old bones in the undergrowth. Eric overheard Sharfy and Anfen quietly talking of massacres, mass executions of soldiers marched here in lines from trapped or surrendering armies, their bodies left in shallow ditches and the woods left full of angry spirits.

They bathed in cold clear streams when they found them, without time for modesty or embarrassment if the mist was thin. Eric soon found that Sharfy had just as many scars on his hairy backside as on his face and arms, and deep crisscrossing grooves on his back which could only be from distant lashings. Siel meanwhile did not much speak to him or anyone else, only to say necessary things. She had distanced herself on purpose and he didn't know why. Again and again he thought back to the hilltop, and always he saw her head turning away from him, denying her mouth to him, then passively giving it with her eyes looking sideways into the distance as though at nothing, as though waiting for him to hurry and finish what *she* had willingly started. Like he had caught her and thrown her down instead. Did you? he wondered. If she thought you were a prince, was it not a lie that got her to offer herself? How is that different? As the days of travel went on, and they got further and further from the world he knew, a desire grew in him to do that very thing, right and wrong aside: throw her down and have her.

In the nights they spent in those lonely silent parts, white orbs glinted on the edges of their sight, seeming to press in, bringing with them a biting chill. A wind they couldn't feel whispered and rustled through the grass and bushes with faintly heard sighs of pain and weeping. But when they turned to look closer, the lights fled their vision, staying always at the edges of it.

'Silly old ghosts!' Loup cried one night, when the lights sat at the edge of their small hilltop clearing and no longer fled, bathing the whole campsite in eerie flickering white. 'Go on, leave us a while. You and your whines and moans, trying to give us nightmares. Here! Come with me, come tell me all about it, get it done with. Yes, yes, you've got your troubles, so do the living, curse it, so do we . . .' He marched grumbling off into the trees, the glimmering lights following him. He was out of sight for a long while, but when he returned, the lights didn't come with him. 'Ignore em,' he said with a yawn, as though they were no more than loud neighbours. 'They make the air cold — so what? They're no harm, just seeing who we are and why our feet make such a noise through their scrub, whether we mean harm to kick their bones with our steps or no. They'd need lessons from foul dead-meddling spells before they could make *real* trouble, oh aye. These poor sad ones don't know how.'

Siel for some reason was not so easily assured; she moaned and whimpered in her sleep. Eric suddenly had to fight no lust, only a desire to stroke her hair and tell her she'd be all right.

Loup saw him watching her and whispered: 'She can see what happened here, back in the day, that's all.' Seeing his surprise: 'Oh, aye. Got a little Talent, she does. Can't control it or help it, of course. But bad things happened here at this very spot, very bad things. She can hear em, loud as if they're going on this very moment, just over yonder. Kept it hidden, she has, brave thing, but it's harder tonight. This is a bad place. Men of honour died here in a way they never deserved, lots of em at that. She hears it.'

In the night's quiet, with just the faintest of breezes whispering through the branches, Eric lay back and imagined he could hear the sounds too: horrible screams of pain from the strangers whose bones littered the undergrowth, whose torment would never really end, but was in some little pocket of time forever locked away, their screams still trailing on and ricocheting faintly off the tree trunks, which stood as indifferent to all this then as they did now.

26

There followed one of those days when the mist eased, perhaps as the ground rose. It didn't help much, as any stretch of woodland seemed identical to the last, down to the moss-covered stones. Anfen turned and gave Eric an expectant look and a half smile. 'Well?' he said, nodding towards Sharfy. 'You are walking next to a great source of knowledge. A vast pool of it. Why not scoop in your hands and drink? Do not drown, I warn you. It could become a flood, a storm of words, and we could all be swept away. Just a drink, for now, of his wisdom. It may distract you from . . . other troubles.' Anfen's smile was ambiguous.

It's as obvious as that, is it? Eric thought; he had spent the last day and a half determinedly not looking Siel's way, and succeeding some of the time. Now that he learned she had magic about her, the intensity of his fascination was almost overpowering. Sharfy meanwhile seemed to take Anfen's words quite earnestly, and held his head up proudly.

'What's to be your first lesson?' said Anfen, and Eric saw he wasn't entirely joking. 'Our worlds are very different and you'd better learn *fast*. We are in the wilder parts of it now.' The tall trees seemed to agree with their silence. The group's footsteps cracking on fallen branches and undergrowth sounded unnaturally loud, as though any kind of netherworld demon might be called by it and come screaming their way.

Eric shrugged. 'How about magic, then? What makes a folk magician different from a war mage?'

Sharfy gladly replied without delay. '*Folk*'s just a word for a whole lot of little bits, mixed from the major schools. Passed down by mouth, not books. Be lucky to meet two folk mages who know all the same things. Other kinds of mage all got killed off or ran into hiding for good. 'Swhat war mages were *made* for, see? Mage hunters. Got to be careful with spells, cos they can see it from a long way off. That's why you see Loup pick up a sword or knife in a scrap, not start waving his arms, making funny lights.'

Eric glanced back at the senile-looking old man, no teeth, no shirt no matter how cold it got, now sharing a joke with an unsmiling Case at the back of the group. Loup wheezed laughter while Case looked like he only wished the magician would shut up and leave him alone. 'Could Loup really make funny lights and all the rest?'

'Doubt it, I never seen it,' said Sharfy. 'Mages get offended if you ask em what they can or can't do. But you can bet he probably blessed the sword he picked up. So you'd best be careful, if you mean to scrap with him.'

'Hey, he's OK by me.'

'He's handy enough for us,' Sharfy continued. 'He's why we'll get through these woods alive, despite this cursed mist. He can sense which way's best to go. But in the old days, when the five schools of magic were strong, they would've handed him a broom if he showed up at their temples. He's worth more, these times. Casters are rare. Not many left to teach, not many game to wield magic, in Free country or Aligned. War mages still hunt em down.'

'You said there weren't war mages in Free Cities.'

'No. But castle pays bounties, so people got rich hunting em. In Aligned places, magic's been outlawed a hundred years.'

'Outlawed. What a pretty word,' said Anfen. 'Ditch full of bodies, it means.'

Said Sharfy, 'Castle can wreck a lot of things, even in just a century. Rip up books, burn huts and villages, knock down temples, steal wards and charms and totems. Stuff that'd been around through it all, theirs now. *His*. The magic schools, their High Elders wouldn't have believed how the world would look today, if you told em, back then. They were so strong and wise. Wiped out *quick*.'

'How about the magic schools then?' said Eric, suddenly likening Sharfy to a kind of knowledge-jukebox, and imagining sliding a coin into his mouth.

The song played: 'Used to be five schools, one for each Great Spirit except Valour, who don't have magic. A bunch of small temples and such too, which were nothing to do with the gods: local to a region, usually. You'd know where to go to get healed, or blessed, or get charms made or charged up. Some'd train your horse for you so it was almost as smart as you were, could understand every word you said. All for a price, of course. Not cheap, and people didn't like em for that. The big schools were sometimes hated. Would you feel bad for someone who refused to cure your son cos you couldn't pay up, when it'd only cost em a spell, and maybe some pain to cast it? So no one cared too much back then when the new castle lords said they were going to do something to the magic schools.

'But people didn't understand, the magic schools stopped the Cities fighting each other. Not always, but sometimes. Just by being there in the background, with Mayors not sure what they'd *do* if war broke. So when the castle got taken over by Vous, no one worried too much. The schools wouldn't let em do anything *too* crazy. They thought.'

'This is recent history, but before our time,' Anfen interjected. He rubbed a dead stone on his blade while he walked, still stuck with the army-issue sword stolen from the dead soldier. 'When we were born, much of the wrecking was already done. Not all, though. Not all.'

'Were these magicians actually a threat to them?' said Eric. 'The schools, or the folk magicians?'

'Not if the castle left the magicians and everyone else alone,' said Sharfy. 'But they meant to do something *no one* would like: take over all the cities, all the land, all the people. That's just for starters. Then there was their "Project", the point of the whole thing, the reason they needed the castle and its air full of magic. Ask Loup what the castle looks like these days to a mage's eyes! Frightening, is what. No decent mage would've let em do it. Soon as word got out, the schools would've done something.'

'I invite you to try telling Vous someone's not a threat to him, anyway,' said Anfen with a laugh. 'Rumour long held he's terrified of his own shadow. I never quite believed that, until . . .' But he fell silent and seemed to reproach himself, as though he'd said too much.

'When it all began, they said they were going to leave the folk magicians alone,' said Sharfy. 'The mongrels who knew a little of this and that, like Loup. Folk magicians didn't like the schools, who looked down on em, tried to boss em around sometimes, told em what magic they could or couldn't do, arrested em if they disobeyed. So the folk mages weren't upset when the castle started taking on the big schools.'

Said Anfen, 'The new lords told each school they only meant to reform one or two of the others. It was easy to play them off — lots were rivals and enemies. But all this talk was stalling for time, so no allegiance between schools would seize back the castle. Which they might have done, if they'd stopped their cursed bickering. Then a thousand war mages poured out of the castle in one flock, before anyone even knew what war mages *were*. No temple was ready for hundreds of them descending at once. It was a terrible battle. Not many from that foul army returned, but they'd done their job. In just a few long nights of death, they'd done their job. Unique and precious charms were seized, and *that* was no trifle. Many of them, Vous wears right now.'

A small-game creature that looked vaguely like a hairy pig burst through two trees and scuttled slowly through the under-growth ahead, not the least mindful of the creatures nearby, higher than it on the food chain. Siel darted after it with her curved knife drawn, not even bothering with an arrow. Soon they heard the animal squeal with surprise as it discovered it was lunch. Eric said, 'Would Loup be able to defend us, if a war mage came?'

Sharfy laughed and slapped his knee. 'He'd be blood in the grass! He wouldn't even try to fight. He'd not get himself near one in the first place. He'd know what paths to take, when to hide himself in the woods so danger can't find him. Maybe he didn't even know there was a war mage after him. He'd just see a cloud's shadow pass over, see something in it, and know he had to hide. That's why someone like Loup looks crazy to us half the time, but we listen to him.'

Dead leaves crunched under their feet, and the trees about them grew denser. Siel returned with the animal already gutted, drained and slung about her shoulders. The ends of one of her long braids had evidently dipped into the beast's carcass, for it was caked in blood. Eric tried to think of her splitting it open, hoping it might douse some of what he felt — a bizarrely powerful feeling moving up and down a spectrum from animal lust to tenderest love — but after days and nights of fear, exhaustion, exertion, he only wanted her more.

'Is she still behind us?' Anfen called to Loup, meaning Stranger.

'Not for a few days now,' the folk magician replied. 'She's trailed back, 'less she knows a way to hide from other mages that I never seen before. Maybe she does! Handy? Oh aye, that one is. Now let's sit down a while. We're not long from being through these woods. But there's danger ahead whichever path we take, and not far either. Rest a spell and we may miss out on some of it. If not we'll be crying and moaning at the next poor group to blunder through, our blood splashed on the tree trunks, bones getting kicked along in the dirt.'

27

That afternoon the mist cleared, but what it revealed was not comforting. Among the clumps of ruins they finally came across remains of recent campfires in a big clearing, the first sign of human life since they'd stepped off the roads and into these haunted woods. Anfen turned to Loup. 'This was the safest way?'

The magician bristled. 'You mark me, it was. By all the signs I seen and *still* see. Never said we'd not have to be on our guard, did I?'

'Weapons,' Anfen called wearily. 'You too, Pilgrims. The peace couldn't last forever. Inferno cultists are nearby.' Eric drew the sword he'd plundered from the dead castle soldiers. The blade had a notch in it halfway up but was sharp enough. It was not time yet to risk showing off his secret weapon, the gun in its holster. Case held his sword like a walking stick with no pretence at combat and yawned like he'd rather be napping, thanks.

They fanned out, Sharfy with his smoking knives staying close to the Otherworlders. Anfen walked in the lead, lithe as a dancer ready to burst into a flurry of movement. They carefully stepped through the stone bricks of a demolished old cottage. Discarded clothes lay here and there, as did cups and plates recently used. There was an open tome set on a piece of log with indecipherable symbols on its torn page, flapping in the breeze. But there were no people.

'Dead wind ahead,' Loup called. 'Steer right.'

Something blew through the ashes, kicking up a little shuddering whirlwind of them. There was a faint shimmering effect half a man's height above where the ashes flew.

'Survival lesson, Pilgrims,' said Anfen. 'That little disturbance there. If you see such when no breeze blows, stay away. Sharfy, demonstrate.'

Sharfy rummaged around in a pile of unused firewood till he found a long thin branch. He approached the dead wind with great care, as though it could change direction and come his way, then poked the branch into its midst. As soon as it touched the shimmering part, the stick wrenched out of his hand with a sound of breaking, then vanished.

'No one knows where the stick went,' said Anfen, picking up a stone and throwing it into the dead wind, where it also vanished. 'Beyond World's End, for all we know. But a dead wind means Inferno cultists have been here. It's leftovers from some of their rituals.'

'Two more, yonder,' said Loup, displeased Sharfy had got so close to it.

'I don't fathom this,' said Siel, peering at everyone with her dark eyes wide. 'These are fresh tracks, two days old at most. Where *are* they? Look over by that fire. Do you see the chopped-off arms and legs lying about? It's fresh, not old bones! A large gang of them had a ritual here. They danced around a huge fire. They had an orgy. See the loosed shackles and ropes? They had victims to toy with, likely kidnapped from the road. They cast their foul magic.' She poked at the footprints with her boot. 'There are some marks here I don't understand. The tracks all rush off, that way.' She nodded ahead, where the ground sloped down out of sight. 'No patrol came through here to clear them out. But *something* scared them away.'

The surrounding trees were tall, silent and watchful. Anfen said, 'So perhaps they're all waiting for us, just over that rise there. Siel, wear the charm please and scout ahead.' He tossed her the Invia's necklace.

Siel's returning footsteps disturbed the leaves and sent Loup into panic, fearing a dead wind coming right for them, until she spoke. 'Come. You should see this. It's ugly.'

'Are we in danger?' said Anfen.

'I don't know,' she replied, removing the necklace and becoming visible. 'But if we are, it's not from cultists.'

'You sound very sure of that.'

'Oh, I am. Come see.'

They crossed the sloping turf and came to an old hunters' hall, solidly built though many of its thick logs were rotting. A kind of shanty town of lean-tos and tents made of animal skins spread around behind it. Tracks were visible here, even to Eric's untrained eye, of a panicked stampede to get away from something and into the hall. Through its windows — no glass, just square gaps in the wood — the scene was far worse. Corpses lay in twisted piles, like a giant thresher had been through the crowded place. From within a horrible reek came that tugged at Eric's memory. 'Sharfy,' he whispered. 'That smell. In the caverns, remember? Back near the door. The dark passage we couldn't see into . . .'

Sharfy nodded. 'Weaker here, but it's the same smell. We walked right past whatever did this.'

Anfen stood in the doorway gazing in. A mask of blankness closed down on him, making his young face lifeless as a stone statue. 'Don't come closer, Pilgrims,' he said quietly.

'Another fine stop-off courtesy of our friendly guides,' Case whispered, pulling Eric by the arm out of earshot of the others. 'Have you had enough of these people yet? Where are they taking us anyway?'

Eric groaned. 'Maybe ask *them*? Case! Who the fuck else is going to look after us here? We're in the middle of nowhere. We don't know a thing about this place and there are dead people every time we turn around! Do you think you know the lay of the land better than them?'

Case said nothing and Eric knew his words had ricocheted without effect.

'Look here. They tried to barricade the door,' said Sharfy. 'Something smashed it in.'

'Can anyone think of anything, anything in the *world* that would scare twenty or thirty Inferno fanatics so badly they'd run screaming for cover? Let alone kill them all in such fashion?' said Anfen.

'Not mid-ritual,' said Sharfy. 'They go crazy. I've seen em at it. Nothing would scare em. Anything that might kill em gets em more excited.' He said in a lower voice: 'That's why mid-ritual's a good time to kill em.'

Anfen moved from the doorway and gazed at the treetops as though to cleanse his vision. Eric noticed that for a good while afterwards, the troop leader was reluctant to look directly at any of them and seldom made eye contact. At his feet near the door there were scratches and gouges in the turf, as though someone had hammered spikes deep into the ground in some random pattern then removed them. They were clustered in a rough trail which ran back past the site of the bonfire, from which the cultists had fled, then turned almost at right angles back to the trees. It had been easy to miss at first, partly hidden by foliage and dead leaves.

Siel donned the charm and followed the trail, little scuffs in the dirt indicating her footsteps. Something screeched from the trees and everyone jumped. A huge black bird flapped skywards, ugly as a vulture, cackling as though amused. An arrow sailed after it from Siel's invisible point in a graceful arc, visible only well into its flight. It landed tip-first in the dirt.

Soon she returned, fetching the arrow on the way. 'Not far in, there's a groundman tunnel gap, larger than usual. The strange tracks lead right to it. Two pit devil corpses nearby.'

'Pit devils didn't do all this,' said Sharfy with finality.

Siel removed the necklace and gave him a rare smile. 'Oh?'

'No way. Wrong tracks. Too far from the tunnel opening. And the bodies didn't look like devils got at em.'

Siel nodded like an attentive pupil. She said, 'That may also explain why one of the devil corpses has been picked up and impaled through the chest on a tree branch, quite high up.'

There was no talk for a moment. '*How* high up?' said Sharfy, as though this changed things.

'Three times a man's height. Both bodies marked by holes like those tracks, punctured by many spikes. Shall I take you? Your analysis will be ... useful.' Eric had a feeling she didn't like Sharfy very much, nor anyone else who ever lived. Except Kiown, perhaps ...

'We're not going anywhere near it,' said Anfen. 'Everyone *move*. We are not camping in these woods tonight.'

Eric took Anfen aside. 'I don't think Case is up to another long march, let alone a long, quick one.' He didn't say, fearing it would sound silly: *He also needs a drink the way a sick man needs medicine* ...

'He's going to have to be up to it,' said Anfen. 'Unless death is his preference.'

'How much further?'

Anfen's jaw clenched with annoyance. 'A full day's march, then the going gets easier. There's a friend of ours out the other side of the woods who will give us shelter as long as we need it. Maybe even a drink for your friend. I see his hands shaking and his temper, but it can't be helped.' To the company he said, 'Let's move.'

At that moment something dashed through the hunters' hall doorway. A young woman in a woven wool skirt and jumper, both torn, running with a limp. She was barefoot, eyes wild with fright or rage. Her clothes and skin were coated thick in dried blood, which made her hair stand stiff. Panting, she stared at them like a wild animal unsure whether to flee from them or go nearer.

Anfen stepped towards her. 'You're safe, don't run.'

'Safe!' The girl — midway through her teens — barked bitter laughter. Her teeth showed white through the dark stains, as though this was the lone part of herself she'd been determined to scrub clean. Anfen unstrapped the scabbard from his belt and let it drop to the ground, stepping towards her again, palms open. 'Safe from us, at least. We'll feed you if you tell us what happened.'

'I've eaten,' she said, and laughed again. It was a horrible sound, despairing and caustic.

Anfen said mildly, 'Very well, but I suspect our food is better. Our conversation, too.'

'Leave the food there, then go,' she said. 'You won't need it any more. They will get you too, if you're worthy. I alone was not. Inferno sent them to collect us. He was pleased with the work we've done.'

'A mysterious Spirit, Inferno, to compliment you this way.'

'Yes!' she said eagerly, teeth showing.

'You have been through a lot.'

The girl's demeanour shifted before their eyes, as though conflicting wicked forces wrestled for her emotions. Her head slumped forwards: something won the battle. She said no more.

Anfen took her arm and guided her back to the others. He left her with Siel then picked up his sword. Siel looped a rope around the girl's waist none too gently and handed the other end to Sharfy, who tied it around his wrist. The girl gave a dark look to them both; she had clearly not expected to be tied.

'Where is your home city?' Anfen asked her.

'I have none. No past. Lalie is dead, I am her corpse.'

'Where was it, before you fell in with Inferno?'

'*Fell* in,' she snarled, mocking. 'He calls all who are worthy.'

'Worthy of death like cattle in a slaughterhouse,' said Anfen. 'Worthy of running to cower in their tombs before they die.'

The girl gave him a look of hatred made terrible by the blood coating her.

'I have fought with "unworthy" men who stared at death and marched towards it knowing where they went,' Anfen continued mildly. 'They did not run screaming into a hall to bar the door. Or hide there beneath their dead friends' bodies.'

'You want to stare at death?' she hissed, shivering with rage. 'Come inside! You are not worthy even of Offering. Come and see, brave man with a sword. See what Great Inferno sent us. All you know is ash.'

'Hey now!' cried Loup. 'That's a curse, what she just said. She's got no kick to give it, but she'd try, if she did! Other things might hear her too, you never know. You watch yourself here, Anfen, and maybe gag her if she keeps up that rubbish chatter.'

Anfen's eyes narrowed. 'It's still in there, whatever did all this?'

She laughed at him. 'Come and see!' She headed back to the hall, dragging the rope like a leashed dog. The despairing laugh rang loud across the clearing. 'Come and see! You won't come, brave man.'.

'Don't go,' said Siel.

But Sharfy and Anfen followed the girl in.

'See by her manner,' muttered Siel. 'From her speech. She's from a good home in a Free City. Elvury I'll guess.'

'Oh aye,' said Loup gravely. 'She'd have been warned of these cult people, but sought them out for adventure. They'd not need much encouragement to keep her. Pass her round the campfire like a bottle of wine. And she'll bite the hand reaching to rescue her.'

'What is this Inferno she was talking about?' said Case.

'He's a sick and weak old Great Spirit,' said Loup. 'Good as dead, buried in the Ash Sea. Other Spirits joined up to battle him, the myth goes, after he spun out of control. Long, long time ago. Weakest Spirit has the keenest followers. I can't figure it. Not even Nightmare's crowd get as worked up as this bunch.' He shook his head. 'They try to revive Inferno, like it's as easy as lighting a big fire. That's why they dance around fires, torture people, eat each other and all the rest. How it's supposed to impress Inferno, no one ever explained to *me*. And he *ain't* waking up ... oh no, other Spirits'll never allow *that*.' Loup sighed, dropped to the ground and took the opportunity for a few minutes' sleep. In moments he was snoring like a dragon, while Case scratched his head in confusion.

Inside the hall, Anfen and Sharfy, weapons drawn, showed no reaction as the girl led them through the carnage, eagerly watching their faces. She grew angry and fell quiet when they did not retch or flee the scene in horror.

Most of the bodies were in the front half of the hall, evidently an attempt to hold the menace out. Or perhaps it was a rush for the exits when it came inside. Two parts of the broken door had been hurled to far corners of the room.

'Your friends did not appreciate Inferno's gift, it seems,' said Anfen. 'That's hardly polite.'

The girl shut her eyes and sat on her heels. She did not want to be here, it was obvious, but had hoped to spite them with the horror of what had happened.

'Is there or is there not anything to show us?' said Anfen, growing angry in his turn. 'You're wasting precious time. If you think we are impressed or scared by death like this, you are wrong. We have seen it before.'

'And worse,' said Sharfy.

She laughed bitterly until Sharfy menaced her with his knife. Anfen held an arm out to stop him. The girl, cowering, pointed to the far corner of the room.

Anfen approached it, steps very careful, blade angled for a quick strike. Something small moved in the shadows there. There was a sound of scratching on the wood floor. A length of something that looked like intertwined tree roots made from dark glass twitched on the floorboards. A heavy two-handed axe lay near it, its blade badly notched. 'I see one of your friends, at least, had some heart,' said Anfen.

'Brave man,' cried the girl, mocking. 'Our High Priest could only cut off a hand, with an axe as big as that! What would *you* have done?'

If it was a hand, long curling spikes — four of them — were the fingers. They looked sharp as knives. Spikes of similar length ran in ridges up the length of its wrist. The finger-blades still groped and clutched. The floor around it was covered in scratches and sawdust.

'How long ago?' said Anfen. 'And how many were there?'

The girl laughed at his disquiet like she'd finally got her victory. Sharfy again showed her his knife. She looked at him hatefully, but spoke: 'Night before last. Three of them. Two did the . . . did it all. One stayed outside and didn't move for hours. Even when the others had gone.'

Anfen put his blade in the middle of the groping 'palm'. The finger-blades closed on it like the arms of a trap, its grip tight. He lifted it from the floor and the three of them gladly left the hellish place, even the cult girl's relief obvious.

Loup, baffled, examined the hand. It twitched and groped at the dirt like a sick crab. 'Nothing like I ever seen or heard of,' he said. 'Some kind of magic in it, hard to see its type.'

'This thing casts?' said Anfen, incredulous.

'Doubt it. The magic doesn't flow in or out. Just kind of packed in there real deep. Might be magic's what made it. Kind of reminds me of some magic gadgets them Engineers make ... whole thing could be an invention, not something natural. Can't say. If that's a hand, it'd stand pretty tall, maybe a tall man's height and half as much again.'

The girl laughed. 'Bigger. And that's the small one. The small one!'

'Oh aye, lass. You've been very brave.' Loup gave her a look of sympathy and her gaze dropped. He and Sharfy wound strong rope over the hand several times, then put it in a leather bag, discarding some things to make room. The hand still twisted and jerked, the fingers bending in many directions.

'Is there any more you will tell us?' Anfen asked the cultist. She scowled at him and said nothing. 'Very well,' he said. 'Cut her loose. Goodbye, Lalie.'

The girl looked suddenly panicked as Sharfy cut through the rope. 'What are you doing?' she said.

'Did you think you were captive?' said Anfen. 'No. You are a mouth to feed and a risk. I could tell Sharfy to do to you some of what you and your friends did to others until you talk, but there's enough on my conscience, and his. You are on your own in these woods with Inferno's gift, since you'd prefer that to a hot bath, cooked meals and a bed. May it kill you quickly.'

'Now don't you leave this girl here alone,' said Case.

'Case, don't,' said Eric.

'Don't yourself. All of you should be ashamed. She's scared and on her own. Something terrible happened here and you can't just leave her.'

'Perhaps she'll tell you how many innocents she helped slice to pieces or burn alive for her dead Spirit's favour,' said Anfen.

'He's not *dead*,' the girl said, glaring.

Anfen strode away, in the direction of the clearing's far side. The others followed. Hot tears brimmed in the corners of Case's eyes. Behind them, the girl stood mute in the clearing, a mix of bitter emotions in her face. Case looked back at her before passing through the trees. 'Lass, maybe you should tell them what you know. You can join us, they won't hurt you. Maybe you'll get cleaned up and taken back to your home and your folks.'

She scowled at him. 'I don't want your pity, old fool, and I don't want the touch of your fingers under a blanket at night.'

Case looked at her. 'Your world must be as sad a place as mine, lass. I hope you'll be OK.'

Her lip trembled. Case didn't turn back as he heard her footsteps hurrying after them.

'Good job,' Anfen murmured to him as the girl ran towards them, tears sliding through the muck on her face. 'But we will have to watch her.'

Case blinked at him, surprised. 'I wasn't playing a game there, friend. I thought you were willing and able to leave her here alone. And I meant it all.'

'I did too.' Anfen met his gaze with flinty eyes and Case backed away from him.

28

In his chamber, the Aligned world's Friend and Lord sat with face and body poised in the exact same way Case had seen when he'd walked invisible into this lonely chamber nearly a week ago.

Again unblinking, Vous's eyes were so unnaturally bright they almost glowed. On some days, they were bright enough to light dim rooms. This was due in part to the powerful charms about his neck, on his wrists and fingers, many of which would have been quite at home in the sky cavern troves of the dragon-youth. (And some of which may in fact have come from that very place, where no man had set foot. Invia were occasionally careless, now and then stealing away with a treasure, only to be spotted by a quick-witted thief in position to strike, and willing to wear a Mark.)

The magic force in sway, constantly ebbing and pulsing around and through Vous, was another part of what lent his eyes their unnatural gleam, as well as his body its youth, and his mind its insanity. Yet another part was this: whatever beliefs were held by peasantry, by soldiery, and by the castle's shrinking supply of enemies, the Project *was*, slowly, achieving its aims. The Arch Mage said changes in Vous would remain slow until they reached a critical point from which things would move fast and unpredictably. Perhaps he would increase in size, becoming huge as Mountain. Or not; Valour, it was said, was only just bigger than a large man. Perhaps he would become ethereal, invisible to all but mage eyes. Or he might assume a form none could guess. But his immortality at least was assured; even Inferno, as close to death as a Great Spirit could be, still writhed beneath the seas of ash above him, and still clutched a link to the world, however tenuous it was.

Vous the man had been but a seed planted by his own hands in historical soil. Now and then he looked back on co-conspirators who never knew they were but tools in his kit, albeit for important ends. He saw the young Arch Mage, not so called back then, just a rogue wizard banished from the schools and shunned for his penchant for forbidden things, lucky not to have been slain in disgrace. But mostly, Vous remembered that young man whose name he still shared, who'd started all this by reading texts in his wealthy father's collection of the rare and forbidden. For that young man he felt intensely sad nostalgia and love, earnest and tender as any mother's. He saw the young man going mad with ambition and power too great for *any* person. And still he embraced the same historic prize that the young man had opened his arms to, whatever the cost to himself or others. Only now, the prize was no longer the ethereal stuff of dreams: it was this throne, this room in the castle, these servants and soldiers, these charms about his neck, fingers and wrists. Just vehicles taking him towards it, perhaps, but all very real ...

Things moved apace. He had more people swearing to him, praying to him. His extended life was blending into history's pages, the lies *and* the truth of it. The Arch Mage's preparations — though Vous's understanding of them was limited — had passed the point of being possible to undo. What could stop him now? The dragon-youth were imprisoned; the Great Spirits would not come near the castle; and the Dragon Itself slept, hidden, unconcerned with the deeds of men.

That unknown critical point may be a day away or it may be another century in coming. Or longer. Vous was impatient for it, afraid of it, and already barely human any more in mind or spirit. He felt now like an unstable force being bottled in his body's shape. He felt like volatile liquid, stirred or gently shaken by any who came near him. They had better be brave, to shake him hard. He waited, and they all waited, for the great Change, the turning point.

And yet . . .

Vous's eyes rested on his wine glass, which was full. His lips were drawn slightly up so the teeth showed. There was a plate of food next to it, just as untouched. Whoever had prepared it knew he would not eat it; he never did, fearing poison, yet he demanded to be served anyway. They theorised that the sight comforted him and brought pleasant memories of good meals, long ago.

Poison would not be likely, with his protective charms, to hurt him much anyway; but to his mind, there was just no *knowing*. Every so often, a grey-robe was summoned to eat his meals before his furious, unblinking gaze.

If bothered enough by hunger — something becoming rarer with time, though he seldom ate — he would steal down to lower levels of the castle, in disguise, passing the mess halls of lesser staff. He would furiously devour half-eaten plates, swatting at whoever's food it had been with furious curses, ripping them from their place at the table by the hair, animal screams tearing high-pitched from his throat, thrown mugs shattering on the floor and walls, tables overturned, food smeared across his finely featured cheeks and chin, slumped back against the wall, inconsolably weeping while the mess hall cleared of people quickly and quietly.

Insanity was one price of it all. He knew he was paranoid, and foolish, and yet it struck at his heart no less: that special fear. For while he knew he was foolish, he *also* knew he was not, for he'd found an insane mind can believe two things or more with complete conviction, even as one disproved the others. The fear was at its worst at night, when all that was still human inside him begged the rest for sleep. It made him jump at movements in the corners of his vision, and cower pitifully.

The theft of his wine, days ago, had had a lasting effect. It had helped to convince the part of his mind which argued against Shadow's existence that the frightened part feared something real. The viewpoints coalesced on the spectrum of his sanity like a distorted shape gaining focus. Even when that same part began to seek other explanations — that he himself had drunk the wine and forgotten doing it, that his cup had been empty all the while — he knew better, and knew that something, or someone, had really been there, and had really drunk it, as if to mock him.

To Vous's left, against the wall, on the surface of the tall mirror, some faces slept, while other faces watched him. Their eyes were adoring and concerned. The faces gently bobbed and floated like dead fish on water, five in all; some still vaguely resembled the people they had been in life, though others had, with time, changed to look like little more than skulls. Of the rest of their bodies, only the occasional hand-print on the glass was ever seen, like fingers pressing on the window pane through which the faces gazed.

In their lives, Vous had known them and plotted with them for the throne on which he now sat. Their original plan — his too, for a brief time — had been to share it. Then other ideas had seemed appealing, for thrones aren't easy to share. One by one he'd killed them, three of the five with his own hands.

In the high upper halls, where the air was thick with power, and in the presence of powerful magic charms, acts like murder sometimes set off strange energies and effects, as did the subsequent thoughts of the murderer reflecting on the deed. Thus had emerged Ghost, his advisor, confidant, his dearest friend, and in some ways his very own unwitting creation, peering back through the mirror at him one day, and assuring him that it — they — felt no ill will, and bore no grudge, and wished only to see him prosper and thrive, he and the Project.

How Vous had screamed and recoiled, at first. How he'd screamed when they — it — followed him through other rooms on window panes, wine glasses and mirrors, for days on end, apologising and pleading, until he got used to their presence enough to listen to them and be convinced they meant him well.

The woman's face smiled placidly, the hair swaying as though it were immersed in water. Hers had been the first murder; he had strangled her as she took her bath. She'd been his lover at the time, had presumed herself his 'queen', had even suggested they plot against the others. He'd been disgusted at how ugly she was during the death. Here, her face was the most whole, the least dead-looking of the group. Another of the faces had begun to resemble a beast, with its two long rows of sharp white teeth and its hard round snout. He forgot what the man had even looked like, whose head he'd gone on smashing into the ground well after the deed was done. The others seemed starved, skull-like, with gloomy round sockets instead of eyes, and sadly set features. They seldom ventured away from this mirror, and longed only to help their Friend and Lord.

Their Friend and Lord had turned his eyes to them. An hour prior, they had told him they had important news, but he had angrily bade them be silent while he explored the thoughts floating through his mind like fast-moving clouds, sometimes assuming shape, sometimes all murk and vagueness, often stormy black. He would not make it clear whether he wished them to speak or not, but Ghost seemed determined to take a risk. If Vous angered, they would probably flee. 'We have heard strange news,' they said.

Vous stood, his hand reaching for the wine glass. It was all still there, every drop. He lifted it to his lips, wanting, suddenly, to shock Ghost.

'Friend and Lord!' cried four of the five faces in distress, the fifth gaping in mute shock. 'Friend and Lord! Please! Take care! Are you sure you should drink that? Is it safe?' They all spoke at once, their voices a jumble.

Vous's hand clenched tight around the finely wrought crystal glass. His arm shook and he gazed around the room in defiance, lip curled, teeth bared. '*Watch*,' he snarled, though he didn't speak to Ghost. 'You go ahead and *watch*.' In his bed at night, tossing and turning, he'd toyed with the theory that Shadow's stealing his wine was an accusation of simple cowardice. Now he threw back the drink in one swallow, spilling blood-red drops of it down his chin. The glass he flung to the wall near the mirror, where it broke.

Ghost's faces were in shock to see their Friend and Lord break so drastically with habit. The familiar display of rage hardly registered.

Vous stepped towards the mirror. He paused only to grab a handful of green vegetables from the plate before his throne and stuff it into his mouth, pleased at having shocked Ghost and wishing for more. Ghost obliged him with more fearful gasps and whispers, until he came near and stood, hands tensed halfway to making fists.

'Grim news,' said the face in the middle, recovering from its shock first. It was the sad-looking round face with big eye sockets, otherwise nearly featureless. Vous had forgotten what its name had been in life. He'd forgotten the rest of their names, too.

Speak, Vous thought, then realised he hadn't given the command aloud. They may have interpreted his posture, for they spoke. 'We heard a conversation, when we ventured to the Arch Mage's window.' Ghost then told him of how the Arch Mage, arguing with two Strategists, had dismissed the importance of the word 'shadow' being found on the rock face where a patrol had been ambushed and killed, a day's march from here. No survivors were reported.

Vous listened with fists tightening. He could not be told *all* tidings, and many things of import escaped his notice. But this? Why had *this* been hidden? 'I was not told,' he said, beginning to shake.

'The Arch Mage claimed ... he claimed ...' Ghost had become nervous; the round middle-face lost the ability to speak, so the female face took over, 'claimed it was better for your health, not to trouble you so. And he further said it was best not to show you what he called "the letter". One Strategist believed otherwise. They argued fiercely. Then the Arch Mage struck his face and banished him. And bade him never again mention "the letter".'

Vous paced before the mirror for a full hour. Ghost watched every step, waiting. At last: 'Did he know you were present in the window glass?' referring to the Arch Mage.

'Nothing indicated yes or no, Friend and Lord. The curtain was halfway drawn, and we hid behind it.'

Another hour's pacing, his body regular as a pendulum back and forth.

Ghost said hesitantly, 'Aziel, she wailed beautifully this morn—'

'Shhh.' Vous strode from the chamber without a further word. He went down to the Arch Mage's room, a place of white bricks and many special iron grids in the walls to facilitate the magic air. It had been too long since he'd visited. A vast library stretched along shelves on the side walls: books on lore of all kinds, magic of all known schools detailed here and only here with such comprehensiveness. Jars were filled with black twisting smoke or fluttering light. Cages held living things that scuttled about or crawled, attacking the glass walls when they felt Vous pass by. A small red drake, perhaps the last of its kind, was imprisoned in an iron cage in the corner. It made a mixed whine and growl, pleading sadly for freedom. Old scorch marks spread out from the floor near its cage, but its fire was used up long ago, and it surely knew by now that it waited here to die. When Vous sat and ignored it, it lay down to sleep, with a long sad sigh.

The Arch Mage wasn't home, yet again. Vous picked at the chair's arms in irritation, then pissed out the wine right there where he sat. He thought of tearing through the room, ruining everything, all the fragile instruments, the glass orbs filled with their mysterious smoky liquid, the charts and diagrams and sculptures, setting loose the creatures. He recalled having done such a thing before, and that the Arch Mage had not reacted other than with a displeasingly mild sadness, hardly even speaking about it afterwards.

Hours passed, then a full day. At last, the sound of familiar limping footsteps. Around the door came the half-melted face, the forked tip of a silver staff, the three horns on his head emitting a light curl of smoke each — he had flown in, then, most likely assuming the shape of a bird or bat. Behind his head was a long trail of black feathers. The one good eye took in Vous in his chair and scanned briefly around to make sure all was in order, before the Arch Mage cringed back from the hostile effects of Vous's charms and wards like someone who'd been shoved hard.

Vous's lip curled; he always enjoyed the sight. 'I left the bad ones in my chamber,' he said, which was untrue — they were in his pocket, where they would be harmless enough unless he put them on.

'What you wear still serves you well, Vous. It is good to see you. How your eyes glow — it shan't be long, I sense. Is something the matter?'

'The letter,' said Vous.

The Arch Mage began to speak, then didn't.

'Where have you *been*?' said Vous, standing. Spit sprayed from his lips. 'Ugly, foul thing. Disgusting, filthy thing stinking of shit.' Vous's rage spiralled away from him and spilled into the room like a small hot wind.

Sparks of fire erupted around the Arch Mage and sent little tendrils of flame up his gown. He winced and frantically patted them out. Hurriedly he said, 'There are things I feared to tell you ... things which I felt you would take badly, which could jeopardise—'

The rage was gone as swiftly as it had come. Vous's eyes shut, his face curdled in pain and infinite weariness. 'The letter. Where is the letter?'

The Arch Mage pointed at his far shelf. Vous ran there, snatched off a sheaf of folded paper, snarled deep in his throat, and sprinted from the room. The Arch Mage gently shut the door behind him.

In his chamber, it was a long week before Vous read what was written therein. He left the letter sitting at times on the floor, as though it were an unimportant piece of litter. His hands moved to rip it to pieces, but always stopped. Most of all, he marvelled that this thing could command his attention solely above all else, that it could have such power over him, though he didn't even know what message it held. That such an object of power over him had come from the Arch Mage's chambers was not lost on him ... not lost on him at all.

Finally he picked it up, startled at the lack of ceremony, the plainness of the act: it was just paper, light and dry in his hand. And the writing was of an ordinary, jagged script, though what it said burned through his mind like fire.

I WILL DESTROY THE WALL. MY NAME IS SHADOW. THERE IS WORSE THAN DEATH. I WILL DESTROY THE WALL. THERE IS WORSE THAN PAIN. I WILL DESTROY THE WALL. THERE IS WORSE THAN MOCKING LAUGHTER. I WILL DESTROY THE WALL. I WILL DESTROY THE WALL.

—*Shadow*

29

The light of afternoon was beginning to dim, but they were able, still, to keep an eye on the forest floor for more of the distinctive marks they'd seen by the hall. They had not yet found any. Loup led them, sometimes changing directions for no apparent reason, once even leading the group in a wide circle, and it seemed he'd done so on purpose. The others traded exasperated looks but didn't question the magician.

The cult girl — Lalie, as they began to call her, despite her ignoring this at first — kept a sullen silence, but briefly inclined her head in thanks when Anfen passed her a strip of dried meat. She ate it ravenously. She warmed to no one, but Sharfy was the one to whom her looks were the most venomous. No one questioned her yet. Nor did Anfen decide — after some murmured debate with Loup — to keep her hands tied, not yet.

When we get near a town, perhaps, he thought. Inferno cultists were not permitted in most cities, Free or Aligned, which meant they were usually killed on sight. Lalie did not bear many of the tribal scars or tattoos of long-standing cultists, but nor did she yet seem willing to lie about her beliefs, or forsake them. The Mayors would hear her story, and they would resort to torture, if she kept it to herself. War was war; no one had to like it.

The doomed hall and its museum of death had done the

expected bad things to Anfen's mind. Only Sharfy's face, Sharfy with whom he'd travelled most out of this group, was free of being split and cracked open in his eyes. Lalie and the Pilgrims he tried not to look at. Lalie especially was the stuff of nightmares, not helped, he guessed, by the dried blood that had caked her real face for so long. And these trees, these fucking trees, how he hated them, more than the old Pilgrim Case did, no matter who complained and who didn't. When he came close to one he had a strong lust to hack into it with his blade. It didn't matter that they'd come through the haunted part of the woods unscathed.

Anfen also knew Case was battling to keep pace with the group, and seemed on the brink of a one-man mutiny. It would be a challenge, when the peevish complaints ceased being quietly muttered and began being grumbled aloud, to keep from cuffing the old man's head, or screaming at him, or more. He didn't want things tense with both Pilgrims. But it was too late now — they would not avoid another night in these woods, and largely because of that one old man's lagging legs.

'We'll be safe if we're quiet,' said Loup as they set up camp for the night on a rise in the ground, away from the mist. 'Could be that the noise and whooping and hollering was what drew the beasties from the ground.'

'Maybe so. Lalie, what time did they attack? During your ritual?'

She answered, to Anfen's surprise. 'After. Late.'

'Go on,' he said, deciding to press her. 'You've been fed. Earn it.'

She shut her eyes and spoke hesitantly: 'We had collapsed, spent, around the fire, when they came. They . . . they stood by our sleeping bodies, we didn't know for how long. Hours or minutes. They were perfectly still, in our midst. Watching us.

Someone woke and saw them. She screamed. We others woke and ran. They didn't follow. They stayed still, perfectly still.' She swallowed and her voice quavered. 'We went to the hall. Barricaded it. They didn't come, not for a while. Morning was not far. We began to wonder if . . . we had imagined them. Then, out the window. I was the one who saw it. Right outside, peering in. It moved strangely. We didn't hear them come. It looked right *at* me.' She was shivering.

'What then, Lalie?' said Anfen, but she fell quiet and he let her stay that way.

They had a small fire with carefully treated wood but after their broth was heated that was all, cold night or not. 'And we'll have two on watch, all night. Siel and Eric first. Case and myself second. Sharfy and Loup third.' Eric's possible link to Siel was one way to nip in the bud any potential mutiny . . .

Lalie tossed and turned, whimpering in her sleep. Loup crouched by her, laid a hand on her forehead and murmured a few words. She soon lay quiet. Whatever Loup had done caused a drop of blood to trickle from his ear. 'Another thankless deed,' he muttered, holding his head in pain. 'But she needs it. Us too, with that moaning. Dreaming of beasties and blood. Silly girl.'

Who needs thanks and praise? They're just accusations of what good you *haven't* done, Anfen thought before drifting to oblivion, where colourless dreams awaited, the kind mercifully overlooked by his memory each morning.

Eric sat by the dead fire and Siel — to his surprise — sat behind him with her back pressed against his. The night woods were quiet around them, save the odd scuffling noise as a small creature lingered now and then at the edge of their camp, sniffing them out.

'You aren't a prince,' said Siel after a few quiet minutes. 'Or nobility.'

To lie or not to lie ... 'No, I'm not. But I'm the next closest thing, an unpublished novelist. That's a joke. How could you tell anyway?'

'At the hilltop. You know of my talent?'

'At the hilltop, I discovered your talent, yes.'

She laughed quietly, which was fine music to his ears. 'I see things,' she said. 'Glimpse through windows into the past. I don't like it. Here where bad things have happened, it's awful. I walked into a room at our old house and one day saw a man strangling an old woman. That was the first time it happened. I was five. Sometimes I can block it out, sometimes I can't. When they found I had talent, they tried to make me a mage in Happenstance. But my tutor was killed by bounty hunters. I'm not glad about that; she was nice. But I'm glad not to be a mage. Glimpses are bad enough.'

'Happenstance ... that's what your magic's called?'

'It's Wisdom's school. Or it was, before they destroyed all the temples and burned the books.'

'Wisdom — another Great Spirit?'

She sighed as if annoyed to be drawn onto an objectionable subject of discussion. 'Yes, but it's misleading. She doesn't really have much to do with their spell craft, though they thought otherwise at first. She's connected to the raw kind of magic they use, but not to the *ways* they use it. It's complicated to explain.' She waved a hand to brush the subject away. 'Anyway. When we mated, I learned things about you. One is that you lied about yourself.'

Mated. That word seemed a fitting description of their encounter on the hilltop. He nodded. 'Is that why you did it, to learn about me?'

'The main reason. I also like it, sometimes.'

'Ouch.'

'Though it is different for me, I think, from how it is for most women.'

'Did you learn also that I'm scared to death here? I was marched to your camp at knife-point, for fuck's sake. I thought this group was likely to kill me, unless maybe they thought I was important.'

'Yes, I knew that too. But you are important. You are a Pilgrim.'

'What does that mean? What's going to become of me?'

She paused so long before answering he wasn't sure she'd heard him. 'You'll decide what becomes of you,' she said. 'I don't know. I can't see the future. Almost no one can, not clearly, or the magic schools would still be here and Vous would never have taken the castle. And I don't know what it means that you're a Pilgrim. Only that it's important.'

'Are you going to tell Anfen I lied?'

'Not if you massage my shoulders.' She wasn't joking, he saw, as she planted herself in front of him and loosed the shirt about her neck.

He worked his thumbs into the knots and tension of her shoulders and neck. He took it no further, not here while they were on watch duty, though he itched to reach around and squeeze her to him, and had an odd feeling she would allow that much, at least.

'I also know you have a weapon,' she whispered. 'I learned it at the hilltop and I think I've seen it. What is it?'

'It's called a gun.' He took it out of its holster and showed her.

She held it. 'But this is small. Is it powerful?'

'Yes, it is.'

'How is it enchanted?'

'It's not. It shoots out a small piece of metal very, very fast. Much faster than your arrows. Don't tell them about it please, not yet.'

'If you carry it to protect us, I won't.'

'Of course I do. I have a feeling it would take care even of a war mage, if it had to.'

When his hands were too tired to go on kneading her shoulders, she turned to face him with her legs apart, reached into his pants, took hold of his penis with no ceremony at all and tugged it until he came, which didn't take long. She did it with about as much passion as a farmer milking a cow. 'You can perhaps relax a little, now,' she said, 'and think more of the dangers around us, less about *me*.'

He laughed. 'It's a deal.'

They said little more for the rest of the watch. He jumped every time something scuttled through undergrowth or flew with swooping wings from a high branch, but soon enough it was time to wake Case and Anfen, then, all too soon, time to rise and set out again.

As they put some distance behind them, the forest floor gave way like a balding scalp to the dark grey rock beneath. Ridges of it battled with the forest for turf. The place felt like distant, remote wilderness, the middle of nowhere; there was no sign of human habitation, no ruins or beaten paths.

Loup, who'd been in a foul mood all morning since they'd asked him to bless the biscuits they had for breakfast (he'd refused), finally perked up at the sight of rocky cliffs, and bounded towards them without a word, gesturing frantically for Eric to follow him.

Anfen, displeased, halted the rest of the company. 'Loup! Don't get my Pilgrim killed, and don't be long.'

Loup held Eric's arm and practically dragged him down a steep slope to the tallest part of a sheer wall of stone, out of sight of Anfen and the rest. The old magician held his palms to the flat wall, muttering, 'Somewhere round here, bound to be one. Bound to be. This far from cities and the road, oh aye! No one to bother him out here, he'll reckon he's safe. There'll be one: cranky, old and lazy.'

Part of the cliff face bulged outwards, and it was here that Loup stopped. 'Here! Here's one! Now let's wake him up.' He stood some way back from the bulge and threw small stones at it. 'Back here, Eric. You won't see him from right close. We got a stoneflesh golem here! Ho boy, this far north's a rare treat. Didn't think we'd actually find a live one!'

Only from back where Loup stood did Eric see the network of cracks and neat cleaves vaguely forming a squarish head. Two holes set wide apart made its eyes; its mouth was a jagged tilted slit above a bulging grey chin. If the rest of its body were below, it had merged with the cliff. 'Wake up, you ugly fat thing!' Loup called. 'Got a job for you! Wake up! Eric, throw stones at him. Big ones.'

Eric picked up some loose rocks and underarmed them at the rock-man.

'Hey now, don't hit its face!' said Loup. 'Aim lower down. Slow to anger, these are. But make it *too* mad and we'll have problems. Hey you! Wake up!'

There was a grinding sound. The mouth-line shifted sideways, grains of crushed stone falling like sand from either corner. 'Good! It's awake,' said Loup. 'Now. Here. Your scales. Where are they?'

Eric handed him all four. 'What've you got in mind?'

'You'll see. This golem's going to help us out.'

Anfen's voice carried over to them: 'Hurry up, you two.'

'Almost done!' Loup yelled back. 'Eh, him and his rules. You, golem! I got a job for you. But I don't think you're *strong* enough for it.' The mouth sawed sideways again, grinding more powdered rock. 'Ohh he's cranky now!' whispered Loup. 'You gotta insult em, make em want to prove emselves. You, golem! I got a job if you prove your strength! Which you *won't*. Weakling! Weak as my mother's pudding, rest her heart. Seen mud puddles stronger'n you. What reward d'you seek? Eh? Speak up!'

The jaw jerked around again with a spray of ground rock. Eric heard and understood: 'Sleep,' its voice like gravel scattering across the ground.

'What'd he say?' said Loup.

'He said sleep.'

'Aha! Wants to be left alone!' To the golem, 'Well, you can help us out first, then we're gone. You don't help us, we stay here *all* day, pestering you. Show us your palm, you fatso. Go on!'

A ripple of cracks wormed up the rock wall, outlining a slab of stone with a round fist at its end. The fist uncurled, the palm open, its fingers fat rectangles of stone. Loup ran forwards, placed Eric's black scale on its palm, then said, 'Go! Crush that up, you weakling! Show us what you're made of.'

'My scale!'

'Oh aye, she's a rare one,' said Loup with a grin.

Eric darted to retrieve the scale but the golem made a fist. There was a loud cracking noise, then a sound like glass being slowly crunched by a boot. The golem's eye holes peered out expressionlessly.

Loup pulled a soft leather pouch from his pocket and held it to collect the black powder running through the golem's fingers. 'Get it all,' he said urgently. 'There, a few grains dropped down. Get em! Quickly.'

The golem's palm opened. Loup dusted the dark powder from it. 'Sleep,' the golem repeated. Its arm still stuck out from the cliff face.

'It'll stay like that till who knows how long,' said Loup happily. 'He'll forget to put it back, you watch.' To the golem, 'Very strong, you are. I was wrong. All right, you go back to bed. Back to your dreaming about stones, stones, stones.' To Eric, 'That's about the only way to crush up scales I know of. Oh aye, strong ones are those stonefleshes!' Loup handed him the pouch. 'Wait till we camp. Hopefully we get a day up our sleeve soon. That'd be best. Then we'll see a thing or two with that crushed-up scale.'

'Thanks, I guess.'

'Spare me a pinch and it's no bother, no bother at all.'

A very impatient-looking Anfen gestured for the company to get up. 'After that little excursion, you owe me a tasty lunch, my friend,' he said to Loup.

'Ahh, I'll bless your lunch.' Loup flashed his gums. 'Stoneflesh, over yonder! Small one, but he was strong as his big old cousins at World's End. Oh, aye.'

30

At last it seemed the march was over. Alone in a stony field before them was a large, one-storey wooden house with several barns behind it. In the yard, a well-muscled middle-aged man bent over the ground with a bucket in hand, digging roots from the ground. He saw them approach and stared as though at peculiar beasts; it was clear this many visitors was not a common thing. Then he recognised Anfen and raised an arm in greeting. 'Faul! It's safe. He's back,' the man called to the house.

Footsteps seemed to rattle the whole house and a huge voice boomed out the door. 'WHO?'

'Anfen. And friends. *New* friends.'

'I DON'T THINK SO!' the voice shot out. It was a woman's. 'TELL EM, NO FURTHER! ANFEN CAN COME. I'LL MEET THE REST OUT THERE.'

'No need for *me* to tell them,' said the man with a shrug. 'They heard you.'

'Wait here,' Anfen said to Case, Eric and Lalie. 'Don't be alarmed. This is Faul. She's a friend of ours but she doesn't like strangers.'

Through the doorway — which, Eric just noticed, was a deal higher than normal — came a huge woman who had nonetheless to duck to get through it. She was larger, even, than Doon had been, round shoulders and arms straining at the plain farm dress she wore. Long straight hair hung to her shoulders, and a broad smile, full of blocky teeth, stretched across the ruddy slab of her face. Her big wooden clogs shook the house, its front steps buckling under her. She looked around at the rest of the company, a crazy gleam in her eyes. 'I KNOW THESE. YOU LOT ARE FINE. IN YOU GO. PANTRY'S FULL. DIG IN. BUT CLEAN UP AFTER!'

Sharfy, Siel and Loup bowed low in thanks, then went inside, taking their boots off at the door. Faul stomped over to Eric and crouched low to stare into his face. He had never felt so vulnerable in all his life, but the feeling was surpassed a moment later when she reached under his arms and lifted him like a doll, holding him over her head as though measuring his weight before setting him down. She did the same to Case next. 'YOUR HANDS SHAKE. WHY?'

'Need a drink,' he said tiredly, his tone suggesting that getting hauled off the ground by a half-giant was just another trial in a long, long day.

'DRINK! WE'LL SEE. YOUR WEIGHT'S GOOD ENOUGH. NOTHING FUNNY GOING ON HERE. MAYBE LUT CAN FETCH YOU ONE, IF ANFEN WISHES. WE'LL SEE.'

When she got to Lalie and lifted her, the big, crazy smile changed, and her brow clouded. 'AND WHAT'S THIS ONE? AHA, I THINK I KNOW. ANFEN! WHY DO YOU BRING SUCH AS THIS TO MY HOME?' Lalie's feet pedalled the air. 'CAREFUL, GIRL. THE HARDER YOU KICK ME, THE FURTHER I THROW.'

'She's the last of her group,' Anfen said quietly. 'Something, perhaps whatever has been causing grief and death in the south, now lurks in the woods near your home. She alone saw it. That's why I bring her.'

'VERY WELL. SHE MAY NOT COME IN. SHE STAYS ON THE PORCH TONIGHT. TIED.'

Anfen sighed. 'Faul, is that necessary?'

'IT IS!' she boomed. 'NEVER ONE SUCH AS THIS SLEEPS UNDER MY ROOF. SOME NIGHTS, WHEN THE WIND CARRIES, WE HAVE HEARD SCREAMS OF PAIN FROM THE WOODS, EVEN FROM HERE.' Faul had set Lalie down, but continued examining her. Lalie squirmed under her gaze. 'WHERE'S MY NEPHEW? WHERE'S DOON?'

'Marching south-west to the Godstears, with the others,' said Anfen.

'HE BEHAVED?'

'He's done himself honour. And you.'

'THEN WHY DID YOU SPLIT WITH HIM?'

'We have acquired another companion, uninvited,' said Anfen. 'She calls herself Stranger and seems to be a powerful mage. I wanted to be doubly sure she wasn't following Kiown or a couple of the others.'

'WHY WOULD SHE FOLLOW THEM?'

'Past deeds of theirs give many reasons. I sent Doon to look after them.'

'HE WILL. AND YOUR STRANGER WILL BE BRAVE TO STEP ONTO MY LAND, MAGE OR NO. FAR GAZE WILL SENSE HER, IF SHE IS GREAT. HE IS OUT THERE, SEEKING YOU. HE CAME HERE IN WOLF-FORM.'

'Far Gaze?' said Anfen, startled. 'Why?'

'HE ASKED OF YOU. THE MAYORS SENT HIM. IT IS ALL I KNOW.' Faul strode up, towering over him as though she meant him harm; she could hardly look otherwise. 'AND YOU, ANFEN. YOU SHOULD NOT LEAVE HERE FOR SOME WHILE. PATROLS SEEK YOU ON EVERY ROAD. TRADE WAGONS ARE SEARCHED. FAR GAZE SAYS CRIERS CALL FOR YOUR HEAD IN ALIGNED CITIES, AND SECRET BOUNTIES ARE BEING PLACED IN FREE ONES. WAR MAGES FLEW BY HERE. THEIR SHRIEKING SCARED THE BIRDS.'

Anfen's face was grim. 'When?'

'TWO NIGHTS PAST. THINGS STIR, RATTLE AND BOIL.'

The interrogation seemed to be over. Faul stomped back up the steps, gesturing for them to follow.

At long last, Case got his drink. It improved his shakes, but not his mood. Faul's husband, Lut — who was hale and hearty enough himself, when his wife wasn't close by to make him seem a midget — poured what smelled like petroleum into a clay goblet with a shake of the head which said he'd seen alcoholism before and didn't much like it. Case, for his part, had seen that disapproving look before, and he had learned not to give a flying fuck about it.

Lut fetched the rest of them plates of cold sliced meat and cheese. He refused Sharfy's offer of a red scale in payment, which Sharfy had counted on before offering the scale (which he pocketed again with some relief). The band laid their mats down across the splintery floor of a huge living room full of caged birds. Every so often Faul stopped to talk to the pets in her booming voice, as though no one else were able to overhear — often as not, talk about her guests. The birds learned that Anfen 'looked a little older and didn't walk so smooth now', that Sharfy 'needed a few scars on the other side to even up that face of his, for all the good that would do', and that the cult girl wasn't to be trusted and should count herself lucky to get a porch, for Faul had a mind to break her legs like twigs.

'AND I STILL MIGHT. DEAD GODS, MY PRETTY. WHAT ROT! LET EM BE IF THEY'RE SLEEPING, SPECIALLY TROUBLEMAKERS LIKE INFERNO. THINK PEOPLE KNOW BETTER THAN THE ONES THAT PUT HIM TO SLEEP? AND THE KILLING AND TORTURE AND ALL. SHAME ON HER. AS FOR THOSE OTHER TWO, THE

YOUNG AND THE OLD, DON'T LIKE EM, DON'T HATE EM. WE'LL SEE, WON'T WE? WE'LL BLOODY WELL SEE.'

The bird angrily screeched its opinion right back.

There were large spaces beneath false floors in nearly every room for Faul to hide in, should a patrol pass through, as they occasionally did. The patrols, Eric thought, would have to be numbskulls not to guess by the huge doorways alone that a giant dwelled here. Perhaps it bought Lut time to bargain for bribes.

'Faul shouldn't live here,' said Sharfy. 'It's too close to them.'

Anfen shrugged. He lay back on his cushions, legs crossed over one another, eyes closed. For the first time he seemed somewhat relieved of his cares, and closer to the young man his years claimed he was. The charm necklace lay across his chest, and he played with it absently. 'Tell *her* that,' he said. 'What was the old saying? If you can change a giant's mind, you can probably beat it in a wrestle too. But since she's here it's a roof and a plate.'

Loup threw himself on a mat and didn't wake up again for the rest of the day, despite the screeching of caged birds and Faul's thunderous passage through the house. Just as Eric lay back in his cushions, and discovered they were indeed the most marvellous invention ever made, a boot poked him gently in the ribs. Sharfy stood over him. 'What do you think *you're* doing?' he said with a grin.

'My people call this *relaxing*,' said Eric. 'It's our custom, after a forced pace march through death and danger and corpses. And frankly, if I don't get an hour or two of rest, I will lose what's left of my bearings and probably have some kind of breakdown.'

'No you don't. No rest for heroes. You want to be one, I'll make you one. But you'll have to work.'

'Later. Please.'

Sharfy dropped an army-issue sword handle-first on the floor beside him. 'Out into the yard and I'll show you how to use it.'

'If you try and get me up from this mattress, I'll prove just how well I can use the damn thing, believe me.'

Siel, he noticed, was watching him. With the heaviest of sighs, he picked up the sword and followed Sharfy outside.

The backyard was hard stony turf with patches of reddish soil, which Lut and Faul had somehow convinced to tolerate small fields of vegetables bordered in by logs, some way away from the house. Barns and sheds poured into the air smells and sounds of livestock, though what in God's name they grazed on Eric couldn't imagine. The line of the woods stretched along the horizon to their right. Mountains stood blue against the other horizon's white sky, behind long stretches of what seemed rubble fields, dotted here and there with trees.

Sharfy jumped down the steps, winced at what it did to his knees, then picked up a handful of pebbles. 'Drop the sword,' he said.

'Forgive me, I thought I got up from the cushions to learn how to use a freaking sword.' He let it clatter to the ground.

'Yep. This is about footwork. And enough with the whining. *That* won't impress her.' Sharfy laughed at the blush rising to his cheeks. 'Yes, I know you're in love. More dangerous than combat, that is. Here. Catch these stones with your right hand. Lunge forwards to catch them, if I throw in front of you. Step this way if I throw left, or this way right.' Sharfy demonstrated what looked like the steps of a dance, then threw the first pebble, which bounced off Eric's knuckle. A second pebble whizzed straight into his forehead. 'That's what happens when you miss.'

'This is going to be a long day, isn't it?' said Eric, rubbing what felt like a bee-sting between his eyes.

'That's up to you. Catch! Good. Catch! Better . . .'

'Least you know how to *hold* a blade now,' said Sharfy at nightfall as they headed back to the verandah, sweaty and tired. 'Holding the sword right might be enough to make someone *think* they're in for a fight, maybe enough to stop em starting one.'

'That's not a ringing endorsement of my potential, is it?'

Sharfy shrugged in reply.

'I'll make the front rank one day, you wait,' said Eric, strangely buoyed as they sat on the back steps and surveyed the darkening horizon.

Sharfy laughed his unpleasant laugh. 'First lesson, you did all right,' he said. 'Your eye's fine, seen worse make it to military grade. We'll work on your defence. Stay alive as long as you can, Anfen or me will kill whoever's attacking you.'

'Cutting the enemy's head off seems a pretty good defence.'

Sharfy nodded. 'Maybe so. Getting yours cut off's a pretty poor one. Hey, before. When Loup took you to the cliffs. What'd he do?'

'Not much, just crushed my most valuable possession into powder.'

'Which one? Not the black?'

'The black.'

Sharfy looked stricken. 'I'll kill him! Why'd you let him? Don't worry. Your other scales, all valuable. Worth a bag of gold each, two bags for the blue. Did he keep the powder or give it to you?'

'It's right here.' Eric held up the pouch. When Sharfy looked at it, a change came over him: his dents and scars had made him seem a hardened old warrior, but now he had the desperate leer of an addict. He looked around conspiratorially, leaned close, voice lowered. 'Might as well do a vision, if it's already crushed. If you can spare a pinch, I'll owe you.'

Eric experimentally moved the pouch left, then right. Sharfy's eyes followed its every movement till he put it away. 'Just why have you lowered your voice there, Sharfy?'

Sharfy blinked and returned to normal. 'Anfen and his rules. He's not keen on scale visions. But listen. You know how I was saying Loup's a bit of a mongrel, in what magic he knows? If he has a speciality, it's visions and other Dreamcraft. Our secret though, just the three of us. And I can see by the look in your eye you're keener than I am. Don't deny it.'

'I doubt you can see that in my eye, my friend.' But it was true enough.

31

All had eaten and bathed, even Lalie, who was again tied up on the front porch and none too happy about it. Sharfy, Eric (and Loup, who had been put on notice visions were to transpire) were all patiently waiting for Anfen to fall asleep or busy himself on some hours-long mission, but as yet he was still around, and hadn't seemed to notice all the furtive glances his way.

Siel now sat on Eric's mat with her legs crossed, heels pushing into the brown flesh of her thighs. He lay with his eyes about level to her knees, chin resting on his hands and pleasantly close to hypnotised while her quiet voice spoke as though telling children a story. The half-giant's footsteps occasionally creaked from other rooms, even her softest tread enough to make the floor shake as she put cloth covers on the bird cages and bade each bird good night.

Said Siel, 'The castle was not always home to its current dwellers. It used to house powerful magicians from many schools. Before that, it housed no one, for it was *not* a castle but a hunk of magic stone, shaped, we guess, by the dragon-youths' very own claws and teeth. But the dragons left no clue as to their use of it.

'For much of history, none dared go close. Not until the mages arrived to start their work: hollowing out stairways, halls and chambers to make a great house of it. They dwelled there for a long time, developing their arts, ignoring the rest of the world, which had so mistrusted them and driven them away from the cities.

'Then five centuries ago came the War that Tore the World. All eighteen cities were dragged into a tangled mess of allegiances, betrayals. More people died in that war than live today, and the Great Spirits intervened to end it before we killed each other completely. Stories are told of Mountain stepping into a valley and sitting, legs crossed, to block the path of two great armies marching at each other. Catapulted rocks flew from both sides, striking his front and back, but he wouldn't move.

'When the War finished, the magicians devised a plan for permanent peace. They relinquished the castle to the Mayors for a staggering price, and retreated to their newly built temples. By agreement, the castle formed its own peacekeeping army, a force greater than that of any *one* city, or any two ... but not great enough to defeat several cities at once. Cities took turns sending wise people to the castle to govern disputes. Of the eighteen cities, six had run of the castle for five years, then six others for the next five years, and so on. They made decisions by court, a charter of principles as their guide. Disputes were settled this way. Not without complaint, of course. But for the most part, peace held.

'If only the dragons could tell us what they had done to that mountainous sculpture to make its airs run so thick with power ... but they keep their secrets. Men who dwell there live longer, untroubled by sickness. Mages bask in the potent airs or at least pay a lower price for the magic that goes through them. It has been a temptation to all who have sat in those thrones, and walked those halls, to remain forever. It took a long time for someone to reach for the prize with enough cunning and luck to seize it. Vous was the one to do it.'

Siel paused to sip her drink, the same strong brew Case had been sipping most of the day. They'd seen Lut begin to make a new batch of it from roots and fat red berries. Eric sipped a far more agreeable drink, the Levaal equivalent of tea, its taste sweet and nutty.

Siel went on, 'He was born of a powerful merchant family in the city of Ankin. He knew sons and daughters of other powerful families across the world. They all resented and mocked the magicians' system, resented its taxes on their wealth, its limiting of their cities' greatness. Their parents and grandparents had mouthed the same complaints, but this generation decided to act. Vous, a gifted speaker, a skilled swordsman, soon earned his cause a small, devoted following. They were few, but had great wealth behind them. They recruited the help of rogue mages, many of whom hated the Schools' decision to sell the castle to the Mayors.

'It was easy for Vous, with bribery, lies and blackmail, to be Ankin's nominated wise-man when the time arose, despite his youth. It was a longer, dirtier battle to get his co-conspirators nominated as their respective cities' wise-men. A trail of intrigue and murder churned in their wake. The families emptied their safes of riches, knowing the prize they reached for would be greater. And they achieved their goal. For the first time, all six wise-men had the same interests at heart.

'The rules *appeared* to be followed, when the newly appointed wise-men set forth for the castle gates from their cities to claim rule. They appeared to rule justly at first, and fears were soothed. But much went on behind the stage of this performance. In five short years, with vast new resources and powers, the six used the same blackmail, bribery, lies, and murder on a grander scale. Soon the ring of cities closest to the castle were the first of what we now call 'Aligned Cities'. Puppets of the conspirators were put in charge of each, generals were likewise replaced, and those cities' armies swelled the castle's ranks. War brewed silently and invisibly. The cities further away did not see it coming.

'When five years had passed, the next six nominated wisemen came to claim their place. They were brought up to the castle halls and killed. This act was kept secret for three years, time enough for more drastic change. The first war mages were created, wilder and harder to control than today's. An army of them began to grow in secret. Many heard their screams, and wondered what foul thing spoke death's tongue.

'People were slow to believe a tyrant had really seized the castle. People in Aligned Cities learned not to rebel when their city's food was withheld. In time, anything posing a threat to Vous and his cohorts was stamped out: the magic schools, folk magicians, half-giants, things and peoples you've not yet heard of. We who serve the Mayors' Command, a fragile alliance at best, are high on their list. There are slave farms, mines, and other places to send us. Six Free Cities remain.'

As Siel paused to drink from her cup, the silence was startling. Across the room Loup began snoring as though to fill it. Anfen got up, stretched, and sat with them. 'I've been listening to your history lesson,' he said to Siel. 'Painfully brief. But the key things were covered. May I join you?'

'Your pardon, good people,' said Case, sitting up from his mat. 'I don't feel right lying in here, comfy and warm, while that poor girl's out there in the cold.'

'She has blankets,' said Siel.

'I'm going to see if she needs anything else,' said Case, 'like being treated like a human being after what she's been through.'

'Don't go further than the porch,' said Anfen, rolling his slanted eyes. Case didn't acknowledge he'd heard.

Eric sighed. 'Sorry about him.'

'What's his grievance?' said Anfen. 'Does he want to return home?'

'It's that Stranger woman. He thinks she's his friend, thinks you've been unkind to her.'

'Yes, her.' Anfen looked troubled. 'I wasn't going to tell you this, but ... the charm Case wore. Loup discovered one of its secrets. If you wear it and hold two of its active beads in a certain way, you have a vision, showing you what Case heard and saw within the castle, right up to his waking on the lawns. I spent the day examining it closely. On the lawns, you hear what *he* says to Stranger. You do not see Stranger, or hear what *she* says to him. Somehow, she has kept herself hidden from the charm, almost as though she knew at a glance what its purpose was, and hid from it.'

'Or maybe she wasn't actually there—' said Eric.

'She exists,' said Siel. 'I saw her and fired at her.'

'But who is she, what does she want?' said Anfen. 'Her powers sound formidable. She does us no harm, but goes to great trouble to remain unseen. If she is really a friend, why?'

Said Siel, 'We have not been unkind to Lalie. She has done many bad things. I would be glad to kill her, if allowed.' She said this as casually as if saying she'd like a bath. Eric pictured her wrist-deep in a mule's carcass, blood glistening down her arms as she sliced off its meat with steady calm hands.

Case crept out the front door, unsure why it felt like he was up to something mischievous. He just wanted to check on poor Lalie, out here on her own.

Didn't he?

There she was, asleep, curled up like the house pet on a soft mat, pillow under her head, blankets over her, a clay jug of water nearby. He peered at her face: so different from the wild, angry thing she'd been, sprinting out of the hunters' hall covered in blood. She didn't stir at the creaking of floorboards under Case's feet, loud though it sounded to him.

Cruel to keep her out here like this, he thought. He gazed around at the darkness. The quiet was broken only by a fresh-smelling breeze rustling the stony yard's stiff clumps of grass. The night's darkness was not total — there seemed as much light as if there *were* stars or a sliver of moon above, and that was probably the strangest thing. Direct from the front porch, that's where they'd come from. The woods stretched out to the left as a thick, pitch-black line. A night bird of some kind screeched horribly from that direction, and he shivered.

It *was* a night bird, he hoped. So many perils, so many horrors. He'd thought the old world was a dark, terrible place. Maybe it was. But at least you knew there it was other *people* out to get you most of the time. Not some unknown, unnameable *things* . . .

He didn't know why, but yes, his feet took him down the steps of the porch. And then, well, it seemed he was walking out through the stony field, a little adrenaline surging in his veins as he spun around, eyes sweeping all directions, looking for something. Or, of course, someone.

He'd known he would see her here, had known it before he excused himself and came outside. And there, not too close: a little glimmer of green.

Case ran for her. There she was! And he wondered: why should he have missed her so much? He hardly knew her. But she stood, that smile on her face, that glint in her eyes, eyes that seemed to see him inside out and to understand: *You can't help but to be what you are. Don't worry! It's not all bad! You're fine. I see you as you are, as you used to be, as you might have been. They are all fine.*

In her hand was a cup, and he knew what was in it. 'I didn't know if you'd come,' she whispered, handing it to him. 'A few nights, I've waited for you. This is as close as I dare get, even though your mage sleeps.'

'He's not *my* mage,' Case said. He sipped the delicious cold wine, felt the buzz cloud his head. 'I don't want to be with them any more. Even Eric . . . well, even he seems to have fallen in with em. I want to be with—'

'Shh, shh. Do they know you're out here? Are all your companions asleep?'

'No. They think I'm on the porch, there. Listen, be careful out here on your own. We've seen some bad things in those woods. Why not come in, introduce yourself?'

'I cannot. There are reasons I cannot, which will make no sense to you, Case, though I know you mean well. I need you to trust me on this: *I* mean well too.'

'I believe you, miss, but *they* probably won't, no matter what I tell em.'

'You need not tell them a thing.' She touched his arm and it sent pleasant chills through him. 'Case, do you know where they are headed? I follow, and keep many threats at bay. You would not have made it this far without me. But it helps to know Anfen's intentions.'

Case thought back. 'He said something about meeting a council—'

'Council of Free Cities?'

'That's it, I think.'

'Good,' she said, nodding. 'He must. And I shall help him get there, though he may not see it. You had better go back.'

'Stranger, look, please be careful out here. I'm telling you.

There's something bad in the woods and we saw what it did.'

She laughed that sparkling laugh — damn it, nothing would hurt *her*, nothing could hurt someone with a laugh like that. 'I am well aware of *them*,' she said. 'Tormentors, they are called. There are none nearby, for the present.'

'What are they supposed to be?'

'No one knows. The castle is as frightened of them as everyone else. Anfen may rest assured of that. They come from World's End, from beyond the great wall, the Land None Have Seen. Few know this. But you must go back. There's another mage, not far, in the guise of a wolf. I must hide, for his intentions aren't clear to me. Sleep well, Case.'

'You too, miss. And thanks for the drink.' Case wiped away a tear, and wondered why he'd shed it. She'd vanished, but her voice came from the gloom: 'Be safe, Otherworlder.'

32

The next day brought more hours of sword craft in Faul's lonely back yard, surrounded by scattered man-sized knuckles of obsidian black stone. When they were done, every part of him ached and some little cuts crisscrossed his forearm where Sharfy's sword had come a fraction too close. They sat for a breather by the back steps. 'Who's going to teach me magic?' Eric asked.

Sharfy's reaction surprised him with its vehemence. 'No!'

'And why not?'

'Want to risk going halfway mad?'

Eric laughed. 'Look, life as I know it is forfeit. Understand? You guys won't let me go back and read comic books or get laughed at by co-workers ever again. Yeah yeah, I know what you're going to say, how it'd be impossible even if you wanted to. The point is I am not thinking long term here. I am thinking: what kicks can I get before something bites my head off in a week's time? To be able to cast a spell, an actual spell, would almost make it all worthwhile.'

'Make *what* worthwhile?'

'Having to see all the dead bodies I've seen, we'll start there.'

Sharfy surprised him by laying a hand on his arm gently. 'If you don't already have talent, no one can teach you. You'd know if you had talent because you'd see magic in the air. If you don't see that already, you won't learn to cast. Don't be sad about it. If I had talent, I wouldn't learn. If you learn, *they* come hunt you, unless you're like Loup is, and can stay out of their way.' Sharfy contemptuously flung the army-issue sword to the ground. During their session he'd cursed the weapon nonstop.

A flock of birds suddenly erupted from the woods' line of dark green in the distance to their right, with a faintly heard explosion of shrieks and squawks. 'And what might that be?' said Sharfy, standing and reaching for the sword again. No one had mentioned the horror of the doomed hunters' hall since they came here, but they hadn't forgotten it wasn't very far away.

Loup suddenly barrelled down the back steps, an excited grin across his face. 'There they are! There's our dancing mages! *Hoo!* She's back on our tail all right. Far Gaze doesn't know what to make of her either, you watch!' Loup jogged off towards the woods, peering at distant things none of the rest of them could see and hopping from foot to foot with excitement. Sharfy ran after him and tried to get some idea what in blazes he was talking about.

On the other side of the yard the man of the house, Lut, was watching Siel push along a wheelbarrow full of bark strips he used for brewing. At that moment she evidently tired of all this toil and hurled the cart sideways, spilling its contents across the ground. She ignored the man calling her back, instead storming directly towards the back steps.

Eric watched her come. 'These people are feeding us,' he said. 'Maybe we should earn our keep.'

'I've earned it by risking my life for weeks,' she replied, tugging on both braids at once, to indicate *extremely pissed*. 'It's not the work I hate, it's his blathering. The man won't shut *up*.'

She sat heavily on the step beside him. He began to speak but she cut him off: 'Shh! I have something to say to you and I'm thinking of how to say it.'

'Fine.' He waited, watching Lut pile the bark strips back onto the wheelbarrow with much angry talking to himself and head-shaking.

'You're to be a hero,' said Siel at last. 'Good. Do you think learning to use a sword is going to be enough?'

Eric looked at her in surprise. 'Maybe not. But I've asked to learn magic as well—'

'Do you think magic is going to be enough?'

'Enough for what? To beat them?'

'*Yes* to beat them,' she snapped. 'They have magic, so do we. They have swords, so do we. Anfen is a better swordsman than most, though you have only seen him lose a fight to an Invia so you may not believe it. *He* is not enough to beat them. So even if you could wield a blade like Anfen, and cast like the Arch Mage, would that be enough?'

Another flock of birds erupted from the line of trees. Out in the yard Loup cheered like someone watching a horse race. Eric said, 'Obviously not, by the way your questions are headed. You're saying we'd need a lot more such people. How do you propose to get them? I'm trying to become Anfen. It's why I have these.' He showed her the cuts on his forearms.

She slapped the step in frustration. 'Listen! What do we have that *they* don't? What weapon, what tool to use, what thing to fall back on, what map to guide us which *they* are missing? You heard what I told of their history! They do anything they want. They stop at nothing. They kill, steal, kill, lie, kill.'

Now he got it. 'Principles. Values. We have principles. They don't.'

She turned to him, brown eyes wide. '*Yes!* Case is usually wrong, but he *has* them. Do you?'

He was taken aback. 'Of course I do.'

'What are they? I've heard you betray your friend's confidence, telling us of his lust for Stranger when he left the room.'

'Anfen needed to know it—'

'Yes, he did. So betraying your friend's confidence was the *useful* thing to do. Was it *right*? You lied to my face without batting an eye. Yes, you were scared, but you also wanted to use my body again, and you kept up the lie for days. I waited, I gave you a chance to see there'd be no danger in telling the truth. But you didn't.'

'Hey, *use* your body? Who seduced who?'

She hadn't seemed to hear. 'You explained why you lied but you never said sorry. You just panted after me like a dog all through the woods, greedy for more meat.'

There was nothing he could say in his defence, other than: 'Siel, please, what the hell brought this on?'

'I've looked into your mind and heart and seen nothing there. It scares me.'

Tears slid down her cheeks. He didn't get a chance to recover from his shock and answer before she'd stormed into the house and slammed the door behind her.

Loup and Sharfy returned, the magician muttering excitedly. 'They were close! And fighting hard. We'll see how that works out. Far Gaze isn't the greatest mage who ever lived, but he's no weakling. She must be something, that one he's dancing with! Oh, aye . . .'

'Are you sure Anfen's sleeping in there?' Sharfy asked him.

Loup nodded, grinning. 'Out like a blown candle. I even blessed his sleep, so his dreams'll be peaceful, not full of blood and guts, the poor lad.'

'Now's the best chance we'll get,' Sharfy whispered, the addict again creeping into his face. 'How long's a black-scale vision take?'

'Depends,' said Loup. 'Maybe he'll go out of body. They got some kick, the black ones.'

Eric barely heard them, too busy replaying Siel's outburst, trying to find which parts he should accept and which he could debate. Point taken on the lust, but given the stress and circumstances, perhaps a little slack could be cut. As for betraying Case's confidence, I don't quite see her point . . . He came back to the present. 'Out of body? Does that mean what I think it does?'

'Means what it sounds like,' said Sharfy. 'Body stays here, you don't. Looks like you're sleeping.'

'Where would I go?'

'Past, future, present, maybe somewhere else altogether,' said Loup, smiling toothlessly. He lowered his voice as Lut strode past with a crunch of boots on gravelly turf, still muttering angrily about young people's lack of respect for the land. 'I heard of people who went to Otherworld, and further places besides,' the magician whispered. 'Whatever happens, you'll *see* stuff, you believe it.' He leaned close, eyes gleaming. 'I heard how you found that scale. No one just finds a black scale like that. That's *meant*. Dragon *meant* you to have it. Why you think I crushed it up like that? I knew It wanted this. It didn't just want you trading for a few passing treasures. So let's go inside and see what It wants you to see . . .'

They gathered in the room's far corner while Anfen snored deeply at the other end. 'He's out for a good while yet,' said Loup. 'But these are *his* rules we're about to break, so hush or we're in it, deep. Here's the story. We're taking a quick nap. Anfen, he don't understand visions, thinks it's risky.' Loup looked suddenly angry, twisting his whole face into a curdled bunch of wrinkles and beard. 'Oh aye, *can* be, but so's taking a step outside at night. And you can't stay inside all your damn life, just cos you might kick your toe out there!'

'Easy . . .' said Sharfy, a hand on his shoulder.

'Oh aye.' Loup nodded. His face uncreased, his toothless smile returned. 'Who's to say? We might just learn stuff that's useful. Aye, you sometimes do.'

'You've done this before with black scales, right?' said Eric.

Loup stared into the distance. 'Once. Girl who did it wouldn't say what she saw, but she was . . . different, after. Glad she went, oh aye. Went on for big things, that one, riches and power. Whether it was what she learned in her vision, or what she'd have done anyway, not for me to say. I miss her.' He sighed, eyes distant for a moment. 'Black visions fade too, sometimes. Might just pass out and wake up, see the vision itself sometime down the track. Hope you're not riding a horse or walking a ledge when you do!' He turned to Sharfy. 'You done red ones and green ones, aye? Done gold?'

'Not gold,' said Sharfy. 'Done purple, bronze.'

'Aye, bronze! That's wild enough, there's your out-of-body. Still, let's see what black puts you in for. Rare treat, a black one!'

'Let's start,' Sharfy said impatiently. 'Eric, spare a pinch?'

Eric opened the small leather pouch.

'Some red in mine,' said the soldier, taking a small battered pouch from his pocket, inside which was a tiny amount of ground red-white powder, fine as table salt.

'You and your mixing. Pure black for *me*,' said Loup, gums glistening. 'And enough left over, Eric, for more down the track, if you're wanting. But don't you do it without me there to help you! Not without risk, oh no. And now listen close, so you know what we're about to *do*. We're about to put in our bodies, in our minds, a little piece of the *Dragon* itself. Fathom? This little scale, all crushed up, still a little bit *alive*, is made of the great god-beast's very *stuff*. Full of secrets, it is, and knowledge.'

By opening the leather pouches, it felt like whatever they were about to do had already begun, that they'd slipped already into some heavy moment that could not reverse course in time. Loup set down four cups before him, three empty, one filled with water. Sharfy's ugly scarred face eagerly lit up, reminding Eric suddenly of goblins and inviting a moment's doubt he resolved to ignore.

Loup poured a dribble of water in the other three cups, pinched a small amount of black powder and added it, stirring each in turn with his gnarled finger. Eric's cup got the greatest share. He couldn't tell if this was a courtesy to him, as the finder of the scale, or whether Loup had other reasons.

'It's a kind of knowledge minds like ours can't hold,' Loup continued. 'Unless you think your hands can hold a mountain. You get half a thought of It — not even! A flicker of noise across Its sleeping mind — and your mind, why, it'll bend just trying to hold it. Just a few grains of Its scale, that's enough. And it'll send us through the very *sky*, brain all full of the same magic that made the world.

'The red, if you must mix,' Loup said to Sharfy, who added a pinch of red scale to his cup. 'When I say,' said the magician, a glint in his eye, 'drink it up. Simple as that; hard part's the crushing. Takes the strength of a mountain to crush up even an old piece of Its skin. Drink, then we're away. See you beyond, and Eric, I'll give you a push over there, if you need it. Drink now!'

His mouth was full of grit. He managed not to gag, but it was a battle to swallow the mix. He fell back, hands to his throat as his airways seemed to close off. From the corner of his eye, he saw Sharfy doing likewise, then rolled his head the other way, where Loup — Loup just watched him, eyes gleaming.

Then he woke to the folk magician shaking his arm. It was dark. 'Awake, at last!' Sweat ran into Loup's beard and covered his torso. A more relieved face Eric could hardly imagine. He sat up and groaned.

'He's back!' Loup stood and did a little dance, elbows cocked.

Eric's head felt like it had been put through a washing machine. 'What happened?' he slurred. 'How long've I been out?'

'Hours,' said Loup, smiling. 'I thought you'd slipped away for good! That can happen sometimes, you know. Spirit goes out of body, sometimes don't find its way back. Happens more'n you might think.'

Eric looked at him in disbelief. 'Thanks for the warning.'

'Ah, you were safe with me right here. What'd you see? Gave you a push over there, but I lost you after that.'

'I don't know what I saw. A lot.' He thought back, sifting through the pictures like trying to recall an old dream. It fell through his hands the second he reached for it, then was gone. 'Something to do with Kiown and the others ...'

'Pff, I saw *that*. Right at the start, that was, before I gave you a push higher up. Don't you bother with that old news. What else?'

'Nothing. My head's completely blank.'

'Ahhh! She's faded on you!' Loup regarded him thoughtfully. 'You'll see it. It'll come, likely some night before sleep, not far from now. Means you was showed something you're not meant to see just yet. Maybe given some instruction, but your *head* can't know what it is, or you might think to do otherwise! Gotta be felt right down in your bones, whatever it is.' Loup's gummy smile was so close Eric could smell his sour breath. 'I followed you in. Out my own vision, into yours. Good at that, I am. Not all mages can do it. Not even the old schools, who thought they knew it all. Lingering around, you was, all confused, so I gave you a boost up high. Meant to follow you, then something grabbed you. Whoo! Did it what? Oh aye, grabbed you hard and yanked you away so's I couldn't see. Didn't want *me* to see whatever was meant for your eyes! More to you than there seems, don't you doubt it. And here, you're just back now!' Loup laughed and shook Eric's arm like they'd shared a grand joke.

'He's back?' Sharfy came in and crouched by Eric's mat. 'What'd he see?'

'Nothing yet!' said Loup, growing more excited. 'He'll see it when the Dragon wants him to. Could be a day from now, could be a week or more. Knew it, I did! It was all *meant*, that whole group of things: him finding the scale, me crushing it up, now the vision. What else? Maybe all of us being here in this very house, *and* whatever comes next, good or bad. As It wills! Anfen's being a fool.'

Eric lay back — whatever he'd been through had made him sleepy. 'So, the boss found out.'

'Yep,' said Sharfy. 'You were out too long. He twigged you weren't just sleeping. Not happy with us. And if anything goes bad in the next few days, it'll be our fault. You watch.'

'What was your vision like?' Eric asked Sharfy.

'Not saying,' Sharfy answered, face grim.

'Ah, he blames the black scale,' said Loup, grinning wide. 'That pinch of red's what did it. Warned you about mixing, I have. Sometimes gives it a kick, but black scales don't need a kick. Skewed you to a bad place, eh?'

'Not saying,' Sharfy repeated, and he seemed a little pale.

Anfen came back inside. He quickly examined Eric as though for physical injury, but said nothing. 'Ready to hear me out now?' said Loup. 'I'm telling you, I saw something important. Real or no, you should hear it.'

Anfen shook his head and kept tensely silent over on his mattress, running a dead stone over his blade.

'He's not happy,' Eric whispered.

'Nope. That was a fine sword of his, and that Invia snapped it like a stick,' said Loup. 'Eskian blade. Heck, it made *me* sad, wasn't even my sword.'

'I get the feeling that's not what's bothering him,' said Eric, though he marvelled again at the often scattered dots Loup managed to connect.

'He's got to understand something about us,' said Sharfy. 'We're never gonna be like his old unit was. Not as disciplined, never will be. We can scrap all right, survive in the wild. We got the balls to come on a mission like this in the first place, can keep our mouths shut about where we been, s'long as they pay us what they promised. That's going to have to be enough.'

'How high up the chain of command was Anfen, in the army days?'

'First Captain, rank below General,' said Sharfy. 'Youngest ever to make that rank, best swordsman around, in his day. There's a tournament, Valour's Helm. Use blunt wood swords so no one's killed. Best sent in from all cities, best from the castle. Week long, it runs, whole lot of smaller tournaments before it to pick the cream. Even Free Cities send their best, kind of a truce. Anfen won it four years running.'

'Three,' said Loup.

'Three, four, may as well be ten. No one won it twice, before him. He's nearly a decade older now; I reckon he'd be a chance to win it still.'

'But *you'd* give him a good fight, wouldn't you?' said Loup, grinning.

Sharfy considered this question very carefully. 'When I was younger, maybe I'd make him sweat, but he'd win. Now he'd cut me up in three seconds, if I really went at him.'

'And I might,' Anfen said from across the room. 'Among my virtues is uncannily good hearing. I was waiting for you to add it to your list.'

Sharfy winced.

'Valour's Helm was pointless,' muttered Anfen, running the dead stone over his blade with aggressive tugs: *scrape, scrape, scrape*. 'You said it yourself. Blunt wooden swords so no one gets hurt. Three years running I was best at wielding a piece of tree barely fit for firewood. Some of those others would have spilled my guts on my shoes with their own swords.'

Anfen tossed the sword aside as though afraid he'd be tempted to vent his anger by using it. 'You think I'm pining for elite soldiers, Sharfy,' he went on. 'Not really. It's common sense not to do magic rituals when a powerful mage stalks your company. And to tell your leader when you're being followed by one. Siel knew, Loup knew, even Case knew before I did. And let's not even mention Kiown's idiocy at the wagon train, which was so stunning I'm almost in awe. Would you people think about this, please? In my pocket is a charm, with a message on it that may change the course of all history: they have shown us their fear and their weakness. All we have to do is get this charm back to the Mayors. Not to mention two Pilgrims with heads full of priceless knowledge. Yet, we are *extremely* lucky to be alive right now, and not in castle dungeons being slowly tortured. You of all people, Sharfy, should be wary of that.'

Sharfy's face darkened, jaw clenched.

'If this were the army,' said Anfen, 'the castle's *or* a city's, on a campaign with one hundredth as much at stake, most of you would be headless in a roadside ditch. And I'd side with the officer who did the cutting.'

Siel gave Eric and Sharfy a look that said, *maybe you should just keep your mouths shut.* So they did, and soon Faul bade the birds good night.

33

No one had been put on watch duty, so Eric was the first to hear it. As he came up from deep sleep, he thought it was only the claws of Faul's birds scraping the metal floors of their cages. The half-giant's snoring from deeper in the house rumbled like an idling engine.

He hadn't noticed Siel climb under his blanket, and it was a shock to find her naked body pressed to his, with his arm pulled around her, her hands clutching it like he was her protector. Fine joke, that — she could probably kill him with bare fists. Her skin felt cool on his and he could smell her body, unperfumed and clean.

The sky had just begun to lighten, so that the sleeping silhouettes stood a little firmer across the long spacious room. Again came the sound that had woken him, *thump thump* on the roof. Like something falling on it. His heart quickened.

With regret he gently prised himself away from Siel, trying not to wake her, but she stirred, and was up a second later. She heard something too. In seconds she was clothed again, bow in hand, stalking through the house with footsteps not making the slightest creak on the floorboards. Eric pulled on his shoes, grabbed the army-issue sword, scoffed at himself and picked up the gun instead, quickly strapping on the holster. It was loaded and ready to fire. He went out after Siel, his steps not nearly as stealthy as hers.

He had just begun to wonder if they'd imagined things when Lalie's voice came from outside, a shrill yell: 'Something here! Help, something here! They're back, they've come!' Her words dissolved to panicked whimpering.

The whole company was up, armed, and rushing through the house. There was a crashing sound as something punched through the roof. Anfen shouted an order Eric didn't catch. He and Siel were out on the porch with Lalie, who groped for them in her terror. Siel told her twice to be calm. Now she slapped the girl, and Lalie hushed.

They stared around the yard. The rocky outcrops, the forest lined down to the left, were black outlines against the bluish gloom. Again came the sound on the roof. And the sound of wings beating the air. All Faul's birds began screeching at once.

'Lalie, do your beasts have wings?' said Siel, pulling an arrow back, angled upwards. Lalie whimpered and didn't seem to hear. 'I don't see it,' Siel muttered. 'Answer me! Do they have wings?'

But Lalie cowered on the floor, stupid with terror.

Faul's snoring still rumbled from within the house. They heard Lut's voice in there trying to rouse her, apparently without luck.

Anfen and the others came outside on the porch with them. Then many things happened at once.

A flash of light flared out in the yard. There, a woman in a green dress — Stranger — had arms aloft, a look of concentration on her face. A fountain of light poured from her, illuminating the yard like a lightning strike that stayed put, but for its slow twisting. She had not made the sound on the roof; she was showing them what had.

Perched on the yard's lone tall tree were two Invia, staring at the house — rather, at Anfen. Wings beat at the air again as two more took off from the roof and flew to join those in the tree. Not knowing who or what else was inside with the clearly dangerous Marked one, they had wanted to draw him out.

'Damn it,' Anfen muttered. He didn't even look at Stranger. He called to the Invia, 'You only want me?'

There was a fluttering whistle in response, like an unearthly bird's coo. Anfen strode down the steps, into the yard. Stranger called, 'Fight them, I'll aid you.'

Siel hadn't looked away from Stranger for a moment. She loosed an arrow which sliced the air and narrowly missed. Stranger looked at her with great surprise. Case gave a strangled cry and threw himself at Siel, who had begun aiming another arrow. It flew well wide, as Siel tripped over Lalie and landed sprawling on the porch.

Anfen meanwhile approached the Invia in their tree. All four creatures watched him and only him, the Marked one, their faces neutral and curious. One by one, they stood and stepped onto the air, wings spreading. Back over his shoulder, Anfen yelled, 'Don't attack them. Take the charm to the council. Sharfy leads. Be safe.'

Whatever Stranger had been planning to do to aid him never happened. A huge white wolf big as a horse sprang from the gloom with its mane flaring. It charged her, teeth bared, a growl in its throat.

'Hoo boy,' Loup muttered, 'still dancing, these two. Far Gaze, that's the wolf. Now what's *she*? Fox, rabbit, or a bigger wolf yet?'

Stranger didn't seem to see the wolf, even as it sprang for her. Then came a flash of green motion and she was gone, the wolf's jaws closing on nothing, the *clack* of its clashing teeth loud even from the porch. It circled back around ominously, its size making it seem slow despite the ground it covered with paws thumping hard on the turf. It leaped at some further point, seeing something the rest of them couldn't, jaws snapping on air. Then again it leaped and bit, and again. Stranger, hidden, kept evading it. She did not seem to fight back. The pillar of light, pouring like a fountain from the ground, remained where she had stood.

Sharfy unsheathed his knives and stepped uncertainly into the yard as the Invia carefully took positions around Anfen. They circled well above his head, cautious of one so Marked, though he *seemed* just a normal man, easily enough dispatched with one swift fist. One sister had mistaken him for such already and flown back wounded; he had cunning tricks, this one. This kill would be as certain as any ever made. They would take great care.

Anfen stood poised beneath them, army-issue sword angled backwards. There was suddenly something unlocked and liberated about him; his movements were smooth and easy, more than just resigned to his fate; rather, relishing it. The beating wings ruffled his hair. Suddenly he dropped his sword to the ground, laughed, and fell to his knees, offering his throat.

One of the Invia experimentally swept down, just a blur of white speed. She came up higher than the others, fearing some counterattack, but the man lay flat on his back, dazed. The others waited; to feign death was an old trick in the wild. Into what trap was he luring them? Dropping the sword had thrown them into slight confusion, and a series of quick whistles exchanged between them too high-pitched for the humans to hear — that was a strange move! Sophisticated, this warrior. A shame about the Marks, for he was worth a long life. Oh well.

Another of them swept down then back, feinting to strike.

Boom. Boom. Eric's gun fired twice. The noise of it was shocking and, in the background, Faul's snoring ceased at last.

The Invia ignored the foreign sounds, assuming it to be something done by the duelling mages. The shots had missed. Eric seemed to be watching from above: someone who looked just like him ran down the steps, out into the yard, fired again three times. One of the Invia screamed and fell writhing to the ground, the tallest and thinnest, with flowing cobalt black hair. The others scattered, flying higher, the deadly trap they'd feared now revealed.

Eric shot as the one with scarlet hair dived at him. A puff of feathers blew and a column of light beamed in the dark night through the hole in her wing. He hit her body with another shot. She screamed loud and spun in the air. *Click* went the empty chamber of the gun. But they fled. It looked like they were divers plunging towards an ocean of dark sky, filling it with their cries, inhuman and beautifully mournful. Blood pattered down from the wounded one and landed like raindrops in the dust.

The pillar of light from Stranger's spell had slowly withered to a trickle, writhing like a thin snake. Anfen rolled to his feet, picked up his sword. The Invia staggered up also, blood beginning to thread down its torso, one wing stretched rigid, the other limp and flopping. She cried out in confusion, trying to understand how and why she was hurt. She made a clumsy lunge at Anfen. He swung his sword at her, the blade flashing fast but missing as the Invia fell, sprawling, away from him. She lay shuddering. 'It's too late, Eric,' Anfen said. His voice was incredibly tired, as though he'd have preferred the rest of death. 'You're Marked. You hurt her on the day of her death. Doesn't matter which of us makes the last blow.'

The Invia darted forwards, summoning some last reserve of that incredible speed, a fizz of motion. Anfen's eye hadn't left her. He swirled on his feet like a matador, spinning, wrists cocked, the blade angled behind him and held still. The Invia nearly decapitated herself on his sword, then fell, a burst of light pouring from the fatal wound, a shriek in her death that, despite her cut throat, spread as far through Levaal as there were ears to hear it.

For what seemed a long time, everything was still and calm. The light from Stranger's spell had faded to a flickering ghostliness and kept dimming, the twisting shape of it no longer distinct. The huge white wolf, Far Gaze, had run back the way he had come, every so often leaping high, jaws snapping at what seemed just air. Stranger, still hidden, fled from him. The wolf chased her until he had bounded from their sight and into the trees. Neither of the mages returned.

Siel got back to her feet and gazed at Case with her teeth bared. Sharfy had seen that look in her eye once before and remembered what her curved knife had done to the last poor bastard on the other end of it. He ran back up the steps and stood between her and the old man.

Case did not know his peril; his eyes were on the yard, where he'd seen something slip from Anfen's pocket. The charm lay in the dirt, and he carefully marked the place, his heart pounding as he watched Anfen to see if he'd remember it.

Eric crouched by the Invia's corpse. He felt sick and numb, his mouth so dry he could hardly peel his lips apart. 'I'm sorry,' he said, not to himself, not to Anfen.

Anfen's slanted eyes caught and held his. 'I know what you're feeling. But it wasn't murder. They aren't as human as they seem.'

Eric swallowed. 'They don't seem human at all. They seem better than us.'

Anfen put a hand on his shoulder. 'This is *our* world, not

theirs any more. The Dragon cleared this world of the dragon-youth, of which this is a servant, so that *we* could dwell here. Remember that.' Anfen stood. 'We're all birds in a cage anyway. We must talk later. You are now Marked. You should learn what that means. And I must know all you can tell of that weapon you used. I wish you'd told me of it earlier.'

Later, when Eric would look back on this moment, on Anfen's words and the look in his eye when he spoke, he would think: I know why you didn't say thank you. I'm pretty sure you seemed happier when you were walking out to die, dropping your sword, offering your throat. Like you'd been waiting for that moment a long time. Like it's why you chose to camp on the hilltop, knowing the Invia would see you, and come for you . . .

Right now, with the Invia's corpse beneath him, and the sound of her death wail still ringing in his ears, such desolation was a feeling Eric could understand too well. Anfen headed wearily back towards the house.

Suddenly in the doorway stood Faul, and she surveyed the sights of the yard in the fading light of Stranger's spell. Her huge face was suddenly ferocious with rage. She stared at the Invia's corpse. 'WHO?' she boomed. 'WHO SLEW THIS ON MY LAND?'

Its blood still dripped from Anfen's blade. His pained smile said it all: *And now this . . .*

Faul moved with speed impossible for something her size. All those on the porch were picked up and hurled towards the yard, the last of them airborne before the first had landed. Case luckily (unless Faul had intended it) landed on Sharfy, not the bare rocky turf. Only Lalie remained, squirming in fear on the end of her rope. Faul loomed over her.

'AND YOU, GIRL. DEATH FOLLOWED YOU SURE ENOUGH, HERE, TO MY DOOR. IT CAN FOLLOW YOU ELSEWHERE. BE

THANKFUL I DO NOT SNAP YOUR SILLY NECK. MY HANDS ITCH TO DO IT.' Faul yanked the rope, pulling free a section of the post it was tied to. She picked up Lalie and hurled her towards Anfen. His arms spread to catch her, but she knocked him over, both of them winded, her leg grazed as it scraped on the ground. The piece of post thumped hard into the turf nearby.

'TAKE BACK YOUR GIFT OF DEATH,' Faul bellowed at Anfen. 'I SHOULD SQUEEZE YOU ALL BY THE GUTS TO GET BACK THE FOOD AND DRINK I MADE, AND GAVE YOU, IN MY FOOLISH-NESS. IN MY . . .' her voice choked up.

'We're going,' said Anfen as they picked themselves up. 'I hope we meet again, when you've calmed. Thank you for your shelter. I'm sorry this happened.'

Faul's feet boomed down the steps. 'I WILL NOT CALM. LEAVE NOW OR I BREAK YOUR HEADS LIKE EGGS.'

'Come,' said Anfen to the company. 'If our host will be so kind as to throw us our possessions, our going will be easier.' Lut emerged, a look of utmost regret on his face as he dumped their packs and gear into the yard.

Eric turned just in time to see it. Case had edged his way around the group, while the company gathered their things, all eyes nervously on Faul. Now Case made a run for a patch of ground just beyond the Invia's corpse. 'Case?' Eric called.

Case looked back at him, hesitated, then grabbed the neck-lace from the ground and slipped it over his head. He vanished. Scuffs of dirt trailed away at the pace of his jog. 'Guys! Wait!' Eric called, rushing to follow before he lost sight of Case's trail.

But Anfen and the rest didn't hear. At that moment, Faul charged like a bull, a howl of rage tearing from her throat, eyes ablaze. They scattered, all of them. Eric had a second to decide which way he went.

In that moment he could smell Siel's hair while her body

nestled against his under the blanket, felt hope and desire bloom through him as it had just before hell had broken loose, a triumphant giddy voice crying: *she's mine!* He also heard *her* voice, saying she'd looked inside his heart and mind and seen nothing. He hadn't realised at the time, nor with the ensuing distraction of the scale vision, that they had been the most painful words ever spoken to him. He knew the choice may right now be: lie with her again tonight, or chase an old man through the wilderness, probably to their pointless deaths.

If they met again, he could explain what his choice had been trying to show her, if it wasn't already clear to her. 'You stupid, *stupid* old fucker,' he muttered, and ran in the direction he'd seen the scuffs of Case's footprints take.

34

It was too dark to see them, but there up ahead he heard it with intense relief, the *crunch crunch crunch* of Case's feet on gravel, slowing to a walk. Eric had followed for a while, not even sure he was on the right trail, calling Case's name to no response. Thin morning light revealed a plain of rubble and stones with no sign of life. Already Faul's house couldn't be seen when he turned and looked back. The wasteland of rocky turf sloped gradually downwards, awkward to walk on. On the very horizon's edge was a raised bridge — a road, running left to right across the plain. Something, at least, to head towards. He hoped Case felt the same way, but there was no knowing, for the old guy wouldn't speak and refused to take off the charm.

'Case. Can you hear me? I hope to hell you're listening. Because we're square now. You think I got you into this whole mess in the first place? Well I'm telling you the ledger is *even*.'

No response.

'Hey. Remember? Switch that lever. Open that door. Fuckhead. Who started it, huh? Yeah OK, jumping through the door was a mistake. Maybe stopping to talk to you under the bridge was a mistake. But look. Think about it. Does this seem a good plan to you?' Eric swept his arm around at the barren grey wasteland. 'Think our next meal's going to be easy to get out here? I can't see any lonely journalists who might put us up and pay for our alcohol. Know any?'

Crunch crunch, Case's footsteps answered him.

'It may not be too late to go back and find the others. Probably is, since they fled for their lives in a different direction, but maybe not. It'd be nice to have someone to talk to anyway, before we starve to death or get killed by pit devils or ringwraiths or whatever else.'

Eric realised the sound of footsteps had ceased. Behind him, there was Case, head in hands sitting on a rock. 'Why'd you follow me?' he said.

'You just heard why. So we'd be even.' And to prove to a certain female I'll probably never see again that I'm able to stand on principle, however pointlessly.

'Why? What a waste, Eric. I did this for *me*. You weren't meant to come. You were happy with the rest of em. I wasn't. Didn't like em or trust em.'

Eric laughed. '*Happy* is maybe going a bit far. But we were fed and protected.' He sat down beside the older man. 'What is it, anyway? You want to go back home?'

Case snorted. 'We're not getting back.'

'What makes you think so?'

'She told me herself. Opening the door, it was real powerful magic, more than people here can actually do, even them mages. She didn't know who did it in the first place. We can't open it. No one'll do it for us.'

Who's 'she'? Ah, Stranger ... 'Case, we don't know that. Someone already did it: there must be a way. We could go looking. Maybe find our way to a city, ask around. Our very own quest. How about it?'

'I'm not going back there,' said Case.

'Why not? You hate it here.'

'I hate it there too. Hate it all. It stinks wherever you go. You get me? I've done my time. What's life all about, Eric? What's the big game, the whole point? I learned it. It's to get to death in as much comfort as you can. Do your time, then bail. I fucked it all up pretty well but now I'm bailing.'

Eric sat beside him, muscles in his thighs twitching from the walk. Day settled a little firmer around them, the sky going white. 'Let's go back, Case. Let's find the others.'

Case snapped, 'To hell with them, and do what you like. I came out here to be with her.'

'Right. You're so certain she was following *you*. What if she doesn't come? Because,' he looked around, 'nope. I don't see her.'

'She'll come,' he said angrily. 'You bring the gun or not?'

'Sure did. But you can't shoot at hunger or thirst.' Eric was overcome by a sudden burst of grief and guilt as he recalled the gunshots and the Invia's dying scream. He moaned.

'What's wrong with you?'

'I don't know.' Eric stood and began walking. He saw again the last fumbling drunken charge of the wounded human-looking creature, wounds he'd inflicted himself. As though despair had been cast on him like a spell, it suddenly all seemed pointless, and he empathised with the old man. Maybe he too had had time enough. The gun was right here — into the mouth, *pop*, and it was done as quickly as one could hope. He could do it at any time. It was not a thought he'd ever had before.

'Where you going, Eric?' Case's voice, edged with worry. Eric pointed at the bridge in the distance. Case's footsteps scuffed the ground behind him. 'Hey. Hey, wait up for me. Hey Eric. That gun. Why not hand it over for a while?'

Am I as transparent as that? he wondered, handing Case the Glock. For a time they walked without speaking.

'Shame about that bird lady,' said Case with a sigh. 'They're pretty, they are. Real pretty. But so what? You did what you had to. Took balls to do it. Didn't think you had it in you, but I was wrong.'

Eric didn't answer.

'I know what it feels like,' said Case with a sigh. 'Believe me, I know. It'll stay with you, but it'll let you have some peace, now and then at least.' He put an arm around Eric, who was surprised to find himself crying.

Little sections underfoot spitefully gave way here and there. Amongst the smooth white stones sharp rocks dug at their feet. They sweated, but not too much, for the ivory-white sky did not bear down with a sun's heat. The distant bridge and road slowly got closer. 'Can't get my head around the temperature here,' Case grumbled. 'How do they work it out, with no sun? Some days are warm, some days cold. Like someone flips a coin.'

'I asked the others about it. They don't have seasons here. What's weirdest is, they still mark the days with the same units of time we do. Days, weeks, months, years, centuries. Hours and seconds, for that matter.'

Case grunted. 'How'd they come up with all that, then, without a sun to work it out?'

'Not sure. We're not the first ever to come here from Earth. And I get the sense . . . no, it's weird, but it almost seems we're not that far *from* Earth, almost like this is just some hidden part of it. Maybe the last people who came through brought our system with them and they copied it. Who knows? It's almost like someone changed the settings by pressing a button, making days and nights fit our pattern.'

'How do they work out north from south, then? If they don't have a north pole ...'

'That's easy.' Eric pointed at the sky. 'Look at the clouds.'

'What about em?'

'They go only one way. South.'

Case stared up at the few slowly crawling threads of cotton. 'Why's that?'

'No idea. But have you noticed the wind too? It mostly goes the same way. Swirls around a bit sometimes, but mostly goes south. I asked Loup why and he said I wasn't ready to know. So there must be a reason.'

Case whistled. 'What've they got up there instead of sun and stars, then? What makes day and night?'

'Not sure. There just *is* day and night, they seem to think. They don't ask where it comes from. But do you notice the way our shadows are sometimes normal, but sometimes fall several ways at once? Like there's more than one light source up there.'

They paused for a breather when some suitably seat-like hunks of smooth stone appeared. The extent of their vulnerability in the eerily quiet rubble plain began to sink in. It felt as though they were little ants crawling across a giant's plate. Even a twisted ankle out here would be grim news — Eric couldn't picture either of them carrying the other very far.

'See that light pour off her?' said Case with a sigh. 'Wasn't that something?' He'd been looking over his shoulder as time went by, concern beginning to creep into his features. It's dawning on him, Eric thought. There is an 'oh shit' moment coming which he's trying to hold off. Before, he thought she stayed away because of the others. The others aren't here, now. So where is she?

He wasn't going to press the point. 'That was something, all right. Magic, they call it. We'd better move.'

Walking took concentration. Pebbles scattered from their feet with noise that seemed huge, accentuating their solitude. Eric's shoes hadn't been made for this kind of travel — he wondered how long they'd last, and just what the hell he'd do about it when they fell apart. His wallet still bumped against his thigh with each step. Why it seemed so important to keep it, he wasn't sure — a souvenir of the old world, the real world? Somehow, being able to pat that familiar bulge was a good feeling.

'Groundman hole ahead,' said Eric.

'You sure that's what it is?'

The gap — like a large open manhole tilted at an angle — was identical to the one Sharfy had pulled him into, near the door. 'Pretty sure. You haven't been down one of those, have you?'

'Nope. Don't like the sound of em, either.'

'Agreed. Rather be lost up here than underground.' They went closer to it, nonetheless, until Case grabbed his arm and yanked him away. 'What is it?' said Eric.

'Look. *There.* Those tracks.'

Just a few of the spiked holes, similar to the ones near the doomed hunters' hall, littered the ground outside the tunnel. They did not spread far, as though the thing making them had come out only for a brief look around. A wind skipped across the plain, scattering dust down the groundman hole. It was too easy to imagine something down there, just out of sight, *watching*. 'Come on. Let's move.'

They were both hungry by the time they got to the bridge. Eric knew the extent of Case's folly — and his own, for that matter — would truly hit home around dinnertime if they couldn't find a meal somewhere soon. He looked at the expanse of plains behind them, and ahead, and saw no evidence of small game, even if they wanted to waste bullets trying to shoot something. Nor did anything even remotely edible grow around them, just the stiff grass clinging desperately to a few softer patches of dirt amid the rubble.

The road to either side of the bridge, at least, gave them hope. It cut across the plain, wide and paved from slabs of stone coloured deep blue, which in many places cracked and lifted from the surface. Nothing and no one passed along it in either direction as far as they could see.

'Horrible place,' said Case, taking in the view of the plains from up on the bridge. It had been built as though water normally flowed through the arches down below it. Perhaps some time back, this whole region had been an inland sea. 'Looks like it's all been bombed.'

'Maybe it was,' said Eric thoughtfully. 'Maybe dragons or gods or something had a big battle, right here. Imagine it. Things as tall as the sky, breathing flames, blasting away green hillsides, leaving *this*.'

That wind kicked up again as though voicing an opinion. Case shivered. 'Don't talk like that, Eric. Not when we're out here all alone.' He sighed. 'Wish she'd show up already.'

Stranger didn't show. Still, they were glad to have paved road underfoot, neglected and pot-holed though it was. They picked up their pace and came to a road sign with strange lettering. 'Can't read it,' said Case. 'You?'

'That symbol there could be a bed, that other one a plate. An inn ahead, maybe.'

'How're we gonna pay for a room, if there's an inn?'

'Three scales, that's how. They're worth something. And you'll be sleeping for free, with the charm on. You're also my secret bodyguard, OK? Anyone attacks us, wear the charm and blow their brains out.'

No travellers came in either direction as they put more road behind them. The land's desolation gave way to grassy hillsides. There were several abandoned villages and farmhouses, long run down. The *emptiness* of the whole place was striking. Eric remembered Siel's words: *More people died in that war than live today* . . .

They stopped for rest every hour or so, both locked in private battle with the road and trying not to think of their growing hunger. It was early evening when at long last, like a desperate ocean crew spotting land, they saw lit windows in the distance.

'Maybe I should take those scales too,' said Case. 'We don't know what people here are like. You might get robbed and there'll be too many to shoot. If you need a scale, I can put it into your hand.'

Eric handed him the scales, and Case had just put on the charm and vanished when something above them gave a deathly shriek. Case grabbed onto Eric's sleeve and spun around. 'War mage! I know that sound. Quick, hide.'

'Hide where, Case?'

The sound came again, close this time. Then above them the war mage came, flying head-first, ten metres high at most, staff clutched tight to its chest in crossed arms. The wind blew its beard and hair, but it seemed otherwise frozen still as it passed directly overhead no faster than a bird. Thin smoke trailed from the tips of its curled horns. Eric could have sworn its yellow eyes locked directly on his. But it kept moving till it had passed from sight. Another shriek pierced the fading day.

'It saw you,' said Case, amazed. 'It must have.'

'Those things don't seem to want to kill me. Maybe it was just too busy, for now. Come on. Let's get to those buildings, get a roof overhead.'

'Food in the belly,' Case murmured.

35

The first building they came to did appear to be an inn. It was built like a large wooden cottage, two storeys, a sign out front with a painted bed, spoon and plate. All up and down a narrow side road running off the main one were several such buildings, perhaps with enough total beds to house a large army patrol. There was a smell of hay from nearby stables. Only a couple of the buildings had lights on, all the others appeared to be locked up. No people walked the street and there was eerie quiet. 'Everyone's hiding,' said Case.

'They might have heard the war mage and put out their lights,' said Eric. In truth he feared walking into one of these buildings and finding a scene similar to the hunters' hall, and it took more courage than he let on to go inside. As planned, Case donned the charm and followed him closely, trying to keep his footsteps in sync so they weren't heard. The inn's lower floor was a dimly lit tavern with round wooden tables and booths, deserted but for a girl wiping the bar and a pair of men, dressed in dark robes like druids, having a secretive discussion over cups of mead.

The girl stopped wiping tables and peered in utter bewilderment at Eric's shoes, business shirt and slacks. She had the peculiar look of heavily Asian features with blonde hair and very pale skin. She seemed unsure whether hostility or reverence was required. The two druid-types also turned to stare, and kept staring at him, clearly unnerved, as though Eric were some kind of omen. 'Your need?' the girl demanded.

'A meal, a bed. Two meals, if possible. I'm very hungry.' Case pushed the scales into Eric's pocket.

'Where from?' said the girl. 'What city?'

'I have no city.'

Wrong answer. The girl backed away, eyes wide with fright. 'There are rules here. We follow them. What *city*?'

'What's the name of a city?' Eric whispered behind his hand.

'Trying to think, give me a sec,' Case whispered back. 'Esk! Esk's one. They kept talking about swords from Esk, remember?'

'I'm from Esk,' Eric said to the girl.

She looked dubious, but approached him with a hand out for payment. He showed her a red scale, and her face lit up with wonder. She curtsied. 'Good sir! I'll fetch your meals. Your room's second door, upstairs.'

'Ale, too, if you please. Two mugs.' She nodded and bustled away.

'Damn it,' Eric muttered, taking a seat by a window, out of view of the two strange men, who had gaped in disbelief on sight of the red scale.

'What is it?' said Case.

'See how she reacted? The scale's way too much payment. And keep an eye on those creepy guys. They might want to see if I've got any more of them in my pocket.'

The girl wasn't long with the drinks, but food took a painful time longer. Eric felt the strange-tasting ale go to his head very quickly after the long day's walk. He reflected that he could feel the softer edges being chipped off himself and hardened with each new day here. He had never been comfortable around hard men, biker types, gang types or even cops. Now he knew what death looked like, knew it was real, and could feel a change coming which there was no choice but to welcome, since it was needed.

The serving girl brought two more full cups without being asked. Case sipped from his discreetly, trying to hide its movements. If he clutched the cup for a little while, it fell under the charm's influence, and vanished until he let it go.

A strongly built man in a kitchen apron, resembling the girl enough to be her father, finally brought out two steaming plates. Leeks, potatoes and slices of meat were piled on it. It looked fairly plain fare but Eric had never been more glad to see such in his life. 'Good sir,' said the man with exaggerated politeness, bowing. He eyed the two half-finished cups for a moment. 'We've had issue with your scale.'

'It's real, I assure you.'

The man chuckled. 'No question there! My heaviest cudgel won't break it. But I've not enough gold in shop to exchange it fairly. None, in fact. Have you coin or other means?'

'I don't.' *And I think you probably know it.*

'Then I'm afraid you'll be paying too much for your room.'

'Exchange it as fairly as you can,' Eric said. 'I'll take as fair a trade as you can manage.'

The innkeeper nodded, departed, and returned with a small tied bag of coins, which he dropped on the table. 'Best I can do, good sir.'

Eric examined the flat copper and silver discs with no idea of their worth, but he made a show of his disappointment. 'Some provisions for the road as well, perhaps?'

'Aye, in the morning if you like. Not many pay for rooms at an inn with scales, as you'd know. Strange accent you have. Esk, is it?'

'Yes.'

'Long way to come on foot.'

'I know that much very well.'

'You have no gear with you.'

'I did, until recently.'

The man nodded, though his look was hard to read. 'So you know, a patrol comes through tomorrow, and all beds are taken.'

Eric nodded as though this were no problem, but cursed inside; he'd hoped for a few days' rest. When the innkeeper departed, Case whispered, 'He doesn't trust you. See the way he looked at the two plates, two cups? He smells a rat, wants us out with no trouble. Bet there's no patrol coming tomorrow at all. He might've said that to see if you'll bolt, see if you're a fugitive. We better be careful here. Take it easy with that drink. Might have to think fast.'

They devoured their meal and their ales without speaking. The meat was of a kind neither of them had tasted before, apparently one of the native species, salty and tender, smothered thick in gravy. Eric ordered two more ales and let Case drink both.

The upstairs room was tiny, but had a sizeable bed with a straw mattress. 'I'll take a different room,' said Case. 'There's plenty, all vacant. You keep the gun since I got the charm. They won't see me in the beds.'

'Hope you don't snore,' said Eric.

'Hope I don't piss the bed, too, but I just might.' His footsteps padded away.

Eric had just lain down and deemed this scratchy dust-smelling excuse for a bed the most comfortable in all creation, when again came the war mage's shriek, not far distant. A minute passed before it came again, closer, as though it had just passed over the very roof of the inn, and was speaking to him personally.

Then there was silence. 'Good night to you too,' Eric whispered, setting the gun within reach as he sank into sleep.

The quiet sound of a familiar high-pitched, maddening laugh was what woke him, not the daylight. He might otherwise have slept for the whole day.

Kiown sat cross-legged on the bed by his feet, head tilted so his cone of red hair drooped down to the right, fists pressed to his chin. 'Good morning to *you*,' he said, head bobbing to accentuate each word like a whistling bird. 'Mmmm! You have come so *far*, Eric of Otherworld, brave worthy Eric, inn-finder, road-walker, magpie-slayer!'

Eric thought he was still dreaming. He glanced at where the gun lay hidden by his discarded shirt. 'What are you doing here? How'd you find us?'

'I stayed here last night,' said Kiown. 'Must have just missed you downstairs! Quite a coincidence. Or ... *is* it?' He cackled.

'Is Anfen here, too?'

'Nope! Which is curious. Because, although he isn't, you *are*. And I thought we'd all agreed you were Anfen's property. He must have a hole in his pocket!'

'I'll explain what happened. Just let me wake up first.'

'I know *some* of what happened to you. But first, that black scale. Still got it? Do I ever have an offer for *you*.'

'Loup has it,' said Eric. He affected disappointment, remembering how Kiown had drooled at the sight of it back at the hilltop.

Kiown cursed. 'That old fraud. And they all thought *I* was the shifty one. Oh well.'

'Magpie-slayer, you said. How did you know about that?'

Kiown's mouth hung open. 'Wait wait, I was joking! As if *you* would have killed it, I thought. Not my timid Otherworld prince who goes pale at the sight of blood. You're serious? *You're* the one who killed it?'

'I just hurt it. Anfen killed it.'

Kiown peered at him closely. 'I somehow don't think you're lying! What a strange tale. Magpies aren't easy to kill. Perhaps I'd better be careful of you, O Eric, inn-finder.'

'Why should you need to be?'

'*Extremely* good point. You understand this means you're Marked? Don't worry. We are probably too far south for them, approaching country where people think they don't even exist. I suppose we had better trade stories. Who goes first?'

'You, please.'

'Very well. After the company split, we got wiped out half a day south-west of Faul's place. We stuck to the road, which was, in retrospect, most unwise. As if the patrols will range *this* wide, I thought to myself. Sure enough, patrol found us, took us out in a mountain pass just like the one near the hilltop. I fled like a coward. Wise coward, however. I *was* supposed to be in charge, and I *did* yell "flee". But they had battle fever.' He sighed, face downcast. Eric, however, found that most emotions Kiown expressed — apart from anger — rang faintly theatrical, as though he performed them for his own delight like someone before a mirror. He said in a lowered voice, 'All was lost and there was no way through. Heavy infantry blocked the road with archers behind them. They fired at Doon, which made him pissed. You seen heavy infantry? There were none at the hilltop. Armour, big heavy armour. Their job on a battlefield is pretty much to get in the way. Almost too weighed down to be dangerous, but you sure as fuck can't kill em. Guess what Doon did?'

'No idea.'

'Killed em. You remember our friend the half-giant? Stomped through em all, knocked em scattering. Not pretty to watch.

One poor clod, Doon slammed down a foot on his chest, and blood gushed out the visor of his *helm*. That's what it means, to be stomped by Doon. But the archers in the back, they just kept filling him with arrows. Rest of us too. Arrow stuck me like a fork into mutton. See?' Kiown lifted a sleeve of his shirt, where thick bandages showed old blood.

'You should probably change that dressing.'

'I'm kind of proud of the blood, to be honest. Looks good for the ladies. Lucky the arrow ricocheted off someone else and hit me weak. Serrated arrows! Ouch. I cried, honestly cried.'

'Then what? You caught up with Anfen and he sent you to find us?'

'Patience, patience. Even after Doon trampled half their infantry, there was no way to reach the archers behind em. So what'd I do? I fled. Say what you will. The others kept trying to get at the archers, even after I yelled retreat. Idiots. And when Doon gets in that mood, he sure doesn't take orders. But he was only ever going to make a dent in them before they got him. Just a *few* too many foes, this time.'

'What happened to him in the end?'

Kiown sighed. 'Last time I looked back, he was busy stomping his way to happiness. But they sure had a lot of arrows in him by then. A lot. And they were drawing back those shitty little standard-issue crossbows to fire another round.' Kiown was quiet for a moment, staring out the window. 'No other way to go but through that mountain pass. Somewhere along the way, they knew we were coming, and knew to wait there. Anfen shouldn't have split us up, if I may be *ever* so briefly critical of His Perfection.' He sighed and was quiet for a while. 'Such is war. *Valour return him.* Now. Your turn.'

Eric told Kiown what had happened, though he didn't mention the gun.

'Mmm, I see,' said Kiown when Eric had finished. 'Or I think so. I guessed Anfen would be at Faul's still, waiting for the patrols to die down. I'd hoped to come back and meet you all, but just missed you. I did *not* know the woods I travelled through were full of monsters, however. Inferno cultists, yes, and ghosts. Not monsters.'

'How was it at Faul's, when you arrived?'

'Faul was pissed,' said Kiown, shrugging. 'And that is not nice to behold. Worse than Doon almost, with those big teeth of hers. It was not time to impart grim news of her nephew. She chased me away as it was. She never liked me much. But I saw the magpie's body, and went "aha!" inside. She was digging a grave for it, her and that weird husband of hers dressed in mourning garb and everything. That pair are funny in the skull — it's a magpie, I mean come on. I bet they didn't even loot it for trinkets. She wouldn't say which way you'd all gone. I had to guess from tracks but they were hard to read. Guess I followed yours, not Anfen's.'

'Lucky you found us here,' said Eric, wondering at the source of the apprehension he suddenly felt. Was it the feeling of being captive again — 'property' of Anfen's band?

Kiown shrugged. 'Only lucky I decided to stay at this inn, rather than camp off road. I was always going to travel the same way you had. Basically one road leads past Faul's, from River City through to Hane. These inns are the only place for a long way to spend the night under a roof. It has been a long while since I had a bed. On the off-chance, I asked the girl downstairs if any strangers had passed through. Didn't expect her to say yes. For a coin, she described you. Didn't ask her what she'd do for ten coins, but I bet it's coin well spent, with that pretty mouth of hers. Mmmm. She found you most peculiar indeed. You also scared off their only other two customers,

Nightmare cultists. If you can scare Nightmare cultists, you have done well.'

'Hane is a city, I take it.'

The cone of red hair bobbed to and fro. 'Aligned. Pretty newly Aligned, so it's freer than the others, but getting worse. We may be able to get in and out, still. Most people aren't able to leave, but I got contacts there . . . or I *did*. Been a while since I was there. We'll scout it out. In a way, it's good we're not with Anfen. We'd be a lot less free to travel if we were. They're putting up road signs with his likeness, and posting rewards. Serious business!'

And no thanks to you, right? But you seem cheerful enough, Eric thought. Aloud, he said, 'Where are we headed, then? You're our guide, it'd seem.'

'And I work cheap! We'll meet Anfen. He's off to the council of Free Cities over in Elvury. We'll stop in Hane, grab supplies and get you some more normal-looking clothes, so you don't stand out so much.' Kiown stood. 'The girl downstairs said you paid with a red scale! Tut tut, what a waste. But believe me, that'll cover our breakfast, and they can serve it with a song and a kiss, for what you've put in their safe. Where's your grandpa?'

The door creaked open. 'He's right here,' said Case, his footsteps padding in. 'And he didn't piss the bed.'

'Then we shall celebrate,' said Kiown.

Downstairs they had eggs and sausage, the innkeeper stacking food high on their plates, apparently mindful he'd been hugely overpaid for the room. 'Don't believe him either,' Kiown muttered. 'He's got plenty of gold in the safe for an exchange. No matter. I'll be back through here and I'll rob the bastard. I've robbed this place before.'

'Got away with it?' said Case, who sat hidden by the charm necklace.

'Sure did. They thought their help had done it. Hanged someone for it. I didn't mean *that*. Dragon's will, eh?' He laughed. 'Got a tidy sum of gold, even pissed in their ale barrel. Customers commented on the tang and drank it down in record time.' Kiown downed his cup of mead in one long pull, spilling much down his shirt, then slammed it down, screaming obscenely across the room for another.

'Pipe down,' Case muttered. 'One thing I learned in life, don't ever mess with the people preparing your food.'

'Good point,' said Eric. 'The innkeeper's packing us supplies for the road. Or he *was*. We should stay in his good graces.'

Kiown waved this away. 'They respect a rowdy drinker in these parts. First thing in the morning, even better.'

The innkeeper emerged with two small sacks, filled with bread, fruit, blocks of hard cheese, jerky and salted meats. 'Patrol's through soon,' he said quietly. His eyes said it quite clearly: *You are hereby invited to get the fuck out.*

Kiown looked in the sacks. 'I see you've disposed of your spoiling food! Here's a thought. Get your scaly hide back in that kitchen and get us some fresh stuff for the road. I want two more sacks at least as full as this one. An old cook-fire pan while you're at it. And when you get back here you can do a little dance for my amusement. And by the way: you are an ugly, ugly man.'

The innkeeper said nothing, but did indeed return to the kitchen. 'Enjoy that?' said Kiown. 'Scaly hide? Hint, hint. He knows it too, the dirty thief.'

'This food looks OK to me,' said Eric. 'Bread, fruit, meat. Even skins of water.'

'It's fine, but he can do better than that for a red scale.'

The innkeeper returned with another sack and dumped it heavily on the table, but behind it was a long knife. Very quickly it was at Kiown's throat. The man snarled, 'I hope these supplies are more to your liking, good sir. As requested, an old cook-fire pan in there too. Now enjoy guessing which of these food items were rubbed against the rat dead of poison overnight in my kitchen. The foam on its mouth was green. Get out.'

Behind the innkeeper's shoulder, his daughter stood with a crossbow braced on her forearm, aimed at Eric. Kiown's hand had found his sword hilt, but he weighed things up, smiled and said, 'And thank *you*, tavern master, for breakfast. My meat was a touch overcooked, but only a touch.'

The innkeeper backed away, knife still at the ready. Kiown stood, and looked to weigh things up again. 'Don't do it,' Eric said nervously. The innkeeper's daughter had followed him with the crossbow.

'Wise,' said the innkeeper. 'She's a fine shot. You'd be her second this month. Now. I'll forget you, should the patrol ask of wayfaring travellers. In return, you forget me, if you start to pine for that scale.'

'Haven't *you* done a handy day's trade,' said Kiown pleasantly, twitching fingers the only indication of his rage.

'I know my business,' said the innkeeper, a glint of humour in his eye. 'And I'd be careful paying your way with scales. No one has done so in this country since my grandfather's day, and I hear a castle wagon train was robbed. A grand mystery, that. Swift travels t'you.'

36

They set out through what looked like English countryside, with the occasional farmstead and patch of scenic woodland. They went largely off road, since the terrain easily allowed it, sneaking a look through the foliage at the rare people going by road. There was something secretive and hurried in the manner of most travellers they saw. Soldiers sometimes walked by in light chain mail, always in pairs, chatting and laughing: they alone seeming light of spirit. 'Always this way in Aligned country,' said Kiown. 'People try not to stand out.'

'Too bad we do,' said Eric. Even Kiown dressed unlike any other natives, with his long black sleeves and pants nearly skin tight about his lanky frame.

'Mmm, we do. But we wouldn't dare walk around dressed this strangely if we had something to hide. We must be important, maybe even on castle business. You watch, if there're any roadblocks, they'll think that very thing as long as we stay calm.'

'They'll think we're top secret castle crack troops?' said Case.

'You jest,' said Kiown. 'Such people *do* exist. You'd be surprised. They're called Hunters; I've encountered them. And they strike terror in the common grunt. So shall we.'

They put good distance behind them without incident, stopping off road now and then to eat the more perishable of the innkeeper's goods. 'Worried about what he said of poisoned rats?' said Case as they sat on boulders near a crystal-clear stream through which black fish sluggishly pushed against the current, ignoring the pebbles Kiown skimmed at them.

'Rats? Nahh,' he said, stuffing into his mouth a hunk of soft, flavoured bread. 'That was just play. But he *was* pretty close to cutting my throat. Made me sweat, I tell you. Even though I had a magpie-slayer there to help.' Kiown turned to Eric. 'Let's hear the tale again.'

Eric groaned, not wanting to relive that trauma.

Kiown patted his arm. 'Reluctant, I see. How odd. I'm used to travelling with Sharfy. He squashes a fly, and it's a four-hour saga. If he killed a magpie, the tale would never end.'

'It's as I told you. I just hurt it. Anfen finished it off.'

'Hurt it with a sword? A crappy little standard-issue sword?' said Kiown, an eyebrow raised.

He still hadn't mentioned the gun. 'Yes. What else, my bare fists?'

'Mmm. Brave of you.' His look clearly said he sensed something missing from the tale, perhaps thinking Eric had lied to impress him. Eric changed the subject. 'Did you see the war mage last night?'

'Heard it,' said Kiown, wolfing down the last of his bread and crouching by the stream to refill their skins.

'What's the plan, if it comes back for us?'

'Run. Scream in fear, too.' Kiown pondered. 'Odds it was here for *you* are most slim, O Eric, inn-finder. For had it been, you would right now be a steaming mound of cooked flesh.' Kiown stood, stretched. 'Night approaches! One more hour and we'll make camp.'

Despite the day's exertions, Eric and Case both struggled to sleep in the little enclave he led them to, with its piles of soft dry grass set up as though he, or someone, camped out there frequently. They risked a small fire, though no mage was there to keep its smoke and light hidden from prying eyes, and ate well of the innkeeper's food again, not too mindful of dwindling supplies; Kiown could hunt game, he assured them, and they'd be able to buy more when they reached Hane.

Finally Case's snoring began in tandem with Kiown's, and Eric alone lay awake, trying not to think of the Invia's dying scream, or the unearthly beauty of the others escaping skywards, one of those also wounded by his cruel weapon from another world. But the images wouldn't leave his mind. They'd want to kill him, now; so be it. He just wanted to find the surviving ones and say he was sorry.

Giving up on sleep, he went to the enclave's opening, leaned on it and gazed at the starless night. Then he saw something that took the breath out of him. In the distance, something *huge* moved across the sky. His first glance had taken it to be a massive bunch of clouds, but it was far too distinct, vaguely human-shaped and lit by its own glowing light. Two huge arms stretched out before it. A hooded face turned slowly left and right, sweeping across the ground below, and casting a faint luminescence like a thick beam of moonlight. It wheeled around, the tail of its hooded gown trailing far behind it, like a stream of smoky black cloud.

Eric's heart beat fast, though the huge apparition was nowhere near them. Should he wake Kiown? He had to know what that was, whether he really saw it or whether he was mad. He shook the bandit's shoulder gently. Kiown was awake, blade drawn in a second. 'Eric? *Yes?*'

'Look at this.'

'It better be good,' said Kiown, getting to his feet and yawning.

'I dreamed of innkeepers' daughters, and the things one might do to them.' He peered out into the gloom.

It took a moment for the huge shape to reappear, for it had floated out of sight. Shivers went down Eric's back as it turned back from beyond the horizon. '*Look* at that! Do you see it?'

'That's just Nightmare,' said Kiown, yawning. 'Haven't seen him for a while. Year, at least. My, he's a long way north. Well done, O Eric companion-waker. You've seen your first Great Spirit.'

'That's one of your gods?'

'Yes, now let me sleep.' Kiown staggered back to his dry grass bed, and was snoring seconds later. Eric stood watching for a good while after Nightmare had wheeled out of view, but the Great Spirit didn't return.

They rose to a pale, cool morning, bundled up the piles of straw for the next secret travellers to come through, then headed back towards the road. 'Are the other Great Spirits like Nightmare?' Eric asked Kiown.

Kiown shrugged. 'I've seen only Nightmare and Wisdom. Valour, no one sees him, but Anfen says he's real enough. He's not huge though, like Nightmare. Wisdom is. She flies around at night too.'

'It sounded pretty evil from your talk of it,' said Case.

'Evil? Nightmare?' Kiown frowned. 'Does he roam around eating people like apples? He does not. Does he look scary? He does. *Some* think to see him's bad luck, but that's tosh. I'd be more worried about his worshippers, the creepy shits. Not half as bad as Inferno's, but I wouldn't go to *their* parties either.'

Late in the day they saw a roadside vigil manned by guards wearing Hane's colours, orange with white bands. They were seen before they could go off road. Kiown said, 'Easy does it, everyone calm. Case, wear the charm. Eric, wait here and look important.' Kiown rushed ahead and had a quiet word with the soldiers, who listened, then waved Eric to come through without saying a word.

'What did you tell them?' said Case when they were safely past.

'Trick with soldiers on watch is to pretend you're on urgent secret business for their city. Just make something up. Watch duty's boring, they like a good yarn. One or two harsh words about the state of their uniforms doesn't hurt at all. Anfen taught us the right things to say to make em think you're connected to the high-ups. Those chaps back there think they'll get promoted for letting us through. Ready for another night in the wilderness?'

Case groaned.

'Don't worry, I know a good spot. Just a short climb. Pretty view.'

The climb was hellishly steep up stone steps winding around a tall pillar of rock. It had been built as a roadside lookout tower but abandoned halfway through. The result was a hunk of dark grey stone tall as an office building and about as wide at the top. The steps were wide and solid underfoot but had no railing to grasp. The Pilgrims clung nervously to the pillar's wall, trying not to look down. Kiown laughed at them and bounded up two or three steps at a time.

There were signs of past campfires on the platform, as well as rolled-up mattresses of soft grass to sleep on, tied and weighted with rocks against the wind, again left as a courtesy by others who'd stayed here in secret. Old bones too small to be human were scattered about, presumably someone's meal. Sometimes people stayed up there for weeks, Kiown said, despite the road running directly below.

Case — who'd been so exhausted halfway up the steps he'd deduced, in all sincerity, that Kiown was in the middle of a murder attempt — lay prostrate on the platform's middle. Kiown whooped from exhilaration at the view. Eric found it funny: the sight of a Great Spirit was normal to Kiown, but a view from high up amazed him, despite being less remarkable than that witnessed by any window-seat aeroplane passenger. The road they'd been walking stretched in a long winding line into the distance. 'That way's the inn,' said Kiown, pointing north. 'See that flat space there? Blasted Plains. You were all the way over there, just a few days back. You only cut across one little part of its edge. It stretches further southwest, gets impossible to walk through. Elementals there too, and other nasties.'

'Which way's the castle?' said Eric.

Kiown pointed in approximately the direction of the road they'd come by. 'Right now, we're about a fifth of the way to World's End,' he said, 'which, I suspect, is where Anfen is eventually headed. And I suspect I know why.' But he wouldn't be drawn further on the subject.

To their immediate west was a cluster of round hillsides. From behind those, many trails of smoke wound skywards. 'That's the edge of Hane,' said Kiown. 'And there,' he pointed beyond, where the fading daylight sparkled on a distant patch of what looked like ocean, 'is the Godstears Sea. It's where Anfen tried to send me. It's a very big puddle. Tasty fish.'

From his backpack, Kiown pulled a tightly rolled-up blanket. 'We'll be snuggling up tonight,' he said. 'Gets windy up here. But we're safe. Let's eat.'

There was no wood for a fire, even had they wanted to risk one. Kiown traded jokes with Eric as night fell, obscuring the grand sweeping view. Drawing in the dust with his finger, Eric introduced noughts and crosses to Levaal. 'Stupidest fucking game I've ever seen,' Kiown muttered.

Some distant homestead lights could be seen for a while, but they were shut off before long. Case either slept early or pretended to. The shakes had returned to his hands from lack of drink, and he'd all but admitted Stranger was probably not going to show up.

It got windy up on that platform, but Eric went to sleep with his belly full, his mind at peace, and happier than he'd been since he came to this world.

37

Nightmare drifted. Spread out below him, the people and the creatures swarmed across Levaal's night-time surface slept, lived, died. He saw not *them*, he saw patterns: some were pleasing, but some disturbed, disquieted.

It was not the patterns as they were *now* which disquieted him; it was the way they shifted and moved, how some invariably swung towards others to meet like waves in a pool, and what, from that, would result.

He switched perspective as he drifted, the way others may shut one eye to look out from the other. Now down below appeared as machinery, pistons moving, spoked wheels spinning in place, steam bursting from a vent. This way, things seemed a little more sure . . . but there were many ways to view things.

There, look at that interesting little bolt, up high on the tall rocky platform. Important, that one was, tucked in between many other key parts. Yet something hindered its function. Nightmare would have to think about it, later.

Actually not much later . . . for the bolt was a human, and those did not function for long. Should he act? He thought about it, foresaw two likely futures spreading before him. One was terrible, one most desirable. And if he did nothing, just drifted and watched? Five other likely futures stretched before his view. All were bad, *very* bad, save one. This part of the machinery should therefore function well.

Nightmare switched views again, and now saw the world as music, mostly playing as it should, though a dramatic crescendo approached, booms and crashes coming loud indeed. The futures he saw through this lens boded similarly to those seen through the others. There, that one important instrument named Eric was not playing its notes correctly. Much of the symphony relied on it, and soon the instrument would break, the man be slain. He switched view to the patterns he'd seen before. Again, a fault in the complex web of colours and shades, a smear of jarring red, a stain spilled across it.

It was becoming clear, now. But an hour longer to think wouldn't hurt, so he stayed in that space of sky, above the rocky platform, and thought. He *could* think quickly when he had to, distasteful though it was.

It was that Invia's Mark causing all this trouble. Nightmare would have liked even a year to consider it longer, to have the impressions swirl about the deep volatile mix of his thoughts before choosing an action. But the man would be killed in so little time.

Nightmare reached down and smothered out the Invia's Mark like a hand snuffing out a candle.

38

Eric did not have breath to scream. His eyes had opened just as the huge hand descended. Its palm — which seemed to be made of night itself, only stuffed more densely into the hand's shape, so that it stood boldly out against the night surrounding — came down over the entire roof of the platform.

Whatever it was made of, Nightmare's flesh passed through Eric and his sleeping companions as would cold ozone-scented air. All went pitch black and the wind could no longer be felt, not until the huge hand retracted, making its slow way skywards. When it had moved sufficiently, Eric looked up at the face within the shroud's outline; it was mostly featureless, or else its features were obscured by the shroud's shadow. Eyes, black slits small in proportion to its face, expressed nothing human, but he knew they gazed at *him*, which was the most terrifying and yet exhilarating thing he'd ever felt. A mouth, some way down, could just be discerned as a motionless crisscrossed row of upper and lower teeth, similar in style to a tribal wooden mask. If anything, this thing in the sky looked like Death. But Eric knew it wasn't there to hurt him.

The arms spread slowly, ponderously outwards again. Nightmare drifted away like a huge cloud blown on steady winds.

Eric looked sideways at his companions. Should he wake them? Would they believe him in the morning otherwise, when he told them what had happened? He didn't, and it wasn't because they needed their sleep. Rather, it felt that somehow this had been *his* moment, his alone whatever it meant, and selfishly he didn't want to share it.

Nightmare drifted languidly away, till he was gone over the horizon.

In the morning, Kiown simply didn't believe him. 'And then did he do a little dance? Challenge you to an arm wrestle? Blow kisses?'

'I know Eric, and he's not lying,' Case said testily.

'Sure, he was *here*,' said Kiown, rolling his eyes, 'I believe that. Maybe he even looked right at us. But no way would he reach down and *touch* us. You dreamed, that's all. Nightmare doesn't touch people. Doesn't give a shit about us. He just exists. That's about all he does. Like old Case here.'

'What if it had happened?' said Eric. 'Just for argument's sake. What would it mean?'

Kiown shrugged. 'No knowing. A blessing, a curse? I have enough trouble understanding mages, let alone Spirits. Hmm. If he cared about you enough to curse you, he'd probably just kill you like that.' He snapped his fingers. 'Which is why it's good he didn't actually do what you dreamed. Vivid dreams up on the tower: you're not the first.' Kiown patted Eric on the head condescendingly and smiled. 'Now, no more of that silliness.'

The morning was like a veil being lifted from the landscape. Smoke rose in a thick hazy pall beyond the hillsides from homes in the city of Hane. 'Eat up!' said Kiown, digging into the provisions sack. 'Long day's march ahead.'

'But Hane's just over there.'

'We can't cut through those hills, alas,' said Kiown. 'Lesser Hane is not where we want to be. Crazy place. Population's fenced in and starving. It's where they've been putting the misbehaving ones who haven't sworn to Vous yet. Got to go around the long way to the other side of the city. Another day's march. And we'd better stay off road as long as we can.'

They'd only just finished eating when noise below caught their attention. An army unit marched past, two abreast. Further north the procession reached as far as they could see. Kiown gazed at it for a long while, troubled. 'Hmmm. Those are soldiers from the castle's own army, not from a city. They are a long way from home.'

'What's this mean then?' said Case.

'For us? We wait right here. For someone else? It means trouble, and a hefty pile of it.'

They waited. When the castle soldiers had finally trooped past, they began their climb down. Then from further up the road came another procession walking two abreast. Kiown cursed viciously. 'Back, back to the top. Lie flat. What the ... ? *Those* aren't castle soldiers. They're wearing city colours. They're from River City!'

The whole day passed them by in similar fashion. Kiown gnawed his fingernails down to bloody little nubs. When one army unit had passed a safe distance away, another would follow, sometimes only a small patrol, sometimes a line stretching to the horizon. City soldiers in plain colours, castle soldiers in their drab grey.

Kiown seemed to take all this as a personal slight. At times he ranted and swore like a madman, inconsolable. He was no longer willing to risk going down even when there were ample enough breaks between the marching units. 'By the time we get down there, there'll be another,' he snarled. 'I bet they're going to Elvury, the bastards. They'll clog the roads all the way there. I knew something was cooking.'

'Sounds like a war cooking to me,' said Case, who didn't mind a break in travel one little bit. He lay with his feet crossed and eyes closed.

'Course it's a war,' Kiown snapped. 'The castle and Free Cities are always at war. Damn it! My Hane contacts are expecting me. They had to come this way, didn't they?'

As evening came and a marching unit made camp by the roadside not far from where they would have to climb down, there seemed no choice but to spend another night up on the platform. Their dinner was a little more modest than recent meals had been, for the innkeeper's supplies had begun to dwindle. 'We had our chance to worry about that,' said Case, looking pointedly at Kiown. 'Chose to stuff our faces instead.'

Kiown's hands twitched. 'Every time you talk, old man, I get a most peculiar urge to take out my sword and *rub* it. Not to cut you, not to fight you. Just to tenderly, lovingly rub my sword. It's the strangest thing.'

'Do what you want,' said Case placidly. 'You think I give a shit about getting sliced up these days, you don't know me.'

'Oh but I could make you sing a pretty song, if I did it slowly.'

'Relax, you two,' said Eric, tired of both of them complaining. 'Maybe Nightmare will come back and you'll believe me this time.'

Nightmare didn't return, as Eric lay there sleepless, the other two quietly snoring into the wind. But something else happened he hadn't counted on: he was back in the room at Faul's house.

39

First came the darkness of sleep, with only Loup's voice, as though in conversation with itself:

'*It's a kind of knowledge minds like ours can't hold . . .*'

'*. . . know what we're about to do. We're about to put in our bodies, in our minds, a little piece of the Dragon itself. Fathom?*'

'*. . . this little scale . . .*'

'*. . . thinks it's risky. Oh aye, can be, but so's taking a step outside at night . . .*'

'*Girl who did it wouldn't tell me what she saw, but she was . . . different, after.*'

'*As It wills! Anfen's being a fool . . .*'

The room in Faul's house spun around slowly, till it was upside down and tipping him out of itself. Then with a rush of acceleration he felt in his belly, the house fell away, the surface of the world falling with it, way down below, very fast past his feet. He was caught in the sky, like someone who'd been dumped in an ocean, on swelling waves of rising and falling air.

His hair and clothes were ruffled by winds that weren't winds — were, rather, currents of magic, the very stuff that passed through a mage's body and made a spell happen. Mages could see it, and so now could he: threads and streaks of energy glimmering, twisting and winding about each other like smoke.

Below spread out the woods through which they'd travelled to get to Faul's. Was this the past he looked into? He saw them as his sight zoomed down through the green treetops: Anfen's band, he himself among them quietly talking to Case, arguing some point as they threaded through the trees beyond the doomed hunters' hall, Lalie in tow.

And there was a white wolf running below too, chasing something that wore a green dress. He knew that though it seemed she in the green dress retreated, *she* was the one in pursuit, drawing the wolf along, playing some game for a hidden purpose, until they both vanished.

His view panned back up and beheld the world like a map. West, there, he saw Kiown's tall flopping cone of red hair, and Doon's huge broad shoulders, the cartoonish sights standing out like geographical features as though to get his attention. He flew over that way and they shrank back to their normal proportions. Something was about to happen, something bad. The group approached a mountain pass, Doon leading, Kiown at the rear. An army patrol waited around the bend, and knew the bandits came. With little warning a volley of arrows flew and thickly rained down, Kiown alone out of their reach, for he'd hung back in the road. Now he drew his sword.

The other bandits dropped quickly. The half-giant alone fought, smashing down infantry, but Kiown — surely not! Kiown had run forwards, hacking his sword into Doon's back, with fast angry slashes of his arm. And the soldiers didn't fire their arrows at him.

Doon fought, but points of halberds and spears surrounded him now, impaling him, and arrows stuck out thickly over a shocking red coat of gushing blood. Kiown's sword rent his back ferociously. The half-giant fell to one knee, then onto his back. His wide, horrified eyes saw Kiown above, smashing down with his boot, then his blade, till the half-giant stopped rolling around to ward off the blows, and lay still. The patrol swordsmen swiftly finished off the other wounded.

Kiown, panting, talked for a while with the patrol's commander. It seemed he, Kiown, gave the instructions and was displeased about something. The commander nodded, looking chastened. Kiown pointed at his shoulder, braced himself, and let a trooper stick it lightly with an arrow, a wound to show the others. Then they bandaged him.

Loup's voice, not far away, suddenly called his name. *There you are, Eric! Not pretty scenery here, eh? Oh no. Higher up, go higher, don't waste it on this stuff! We've seen enough and plenty of all this.*

Eric looked around for the folk magician but couldn't see him, though Loup's voice was loud enough to be speaking by his ear. *See how high you can get, see what It meant for you to see. I'll follow if I can. And don't think about what you seen yet, or you'll steer yourself back here. Thinking about it's for later, when you come back to yourself. Keep that head blank. Just watch now, just watch ...*

Eric tried to push the sights from his mind, as the mage asked, and found it easy. Loup's voice again: *Up we go now, lad ...*

So, higher up he went, legs kicking at the pockets of air and magic like he was kicking through water. The land receded further below, further and further, till what seemed the entire world lay between his feet, or perhaps had its image warped to fit his newly seeing eyes. Ah, now he beheld it properly: a large oblong shape, cut off at the southernmost part they called World's End by a huge barrier. At the other end, the northern-most point, was the castle; in the thin strip of land behind it, the entry point, the door. And he suddenly knew as though the wind whispered secrets to him that this world, Levaal, was not a world at all; it was a place *between* worlds, like two balls that swung on a chain-link ... that Earth was to one side, that Levaal was the link. World's End is really the world's *middle* — there's another half of Levaal, and behind its own entry point, at the southernmost tip, *another* world! This half was Earth's side. Perhaps that is why it resembles our world in some ways, he thought. But what is on the other ... ?

He breathed in the magic wind of the upper sky, purer and stronger in its power up here. It combined with the little specks of scale he'd consumed. He could feel them buzzing around inside him, dissolved and in his very blood, each tiny piece alive and in conversation with the others, discussing Eric himself. Wind, strong-blowing wind, suddenly caught him in a tunnel and wrenched him along towards the castle.

There it was, coming at great speed, not far now, a mass of gleaming white. And he saw that the Dragon had to be close to it, for there, almost visible and tangible, was the god-beast's *willpower*, pouring through the castle's mouth as a tangible force, distorting and rippling reality itself about it, faintly visible. Swirls of magic poured from its mouth too, given to the winds to carry through the world.

The castle called him, the castle drew him closer. It bade him look below.

His sight cut through far distances down to the roads, along which patrols marched like something unhealthy plugging the lands' veins. He saw them crossing grassy fields, kicking down village doors, saw people killed by the roadside, bodies cast away like trash. He understood that this was a message for him: whatever else would happen in this mini-world, the way things headed now, people would soon be dead as stones littering the ground, and that could not be allowed for reasons not explainable yet. He sought a clearer answer to this, asking the little pieces of scale humming and buzzing through his body, but to ask made his whole being shudder like he'd tried to lift a weight of under-standing far too large and heavy. Recoiling, he turned away from the sights below and lay on his back instead, while the wind pulled him closer to the huge white castle.

The white sky above was made of gargantuan slabs of light-stone. As they brightened and dimmed, so came day and night. It was not a sky, it was a *ceiling*! Eric laughed, for now this seemed obvious, simple, and a delight. Behind this thick layer was dark grey stone bent in an enormous and gently sloping dome curving over all the land.

He spotted the gaps which led into the sky's roof, wide enough for Invia to fly through. Look, there one passed now with her beating wings, on her way up to speak with the dragons. The sky-roof's open spaces were too narrow for the dragon-youth to fit, the stone walls too powerfully made for them to break, great as they were.

And now he passed through such a gap, like slipping between two bars into their cage. Further up the long winding tunnels of rock he went, twisting into the sky-roof's caverns. The space opened up ahead and through a split in the wall two eyes gleamed like dark stars. A paw covered in sparkling scales reached down through the gap, the tips of its claws fumbling blindly, grasping outside its cage. Vyin, this imprisoned dragon's name. How it longed for freedom, how *all* the dragon-youth longed for freedom, and had since they were shut in these sky-cages, when men began to swarm across what had once been their world.

Imprisoned. As the Dragon-god willed.

Vyin saw him with its dark-star eyes: Eric, little more than a fleeting cloud's shadow here. But those eyes saw much. The dragon's jaws opened and it spoke a single echoing word which had so much meaning Eric's mind filled up with it like a bowl catching a flood of water pouring through the cavern, all else pushed aside, the echoing word spilling over, only the smallest part of it held on to. His mind translated it to something sense-less which just sounded like: *All things are all things, all things are all things, are all things, are all things.*

Away and thoughtless he drifted from those dark-star eyes, back through the sky's caverns and into the sky, while the Invia, who gossiped just outside the sky-prisons for the dragons to hear, who listened to them and understood, now dropped in a swarm through the gap and dived, left, right, down, wings spreading as they soared in all directions. One of them came right by him, paused in the air, her head cocking left then right, ruby-red hair flying behind her, mouth parted. She grasped Eric in her arms, clutched him to her naked body then dived straight down, taking him away from the sky before the castle could draw him into its maw with a deeper breath, as it wished to.

Instead down they plunged, back towards Faul's house, the roof approaching very quickly. She let him drop back to where his body had flung itself on the floor — but, surely, she saw Anfen's Mark. She flew skywards and sought her sisters for help in killing one so dangerous.

Of this, Eric knew nothing. His ears, mind and soul were filled with that one word the dragon-youth Vyin had spoken. Too much meaning for him, despite his partial understanding of it. And he would walk the path he'd been going to walk before, knowing only that it was as it should be and that he should not stray from it, though perils shoved him or lured him from either side.

40

It was still night. Dazed, he opened his eyes, and let the memories of the vision come back, little pieces at a time slotting into place, like a dream whose every last detail could be remembered. He felt the vision had not ended as it had been meant to, that there was more to see ... perhaps inside the castle, where he had felt himself being drawn, before the Invia had grabbed him against the vision's natural flow and taken him back.

Why had the creature done that? A sinking feeling in his gut came as he knew then that they *had* brought the Invia to Faul's house, that they *had* caused that disaster. Loup had been wrong: Anfen had been no fool at all. He'd known very well there were dangers.

Eric lay with the stone of the rock tower cool beneath him, Case and Kiown snoring either side of him. Somehow, he felt as rested as if he'd slept a full night and more. In his eyes were effects like the after-image from looking at light: there, swirls in the air of shimmering colour, veins of pulsing light on the night sky. He blinked, rubbed his eyes, but the colours remained. In his vision, he'd seen these too, and known what they were. Magic. That stuff's magic, what makes a spell happen ... He could still see them; thinner, here, than they had been higher up in the sky.

Waving a hand past his face, his fingers blocked them off. So, it was no trick of his eyes — they were really there, and perhaps had been all along, albeit hidden. Loup's voice: *Wouldn't tell me what she saw, but she was ... different, after. Glad she went, oh aye. Went on to big things ...*

Could Loup have been just as right as Anfen? That having the vision was important enough to risk whatever had gone wrong? His eyes fell on Kiown, still sleeping right next to him, issuing that thin, high-pitched snore. The first part of the vision suddenly blared in his mind like an alarm.

Heart beating fast, Eric carefully got up from under their shared blanket and stepped away, watching Kiown's sleeping face, head tilted and mouth open as though to catch raindrops. His snoring paused at the disturbance, but he didn't wake. Eric feared suddenly for Case lying next to him. And for himself.

Stay calm, he thought. Kiown could have killed us already. That's not his plan. He intends something else. Pieces of conversation, little things, suddenly came back to him: *My contacts in Hane.* The city was Aligned — why would Kiown have contacts there? And how would they know, as Kiown had said, to expect him?

Anfen says hello. Impulsive foolishness, at the wagon train raid? No, but intended to look like it. A message to the 'high-ups' as he called them. How obvious it seemed now.

The way Kiown had 'courageously' approached the roadside patrol. Perhaps he'd known he wouldn't be harmed. Had they expected their spy? Kiown's voice: *Such people do exist. You'd be surprised. They're called Hunters, I've encountered them.*

Eric didn't have the gun — Case did. It would be easy enough to get it and deal with Kiown while he slept. Deal with? he thought. How gently phrased. Kill him, you mean. Point, click, boom. In his sleep, or do you warn someone that they're about to be killed? Look them in the eye first? It won't be pretty. You'll carry it with you for life. You be careful here ...

And if he didn't do it, would Kiown lead them to their deaths? Did a bounty await him in Hane? But if he was on the castle's side, why had he kept them all up on the tower to avoid the passing armies? Then there was the little issue of being stranded here, in Aligned country, on their own. With rapidly dwindling supplies. Supplies he's been very anxious to get through — so we're more dependent on him ...

Eric looked at the horizon, wishing he knew how many hours the vision had taken. The night sky showed no sign of dawn, not yet. He paced, his heart beating fast, not knowing what to do. He had to think. Loup had said: *this is meant.*

What was *meant*? Perhaps that he should see the vision now, but *not* before setting out with Kiown. Why?

If I'd seen it before, he thought, I might have shot him in the inn that morning.

And they'd have wandered, lost and aimless, perhaps head-first into death or capture. Was he *meant* to travel with the spy, the traitor? Was Kiown meant to guide them to a certain point? How would he know when that point had come, when it was time to run?

If he'd seen the *vision* now, perhaps the time to leave was now.

In Eric's pacing, he hadn't noticed that Kiown had stopped snoring, that his eyes were open, and were on him. 'Has Nightmare returned?' he said drowsily. 'Perhaps to seek your counsel, O Eric, road-walker?'

Eric laughed, nerves betraying him. 'Just can't sleep.'

'Mmm. Your world must be very different. When trying to

sleep, we lie down. Happy pacing, then.' Kiown's eyes closed and, after a time, his snoring resumed.

Over breakfast, Eric didn't let on what he knew, though he hoped it wasn't written as plainly on his face as he felt it was. How badly he wanted five minutes alone with Case to talk, but he was afraid to ask Kiown to leave them be. Kiown meanwhile seemed his usual chirpy self, babbling about what comforts awaited them in the city. If he suspected Eric knew something, he didn't show it. He kept teasing Eric about Nightmare as they polished off the last of the innkeeper's goods for breakfast. The bread was stiff by now, but the meat and fruit were still good. Down by the road, the army patrol had gone.

'One last day's walk,' said Kiown, stretching as he stood. 'Hot baths, steam rooms, whores, cooked meals. That awaits us, O Eric, breakfast-eater, O Case, his loyal steed. I am going to hire three whores at once, I think, and pay them extra to battle naked for the right to my cock. The winner gets it first. The others will just have to make do with what they have. For a while.'

'Is all this available in an Aligned city?' said Eric, hoping the question sounded casual.

'If you know the right places and people,' said Kiown, gazing across at the chimney-smoke rising from beyond the hills. 'Or the wrong ones. The wrong ones are usually more fun. And yes, I know them. Just because the castle owns the city doesn't mean everyone there loves them for it. Most don't, and wish to leave. They can't. The soldiery and a few overseers are the only ones living well.'

'Are you absolutely sure we'll be safe in such a place?'

Kiown now gave him a look which seemed, for just a second, to be shrewdly appraising him. He said, 'Safe, you ask. Nowhere's safe. Even if we had run of a Free City, it wouldn't be safe. The world is deadly dangerous, O Eric the timid. Haven't you noticed?'

Eric said evenly, 'I have. Here, danger has a way of . . . sneaking up on you, I suppose, from unlikely places. When your back's turned. As it were.' The instant he'd said it, he wished he could just suck in a deep enough breath to take the words back with it. Why do it, why turn this into a game? he furiously asked himself. The answer: he wanted to be sure what he'd seen was real before potentially taking a life. It had *seemed* real in the vision, and his bones still felt it was, but here, now, in the light of morning . . .

And he got his wish. Kiown looked at him without talking, seeming shocked for just a moment then suddenly wary, eyes darting from Case to Eric. A laughed forced itself belatedly out of his mouth. 'Yes, yes, yes! You are quite right. You may even say there is no such *thing* as an unlikely place from which danger should spring upon one. But, how cryptically phrased, O Eric the intriguing. Is there something on your mind?'

'No,' said Eric, affecting casualness again, though too late, he sensed. He stood and gathered up his things.

Kiown still watched him. 'Unpleasant dreams? Eric?'

'Yeah. Don't worry. It's nothing. I dreamed we went to the city and something bad happened to us.'

Kiown nodded. 'When your . . . back was turned. As it were.'

'Well. Yes.'

'Scuse me,' said Case irritably, 'can you two poets let me in on all this? You're talking about *something*, and it's pretty serious near's I can tell. Want to try it in plain talk for the elderly among us?'

Kiown shrugged as though Eric were the one being strange. He seemed, however, to have been put at ease by Case's outburst; perhaps it was evidence that Eric and Case did not share any plots or suspicions. He hummed a tune as he gathered the soft grass in rolls and put it back in place for the next campers to come up here, weighing the bundles down with rocks. Then he went to the corner of the platform they'd reserved for such functions and pissed down the side.

Eric saw his chance. He whispered, 'Case, when I say now, put on the charm and get the gun ready. Be ready to shoot him. I'm serious.'

'What's this about?' whispered Case.

There wasn't time to talk more. 'Let's away,' said Kiown, bowing flamboyantly. Eric had a moment's doubt, then thought of walking down the steps, no railing beside them, Kiown within reach of them both. 'Case. *Now.*'

Kiown looked the question at them both. Case hesitated, then reached into his pocket, the charm in one hand, the gun in the other. He showed Kiown the gun then slipped the charm over his head, vanishing.

'Wait, wait,' said Kiown, one hand going uncertainly to his sword's handle. 'What are you two cooking here?'

'First, let me tell you something,' said Eric. His heart was beating wildly, but he tried to keep his voice level. 'Don't come any closer, don't try to run away. There's something you weren't told about how I killed the Invia.'

'Wounded her, you said . . .'

'Yes, within an inch of her life. I brought something with me from Otherworld. A weapon. You have magic here, we have technology there. There's maybe not a lot of difference, except any fool can use technology. My weapon's a simple one. Point, make a fist, and boom.'

Kiown laughed. He spread his hands. 'O Eric the strange! What *is* all this talk? Do you resent being Anfen's trinket and yearn to be free? Is that what really happened, is that why you left?

Listen! It's simple. *Bargain* with him. Or with whichever Mayor he hands you to. Demand a price for your labours. You'll get it. You could be rich.'

Eric said, 'Take your sword out and toss it away, handle first.'

Kiown laughed in disbelief. *'What?* Have you gone funny in the skull? Case! What's wrong with him?'

'Do what he says,' said Case's voice, to Eric's right.

Cunning, Eric thought, seeing where Case is. Eric moved away from where Case's voice had sounded, so it wouldn't be possible to attack them both at once. 'Drop the sword, Kiown.'

'Pardon me, I think I'll keep it. It's *me*, Eric. You've spent many nights right beside me and come to no harm, apart from the gas and bad breath. I thought we were companions.'

'Did Doon and the others think that of you, as well?'

Kiown's eyebrows shot up. For a moment, he couldn't speak. 'What?'

'You heard me.'

'Yes, I did.' He shook his head as though baffled. 'Doon? I told you what happened to him. Soldiers got him.'

'Just soldiers?'

'I told the group to retreat. They didn't. They didn't respect my leadership. It happens when Anfen puts doubt in their minds at the outset. Did you hear him? *Kiown leads you, wisely I hope.'* He laughed. 'Have you been listening to Sharfy? Or to that fuzz-brained coot, Loup? I know they think I'm no good, they have for a long time. They forget the times I saved their lives. Ask Anfen to tell you those tales. I saved the whole band, more than once.'

'That's not really relevant to what we're discussing now.'

'What are we discussing?' Kiown said, anger rising in his face and extravagant gestures. 'I've half a dozen deep scars that were meant for Anfen's delicate places. Siel's too. There were fights where the whole group walked away alive because of *me*. Look at this!' he lifted his sleeve, showing his bandaged arrow wound.

Eric said, 'You got off lightly in that fight, didn't you?'

'Lightly? I was *shot* with an *arrow*! I'm lucky it wasn't *poisoned*!'

'Remarkable luck.'

Kiown's hands began to shake, his eyes now blazing with rage. He took a step towards Eric, hand closing on his sword handle. Eric stepped back. 'Unbuckle your scabbard and drop it to the ground, Kiown.'

'Case? Can you reason with him?' said Kiown.

'Don't speak, Case. He's trying to find where you are. Kiown, put down the sword. I'm serious.'

'You're seriously funny in the skull,' said Kiown. 'Here's my sword.' He drew it with a flourish. 'Sharp one, nicely weighted. Got a thin core of dead stone, so you don't need to rub it on every day. Worth two red scales. Come take it.'

'Do what he says,' Case said tiredly, his voice closer to Kiown.

Kiown's wrist moved fluidly, the sword slicing a figure-eight through the air. He had moved towards Eric, two steps taken, when Case fired: *Boom*. The bullet struck the ground just before Kiown's feet, chipping the rock. He dropped his sword in panic and leaped backwards, hands to his ears, not knowing in that instant whether the Otherworld weapon had harmed him or not.

Eric too had jumped at the Glock's enormous noise. He recovered first, rushed forwards, grabbed the sword by the handle as it still jumped and clattered on the rock floor, then stepped back, the blade held the way Sharfy had shown him.

Kiown laughed, though his face showed dark hatred. 'Had some lessons, have we? Anfen teach you? Not Sharfy, surely. Hope you're a prodigy. I could kill you bare-handed.'

'Wouldn't try it,' said Case wearily. 'That was a warning shot. Next one won't miss you.'

Kiown laughed again. 'I thought you were fibbing about the weapon. I really did.'

'It's like a bow and arrow, or crossbow,' said Eric. 'It shoots a little piece of metal, faster than anything you've ever heard of. As we speak, Case has it pointed right at your chest. Want to talk honestly for a while?'

Kiown began to speak several times, then he laughed bitterly. 'I've been nothing *but* honest. This is all a big mistake.'

'Don't make me do it, please,' said Case quietly. 'I've had to do it before. I didn't like it then, won't like it any more now. Though it sounds like maybe you deserve it.'

Something in his tone — sombre, regretful — sank in. 'Fine,' Kiown muttered. 'Fine. Let's talk.'

41

'Where are you taking us, and why? Let's start there.'

They'd told Kiown to sit cross-legged, directly in the middle of the platform. Case was behind him, still invisible, Eric to his side, well out of reach of a lunging charge. 'To Hane,' Kiown answered, 'like I told you. I have contacts there.'

'Then where?'

'Then to find Anfen,' said Kiown. 'Believe it or not, that much is true. I'm supposed to take you back to him then carry on in his group, give them the same story I gave you. I suppose now I'll have to dump you at his feet and run, since you have things to tell him about me.'

'I don't believe it,' said Eric. 'I have trouble trusting the word of someone who can kill the companions they slept beside the night before.' Not just kill, either . . . kill like someone possessed. Eric recalled the manic viciousness of Kiown's sword slicing into Doon's back, the savage way his boot had stomped down.

The conflict across Kiown's face was visible — admit it, or keep denying? 'Let me ask you something,' he said. 'What makes you so sure you know these things? Who'd you speak to? Something happened, something changed, from dinner last night to now. Something made you go from regarding me as a friend to . . . to *this*.'

'I'm not sure we were friends.'

'We can be!' said Kiown. 'I don't hold a grudge. Maybe we have a lot in common, more than you think. Our best interests, at least.'

Eric laughed at him and saw the sincerity instantly crumble to make way for the swiftly rising anger he'd seen before. 'Do you know what Anfen and the rest really *are*?' Kiown snarled, giving in to it. 'Do you know what the "Free Cities" really *are*? They hold back the progress of the *race*! They always have. They're parasites, they're pointless. Do you know what we are creating at the castle, right now? We're making ourselves *gods*. Do you understand that? Do you know what secrets we will learn, what power we'll command? And you can be part of it. Lay one brick down in the great structure, you share in the glory.'

'You used the plural, I notice,' said Eric. 'Who gets to be the god?'

Kiown shifted uncomfortably.

'I bet I know,' said Case. 'Vous does.'

Kiown looked around wildly. 'You aren't fit to speak his *name*,' he spat with great venom. 'Not in *any* tone, let alone that grim foreboding one, you filthy pathetic old shit.'

'A custom in our world,' said Eric, 'is to speak a little more politely when someone's standing nearby with a gun pointed at you.'

Kiown calmed down and rolled his eyes. 'This is fine theatre and all, but can I have that sword back when you two have had your moment? I paid a lot for it.'

'Sorry, no,' said Eric. 'I'll keep it. Now you can tell us more about ... what was the name, Case?'

'Vous. And I could tell you things about him would make you shudder.' Kiown sensed he was being baited now, and shrugged passively. 'What kind of idiot wants to be a god anyway?' said

Case. 'And tell me this, what kind of *crackpot* gets all steamed up following such a person? You sounded like that Inferno girl a minute ago.'

'You are quite, quite right,' said Kiown mockingly. 'What was I thinking?'

'So, the castle's interested in us. How do Case and I figure into these grand plans? If it's true they want Case and me back with Anfen, what comes after that?'

Kiown shrugged. 'Talk to me, Kiown,' said Eric, but Kiown just stared into the distance.

Here's the problem, Eric thought, pacing. If our roles were reversed, if it was me holding back info on him, it'd be easy enough: he'd start breaking bones till I talked. For him it would be the logical action. I can't do it, and he knows it. That's why the bad guys win.

Eric could not invoke the required sadism, but he could mimic it. He said, 'You'd better tell us the rest, so we can decide what to do with you. We could fire into your knees and leave you here. Won't be fun getting down those steps. It'd hurt a *lot* more than that arrow's scratch did. I don't want to do it but I will.' I hope he believes it. 'You say we can still be companions. Make your pitch.'

Kiown rubbed the bridge of his nose, eyes to the ground, as though it hurt to speak: 'My mission is to get you two back to Anfen. Alive and well. I know no more. I get the minimum I need to know, in case I end up in this very predicament. And that's all.'

'What are you, exactly?' said Case. 'Spy? You one of them grey-robes I saw?' From the direction his voice came, it sounded like he'd sat down. 'And hurry this up, make it honest. I'll shoot you the second Eric asks me to. We're out of food and I like an early lunch. We aren't going to be up here all day.'

'I'm what they call a Hunter,' said Kiown irritably. 'We're the elites. We know more than the soldiers, the First Captains, probably more than the Generals. We speak directly to the Strategists, sometimes even higher. Some of us in every city, no more than a couple hundred of us, all told. They train us harder, tell us more. We're not necessarily the *best* swordsmen in the military, though we have to be good.'

'Then what makes you special?'

'We can be trusted, they know it. We have to be good at many things.'

'Like acting.'

Kiown smiled. 'Yes, O inn-finder. But believe it or not, I've been my real self the whole way through. Even around Anfen's band, and the other enemy bands I ran with. I was their ally as much as I could be.'

'But you never told anyone you worship Vous,' said Case.

Anger flickered across Kiown's face, and he fought visibly to bury it. 'It's not your fault. You just don't understand it. It's not merely the man I swear to. It's the *Project*. He's already halfway to being a Great Spirit. If *he* can, we *all* can, any one of us. They're going to watch the process, see how it's done, then repeat it. He's just the first, the experiment. It may happen in our lifetime or in our grandchildren's. Or tomorrow! They'll learn a lot when it does and perfect the process.

'And ah, what then? What happens if we find the step up from being a Great Spirit? The next rung on the ladder of greatness, of evolution? Sooner or later, we become so great we surpass the Dragon! One day, we make our own *worlds*. Perfect worlds. Imagine it. Don't dwell on what things must happen today — imagine that perfect future. That is what the Free Cities obstruct! Just what is the point in human lives scuttling about like the same old insects, asking and answering the same old pointless questions, living and dying, repeating it all, never reaching beyond?' His laugh sounded tired. 'You're new here, you old twit, you don't know our history. Since time began, since men began to play with magic, some of us wondered if it could be *done*, the grand elevation. But the magicians were too cowardly even to ponder it. Then after the War their stupid system didn't allow us to try, not properly. *Vous* was the one who outsmarted them. *He* was the one who dared get his hands red, risk his own life and others. He is a hero. You hear me? A hero.' Kiown turned his head Case's way, lip curled. 'You didn't know what you saw, when you looked on him. Yes, he's mad. Such visionaries have to be.'

Kiown began to stand. 'Stay there or you're dead,' said Eric quietly. Kiown sat back down, surprised, as though he felt his impassioned speech should have changed the situation. Eric said, 'You were to take us to Anfen. Now what do you propose?'

'To take you to Anfen. If you kill me or leave me here, do you think you'll find him? Especially with angry magpies on your tail, armies all over the roads? Grunt troops wouldn't know what to do with you. You talk strange, you look strange, you know nothing. They'd put you through the usual, beat confessions out of you or kill you. Grandpa here would not survive long as prisoner, believe me. And you don't look that sturdy yourself. Listen. Here's our plan. We stop off in Hane. We get fed, new clothes. See this?' Kiown thumbed down his shirt, showing his collarbone tattoo, which only appeared when he flexed the muscle there. It was a little tower, simply drawn of thinly inked red lines. 'I show this to my contacts, I get the resources of *any* Aligned city thrown open to me. Anything we want, take it. Women, food, rooms at the best inns. With me you are above the law. Your pick of the stores, the smiths. Fine clothes, swords better than that one. Can get us a horse-drawn wagon on loan, even drakes to ride, if you're game and if they have any. No more walking. We'll rest up a few days, live like princes, enjoy every second, then ride the rest of the way at our leisure. What say you?'

Despite what he knew, after all this rough travelling, the offer was more than a little tempting. 'Is lying one of the skills you hunters need to be good at?' said Eric.

Kiown waved this away angrily. 'Of course it is! But so is knowing when to tell the truth.'

'Then maybe you can admit what you did to the band you were meant to lead.'

Kiown spread his hands. 'Must you do this to me? Do you think all my orders fill me with joy? Fine, I did it. I helped kill the giant. Led the others to the patrol, who knew we came. Thanks to me they knew, all right? There. I betrayed them because my mission was compromised and I had to. It was not my idea of fun. Had Anfen not separated us it wouldn't have happened.'

A thread of magic like a crimson ribbon twisted languidly across the platform, passing through Kiown and parting around his body the way smoke would, some thin tendrils hanging for a moment around his neck and shoulders. Glimmering strands could be seen more thickly in the distant skies, but over towards the city, there were none at all. 'What about when we catch up with Anfen?' said Eric. 'What will you tell them?'

'Nothing,' Kiown snapped. 'Think I'll run with that group again? I'll get you close, point you to him then flee. You can tell him who and what I am, for all I care. I'll have done my mission, I'll be paid. I'll retire in the new cities, since I'll be known as a Hunter and never be able to go undercover again.'

'Something I don't understand,' said Case. 'It helps us out, sure, if you get us back with Anfen. Helps you out too. Even helps out your bosses. So *everybody's* happy. There are no mutually beneficial moves in chess. Who's worse off? You say the high-ups don't tell you everything, I bet you're right. But you know them better than us. So you can probably make a good guess.'

Kiown frowned, thinking. 'The Tormentors,' he said at last. 'The castle's trying to use Anfen. And you, I assume. How I've no idea. That's how two sides can be happy in war: when there's a third entering the fray.'

'Tormentors?' said Eric.

'You told me of monsters in the woods,' said Kiown. 'That's what they're called. Yes, I knew of them, but not what they look like, nor that they'd come so far north. I don't know how many there are. Maybe a few dozen. Or hundreds, maybe thousands. The castle bosses are scared to death of them. So should everyone be. But guess what? The Free Cities are in more immediate peril.'

'What are they? Where are they from?'

'I've never seen them,' said Kiown, shifting uncomfortably. 'They come from beyond the Wall at World's End. The castle fears the Free Cities will find a way to use them, maybe tame them as pets or soldiers. Both sides have lost men and resources to them.'

'Beyond the Wall,' Eric said, thinking aloud. 'So they come from the other half of Levaal even though the Wall stops everything *else* from getting through. So how do *they* get through?'

Kiown shrugged. 'Grandpa here told me to guess, so I'm guessing.'

'Keep guessing.'

'Fine. Underground. Far underground. There must be a point down there where things can pass *beneath* the Wall. In the groundmen tunnels, when Sharfy was oh-so-baffled at all the pit devils? I knew why.' He laughed. 'Something's entered the southern tunnels, something bigger and meaner than them. It's driving the devils north. And I tell you this, there must be a *lot* of those fuckers down there, to drive that many devils that far north. Now can we please end this chitchat and come to a decision? I've told you all I know. Whether you bring me along or not, time matters. Do you want a guide and protector or am I more useful to you as a corpse?'

42

Eric and Case went to the top of the winding steps, where Eric quickly told Case about the scales and visions. Kiown stayed put, hands linked around his knees, head slumped like he was defeated and lonely. Despite what he knew, a touch of pity stirred in Eric, to see that lively figure brought low like this. 'What do you think?' he asked Case.

'I won't lie to you, I never liked the sonofabitch. In that little talk he was being sometimes honest, sometimes not, but there's no knowing what part's not true. He's not telling us all we'd want to know, that's for damn sure. As for being treated like princes in that city, I doubt it. If I was in his shoes, I'd say that kind of thing. We can risk our lives to find out, if we want. I'll leave this one to you.'

Eric gazed at where the road wound past ahead, dividing just at the edge of sight, one part curling to the right, around the base of hillsides and towards Hane. He still saw streaks of colour glimmering on the wind, streaks of magic, and they kept distracting his thoughts. 'Can we trust the road if we're on our own, is the question.'

'We can try. Better than going to bed with a known snake,' said Case. 'With the charm and the gun, one of us is invisible, the other dangerous. Could be worse.'

'So. Here's the fun part, I guess. What do we do with him?'

Case chuckled grimly. 'When you tell me what you saw, he's led five people to their deaths. Five who made the mistake of trusting him, like we're talking about doing. If he gets one-fifth done to him of what he done to others, he's getting off lightly.' Case sighed. 'I'm willing to fire the shot. You decide if I should: you got more at stake here than me, more years of life to lose if we fuck up.'

Eric looked back at Kiown, who'd turned his head their way. Again he remembered what he'd seen in the vision, made himself see the betrayed, surprised look in the half-giant's eyes as he was killed. Hard to kill quickly, half-giants, and so much pain to go through before they finally died. Siel's accusing words came back to him, and in fact had never left him: *What do we have that they don't? What weapon, what tool to use, what thing to fall back on, what map to guide them are they missing?*

Survival — was that not a principle too? Justice ... would killing him not be just? And yet ... 'No. We won't do it. For your sake and mine, more than his. He's not worth carrying that burden for.'

'A shot to his foot, maybe. That way if he wants to follow us, it'll be hard work.'

'What about that rope tying up the grass bundles?'

'Better yet. Not a bad idea to save a bullet. Mind you, he says he's some crack trooper. Few knots won't stop him for long.'

Case's invisible hands expertly tying the knots was an eerie thing to watch, especially as little sections of rope vanished when grabbed and brought into the charm's spell. Kiown was co-operative enough, sensing that being bound meant he wasn't going to be slain. It seemed Case was right — the ropes wouldn't hold him long, for he didn't seem concerned about starving up here. 'Look after that sword,' he told Eric. 'Take the scabbard off me and keep it in there, out of the weather. And be warned — when I see you again, I *will* take it back, maybe with a finger or two.'

'You seem pretty sure you'll see us again,' said Eric, already doubting the wisdom of letting him live. He took the sheath from Kiown's belt and fixed it to his own.

'I was joking about the fingers, but not the sword. A very good smith made it and he's no longer alive. An Engineer, actually, though the sword's not magical. Look. I'll be honest with you. I *will* come and find you. But not for revenge. I have a mission, that hasn't changed. I must bring you safely back to Anfen. They — my bosses — don't like Hunters who fail.'

Case said, 'You can start by telling us which way the road forks ahead, down there.'

'Middle road goes to Elvury. That's where the Council of Free Cities meets. That's where you'll find Anfen, if you hurry. And if *he* makes it there. I am telling you, there are so many patrols right now you probably won't make it far without me. War mages, magpies, Lesser Spirits . . .' he sighed. 'As you like. I hope your luck holds. Stick to the main path but stay off road until you're out of Aligned country. The road's right fork goes to Hane. Stay away from there. The whole city is a prison and there's no food. Ah yes, you've seen woods full of nice meat running about, waiting for Siel to stick arrows in its butt, haven't you? No good if you're not allowed out to hunt it. If you're not with me you won't last long at all. Listen, the pouch on my belt. There's a green and a blue scale there. Worth more than the ones you have left, the green especially. My share from the dirt cart. Take them, they'll help you along. Take the coins too.'

Eric did so, knowing full well Kiown had expected them to rob him anyway. 'Very generous of you.'

'Isn't it? You can do something for *me* now, Eric. Please.

Something happened between this morning and last night. What was it? No one came up here and spoke to you. Or did they? It can't have been a scale vision Loup took you on, or you'd have been wary of me back at the inn. Did you have a vivid dream last night? Something else? Some device from Otherworld? Can you tell me how you knew?'

'Goodbye, Kiown. I'll look after the sword. Good to know there's something you care about. I won't even stain it with my companions' blood.'

'Was it Nightmare?' Kiown struggled in his bonds. 'OK, maybe I believe what you said, he reached down. He blessed you? Or did he just tell you what had happened? Come, you can tell me that much. I helped you get past the devils, remember? I helped you get here from the inn. That sword, those scales I gave you. Tell me!'

Eric and Case began their way down the steps, Kiown's voice eventually fading from earshot. They both held their palms to the tower's cool flank and tried not to look down, and the view gradually got less dizzying. On the road below, no soldiers passed, just a few travellers eager to keep their eyes low. Eric tried to see in these people any sense of the glory Kiown had expressed, any pride to lay just 'one brick' in the grand project. There was only weariness and fear.

43

Panting, they stopped. At last Faul had quit chasing. Luckily the company hadn't scattered too far — time spent fucking around finding people was the last thing Anfen needed.

The house was now just visible set against the northern horizon's whitening sky. Faul's booming threats and admonitions faded with distance as she ambled back there, weeping.

Anfen shook his head, watching her go. She'd had a long association with the Mayors' Command, and owed them far more allegiance than a dead Invia. That was surely something she'd remember soon, but once roused, giants did not quickly calm down and see reason. As it was, Anfen couldn't tell if Faul had really meant to catch them or just scare them away.

He sighed. The day had just begun and already he'd twice nearly been killed. At one time, such excitement would have stirred his blood with joy.

Siel had had the sense to stick close to Lalie. Good. Sense had been a touch lacking in this bunch, just lately. The girl looked cagey again, examining the surrounds like she was ready to bolt. She'd been lying low, he sensed, trying to lull them after the insult of being tied to the porch. They'd have to keep her tied from here on lest she stab them while they slept. She would already know how to kill, however young she was; Inferno cultists didn't go long without performing their first Offering. Nor did they change back to normal people overnight, if ever.

He counted heads. Oh, shit. 'Loup! Where are the Pilgrims?'

'Ehhh,' gasped Loup. He lay splayed on the ground, sucking deep breaths like he might soon expire from the run. And, just a second — who had the charm? Anfen did. He felt his pockets. Correction — he *should* have it. 'By Nightmare,' he muttered, sinking to his heels.

Loup sat up. 'You upset for the reason I think you are?'

'Why not try a scale vision and see?' Anfen walked off, running a hand through his hair. *That* had been part of this, he knew it, their games with visions. Idiots. In controlled conditions, their own lives at stake, they were welcome to their fun, not in Aligned country with the hornets' nest kicked. Sharfy should have known better. He *himself* should have, too; foolish, to think the band had meant it when agreeing to his rules … Calm down. It's done. Look forwards.

He'd look forwards all right, until they were safely at the Council of Free Cities. But he'd never trust this crew with any missions of importance ever again, and he'd warn the Mayors' Command not to either, if not get them brought up on charges.

'Far Gaze'll find them,' said Sharfy, referring to the Pilgrims.

'No, *we* will.' Anfen's voice was harsh as his anger threatened to boil over. It's all unravelling. Stay calm, or *they* won't. 'First we go back for the charm. It fell from my pocket during the fight.'

Whether or not Faul had meant to catch them last time, she *really* meant it this time. Lut was digging in the yard's stony turf with a shovel, making a grave for the Invia, whose body lay nearby under a draped sheet. 'COME TO ADMIRE YOUR

HANDIWORK?' Faul roared, thundering down the steps, dress rucking up around shins and knees like pillars as Siel neared the Invia's corpse.

As they'd planned, Siel being the fastest of them tried to lead Faul around while the others hid, but the half-giant's speed made it risky. If not for her head start, Siel would have been easily caught. Thankfully Faul, already puffed from the last chase, couldn't keep up her long-striding bursts of speed.

It bought Anfen just enough time to run past the ground where he'd fought the Invia — where he'd marched with relief to his own death, or so he'd thought at the time. The charm had to have slipped from his pocket there. He *knew* he'd taken it from the house.

Nothing but rocks and soil. Faul or one of the Pilgrims had taken it. It had to have been Case ... maybe he'd felt all along the charm was rightfully his. With so much at stake, all of history had been set on a different course thanks to one petty old man. Anfen could only sigh.

For hours they could ill afford they combed through the scrub, calling the Pilgrims' names and seeking tracks. The day was halfway through when they gave up, and Anfen, eyes nervously on the sky seeking shapes in the clouds, had no more time to search.

'I don't fathom it,' he said, despairing and trying not to show it. The group laid out their mats as night fell on an afternoon's travel. Two or three hours of sleep was all they could afford — another aspect of life on the road which was wearing very thin on him, as was needing to confide in a crew he was tremendously angry with. 'The old man wasn't happy with us, but Eric seemed an ally.'

'Eric was,' said Sharfy, sucking the smoke of a reed pipe then coughing horribly. 'If he wanted to leave, he had plenty of chances before today.'

'Better country to do it in, too,' said Siel. 'They won't last long here without a guide.'

'Perhaps the mage called Stranger will be their guide,' said Anfen. 'What did she have to do with this? And where's Far Gaze? Loup, is either of them close?'

'You keep asking, I keep telling. Neither's close,' Loup said sullenly. He sensed he was being blamed for much of this, 'unfairly' no doubt. 'Ain't been close since Far Gaze chased our Stranger into the woods. They're still dancing in there, I'd reckon. When mages that level get in a scrap it can go on a while. They get lost in the games and tricks of it. Powers they use start playing with *them*, not just the other way around.'

'One mage alive could give Far Gaze that kind of fight,' Anfen muttered.

'That you *know* of,' said Loup. 'But he *wouldn't* give that kind of fight. Why play around? He'd kill Far Gaze in a minute tops, dance on his bones. Then on to whoever's next to kill. You think he'd let a folk mage like Far Gaze roam free?'

'We know less of the Arch Mage than we think.' But Anfen knew Loup was probably right. Anfen had seen the Arch Mage up close, one of the only free men to have done so. He had taken personal orders from him, had felt the terrible gaze lingering on him from that half-melted mess of a face, the intensity of its mind weighing and considering him. He hadn't known much about the Arch Mage but even back then, not knowing half of what he'd soon learn of the castle and its designs, he'd known evil when he saw it. It had been the first seed of doubt: *this is the face of those you serve . . .*

'We'll see,' said Loup. 'If Far Gaze is still *alive*, we'll know Stranger's nothing to do with *him*, or the castle.'

'You may be right.'

'Sometimes I *am*,' Loup said bitterly. 'She's not him in a dress or disguise. I pondered *that* chance back at the hilltop when I first felt her close by. I know what *he* feels like to be near. And he doesn't leave his rat's nest to help out sworn enemies like you and me.'

'So you do believe she helped us?' said Anfen. Stranger *had* helped, it seemed ... but he badly wanted to speak with Far Gaze and know why he'd attacked her. On the other hand, mages were not renowned for their powers of reason ...

Loup said, 'She *tried* to help us. Far Gaze saw her starting casting and didn't trust her enough to let her.'

'Nor did I,' said Siel.

'Oh aye?' said Loup, now openly angry. 'I had no clue to that, young miss. I thought you lobbed *friendship* arrows at her. Old Case, he did right to give you that shove. And you got up wanting his head next, aye? It's always the *mages* you all don't like or trust. I warned you about that Kiown too. You'll see about him with time, mark me now.'

This nonsense again ... 'Kiown made mistakes,' said Anfen. 'But have you forgotten? There were times when he made the difference between life and death for us.'

'Pff! All show. And it was his own hide he was saving, not yours. You didn't see what I *saw*! Even if you don't think the vision's real, his mistakes've got us in a nice mess, all these patrols on the loose. You all still trust *him*, but find arrows for a mage.'

'Loup, hush,' said Anfen quietly.

The folk magician stormed off, rankled and muttering to himself.

'We're wasting sleeping time,' murmured Sharfy. 'Talk in the morning.'

Anfen closed his eyes, hoping his mind would stumble on the best course while it rested, as it often did. Yes, he'd had his doubts about Kiown too, had done for some time. What he'd said had been true: Kiown had shown nearly suicidal bravery defending the band, three times in particular standing out. Not always wise, but if a mission was dangerous, he was the first Anfen would choose. A 'vision' alone wasn't going to change that.

Getting to the Council, that was what mattered now. Damn them for taking that charm, he thought, trying not to give in to an inviting surge of despair. Without that charm in my hand, will the Mayors believe my account of its message?

Its impossible message: the Wall at World's End must be torn down. By all the Spirits, how?

44

They were already days behind their expected arrival in Elvury. Anfen led them south-west at a harder pace than they'd managed before, through shrouds of wood and plain fields. It was nice country, that way, picturesque, good soil and farm land, though the farms there were now the castle's. They passed them every so often, covered in huge glass-like domes, azure blue shells reflecting the world around them and hiding what went on inside. People of the cities never saw *that*, only ever (if they were lucky) the corn and maize and bread that were run underground on wagon trains like the one Kiown and Sharfy had robbed.

Sharfy had done a year-long spell on the slave farms, and never even found out what his original crime had been. Right under those impenetrable glassy domes people were being worked to death that very second. Not many escaped.

Sharfy remained silent until the domes passed behind the horizon. Every minute of his time there, the whole year of it, was imprinted on him like a tattoo. His own slave farm had been further east, its food bound for Ankin, the very place Vous's ascent had begun. But the farms were all much the same.

Like Anfen, Sharfy had been a proud servant of the castle's army. Like Anfen, he was *still* proud he'd chosen that honourable path, even if for the wrong lord. It wouldn't be honourable for long. Already signs showed these things had begun to change as the new generations were told to ignore Valour, that Vous was their Spirit of courage and honour now, that his values were of a superior kind. The battlefield wounded were no longer slain quickly, with respect and regret.

He remembered the endless raking, digging, hauling under that glassy blue dome, eighteen daily hours of it, sticks and whips randomly lashing down around the slaves as they went. He remembered hauling out the dead who'd dropped, starved and exhausted, and searching their pockets for handkerchiefs, forks, anything that could be traded for morsels of food. He remembered soup in the mess hall, funny stories traded in the barracks, untreated sickness, and hunger. *Real* hunger. The way starvation made a man entirely willing to kill his friend for literally a mouthful of gruel. He remembered bored overseers throwing two random slaves a kitchen knife each, ordering a fight to the death, whooping and yelling as they watched. Sharfy was sometimes picked for this, the ex-army slaves known for a good entertaining scrap. He never lost those duels.

He remembered the day's work done early and the commanders assigning pointless tasks to fill the time rather than allowing the slaves to rest in their shit-stinking, overstuffed cells. He recalled spotting his chance in the underground while loading a wagon with grain bound for one of the cities. He'd had to be quick. Was he good at hand-to-hand? Two overseers who'd made the mistake of relaxing on the job might have said so, if not for the pieces of nose bone lodged in their brains.

Such were Sharfy's thoughts as he stayed quiet on the way past the farms. He did not turn to look at them, and hoped never to see them again, but *someone* would, whether or not it was him, so what was the difference?

45

After days and nights of travel, Anfen had accepted he had the helplessness of a falling body.

He'd led castle armies through these very parts, subduing villages and militias, herding them back into Aligned cities where they'd be unable to leave, nor live so freely. He knew these lands well, had camped and hunted game in these lush green fields and scenic woods. Not far, there were places where, a few shovel-scoops deep, lay clusters of bodies just a few years dead, killed on Anfen's own orders.

Their orders, spoken through his mouth just as he began to doubt them. But he'd spoken them anyway, while at night he'd slept badly and pondered his course, the conclusion stalking him fast, however he ducked and hid from it in fear. Oh how he had feared that truth finding him, and had run from it, for he had already done so much in their name.

Danger wasn't the worst part of the road these days, Anfen realised; it was this, the long stretches of uneventful travel when he had no choice but to delve into himself, the last ten years eclipsing all of childhood before it so that he barely remembered more innocent and happy times. How he hated these thoughts, yet they were everywhere.

They pushed on as the countryside rolled by, crossing the

road only once, sticking to the hillsides where shells of home-
steads, newly burned or abandoned though they were, sat like
ancient ruins. Troops still moved south in worrying numbers,
as recent tracks and the not too distant thud of many passing
boots sometimes reminded them. What for? Why now? Elvury
was about to Align, Faul had guessed that first night as they
spoke privately. She'd 'seen signs', she said.

They had claimed before that Elvury would fall and been
wrong. The city was high up, easy to defend, and would be a
terrible fight for an invasion or siege. Many had learned this
the hard way, many good men sacrificed so some vain general
could attempt to go down in history as one of the greats, to
have taken the impossible city. It could be that such a general
had convinced Vous, the Arch Mage, or some other ruler lurking
in the castle's high halls, that it was time to try again.

Three days' march had gone uneventfully when they came
to a bandits' cave, tucked nicely away in woods noblemen had
used in the past as a venue for sport hunting, with corridors
through the widely spaced trees to allow horses. These woods
had been given over to Inferno cultists for a time, part of the
castle's plan to discourage life outside the protection of Aligned
cities. Anfen wanted to push on, but this hideout was the last
good shelter for many miles, as safe as anywhere they were
going to find before they reached the city.

Siel brought back two small pigs by the feet, arrows still in
their backs. She'd been gone a long time. 'Hard hunting,' she
said, dropping the pigs down. She began cutting off the meat
but they were scrawny ones. They cooked and ate, not asking
Loup to bless the food, for his mood had been volatile. Lalie's
too: she didn't like being tied like a dog and didn't like bathroom breaks while a minder watched, which Anfen thought
was reasonable enough. Just as reasonably, he didn't like Inferno

cultists on the loose with swords and knives around. Call it even.

He decided they would take an extra hour's rest tonight, given a possible war lay ahead of them. There were secret ways inside Elvury, even if it was under siege. Siel took the first watch, sitting at the cavern's mouth. Anfen dropped to sleep with as much ease as blowing out a candle.

Behind him, Loup had been perfectly secretive when stirring a tiny amount of black scale powder he'd filched from Eric's supply into a cup, with an inch or two of water, mixing it with his gnarled old finger, and swallowing it down. There was one choked snorting breath, then it looked like he was sleeping.

Anfen felt Siel's hand gently shaking him. An instinct on the road in bad country was to be instantly alert upon waking, sword to hand and drawn to swing in a heartbeat. But her touch, somehow, always felt like a friendly hand. He had never lain with her and would not. Nor did he think the offer was there; she knew she'd learn things about him that would make it hard to follow him, or respect him. Still, he was no stranger to the sight of her naked body, thanks to their hurried bathing in streams, and he longed for it the way he longed for meals or hot baths not available on the road. 'Nothing?' he said.

'Nightmare's out,' she whispered.

'Do you believe he's poor luck?' said Anfen, stretching.

'If so, he's a few days late, for us,' she said, slipping onto his mat so his warmth wasn't wasted. She was asleep very quickly.

Have we been unlucky? he thought. I doubt it. We've been very lucky despite ourselves. He went to the cave's mouth. Lalie slept curled in a ball. That girl looked so young and innocent when she slept . . . how her parents' hearts would have broken, if they knew where she'd ended up. Loup, who could cure others' snoring but who usually snored himself, was silent tonight, a small blessing. The breathing of deep sleepers, like lapping waves of air, made the cavern seem a peaceful cove, safe and sure: a most wonderful illusion.

Anfen leaned on the wall out front, a hand on his sword hilt. It was an old habit and a silly one, for he'd taken watch more times than he could count on these missions and only twice needed to draw a blade. Sharfy's watch traditionally brought trouble, something they joked about.

Ah yes, there was old Nightmare, off east, not far from Hane if he judged right. It had been a while since he'd seen that Great Spirit. He remembered when a low-ranked trooper, dared by friends, was lashed for firing up an arrow at Nightmare. The arrow of course hadn't even gone close, nor had Nightmare seemed to notice, though the story grew, as stories did on the road: Nightmare had turned his head their way, some claimed. Then his eyes had sparkled with malice. By the end of their march, some swore, and seemed to actually *believe*, they'd heard the Great Spirit speak.

Anfen smiled at the memory, though it was tinged with pain as well, for he knew many of those with whom he'd served, and had called friends, still served. Good men, still good men; that was the shame of it. Friends no longer. How our rulers betray us, and herd us like malicious shepherds. Is it the same in Otherworld? I must ask Eric, if we meet again.

Nightmare was still at the moment, an arm reaching down . . . an arm reaching down! Anfen watched with renewed interest. They'd never have tried to claim this, that old patrol, he thought. What did this mean? He tried recalling what he'd read in the scrolls and books he'd saved from burning, but little had been written in them of Nightmare; only the necromancers and ghoulish men of his cult could explain this.

So intently was Anfen watching the ghostly shimmering image, as Nightmare withdrew his arm and again began to drift, that he didn't notice the woman in her green dress standing some way down from the cave, watching him. A small amount of light radiated about her, making her stand out in the gloom. When his eye did find her, it was with a shock that sent chills through him. A moment later, she was gone. That was real, he thought. She's here.

Later, he would wonder: what was it that had made him draw his weapon and step out into the night without alerting the others? What instinct, what suicidal impulse — yes, he had them — what vain desire to be the band's hero? After berating the rest of them for their lack of sense, after reminding himself over and over of the importance of getting back to the Council of Free Cities with his news, why did he now unsheathe his weapon and walk out towards the place he'd seen her?

At that moment, though, he did not reflect on any of this. His actions felt natural, logical. He felt only the blade's grip in his hand and the calmness of his pulse, where years past had seen him intoxicated on far lesser danger than this. His pulse had been just as calm walking down Faul's front steps to face the Invia, all four eager to kill him.

The forest was made for hunting, the trees nicely spaced, the footing sure. She hid. His ears were keen, and they picked up little cracks and rustles in the growth. The army-issue blade was a poor one, but right now in his hand it was ready to deal her death, if she got near enough and made him do it.

'You may trust me,' her voice. A pleasant voice, reasonable. Trust you. Far Gaze did not.

She was there, near him, close. Too close. Did she not *see* his weapon drawn? Backhand, his wrist held straight, the sword lashed through the air and caught her midsection lightly. He was fast, his eye good, body poised a moment later for advance and another cut, feet moving with a dancer's speed, all instinct. Others had had to practise for years for these movements which had come to him naturally and so impressed his tutors. They had joked he must have been born with a sword in hand and cut the umbilical cord himself.

A sound passed her lips like a sigh through teeth. She leaped backwards, falling a step or two, then was gone from sight. 'You may trust me,' she said, a little strain to her voice now.

He could not quite locate her through her voice, but she wasn't far. *Keep her talking.* 'Did I wound you?'

'Scratched. My dress torn. There was dead stone on that blade, was there not?'

'Yes.'

'It must be why I misjudged my distance from you and came too close.' Her voice seemed now to come from several sides at once.

'Why are you here?' he said.

'There are things to show you.'

Anfen went carefully towards a thick tree trunk, pressing his back into it. 'There are things to tell me too.'

'Time's pressing. Ask, quickly.' Her voice was just ahead of him now.

'How are you here and casting while my mage rests nearby? He should sense you.'

'He is indisposed.' The knuckles gripping Anfen's sword tightened. She said, '*I* have done nothing to him. He is off on a vision.'

Fool!

She said, 'Don't be angered. He is seeking the Pilgrims, to help them.'

'And where are they?'

'I don't know. May I show myself?' She did so, a patch of shimmering green directly before him, a comfortable distance from the range of his sword. There was a neatly sliced line of fabric above her belly, two hand-lengths long. Her hand ran along the cut lightly. He found the sight of her long finger soothing to watch, the way it traced across the dress's slit. He made himself look away from it. He said, 'Do you wish to travel with us? Is that why you stalk my company?'

'I am more useful to you coming and going as I please. You aren't aware of the many ill things I have steered away from your path.'

Anfen's own thoughts echoed: Have we been unlucky? I doubt it. We've been lucky ... 'Where's Far Gaze?' he said.

'The wolf? He fled. I did not hurt him, though I could have — I am greater than he.' Anfen heard with perfect clarity what she didn't say: *I could hurt you, too.* 'He too seeks the Pilgrims, I believe, and means to bring them back. I wish he would believe that we are of the same purpose.'

'That remains to be proven. I know only that a trusted friend has treated you as his enemy, that you have stalked my company, and that the last time I saw you, trouble befell us.'

'I had hoped to prove myself that morning when the Invia came,' she said, face sad. 'There was not much time for me to do it. Arrows were fired, your trusted friend leaped for my throat. And you yourself are fast with a sword, Anfen. I'd not have liked to be an inch closer to you, just now.'

He looked her in the eye. 'I'm not sorry. You've been like a distant shadow. Your magic is powerful — my mage hardly believes what he's seen and heard. And you cast spells right on the castle lawns when all free mages have long been killed on sight. You are either in league with them, or you have abilities of a kind as yet unknown, even to those of us familiar with the old schools and their devices. Explain yourself.'

'You're right. It's best to show you. You will see what I am. It requires us to walk a short way. There is an underground tunnel, not far. There are castle soldiers down there, but they won't trouble us.'

Anfen shook his head. 'You can tell me what you are, here and now.'

She smiled. 'You have described it perfectly. I am a New Mage.'

He waited.

'The castle is producing more of us, this very moment. I escaped. Unlike me, the others won't be here to aid you. You are best to acquaint yourself with this new threat before you find your way to the Council of Free Cities, for it shall be dire. The more you know, the better you may deal with it, when the rest of the new mages are set loose.'

Anfen studied her face. She calmly met his gaze. It could not be denied: if she was as great as she seemed, she had the ability, if she wished, to kill him this very second with minimal effort. If *that* was her intent, why risk luring him to some other place to do it?

Luring him for capture? That was possible . . .

'How long would we be gone?' he said at last.

'An hour.'

46

The groundman hole wasn't far — groundmen had a knack for keeping them hidden in plain sight. As though reading Anfen's mind, the light about Stranger illuminated the ground around it so he could examine the way for those odd spiked tracks. Watching him do it, she said, 'I know what you fear.'

'And what can you tell me of that fear, Stranger?'

'For now only a little, as we will soon risk being overheard.' They crawled down through the tunnel, its rock walls bare of lightstones. Stranger lit the way with the green gleam about her, otherwise the tunnel would be purely dark. '*Tormentors* they were named by survivors of the mining station wiped out by them. Apparently no written record of the creatures exists. They play with time, they come from beyond World's End. Some are small — man-sized — some huge. A few small ones, an army patrol could perhaps handle, with some deaths. The large ones are . . . a different matter.'

'And what do we do about them?'

'You, I am unsure. I will tell you what the castle is doing about them. Us.' She pointed to herself.

'New mages?'

'Yes. And if the new mages succeed in destroying all the Tormentors, what do you suppose their next task will be?' She let that sink in. 'We are an old project of theirs. So for how long have *they* known of Tormentors? But we must be silent, now. The tunnel walls are thin here, and castle guards are on the other side.'

It was clear they'd be gone longer than an hour, for at least half that time had passed before Stranger gestured to halt. She felt the rock wall with her hands, seeking a secret door, then found it. It appeared she stepped head first into stone that swallowed her up, for that section of wall was illusion, nothing but air. She kept an arm protruding through it to guide him in.

Soon, with greater frequency, voices could be heard to either side of their tunnel. Then the passages widened out and the walls' lightstones were thick, large slabs. This was a thoroughfare commonly used, for military bric-a-brac lay here and there, and signs had been put on the walls with stern written orders and warnings. Small statues and portraits of Vous were everywhere the eye fell. Even as they watched, a man in leathers marched past and paused to wipe dust off the shoulders of a statue which showed the man's Friend and Lord grim-faced on a drake, with a spear in hand, brass eyes staring at the horizon, seeing further than any mere man could . . .

Other tunnels led off away from this passageway to more secretive places, the entrance of each barred by iron lattice with heavy locks. After making certain no one was around to see them, Stranger ran out into the open and Anfen followed. Between two barred tunnels she found another secret wall, and again the rock seemed to swallow her.

Anfen knew they were heading for places not well known to the common soldiery, or to anyone else but a select few, despite the troops traversing past those very secret places day to day. He also knew he would *not* find his way back through these winding tunnels to the surface without Stranger's help, which began to worry him. Every ten paces, he now gouged little marks with his sword's tip in the rock wall. If Stranger noticed this, she didn't comment.

Finally they came to a lightless tunnel angling downwards to a dead end. A secret door was doubtless let into the rounded back wall, or else she'd chosen this to be the place of his death. The air was warm and stuffy.

Stranger turned to whisper, 'It is just ahead of us. It's safe to talk in there, as long as no guards come. The mages may hear your voice, may even react to it, but they won't recall it any more than a sleeping person would.'

He wiped sweat from his brow. 'Mages?'

'You will see. They won't be able to harm us. They won't even see us, though their eyes may be open.'

He nodded. 'Let's hurry. We've been longer than you promised.'

'Yes. I'm sorry.' She felt the dead end for its secret door. Not only was it well hidden, it was just big enough to crawl through, likely put there by groundmen when they alone owned these tunnels. Anfen struggled to fit, Stranger's feet just before his face. It wasn't lost on him that she'd exposed her back to him in these dark tunnels, especially after she'd already felt his blade's edge. *I trust you*, it meant. *Do you trust me?*

The lightstones were tinged golden in the large cavern opening up before and beneath them. At first he thought she'd brought him to a prison, for down below, on the rounded walls, people were fixed in place with some kind of shackle. Men, women, all naked, their heads slumped forwards on their chests. None spoke or moved. A horrible smell filled the air: the way hair smells when it catches fire. Stifling heat rose from below, the air hard to breathe.

Stranger gazed down there, seeking guards, and held up her

hand: *don't move, quiet.* One of the castle grey-robes passed along the rounded wall, moving from one of the shackled bodies to the next. In one hand was a bucket, the other held a sponge with which he cleaned the prisoners. The grey-robe — under some sort of mind-control spell, by the way he moved — didn't spend long on each before moving on. Soon his task was done, and he left the chamber through a secret door, the wall seeming to swallow him. Stranger whispered, 'Now, go.'

A ledge ran down to the ground from below where they stood, though it was a perilous jump to land on it. Nimble as a cat, her leap made it look easy. Anfen glanced down — the drop wouldn't kill him, but broken bones were likely, followed by certain capture. 'As It wills,' he muttered, and leaped not quite as nimbly, his boot slipping when he landed, and only Stranger's grip stopping a painful slide down the slope on his butt. Their scuffing feet seemed very loud in the chamber's oppressive silence.

The stink was worse as they went lower. The bodies were trapped not by chains or shackles; many parts of the wall were covered in what looked like large war mage horns curled around the prisoners' arms, ankles, knees and feet, like long pinching claws. From some angles, the illusion was that a cruel inhuman hand held them in place. They were young people, late teenage perhaps, ranging up to mid-twenties. All had their eyes shut, faces blank. If they breathed, their breaths were too shallow to move their chests.

The horns that gripped them were dark in colour, black or deepest red. It was these that made the cavern's air like that of an oven, though the bodies' skin showed few burn marks. Those horns that hung spare, like unused shackles dangling in a cell, seemed not to be 'switched on' like the dark ones; they were the same dull hue as those on a war mage that hadn't cast for a while. No heat emanated from them.

Stranger watched him examine it all. He looked to her, knowing now that she had been here, on the wall like these unfortunates, yet was somehow freed. Again, she seemed to read his face. 'One of the guards liked to use my body, from time to time,' she said matter-of-factly. 'Mine and others. The bodies can be removed and set back a while later, and not awoken. That time, he took too long. I woke.'

Anfen nodded, not needing to ask what had become of the guard in question. The curling hot mage-horns seemed to be growing *into* the flesh of those bodies nearest, though the wounds were bloodless, as if the horns were now a part of them. 'These people cannot be easily removed, it appears,' he said. 'I assume your escape was early in the process. Do these horns give them their power? Is this how you were given yours?'

'Yes. They alter mind as much as body. This process usually kills; most don't survive it. I probably wouldn't have, if not for the guard. I am also probably the first to live. The mind control is the hard part, from what I've learned ... some early experiments lived with my powers or greater, but no thoughts in their mind to wield them. They sat drooling. Perfectly useless bodies. The castle will be lucky if four or five of these live to become mages. Maybe none. But they learn more each time they try.' She gazed around at the bodies along the curved wall and sighed. 'The point is to stretch the human ability to endure what greater magic does. The horns also teach spells, making them as instinctive as moves of your swordplay, no longer a need to compose as you cast the traditional way. I emerged early, so I know less than these ones will, if they make it out alive.'

'How many more caverns such as this?'

'There's no telling,' she said quietly. 'I know of four.'

'How great will these be, as mages?'

'Imagine a war mage who can cast for an entire day, or longer, unhindered by the burn.'

'Burn?'

'Magic's poisonous effects. It has other names, as you'd know. These casters will have all of a war mage's destructive abilities, with more creativity and more sanity.'

'Like you.'

'Greater. Spells of disguise, illusions, mind control, necromancy, happenstance, elements. What's more, they'll get great use out of only small amounts of power; if the airs are weak, it won't matter as much. Their bodies store it.' Her hand touched the cut Anfen's sword had made in her dress. She lifted the material and Anfen saw something hard and crusted below, which her fingernail tapped on like wood. It took a moment for him to recognise that part of her skin was made of the same material composing the shackles burrowing themselves slowly into these prisoners' bodies.

'It's why I have no horns,' she said. 'Not on my head, anyway. You can hide from war mages in cities, where magic is thin or gone altogether. What if they take a store of magic in with them? There'll be no hiding from New Mages. All of them utterly blind and fanatic with loyalty to the castle.' Seeing his look, 'Oh yes, there is great emphasis on *that*. It is also part of the process I escaped.'

Anfen imagined it and it filled him with dread. And yet . . . 'It would make these magicians greater than the Arch Mage, if I judge right. Does it not seem strange to you that he would create underlings greater than him?'

'I do not claim to know how his mind works.'

'How long until they complete their research?'

'I know only that it's not complete yet.'

When it was, there would be little need for soldiers or armies. A hundred such mages and there would be no real answer. But it was the cruelty of it that sickened him, the heat, the smell of burning flesh. Not that it surprised him. He wondered how many had died, painfully and slowly, as the castle, completely indifferent, experimented and learned. 'You're brave, to return here.'

She smiled, though her eyes showed little of it. 'We're both brave. We should not tarry here long. They come through every so often to clean the bodies and push pellets of food into their mouths.'

'Thank you for showing me this.' He turned to her, wanting to put a hand on her shoulder in comfort, but for some reason feeling he should not, not down here. 'Are you sure you don't wish to journey with us?'

'No. Thank you for the offer and for your trust. But I will remain at a distance. And I will help you as I can. Let us depart.'

'Not just yet, please.' Anfen gazed around at the bodies, counting them: forty. 'How long have these ones been here? How soon until they are freed? How long were you held?'

She shifted uncomfortably. 'I remember little. Only that I was one of those who came from the cities to the castle seeking work, as my parents wished. I was accepted, my aptitude tested. They took those who had magic talent. I had much — I knew it before they tested me. They sent coin and a letter full of lies to my parents, brought me with a few others underground, and that's where memories fade.' Her eyes closed. 'Or, at least, change. Please, let us go.'

'And these ones, you say, will be of different inclination from you, if they survive to become New Mages? They are certain to be a threat to the Free Cities?'

She frowned, watching him carefully. 'Yes. When this process is complete, they will be unable to do anything other than serve the Arch Mage.'

'Even if we free them now?'

'There is no way we can. Your sword will not break their bonds.'

'Are you *absolutely certain* all that is so?'

'Yes.'

Anfen nodded. He drew his sword.

She looked at him, eyes wide. 'What are you doing?'

He looked back, surprised at her. 'You have told me yourself, this is a threat awaiting us.'

'Please. Some of these were with me at the castle gates. Some were my friends. They were just like me. Their parents think they are spinning wool or learning trades.'

'I am sorry, Stranger. Such is war. Look away if it distresses you.'

'*Don't . . .*'

He didn't look back at her, did not wish this moment or this act to be extended. His arm moved, that was all, and he distanced himself from what it did, made it a mechanical thing, a killing machine. He made himself distant from Stranger's blazing, hateful eyes, glaring at him with — he imagined — heat as strong as that coming from the claws embedded in the walls. How shocked he'd have been by the change in her just then, had Anfen really been present in the room as his arm lashed out and killed, rather than watching it all from a safer distance, and trying to bury the memory even as it occurred, to make it meaningless sounds and blurs of colour.

The poor souls trapped in the Arch Mage's embrace did not make a sound. Anfen's sword thumped against the stone wall behind them with impersonal regularity. Finally the last of them was dead. Sweat poured from him and he felt dizzy, wanting a drink of water more than anything else. He felt Stranger's rage, felt it seething. She could kill me, we both know it, he thought, as Anfen returned to himself.

'We may be allies,' she said, 'but from this moment, we will never be friends.'

Anfen cleaned his blade as best he could. He looked at her sadly. 'As It wills.'

47

As they headed back through the tunnels in the ghostly glow of lightstones her mood cooled, and she finally broke her silence. 'I had hoped to win them over, when they were freed.'

'Yet you told me that was impossible.'

'I thought I alone could do it. I, who knew where they had been and what they'd been before. Of course I couldn't promise you success.'

Anfen would have liked to put that memory in the place he kept all the others, where other blood had been spilled in such fashion. Yet part of him was glad for the chance to explain it this time, to reconcile his arm mechanically slaying with a mind that knew its purpose, and (this time) stood by it afterwards. 'How well do you know history, Stranger? How well do you really know *them*? The ones who put those people in that cavern. And put you there.'

She didn't answer. The caverns echoed with the phantom *drip drip* of unseen water, though Anfen now imagined it as blood. He spoke quietly. 'Did my arm seem practised to you, just now? Professional? Do you know that I have had to do that sort of thing before? Only not to people little more than suffering bodies. And not to those who will soon be a powerful weapon in evil hands. I have overseen the slaughter of entire *villages* of people deemed trouble, or inconvenient, or simply in the way of some construction and refusing to move from their land. Sometimes it seemed they were killed for no reason at all. I executed with my own hands wise people who owned forbidden books, who practised folk magic. Some of whom *did* do foul things, rituals of sacrifice and perversion. But mostly others, whose crime was to cure their children of fucking *colds*.'

Easy. Easy. Detach. Breathe.

A swirl of dizzying thoughts spun through him and his knees felt weak. Funny — no, plain incomprehensible — that all the while Anfen and his men had done it all believing, honestly *believing*, that these pitiful clinging remnants of the old world *did* present a threat to the castle's great strength. Small-time folk mages like Loup, farmers, refugees from Aligned cities who'd banded up for one last stand. Their tenacity, their bravery ... he'd thought himself charitable, as an opposing commander, to recognise it and grant them mercy where he could, a swift kill, ordering his men against rape and plunder. *Drip drip* went the phantom echo between their scuffing footsteps.

'I know the history better than you may think. Keep your voice low,' Stranger replied.

It was indeed the last thing either of them said for a while, as muttering voices could soon be heard in passages beside theirs. In silence she led him back the way they'd come, illuminating the way with her green light when the dark grey walls were free of lightstones.

The walk it seemed would never end, but Anfen watched that too from a distance, while his tired legs propelled him along, mouth and throat dry as sand, body sick with what he'd done, his consciousness hidden in a small quiet corner of his own mind.

'Maybe you were right, back there,' Stranger said as they neared the surface at long last. 'Maybe it was necessary. I know it was hard for you. I take back what I said.'

He barely heard her. He was exhausted, as though he'd just marched for days straight, not two or three hours. He found his way back through the woods, not even noticing at what point Stranger parted from him, nor caring. It was still night, well past someone else's turn to take watch. Anfen woke Sharfy and murmured, 'Another hour, then wake me and we leave.'

'Where you been?' said Sharfy, smelling the sweat of Anfen's exertions and watching the speed with which he emptied a full skin of water. Anfen waved the question away and dropped onto the mat Sharfy had vacated.

48

There was no point chastising Loup for taking another scale vision; they had four days' march ahead, less if they really laid boot to road, and having the folk mage storm off, disgruntled, was very likely a death sentence. There were elementals between them and their city, perhaps even Lesser Spirits, and Loup would make sure they avoided them.

'We had a visitor,' Anfen said to Siel and Sharfy as morning set in and they set out in the woods. He'd debated whether or not to tell them about Stranger, and decided he'd better, lest Siel put an arrow through their new ally, or lest he be killed and news of 'new mages' never reach the Mayors. They listened to his account of last night without interruption.

'So she's our *friend*,' said Sharfy, clearly not convinced.

'I deem her such. I do make mistakes. But she had ample time to kill me. And she may have wanted to. She did not enjoy my actions in the cavern. Yet she led me through guarded tunnels safely, and back. If she is in league with the enemy, she passed up a chance to deliver them their most hated defector.'

'You need more sleep than you got,' said Siel.

'Welcome to the road,' he said, a stock reply to complaints among soldiers about rations, foot sores, tiredness. But she was right. This campaign was draining him, this *life* was draining him, and no pleasant idle retirement waited at its end. Only this war, sure to last more than *his* lifetime, unless the castle won it sooner. Then oblivion.

Welcome to the road. When they came to a village, Sharfy's scales bought horses and the villagers' promise of silence, should they be questioned. Though Lalie had never ridden before and had to share a steed with Siel, they made good speed for Elvury, only the Elemental Plains between them and baths, beds and proper meals, the mountains already rising in the distance.

They spotted an elemental in the far distance on their second morning on the plains, just a ripple of disturbed air like a tiny cyclone moving in fast lurches, but it didn't come closer and their luck held. Stranger? Anfen wondered. Loup claimed she no longer followed, but he didn't believe it. Their crossing the plains was filled with peace that seemed miraculous.

They prodded Sharfy for war stories, of which he had no shortage, nor a shortage of delight in telling them. Anfen allowed himself to be lost in their fiction, and noted the numbers of dead left in a trail behind Sharfy's heroics had increased from the previous telling. Sharfy was unaware that humour was the appeal; he felt the stories were swallowed whole and that his listeners' admiration for his great deeds was genuine, even as they jested. They didn't know his newest story had borrowed pieces of its plot from a *Batman* comic, but for that matter, nor did he . . .

The plains became foothills. They encountered no one but saw in the distance a few tribal nomads, the rare dark-skinned kind who conversed with elementals and took great pains to avoid other human company. The mountains soon loomed over them like an enormous frozen wave, slabs of blue high on the horizon's white sky. They paused to bathe, then fished for an hour in the River Misery, catching only two small things not even worth filleting, until it occurred to Loup to bless their lines and bait. Minutes later, Sharfy pulled a fat black dirtfish from the water, flopping sluggishly on his hand-held line. Anfen caught a bigger one moments later (Sharfy needed many measures to be sure of it), but they'd wasted too much time here, and headed onwards again, muttering under their breaths in exasperation. 'Good eating, dirtfish are,' said Loup, oblivious. 'Oh aye, if you cook em right.'

At last the land began to climb, building to the ranges that acted as Elvury's shield from assault. If a war brewed there, or if it had begun, they would begin to see signs of it soon. By now, it was almost certain that the looming hillsides were thick with Elvury's hidden lookouts, who watched them approach with arrows fixed. To the group's chagrin, Anfen led them by a path that lengthened the trip by several hours, but also gave them a good look at the road leading to the city. And soon the mystery of the south-marching armies was partly revealed when they rounded a bend on the high shoulder of the sheer cliffs, looking down at where the road led into the mountain pass.

Masses of troops were gathered in the fields and plains just beyond the road, the only way to the city from the north. With good reason, they had not ventured through it; a few hundred well-positioned defenders could make deathly hell for even a large passing army like this; a man-made avalanche to trap them in the pass could be the opening hand played. From there, target practice.

From this high up, the soldiers seemed to swarm like insects over the fields, wearing the colours of many Aligned cities, and some the castle's own uniform of course. It was nowhere near what they *could* send, if they dug deep for numbers, but it was a big enough force to be gathered in one place — a little scooped from each pool of soldiers, so as not to leave any single Aligned city's defences weak. Supply trains could be seen even now making their way from the road to the encamped masses.

Anfen knew what kind of effort such a gathering would take in organisation alone. This would not have been done without strong purpose. Though if it was a siege unfolding . . . 'No catapults,' said Sharfy. 'No siege towers. No machinery at all.'

'Yet they have this bunch sitting here, who must be fed and kept disciplined, who must forgo bathing unless it rains, who must shit in the fields and grumble about being away from their wives. All while anticipating a charge to their own deaths. And they surely don't have forces at the southern gates. So what is the point?'

As they went through the hidden paths carved high above that lethal stretch of road to the city, there were indeed defenders in place and, by their bustling activity and the tension in the air, they expected something to happen soon. Many knew Anfen's face, and he knew the words to grant his group passage. 'How long have the forces been there?' Anfen asked a passing commander.

'First group, a week ago. Building since.' The commander rushed away, a trail of nervous teenage archers behind him.

'A week!' Anfen said in disbelief. 'They could not have set this up better for a complete massacre of their own men. They gave the city a *week* to prepare?'

'Vous is mad,' said Sharfy simply.

It was true, but . . . 'His Generals and Strategists are *not*. The worst we could do is assume all this happens on a lunatic's whim, however it looks. Something foul rides on the wind here.'

At last, there were the walls of the city: high turrets pocked with silhouettes of archers, and gaps in the wall and gate likewise occupied all the way down, sometimes up to twenty men on a ledge, all with a great view of the road below. Any invaders who did survive a march between the mountains would be welcomed with a terrible storm of arrows, spears, weighted nets, boulders and more. If they meant to go through with this, maybe it really *was* lunacy, simple lunacy.

There were secret upper tunnels into the city for those coming from business in Aligned country. The group were inspected by border troops, strip-searched, quizzed, threatened. All expected and endured without complaint, but there was a tense hysterical tone to it all and, inside the city, that same charged atmosphere filled the air. Armed men in big numbers milled about the gates inside, the air rife with the clash of swords as they sparred, the burble of their talk like a noisy sea.

The secret way opened out to a high ledge which ran around the entire rim of the city like the top edge of a giant bowl. Many of the important buildings were up on this shelf, safely away from the charge of potential angry mobs, a lesson history had taught past city rulers the hard way. The streets below teemed with what *looked* like business as usual: the normal massive swarm of people through the trading Bazaar, itself the size of a small city. This was the rich city's economic hub, the home of its tradesmen and guild halls.

Anfen knew, as did the Council of Free Cities, that in those bustling crowds were spies in the castle's employ. He gazed down there as they marched the last few steps of their journey, wondering just how many there were, feigning the life of ordinary citizens, quietly working their way up the city's political ladder, eyes keen for Elvury's weak spots, sending reports off in secret. How many were assassins waiting for their assigned targets and orders? Anfen knew he would now be at the top of their hit lists.

The young guard guiding them to their inn sent someone to alert the Mayors of Anfen's arrival. 'The Mayors were making ready to depart,' the guard explained. 'Gave you up for dead, methinks.'

'They weren't far from being right,' said Anfen.

'That's the road, eh? Much trouble?' The gleam in the young guard's eye said he longed for such missions too. It was the same eagerness for war and spilled guts many young soldiers felt, tavern stories ringing loud in their ears, until their first real sight of it up close.

Anfen saw part of the young man's face slip off and spill down his shirt with a trail of dark blood. 'Much trouble,' he sighed, too weary to impart any kind of wisdom. It would all find him, soon enough.

At the plush inn reserved for high officialdom, Lalie was taken aback at all the luxury on offer — the food, hot baths, musicians, steam rooms and massages. 'This is your reward,' he told her, 'for your loyalty. You have been a good companion to us. More of this awaits you, if you help us further.' It was a lie — she had been a surly companion, adding greatly to their tension, needing to be tied and constantly watched, lagging further behind in pace at times than Loup, who at least had the excuse of age. But he needed her to tell her tale to the Mayors. For that matter, he had to tell his own, and he had too little time to prepare it before another messenger came to summon him to them.

49

There were six Free Cities, yet seven Mayors sat around the crescent-shaped table, in a discreet cabin built beyond the noise of the Bazaar's dinnertime bustle far below. *Discreet* was important with so many prominent targets gathered in one place. The city's lights burned bright outside the high window, stretching further than the eye could see. Plates of delicacies were laid on the table before the Mayors, mostly ignored. After weeks of rabbit stew, jerky, foraged roots and other such fare, Anfen had a powerful urge to walk over and crudely stuff his face with the cold meats, cheeses and berries.

It took him a moment to comprehend why seven Mayors were here: ludicrously, the 'scattered peoples' had finally gained a vote in Council affairs. At least the man was not introduced as a Mayor; rather, as 'spokesman' for a couple of millions spread across vast distances, from little groups of nomad wanderers to the large fishing villages about the Godstears, themselves not far from status as city-states in their own right. To top it off, the spokesman came from High Cliffs, which already had its Mayor at the table. Anfen did not show his displeasure at this idiocy, for inter-city politics was not his trade, but he thought he sensed similar displeasure in a couple of the Mayors when the 'spokesman' was introduced.

All the other faces he knew, bar one. Tsith had sent their Mayor's advisor, not their Mayor, doubtless another sore point for those about the crescent-shaped table. And another obstacle for Anfen, if this matter went to vote; a Mayor's advisor could not commit his city to something as extreme as destroying the Wall at World's End. *It may be your Mayor is too old and ill to make the journey here,* Anfen thought angrily. *That means it's time for your city to get a new Mayor.*

The Tormentor's arm was in a bag by Anfen's feet. A few curious eyes turned to it and invited explanation, even as they waffled on through pointless formalities. He sat heavily on his chair well before they'd finished, a slight breach of protocol earning him a sternly cleared throat from the Mayor of Faifen. *If she begins to swoop around the room like an Invia, consider me chastised,* he thought sourly.

'A long journey?' said Ilgresi, Elvury's Mayor. A smile creased his cheeks, though his eyes, black and blind as two rocks, showed nothing.

'I thought we could cut through some of the—' he'd almost said *nonsense* '—niceties, given the forces building up on your doorstep, Mayor.'

'Ah yes. Have you been informed of the latest?' said Ilgresi, smiling with real mirth. Anfen wished the man wouldn't, for his teeth were metal and as black as his eyes.

'No, but I saw the build-up on my way here, some hours ago. Ten thousand, I'd have guessed it.'

'A siege, you'd have thought?' said the Mayor.

'But for the lack of artillery, yes.'

'And the lack of force at our southern gate! But it may be they mean to send some there. After all, they asked us for passage.'

Anfen blinked. 'Ridiculous. Passage to where?'

'Ah, that's what they do not wish to tell us! They have asked us — their messenger straight-faced — to allow them through the pass, then through the eastern roads skirting the city walls. Which, as It wills, gives them access to our southern gate.'

'What do you think of this?' said Liha, leaning towards him. The Mayor of Faifen, she was the only woman present.

'I don't know what to think,' Anfen answered, knowing full well they'd have had every angle of this discussed already with their best and brightest — why bother asking *him*, unless there was some implied test of loyalty or competence in it? 'It could be the request was to buy time, or they're overstocked with soldiers and wish to cull some on a suicidal mission, and measure your strength into the bargain.'

'It would also make veterans of our forces,' said Ilgresi, shrugging: *let them*. 'Our army is a young one. It would be good for them.'

Anfen groaned inside. Good for them, to participate in a massacre? Good for them, how? Do you think they thirst for the sight of spilled blood and cracked heads? Will getting it help them sleep at night? Tipping big rocks down a cliff face and lobbing arrows down a valley at helpless targets is not combat.

He saw his thoughts echoed on two other faces before him, the two Mayors who'd seen combat themselves, and knew it as more than an abstraction. One of them — Tauk, another former winner of Valour's Helm and Mayor of Tanton — said, 'Their actions will tell the story. So far they do not turn about and take a longer road ... rather, they wait and more forces come. Now let us hear Anfen's news. He has had a long journey and we prolong it.'

Anfen said, 'One question. You sent Far Gaze after me. May I ask why?'

'To see you were still alive, and to guide you back, if you needed it,' said Tauk, his look indicating he told most of the truth, but not all. 'We were due to depart — our cities don't run themselves. The ambitious ones will be clearing their throats for speeches. I'm sure my capture and death are already common knowledge.' The other Mayors chuckled. 'I trust your tale will explain why Far Gaze isn't with you now.'

They were largely quiet as he told them what had occurred since he set out. The base directly under the castle had failed, thanks to the groundmen, though Anfen had expected little different setting out — this despite having freed a number of their slaves as a gesture of good will, and despite enormous bribes. He could see by the Council's faces they would send him, or someone, back to try again. He reported success in mapping out some of the tunnel sections close to the castle, even directly beneath it, for they'd found a staggering amount of underground space apparently unknown to the castle, near the entry point to Otherworld.

Which brought him to the Pilgrims. That part of the tale got them interested. A hundred questions were ready to leap from their mouths, he saw. He told them all they *needed* to know, and was annoyed at their fascination with trivial things: the Otherworlders' personalities, dress styles. He held up his hands. 'Please. Time wastes. It was the charm I found with Case you now need to hear of. It was given to him by the Invia, who then placed him in the castle's high towers.'

That got their even closer attention. He held it too, telling them with as much conviction and detail as he could what he'd seen on the charm: the conversation between Vous and the Arch Mage, the Arch Mage's fear of the Wall's destruction, his apparent fear of a 'plot' to destroy the Wall. But Anfen also saw on the Mayors' faces scepticism and doubt.

'We will vote on this business with the Wall,' said the Mayor of the other 'Great' Free City, Yinfel. 'You've more to tell, I'd venture? Is it time yet to show the contents of that bag at your feet?'

Anfen had had trouble getting it past the guards. He undid the satchel's buckles. Inside it was the Tormentor's hand, like twisted threads of dark glass rope wound into muscle and covered in spikes. It had stopped twitching only two days prior and had shrunk a little, but the spikes of its fingers were still sharper than daggers. Anfen demonstrated this by digging it fingers-first into the floor at his feet.

He said, 'And now, it's time for you to meet Lalie. She waits outside. Shall I bring her in? I may as well tell you now, she is an Inferno cultist. I use present tense as she's not yet repented in my hearing.'

That also got their attention. Izven, Mayor of the one city in the world which allowed Inferno cultists to dwell within its walls, looked around at the others' reaction and shook his head as though baffled by it. 'Well yes, bring her in!'

'And make her very welcome,' said one of the others sarcastically. Izven, in his own opinion clearly more enlightened than they, rolled his eyes. The others smiled at his expense.

Lalie seemed not to know whether to snarl at the Mayors with her teeth bared, or to shyly say nothing and hide her face behind her hands. For their part, they stared at her baldly and waited. Anfen had tried to groom her for this, on top of all else he'd had to prepare, but it seemed that job had been poorly done. When she saw the Tormentor's hand sticking up from the floor, she yelped and turned to run. Anfen grabbed her.

'Come now,' said Izven, smiling kindly at her — and he *did* have a kind face, alone among the Mayors: a small, soft-looking man who looked like he belonged among books, not planning wars. 'You need not fear. I will bring you with me to Yinfel, where we have some of your people. There are rules, of course. Some rituals are not permitted within our walls, nor with our citizens, but you will not be hurt.'

The others rolled their eyes at this; yet another sore point, for no Yinfel law prevented the cultists using people of *other* cities in their rituals. After some more coaxing, Lalie told them what had happened.

Said the Mayor of Faifen, 'It may be painful to you, dear, but what about their method of killing? I see the sharpness of its hand, but what makes them any worse than, say, men with swords?'

'Everything slows down,' Lalie said quietly. 'It's like you're stuck in mud.'

'Just by being near them?'

'Not exactly. One reaches for you, and you run. But your legs feel very slow, and so does everything around you.'

'And they move fast, while you move slowly?'

Lalie shut her eyes in concentration, remembering. 'No ... *they* move slowly, too. Time all jags around, fast, slow, so you lose balance too much to fight back or hide. And when they pull you apart and cut you to pieces, they do it slowly. But if you watch them do it to someone else, it looks normal speed.'

'How do you know that? You seem unhurt.'

'One reached for me. It hadn't finished with the one it was already killing. I kind of ... kind of slipped into ... what seemed like a bubble of weird time. It did it slowly, just cutting him apart, and he looked like he could feel it all, over a long time—' She didn't finish.

'How did you survive, dear?'

Lalie didn't meet their gaze. 'The High Priest was a big man.

I was . . . I was his favourite. He saw it go for me, and he swung an axe and surprised it. He cut off that.' She pointed to the hand sticking from the floor. 'It killed the High Priest. But since it had only one hand left, the High Priest wasn't as badly cut up as the others. There was enough of him left for me to . . . hide amongst his . . . his carcass.' She swallowed. 'I crawled in—'

'That's enough, dear, that's enough. We see.'

They sent her out, leaving Anfen to tell them of the new mages, reliving his own trauma for their questions and clarifications, just as Lalie had. Said Ilgresi, 'Our thanks, Anfen. May we have a summary of your thoughts before you leave us?'

If he hadn't been so worn from the road, he would have made this speech impassioned and rousing, he knew. But he'd spoken for a long time now, and his voice sounded hollow and tired to his own ears, and, he was sure, to theirs. He said, 'I believe we have found something that could turn the course of history. The castle rulers have one great fear. Thanks to the Invia and the Pilgrims, we have learned what it is. The Wall at World's End must come down. I don't yet know how, but from the Arch Mage's own tongue, it *can* be done, and it fills them with dread. We will find a way to do it, if we combine our minds and our resolve. The invaders beyond your doorstep are a sign this war nears its end. Your cities have held out so far but they won't hold out forever. With new mages on their way, the last seconds tick down.'

A heavy silence drew out. Anfen sensed their mood and his heart sank.

'What would happen, if the Wall was destroyed?' said Liha of Faifen. 'What do we know?'

Anfen was forced to admit: 'Nothing. We know nothing.' Liha settled back in her chair as if that settled the discussion.

'Correction,' said Anfen, growing angry, 'we know our victory is impossible as things stand. We know the heavy pendulum of this war swings against us. We know that if it *does* swing back against them, too much will have been left in ruin behind it for the old world to recover. One lunatic with the power they're seeking could decide the rest of us are no longer needed. He could kill everyone in the world, and *he just might*. We know the doom of the Free Cities comes as certain and steadily as the night, and that if a time ever existed for drastic action — even with unpredictable results — it is now.'

'What is on the other side of the Wall?' said Liha, in tones a schoolteacher might use.

'We don't know,' Anfen had to admit.

'Yes. Well, there *is* talk these things, these . . . "Tormentors" come from that side. It is, of course, just talk. We simply don't know.' Again, maddeningly, she sat back in her seat: *that's settled, then.*

'Consider this,' said Anfen. 'The Arch Mage said he had *already* discovered a plot to do it. Since none of you knows of any such plot, it may be a figment of their paranoia, or it may be some hidden ally in an Aligned city, who has stumbled across knowledge we don't have. But the *castle* considers it a plot *we* would consider. That means it cannot be as contrary to our interests as we may fear.'

Liha looked at him almost with pity. 'We don't know *who* their hypothetical plotters are. It may be some suicidal fool who wants the whole world brought to ash. It may have been a drunk on a street corner, a confession beaten out of a prisoner. It may be someone was misheard, it may be anyone at all. Or no one at all. And we are venturing, now, even further from what we know. I don't think the matter even warrants a vote.'

The others were quiet. 'We have not seen this charm you speak of,' said Ilgresi at last.

'Has my information seemed good to you, so far?' said Anfen, though he knew it was hopeless. 'A military action always has objectives and costs. Our cost is unknown. Our objective is to take away the power stolen from twelve cities and placed in one man's hands.'

The Mayor of Yinfel, Izven, added: 'The objective of leaving the Wall alone: not subjecting ourselves to some unknown consequences. The cost: Vous stays in power and one day claims all our cities. An unacceptable cost. I have heard enough. I vote in support of Anfen's proposal.' Anfen blinked, surprised. He waited.

Tanton and High Cliffs were two cities in sight of the Wall. Their Mayors had sat grim-faced, saying nothing, while the discussion unfolded. Anfen did not expect their support. Sure enough, High Cliffs Mayor Ousan's voice was heavy with sarcasm: 'How do you propose we do it? Have you *seen* the Wall, Anfen?'

'I have never gone that far south.'

'Then let me help you. It stretches from deep underground to the highest point in the sky. It runs so far belowground we are unable to tunnel beneath it. The Wall itself *may* be thin as a glass window, it may be thicker than a mountain. Stoneflesh giants stand before it and guard it. They allow nothing to get near them, even other stoneflesh giants.'

Erkairn, representing the scattered peoples, saw an opportunity to gain credibility with the other Mayors and grabbed it: 'Have you seen a stoneflesh giant, Anfen? They are the size of a Great Spirit. How would you combat them? Your plan is insanity.'

'Enough from High Cliffs. Erkairn, you will not be voting on this matter, unless my colleagues disagree,' said Ilgresi. Erkairn began to protest, but Ilgresi ignored him. His black teeth showed in what seemed a grimace directed at Anfen. 'For the purpose of this discussion, let us assume it *can* be done. The discussion is not about how, it is about whether we should. And though

the matter certainly warrants a *vote*, Liha, my decision is made.'
Ilgresi took a deep breath. 'I vote against.'

Ousan of High Cliffs: 'Against. My city is closest to the Wall.
Show me the message on this lost charm and I will consider
the question again.'

Liha of Faifen, shaking her head as though the room had
descended into a circus: 'Against! Even had I seen this charm
and its contents, I would deem the whole proposal an insane
distraction from armies massing nearby as we speak. Our best
hope is subversion of Aligned cities from within.'

'They play that slow game far better than us, or else we'd be
winning,' said Anfen, but he was ignored.

Wioutin, advisor to the Mayor of Tsith: 'I believe Anfen's
reasoning is best. If the decision were mine, I would vote in his
support. But I am not Mayor of my city and cannot commit it
to such an action. I vote against, until I am able to speak with
my Mayor.'

Mayor of Tanton, Tauk's eyes had not left Anfen's face
throughout. Now he looked sidelong at the Mayor of High Cliffs.
'My city too is in sight of the Wall. *This* city is in sight of Vous's
clawed hand and we'll all be weaker, should it fall. As one who
has fought against him with a sword, not just words, I vote for
Anfen's proposal. His reasons are mine.'

'The count is two aye, four nay. But Tsith's Mayor is yet to
have his say, and his advisor supports the action.'

'I am but one of five, what they call the "high advisors". There
are a further two dozen experts in various—'

'*Thank* you. Assuming Tsith votes in support, we are tied three
for, three against.'

'Then perhaps the scattered peoples break the deadlock,' said
the flustered Erkairn. 'And I vote against. I would give *my* reasons
but you don't seem especially—'

'Then that matter is settled,' said Ilgresi with a sigh. 'Anfen, have you anything else to discuss? No? We thank you. Enjoy my city. And do be careful to wear a hood if you venture down to ground level. Assassinations have been foiled, just this week.'

50

Anfen slumped in a seat outside the door. Gusts of deliciously clear and cool mountain air puffed curtains at the window, making them rustle. The city beyond had turned out many of its lights.

The Mayors talked a little while longer, though their voices did not carry outside the room. When the door opened they emerged and passed down the hall in pairs, deep in conversation. Most didn't see Anfen, but Tauk paused to clap his shoulder. 'We should spar while I am here,' he said, a smile in his eyes. 'I fear the standards of Valour's Helm have slipped badly. I may have to run again, to show them how it *used* to be done, in days when men were men. I hear some stone-footed rabble won it three times, though they say his opponents were cripples.'

Anfen smiled.

'I'm sorry,' said Tauk, sighing. 'If your charm reappears, bring it without delay.'

Izven lurked in the doorway till Tauk had gone. He looked nervously around, as though fearing to be overheard, then leaned close: 'You have at your disposal what resources my city can *discreetly* supply you. What do you need?'

Anfen's heart sped up. *This* possibility had not had a chance

to bloom in his mind. He laughed nervously. 'Five strong catapults would be a start.'

Izven winced. 'Hard to keep that a secret: our city doesn't
have many. I was hoping you'd ask for cavalry, but that's not
much use for destroying the barrier, is it? How's two catapults
sound? They would have to be assembled on site. I cannot have
them rolling out the gates or people will talk.'

'Two is better than none. I will send word of a time and place
to send them, if I may?'

'You may.' Izven turned away, then paused. 'I have always
had . . . the *utmost* admiration for you.'

Surprised by this, Anfen had no answer. Six years back, when
he had first defected, and first been called to explain himself
to the Mayors, to tell them all he knew of Vous's army, their
deeds and methods, he'd asked with head humbly bowed to
join their fight, asked for the most dangerous missions they
could give him. There had been no admiration on this Mayor's
face, nor any of the others. Aside from Tauk, their suspicions
had never completely left them, Anfen had always felt. Perhaps
he'd been wrong.

The Mayor strode over to Lalie, who waited in company of a
guard, put his hand on her shoulder and spoke to her. She left
with him, turning once to wave goodbye to Anfen. He nodded,
but barely saw her, for his mind was far away.

Back at the inn, he woke Sharfy, Loup and Siel in their rooms,
telling each to meet him in his at once. When they were gathered, he told them what had happened.

'So why couldn't this wait until morning?' said Sharfy.

'Tomorrow we set out,' said Anfen.

'Set out? Where?'

'To World's End.' There was a silence, and many looks Anfen's way that suggested he'd cracked up. 'Speak your piece,' he said.

'Anfen, do you know what it is you're saying we should do?' said Siel.

'You tell me. I'm proposing to defy the vote of the Council of Free Cities. For which I'll most likely be executed, if any of you let it slip. At the *very* least I'll never be trusted again. You can decide if that's in our interests or the castle's.'

Loup, seemingly uninterested in the conversation, ducked out the door and wandered to the kitchen. The others looked at each other uncomfortably. 'I don't think anyone's going to inform on you,' said Siel. 'But we serve the Mayors' Command. Which means we take their orders, however wrong they are.'

Anfen stood. 'I would love to sleep here for a week, stuffing my belly with good food and drink. It's open to you. Enjoy. Future generations may learn of your heroic deeds, in our Friend and Lord's schools. Or his slave farms.'

'Why are you getting dressed, boss?' said Sharfy as Anfen strapped his boots on with angry, jerking tugs.

'Changed my mind. I set out tonight.'

'Tonight?' said Sharfy. 'Wait. Sleep on it, Anfen. In the morning. We'll talk then.'

'Enough *talk*,' Anfen snarled.

Loup returned, a cup of milk in his hand and a drop of blood running from his nose. Even small spells took a lot out of casters in a city, where there was not much magic. Big spells were usually fatal. 'At least drink this, before you go,' said Loup. 'I blessed it a touch. Strength for the road, protection from disease, heal your bones, this little brew. Improve your luck too, I shouldn't wonder. Just a little.'

Anfen took the cup, sniffed it, downed it in one gulp. The others watched him without speaking. A minute later, his boots and scabbard on, backpack shouldered, he stood to leave, swayed on his feet, and fell back on the bed.

'Heals your bones all right, I told him true,' said Loup. 'Strength for the road, oh aye. Can't beat sleep for that. Now let's go get some and leave the boss to his dreams. He needs em more than he thinks.' Loup winked at them, his gummy smile lopsided.

51

Case sighed as they caught their breath at the tower's base after the long climb down, its huge shadow leaning over and swallowing theirs. Thick grey clouds rolled over the hillside from the west, threatening rain. 'Got a bad feeling about him. I'd go back and shoot him, if it wasn't a bitch of a climb,' he said.

'I have that same feeling,' said Eric, unstrapping the army-issue sword and tossing it away. 'But we're the good guys, Case. That's the point.'

'No, it isn't. You said it yourself some time back. The point's not good guys and bad guys, it's to survive. And I think we just made a mistake.'

'It'll help me survive knowing I'm one of the good guys.'

Case scoffed. 'Until he shoves a sword in your guts. Then I'll get your opinion.'

'You may be right. But before I came here, I couldn't have killed a guy in cold blood. I don't want to go back as someone who can. And if we ever meet the group again, tell Siel what I just told you, because she thinks I'm scum.'

'You think she'll be impressed we let a traitor live, who killed a few of her friends and will probably kill her if he gets the chance?'

Eric pondered this. 'Fuck!' he screamed, kicking the base of the tower as all the frustrations of the recent past suddenly boiled over. 'I don't care any more, all right, I just want a goddamn shower and a coffee, and maybe five minutes alone with a *Playboy*. Go kill him then. I'll go back to being noble later.'

Case fidgeted with his battered old hat. 'I'm sorry, Eric. This is my fault. I was a fool.'

He shoots, he scores ... 'Whatever do you mean?'

'Leaving the others, like I did. Thinking she was going to come for me. She wasn't following us all around for my sake. She had her own reasons, nothing to do with me.'

Eric had opened his mouth to say *hell yes* when he was startled to see a tear go down Case's face. Hesitantly he put an arm around his friend's shoulder. 'Hey, come on. Of course she was there for your sake, handsome old guy like you. Why do you think I still hang around you? It's not for the conversation.' That got a smile out of him, but he could see Case was sick with embarrassment.

'Onwards, anyway,' said Eric. 'We're the good guys, at least we have that much, even if it gets us killed. Elvury, wasn't the city called? That's where Anfen's bunch was headed. That's where we're going, if I'm calling the shots now.'

Case nodded. 'Here, hand over those coins he gave you.' Case took them and slipped on the necklace again, vanishing from sight. 'We'd better set off.'

A fast-moving shadow passed just off the road. The war mage did not seem to be looking at them as it flew, arms crossed over its chest, two trails of smoke in the air from its horns behind it. Eric was sure it was the same one they'd seen near the inn. He ducked behind the pillar, while Case just watched it, the gun ready if it came back. Instead it veered away from the city and up for higher air, where the magic was denser. 'It's gone,' said Case.

'If I didn't know better, I'd say that thing was keeping an eye on us. Let's get moving.'

There was nothing to make the morning's daylight any different from the afternoon's. Nor did they have a means to track time by following a sun's path. Some regions of sky seemed to glow brighter than others but there was no obvious pattern to it. Since a brief heavy rain shower had come and gone, today was one of the warmer days, though where this heat actually came from was hard to tell; it was just *there*, in the air about them.

Eric still saw the swirls and streaks of darkly glimmering colour twining on the wind like smoke. Higher up, it seemed to be background mist in some places, with the odd vein of darker shades woven through. In the sky over Hane, this stuff — this magic, he supposed; how strange to think in such terms — was barely there.

Soon enough, the rock pillar was gone from the view over their shoulders. Case kept the charm on and the gun ready in case of trouble, but the roads, though wide, were eerily empty of people. It was many hours of this emptiness before they passed a merchant train, accompanied by mercenary guards in Hane's city colours. Too late Eric and Case rushed off road, but from beneath their helmets the mercenaries only gazed after them, as indifferent to them as were the ponies hauling the wagons.

The only other passing company was a big group of men and women dressed as druids in big dark hoods. They were sallow-faced and unpleasant to look at, similar to the two strangers Eric had apparently scared from the inn. The group's excited conversation revealed they were Nightmare cultists, who'd seen the Great Spirit reach down, and were on their way to find the place he'd touched. 'Hear that?' Eric said once they'd passed. 'They think they'll find treasure there.'

'Wonder what they'd think of you, if they knew he'd touched you?' said Case thoughtfully. 'Might call you a holy man.'

'Maybe I am, Case.' He was joking, but he also wondered: how big a deal would it be to these people, if they knew, to have an 'Otherworlder' in their midst? Would it create the same excitement as an alien coming to live on Earth?

At a lone roadside store, they were able to buy backpacks and fill them with supplies and rations, though the clerk very nearly refused to serve a customer so oddly accented as Eric. While the guard at the door took Kiown's sword from him (testing its weight with approval and looking at Eric as if to say: *how did one such as you come by a blade like this?*), on the shelves, jar lids were lifted by invisible hands as Case pocketed wares, the young clerk only glancing once at creaking steps on the floorboards where there shouldn't have been any.

With Kiown's coins — large silver and gold discs, the rune printed on them spelling their city of origin, he guessed — Eric bought the backpacks, a jacket to cover his business shirt, a big map with totally illegible writing, and a spare set of clothes for each of them. The guard returned his sword at the door, but Eric could almost see working across the man's mind: *To kill him and take the blade, or not?* With a shrug, the guard handed it back and sweetly bade him safe travels, his grin indicating the decision had been a close one.

From the store, the road led directly south, a few twists and turns aside, through country less scenic, bearing many old scars of war. They played chess on an imaginary board as they walked, though only Case managed to keep accurate memory of where the pieces were, which made the results somewhat predictable. They slept in fields and woods some way off road, their new garments keeping them warm or cool, whichever the shifting daily climate required. Soon, three days of travel were behind them. Every day they woke to the sound of birds chirping and a gently brightening sky growing more familiar and gradually less strange, though they were no less alone beneath it.

52

Their first real trouble came at a place where the road split through wilder-looking woodlands to either side. Two women dressed as Nightmare cultists were tied up and sitting by a road-block, while four soldiers in unfamiliar colours inspected their packs. Not knowing if he'd been seen, Eric ducked off road into the flanking woods, Case just behind him and still invisible.

'From now on, we stick to the old arrangement,' said Case. 'That was close.' Earlier, Case had walked twenty metres or so ahead, invisible, scouting for trouble, and they had cut a wide line through the trees around the soldiers. As they would now.

But it became clear this scrub was harsher than the wood-lands they'd slept in a short way back. Swarms of insects some-times flew in angry bursts about their feet. The trees had an unhealthy, skeletal look, many without leaves or greenery, just long hard branches like jutting bones. Every so often the branches scraped at them hard enough to break skin, leaving stinging red slits for their sweat to trickle into. Blocks of such trees and clumps of impassable stone outcrops soon forced them a fair way wider from the road than they'd intended. 'Don't lose track of where it was,' said Case. 'We should head back, right back the way we came and chance the roadblock.

Worse comes to worst, we can spare four bullets for those guards. Maybe rescue the damsels into the bargain.'

Eric looked behind them, not entirely sure he'd be able to find their exact way back even if he'd wanted to. 'Roadblocks are not our friend, Case. There's a reason Anfen and the others went to great trouble to avoid soldiers. We'll do the same.'

Not long after, the feeling of becoming lost gradually bloomed to suppressed panic, as steadily as their very footsteps led them deeper into nowhere. The sky was completely cloudless, offering no hint which way they travelled. Threads of magic like creeping green mist shimmered and coiled shapelessly through the piebald white and grey tree trunks. When the terrain allowed them to cut back towards the road, it wasn't there; it had presumably curved further west, away from them. Case had been the one keeping track of which way the compass pointed, but without the road he'd lost track. 'A little further,' Eric said hopefully, not even believing himself any more.

The sound of running water ahead soon told the story: the road, if it was in this direction at all, was beyond a river they weren't going to get across without drenching their supplies, assuming they didn't also drown. Nor, by now, was the way they'd come any more discernible than the way ahead. 'This is just fantastic,' Eric muttered. '*Blair Witch* here we come.'

Case removed the charm. Eric thought: If he whines, I swear, I'll break his nose ... All Case said was, 'Good place to stop for lunch, I reckon.'

They did just that, finding a place among the dry dead leaves to sit where those angry insects wouldn't hover about them. The roadside store's bread was still fresh enough, its middle soft and flavoured with something sweet. They munched the last of it in appreciative silence. The water's sloshing and burbling was the only sound, inviting a moment's peace.

'If Kiown wants to follow us through this scrub, he's welcome to,' said Case, looking around at the tall bare trees, which seemed to stare right back. 'We'd best follow the river along until we find a bridge, but the scrub looks pretty thick both ways. We're in a mess, my friend.'

Suddenly, Eric seemed to see the ground they were sitting on for the first time. 'Oh shit. Case. Look.' A little beyond their feet were just a few of those distinctive spiked tracks. Had they sat down to eat a bit to the left, they'd have seen straight away the ground there was covered, absolutely covered in them.

Case stood up quickly, knocking the backpack off his lap and spilling out some of their supplies. The woods' quiet seemed to close in like huge suffocating hands. Not a bird call, not a wind to shake the bone-dry leaves. Yet the quiet spoke: *You are alone.*

'They're all over the place,' Case said, examining the compacted dirt shouldering the river. 'Even right down the banks there. They must be good climbers. Christ! Look, Eric, some of these tracks are *big*. Your leg'd sink down into em!'

'Case, I hate to say it, but I think we're in very deep shit all of a sudden.'

'Maybe, maybe not, just stay calm. No telling when these things passed through here. Could've been weeks ago.'

'Could have been an hour ago. I have a feeling we'd better get the hell out of these woods before night falls.'

They went as far back the way they'd come as memory allowed, but it didn't allow much; the sameness of the woods meant the river was their only reference point. Beneath their feet, often partly hidden by the brittle grass, the ground was still covered in those tracks, sometimes thick clusters of them intertwining, sometimes just a few small holes widely scattered.

Each loud footstep crunching on the dry forest floor ticked off the time till nightfall and their deaths. Long stretches of ground showed no signs of the spiked tracks, which looked for all the world like someone had hammered stakes of varying thickness deep into the surface then removed them. Often as not, the smaller tracks led to groundman holes, which were suddenly everywhere in the forest floor. These were larger than they'd seen, almost as though they'd been built to allow large creatures easy passage ...

The last of the daylight had almost faded completely when Case's feet tripped up on a square grid of sticks stuck together and sent it skidding across the forest floor. It had been covering a groundman hole like a manhole cover. 'No tracks,' Eric said, crouching low and examining the surrounding turf. 'I think we've found lodgings. How these sticks keep the monsters away I'd like to know.'

'Don't know, maybe it messes with their ability to see it? But this is smaller than the other holes too. We'll be lucky to fit.' Case crawled in first, pushing his backpack ahead of him down a J-curved bend flattening out a few metres down. Eric went backwards, carefully dragging the grid-stick cover back across. Tiny lightstones gleamed like eyes in the walls behind them, where the tunnel widened a little, curving around left and out of sight. It was the safest either of them had felt since stopping for lunch by the river.

'Why do these little people make their tunnels big enough for us to get through, anyway?' Case whispered.

'I think they used to be friends with humans when they built a lot of them. Don't know when it all changed, but they hate us now.'

'Who gets first watch?' said Case, yawning.

'I'll take it. Too nervous to sleep.'

'Fine by me. I'll be out in five minutes; not the worst place I ever slept, either.' Case tossed him the charm, then nestled into the curves of the tunnel's floor as though into a comfortable bed, hat down over his eyes, backpack as a pillow.

With the very last of the daylight, Eric peered closely at the charm necklace. There was a little swarm of activity in the air around it, much of it moving patterns like bubbles of clear glass. Around one of its silver beads the magic swirled in a slow, small orbit. He'd been going to put the charm on, but it suddenly felt like he was clutching something very much alive. He put it in his pocket and waited.

The hole's opening made a disc of night sky faint as starlight, cutting across the rough lattice of its makeshift lid. He jumped at every little sound he heard or imagined out among the trees. His imagination was all too willing to recreate the hunters' hall from which Lalie had been rescued. The woods were quieter than it seemed they should be — the occasional breeze made the brittle tree branches creak, but if there was any wildlife, small or large, it moved with complete stealth.

Until, that was, he'd nearly fallen asleep. He heard something like wood being bent until it begins to break — *creak, creak, creak* — and there was no mistaking it for the work of the wind. He crawled so close to the stick-grid its poking fibres tickled his nose, trying to judge the sound's direction. There was so little to see: trees hunched up in belligerent skeletal shapes.

Except — there! One of them *moved*, stalking across the patch of sky behind it. It was nearly double a man's height, with lean limbs covered in spikes, some curved, some straight. Its outline was all he could see. A head, if that's what it was, sported a large jagged mane, spiked in the many-pointed shape of a roughly drawn star, each point needle thin.

The thing out there stood still for a time, only the curling points along its body in motion like fast restless fingers. Then it moved with an awkward stiff gait and blended, hidden amongst the silhouettes of trees. For a time silence fell, then came more creaking noises, closer to the hole's entrance. There was the impact of something heavy pressing down its feet, very close, just overhead, but he couldn't see it.

Had it come lured by their human scent, their footprints? Eric crawled backwards through the tunnel, his whole body shaking. The tiniest sound of his knees and hands sliding across the stone floor seemed hugely magnified. He shook Case's shoulder. Case murmured, annoyed to be woken. 'What is it?'

'*Shhh!* Don't make a fucking *sound*. Let's move. They're up there above us, right now. Go.'

Case cocked his head, listening, and heard it close by: *creak, creak* ... He looked uneasily at the tunnel's curve behind them. 'You sure?'

'*Yes* I'm sure for fuck's sake: go!' Case hustled down the tunnel on hands and knees, around its curve to where it ran deeper and wider, so that they no longer needed to stoop their heads. Case turned to speak, and in fact he was about to say this: *Hold on a minute, if this tunnel is supposed to keep those monsters out, maybe there's a chance of those traps the gang kept talking about,* when, with a crumbling sound, the ground seemed to drop out beneath them. They both fell for just a heartbeat, till they were lodged in the floor waist deep and painfully winded.

When Eric could speak again, he muttered: 'Groundmen traps. Beautiful.'

'I'm thinking we should have chanced those roadblocks,' said Case.

Eric shut his eyes and breathed deeply. 'I am going to agree with you on that, for the first and final time. OK? Now please. Drop it. Please.'

'Just saying, is all.'

I am probably going to kill him, sooner or later, Eric thought. There wasn't much to do but wait out the slow hours.

53

Their feet did not touch a floor below, nor did struggling shift their positions in the slightest, though it served to ward off numbness in their legs. The charm in his pocket was out of reach.

There was no knowing if night had passed yet or not. Eric managed to doze for a while, dreams unpleasant indeed, until woken by the feeling of something sharp poking his leg down below. He jerked frantically, feet kicking the air. There was, it seemed, much hilarity from the groundmen in a tunnel directly beneath.

'Cut legs!' said a gleeful voice below. Someone or something yanked up his pant leg and a sharp object gently traced along the exposed skin. 'Hear screams! Uprat, screams pretty. Cut *slow*.'

'Wait!' Eric screamed. 'Toll! I can pay! Toll! Toll!'

'Toll?' a voice below nattered. 'We *take* toll. Dead soon.'

Another said, 'Wait, wait. Go up, talk. No harm. Why they here? We ask.'

'Trick! May trick!'

'No trick!' Eric yelled. 'Believe me, please!'

There was a moment's silence. 'Speak our tongue?' said one of them. Hard to tell with their strange inflections, but it sounded alarmed.

'Speak your tongue!' Eric agreed. 'Yes, yes! So does my companion. We can pay toll! We can sing and dance. Sexual favours, you name it. Will you free us?'

Case groaned. 'Don't give em ideas for Chrissakes. If they want sexual favours, you're their man.'

The voices below gabbled excitedly before fading as the groundmen moved away. Minutes later there was the candle-gleam of their bright yellow eyes as four approached, each holding a small spear. The foremost poked his spear down at the rock floor now and then, and there was a flare of light painful to the eyes as traps were closed off. 'Can't reach the gun,' Case whispered.

'Shh. Let me talk,' said Eric. 'I've seen these things before.'

The groundmen positioned themselves on either side of Eric, ignoring Case, and pointing the sharp tips of their weapons close to him.

'Speak our tongue,' said one, its face angrily bunched. 'How? Spy?'

'I don't know, exactly. But I come from Otherworld. They call me a Pilgrim.'

A burble of excited chatter. The way they looked at him changed: not more friendly, but certainly more curious. 'Why here?' said one.

'Here ... do you mean in your tunnel, or in your world?'

This got him an angry prod by the foremost, the spear point stabbing half an inch into his shoulder. He squirmed and fought not to cry out but the pain was hideous. The other groundmen rushed to hold the angry one in check before it could drive the spear deeper. What Eric had said to offend it he had no notion at all. 'In world, in woods, in ground,' another said, holding back the enraged one as it made more lunges at him. 'Answer all. Why here?'

'We're lost, that's all. We came here to your world, to Levaal, by accident. We were separated from our guides. We moved off the road to avoid guards. And now we're lost. We came down here to escape something outside, but we don't know what it is.'

'Tormentors, Stranger called them,' Case interjected.

'Case, please, as per our agreement, keep your fucking mouth *shut*. Can you help us, tunnel masters? We're trying to find our way to Elvury.'

Chittering laughter broke out. 'Want to die?' one inquired.

'Not especially.' More laughter. 'Is there something in Elvury that's dangerous?' said Eric.

'They want to die!' cackled the angry one. 'In bad woods, while things are loose. In tunnel, walk right in trap. Now, if escape, they off to dead town. Uprat, hate life!'

Eric said, 'Dead town? Elvury? Our friends are going there. Anfen. Do you know him? We were separated—'

'Dead town, yes! Not yet, soon.' The others gestured for the speaker to hush, but there seemed great mirth afoot all round.

Eric said, 'Soon? Why, what will happen?'

'You go, you see.'

He thought of Siel. 'Are our friends in danger there?'

More laughter. '*All* uprats dead. We don't care. Not our work, but we watch. Your friends first. Then you.'

'Now pay toll,' said another. 'Then say why we don't kill *you*, take *more* toll.'

Luckily Eric had a reason — funny how the feel of their spear point had cleared his head. 'I can teach you Otherworld writing. I can show you how to read what it all says.'

The groundmen tried to hide the fact that this prospect impressed them a great deal, but he could see by the widening of their bright yellow eyes that it did. 'The toll is in my pocket. I can't reach it.' There had to be receipts still in his wallet, maybe old bus tickets, and he knew Sharfy had missed a ten-dollar note, back when he'd rifled through it near the door. His key card, driver's licence. Would these interest them?

'Hear close,' said one of the groundmen after a brief whispered conference with the others. 'We let up. But! Can still kill. You big. Yes, sure. But, see? *Sharp.*' He pointed his spear tip very close to Eric's eye indeed. 'See? *Sharp.*'

'Sharp,' Eric could only repeat, pulling his head as far back from it as possible while the spear tip followed. He didn't see what they did but there was a tapping sound and whatever gripped his waist gradually weakened. With tired arms he pulled himself free, making the pain of the spear wound flare up badly. Blood trickled warmly down his chest. The groundmen spear points waved and jabbed around him as though they feared he'd attack. Slowly he reached for his wallet. Out came the two remaining receipts, their print almost completely faded. His key card — how strange to hand that over, in this world where it was perfectly useless, and still feel an acute sense of loss. The spear tips angled away from him as the groundmen fumbled with the receipts, an old train ticket, their mouths open in wonder, tracing fingers over the lettering. 'More,' one said distractedly. They were evidently so fascinated it didn't occur to them to take the wallet itself.

'This is for my friend's safe passage too, OK?' said Eric.

'More! Give!'

'Will you let my friend up too?'

The spear points came back, one jabbing close to his crotch. He gave them all he had left in the wallet, including the ten-dollar note and his driver's licence. The nearest took this, carefully studied it and looked, amazed, from the licence's unsmiling picture to Eric's face. The others did likewise, and all seemed entirely lost for words.

Something had changed here and Eric didn't know what. The groundmen suddenly backed away, their spears pointed at the ground. 'Let up my friend, please,' said Eric.

The groundmen scampered off like animals spooked by a noise. But Case said, 'It's going loose around me. Quick, grab me . . .' Eric reached down to help him up before he fell through the widening hole. 'What'd you do to scare em off?' said Case, once they'd caught their breath.

'Not sure. Something about my licence. The picture I think. They didn't know what to make of it.'

Case laughed. 'Seen some pretty bad licence pictures in my time, too. Let's get the hell out, what do you say? It has to be day by now.'

Sure enough pale daylight poured through the stick-grid. 'Why didn't we buy bandages at that store?' Eric said, prodding the bleeding cut gouged in his shoulder.

'Why buy when you can steal?' said Case, winking. He pulled a white roll of cloth bandages from his backpack and wrapped some around the wound. 'Not too tight?'

'No, it's fine, unless I'm poisoned. Vicious little bastard. Wish I knew what I'd said to piss him off.'

Through the stick-grid's gaps there was no sign of the creatures he'd seen last night. Only when they went outside and saw the trails of spiked tracks in the ground, and some huge ones very close to the tunnel's mouth, was he sure it had been real.

54

Occasional gusts of wind blew thick swirling ribbons of discoloured air between the trees, but the current as a whole was weaker than yesterday, as though magic changed day by day like the weather. The equation now was pretty simple: there was a full day's light to find their way out of the woods, or they were probably dead. Neither of them liked the odds, nor the fact they'd seen no animal life aboveground at all, bird or beast, no longer even the nasty insect clouds that had earlier covered both their arms with itching little red bites. Trees and more trees still fenced them in with no end in sight. Like a clock's ticking hand, their crunching footsteps began the countdown to nightfall.

And that was if the creatures, whatever they were exactly, never came out during the day.

The day wore on. The woods, mile after mile, were the same: nothing but the trees and Tormentor tracks. 'You a religious man, Eric?' said Case, as the very first fading of afternoon light began.

'Don't know. Whatever I was, all this,' he waved at the surrounding trees, 'being on the other side of a door we found in a train bridge ... well, it's changed the maths a little.'

'If you got any prayers or favours to call in, now's the time. Night's coming and we're dead men.'

They came to a large downwards-sloped clearing, surrounded by a ring of patchy bare trees with skeletal branches. Eric was about to insist on a rest break, whatever Case had to say about it, when something at the clearing's edge caught his eye. He said, 'Actually, Case, maybe let's keep our mouths shut.'

'Why, what's . . . ?' Then Case saw it too: seated on a thick branch some way above their heads, a war mage stared right at them, as though it had been waiting for them. Long horns curled from its crown to its jaw line; a thick ropy beard, brows and tangled hair were like a nest about its face. A thick coat of something's skin hung awkwardly about its body.

'Is that the same one?' Eric whispered.

'Can't tell. They all look the same, pretty much.'

Its feet squeezed the thick branch like bird claws trying to strangle it, grinding off little pieces of bark that sprinkled to the ground. Its eyes were locked on Eric's. 'Get the gun out,' he whispered. 'And go invisible.'

Case had already drawn the Glock. The war mage's cat-eyes followed the motions of his hand as he raised it and aimed. 'Not sure I'll hit it from here,' he said.

'Hurry, put on the charm and get closer.'

The war mage's head cocked sideways inquisitively. Its hand slapped the air like it was swatting a bug. The gun was knocked flying to the ground, skidding along across broken sticks and dead leaves. Turning back to Eric, it crouched down on the tree branch, pointed a long finger at him and spoke, deep voice rasping, 'You're Shadow.'

'Should I answer it?' Eric whispered.

'You're Shadow,' the war mage repeated, its voice as deep as a machine's. It clawed at the air, as though trying to express something and struggling for the words. 'A servant,' it said at last.

'It's nuts,' said Case. 'Be careful what you say.'

Thanks for the tip. 'Fuck,' he muttered. To the war mage, 'We don't want to fight you. We're just lost travellers.'

The war mage's head cocked like a bird's, then it dropped down from the branch, thick beard and hair rising as it fell into a crouch. 'You're Shadow,' it rasped. It began to speak twice, then said, 'Four converging points met across a plain. A cloud formed of erupted heat. A battle, a victory. A servant delivered them.'

'Shadow. I keep hearing that,' Case murmured. 'Why?' He had the necklace out. The war mage's eyes were on him again as he slipped it around his neck and vanished. It shifted on its feet, alarmed, bright yellow eyes carefully following the disturbed leaves of his footsteps. When Case neared the gun, the war mage again patted the air with one palm, making the gun skitter sideways along the ground. It said more urgently, 'Heat comes. Much heat. A servant. Your wish, I've *purpose*.' Frustrated, it crouched and scratched the air again.

'Case, stop. I'm not sure it's going to attack.'

'From what I hear, these things don't do much else but attack.'

'It's trying to tell us something—'

The war mage dug the tip of its staff into the ground and wrenched its top around in chopping motions for a minute or more. Swirls of magic threaded through the air from above the tree tops, curling down in a long thin funnel, the thin end drawn to the staff's tip. It sucked air and seemed to inhale tiny threads of magic, curling like smoke between its lips. 'Look at that,' Eric whispered, before remembering that to Case's eyes it would seem the war mage was just breathing air.

'You're Shadow,' rasped the war mage, now staring at him, eyes wide, imploring him to understand. It crouched low and scooped a bunch of leaves, sticks and dirt into its mouth, eyes unblinking on Eric as it chewed and swallowed. He remembered his first encounter with one of these creatures, the way it had eaten the flesh of its victims, and Sharfy's voice: *helps them cool off . . .*

'My shadow,' Eric said, nodding. The war mage listened to this with head cocked then made a hissing noise of frustration.

'Come away from it, Eric,' said Case, worried.

Eric went towards Case's voice. 'We can't leave the gun. Let me try something.' To the war mage, 'I'm going to pick up our weapon. I will not use it to attack you. But we must find our way out of these woods, and we need it. Trust me. I won't attack you.'

It watched him with eyes as uncomprehending as a beast's, crumbled leaves and bits of chewed twig scattered in the beard near its mouth. Eric slowly went to the gun, the war mage's head following every movement as he picked it up. Slowly into Eric's pocket it went, then he backed out of the clearing. 'Where are you?' he murmured.

'Here,' said Case.

He followed the sound of Case's footsteps. The war mage watched, then sprang from a crouch up to its feet and shuffled after them. 'A servant,' it called. 'Dangers. A . . . *guide*.'

'Run,' said Case, yanking off the necklace. He was lurching along slowly and wincing with each step. Sharp, reaching tree branches scratched and cut them both. They did not even notice the darker shapes standing here and there among the trees as they went.

Then Case's feet caught on something and he fell forwards, sliding on his belly for a moment and rolling down a slope in the ground. Eric skidded to a halt and helped him up, but Case was in no shape to run further; he clutched at his knee and grimaced. They had put enough distance between them and the war mage that it couldn't be seen through the trees, but suddenly Eric became aware of something *else* just ahead of them.

Its feet were shaped like tree roots, balancing it on knife-sharp points digging into the dirt. Two arms so long their dagger tips scraped the ground were for the moment motionless, the creature bent over in a crouch from its waist. The whole body looked to have been wound from threads of muscle like dark unreflective glass. Spikes of varying length covered it. A huge mane spread behind it in a fan of long needles. Its face bore misshaped eyes like shards of obsidian embedded deep above a large half-canine, half-human jaw, filled with long curved teeth the same colour as its skin.

Though it faced them, nothing in its face indicated recognition of their presence. The mouth seemed twisted and frozen into the shape of an inhuman smile. Its only movement was the occasional bending of its spikes, one or two slowly curling then going still. Lalie's words echoed in Eric's head loud as an alarm: *They were perfectly still . . . perfectly still . . .*

Case, who lay on the forest floor clutching his knee, had just seen the creature. 'Shit,' he said with a humourless chuckle. 'That's done us. Luck can't hold forever. You go. Run. I can't.'

Eric went to pick him up, but could barely manage the weight. Case let his backpack drop to the ground. 'There's another one, further down,' said Case. 'Can just make it out down there. Two more, over yonder. Don't go that way.'

Eric's eyes never left the Tormentor but still it didn't move. He dragged Case backwards away from it, and still it was motionless, until Eric's feet caught on the uneven ground and they both toppled over.

There was a sound like a wire fence being shaken as the long thin needles of its star-shaped mane rattled. The creature sprang to life as though roused from sleep. Its head swung slowly their way. No change came to its face, locked still in that frozen alien smile. One hand clumsily rose, pointed at them, and then it came, its awkward stiff gait covering ground quickly with long strides.

In panic, Eric tried to run, but suddenly it was impossible to move fast. He felt that he was being sucked towards the Tormentor as though by a powerful current. Everything about him slowed down, from his heartbeat to the way sounds stretched out, dreamlike: crunching undergrowth, Case's voice speaking too slowly to understand, the sound like slowed-down tape. He slowly craned his neck to see the thing reach for him with its long knife-fingers. One hand for him, one for Case. It moved very slowly now too, something almost beautiful in the sight, and in the way each slow deliberate second drew out, promising death still some distance away but inevitably coming. They were pulled towards its stretching arms like people sliding down hill.

The spell was broken with a cracking sound and a flash of fire. The hand reaching for Eric was severed neatly at the wrist with a burst of searing heat, enough to burn some of his hair. Time caught up, seeming far too fast as he crawled away from the creature, dragging Case with him along the dead leaves and scratching fallen branches. There was another cracking noise, another wave of scorching heat, and the Tormentor's other arm split and dropped. It swung round in one big exaggerated motion, no reaction on its face, still locked in a smile. Little fires burned on the ground around both severed limbs.

A little way away from it, the war mage crouched low, teeth bared in a look of amazing savagery, the tips of its horns already blackened and smoking. It quickly stuffed a handful of stiff grass into its mouth, swallowed, then lunged forwards, another wave of shimmering heat spreading through the space between it and the Tormentor, which began stalking towards it. There was a noise like a whip cracking, then the Tormentor's head split and shattered like a rock struck with massive force, shards of its head thudding heavily to the ground. Its feet propelled it two more steps then it stopped still.

'A servant,' the hoarse voice of the war mage. Heat emanated from it in pulsing waves. Thick smoke trailed from the tips of its horns and it panted for breath. Eric saw a great twister-shaped plume of disturbed magic bending and swaying high, high into the sky, and more of them stretching from each other spot where the war mage had cast its spells.

Slowly, the Tormentor's stiff body toppled backwards and fell. Its hands still twitched and grappled. Case and Eric looked at each other. There was a long silence, just the Tormentor's severed hands still clutching at the ground, disturbing the leaves, and the sound of the war mage chewing undergrowth and twigs, its eyes flickering round the woods.

'A servant,' said Eric. 'I see.'

'I guess,' said Case with a shrug, 'he's OK by me.'

55

'There's something weird about this,' Eric muttered. 'Why have they sent it after us?'

'It's nuts. No offence if you can hear me, buddy,' he said to the war mage. It locked its cat-yellow eyes on Case and he took an involuntary backwards step. Heat still emanated from its body though many minutes had passed. Foul-smelling smoke curled off its blackened horns. Case stamped out the small fires starting near the Tormentor's severed hands. The pieces of its broken head showed no sign of interior organs: they were like cleaved stone.

'I think our new friend used up a lot of juice to kill that thing,' said Eric. 'If another one starts moving, or a bigger one arrives, it might cook itself right away.' To the war mage, 'Can you handle many more of those?'

It clawed at the air in some gesture they couldn't interpret.

'That a yes or a no?' said Case.

It skipped towards him and croaked, 'Horse's hooves. Ticks and fleas. Fleas and ticks.' Its head tilted back and its mouth opened to the sky as it gave the curdling scream Eric and Case had both heard before, then cocked its head, waiting, it seemed, for an answering call. If one came, the war mage alone heard it. 'Are you calling for help?' said Eric.

'A servant,' it said tiredly. 'Heat.'

The war mage approached the Tormentor's corpse, its clawed feet finding careful purchase between spikes on the dead creature's chest. Some of the spikes still moved. It poked the body with its staff, gripped a spike and with a hissed breath and a strain that made its arm shake, wrenched the spike free, cutting its hand badly in the process. All this, apparently, to see whether the spike was suitable for eating, for it poked the tip experimentally in its mouth, bit down, cut its gums, then threw the undamaged spike away. Blood spilled through its lips, into its beard, but it seemed not to notice.

The war mage cocked its head. 'A threaded course is narrow,' it said. 'Rival comes. Running fast. I've purpose, too much heat besides, to *death* it. We flee.' It pointed a hand dripping blood in the direction, if Eric judged right, of the river, then set off that way in shuffling steps, every now and then hopping up to levitate a short distance. It crouched at the edge of the clearing to wait for them to catch up. They looked at each other, then followed.

As Eric had guessed, they soon came to the river again. He didn't think there was much point trying to talk to the war mage, but: 'How are we meant to cross? Is there a bridge near?'

It ignored this and grabbed Case under his arms. Alarmed, he reached for the gun before remembering Eric now had it. His legs cycled the air as the war mage jumped, sailed lightly over the river, bore him across to the far bank and set him gently down. It then flew back, grabbed Eric in rough, coarse hands and jumped him across too, seemingly untroubled by the weight, despite him wearing a pack. Case said, 'With your leave, whatever your name is, we're hungry and sore. Is it safe for us to stop a while and eat?'

Again the war mage gave no answer, just raked at the floor with its long toes like bird's feet as though in irritation, and crouched down low to munch the undergrowth. The heat arising from its exertions slowly faded. Its horns had almost resumed their normal dull yellow, and no longer gave off smoke.

Case, taking its reaction for assent, dug around in their supplies pack for food, taking some of the bread — a touch stiffer by now — and strips of salted pink-red meat, which looked like ham but tasted like fish.

'Just what the hell is it doing here?' Eric whispered, nodding to the war mage, which gazed across the river at the far bank, its face watchful. 'We have to assume it's working for the castle. And maybe it's here to help us get back to Anfen. Just like Kiown said he wanted to. Which meant maybe he *wasn't* lying about that.'

Case took a swig from the water-skin. 'A servant, sounds right. What's the other part mean? *Your shadow?*'

'No idea. Maybe it means it has to stay close to us, like it is our shadow.'

'But it only says it to *you*, not me,' said Case.

'Actually, you're right. Then I have no idea at all.' They munched for a while, both ravenously hungry, both aware it was very nearly a meal they'd never have eaten, and for that it tasted better than any. Back where they'd been, the tall winding spires of magic could still be seen towering over the treetops.

'Hey, bird man, you hungry? Try this, it's better than leaves and dirt.' Case took a handful of bread and brought it to the war mage. It sniffed and pawed blindly for the bread, its eyes never leaving whatever it gazed at beyond the far riverbank. Its head occasionally moved as though following something's passage, but they could see nothing across there but the all too familiar trees.

'What the hell is he looking at?' said Eric.

'Maybe he can see more of those monsters in the distance.'

A loud growling sounded in the war mage's throat. It hadn't eaten the bread, and now cast it aside and stood, planting its staff and summoning magic from the air with those chopping motions.

'What's the matter?' said Eric.

The war mage didn't answer. Urgently it stuffed leaves and twigs into its mouth, swallowed, and bared its teeth. Its body tensed as it scanned the line of trees across the water. 'All things put to use,' it muttered, pieces of dry leaves spraying from its lips.

'It sees something,' said Case. 'Hey! There, see that? It wasn't a Tormentor.' He peered across the water. 'It was white, moving between the trees. Fast, too ...'

Now Eric saw it too, looming ominously as it circled towards the river bank: the huge white wolf that had attacked Stranger at Faul's house. Head lowered, its great body heaved with panting breaths as it stared at them across the water.

The war mage shrieked so loud Eric and Case ducked and covered their ears. It chopped the air frantically with its staff, funnels of dark colour threading quickly down from the sky, and breathed this air deeply.

The wolf backed up a few steps then charged towards the bank, launched itself, and made it two-thirds of the way over before sinking with a massive splash. The water didn't delay it long — soon it had paddled to the bank and surged out, water pouring and spraying off it. It ran right for the war mage, paws thumping the ground loud as drumbeats.

Case grabbed Eric by the collar and pulled him back. 'Which is our friend?' he said. 'Who do we shoot here?'

'The wolf is,' said Eric. 'If not both. We're not shooting either. Far Gaze!' he called. 'The war mage saved us!'

The wolf didn't seem to hear him. It veered from its charge and darted sideways with speed that seemed surreal for something that size. The war mage had balanced on one leg, other limbs sticking out like some kind of martial arts pose as it spewed a plume of inky darkness, narrowly missing the wolf. The grass beneath the spell curdled, blackened and instantly died, as though nothing had ever grown there. The stink of it was noxious and even from a distance Eric and Case both had coughing fits. Spent magic from the spell curled skywards in a funnel tall as a tornado.

The wolf widely circled the war mage once, twice, then came at it again. Case's eyes didn't see the cloud of magic sucked in fast about the war mage, forming an instant streaking pattern around it quick as a lightning flash. A rippling wave of heat shot forth, which Eric and Case both felt from some distance away. Leaves on the ground around it were pushed away and spontaneously set alight. Again the wolf veered safely away from the spell. Its plan was clear enough: to let the war mage cook itself.

It would not have long to wait, for already the war mage looked much worse for wear. Its horns had turned black from just two spells; again, it was using far more power for this enemy than its cousin had for the spells which had killed regular people, back at the door. As the wolf circled then came at it again, the war mage, awake to its game, declined to cast. The wolf split into two — one a mirror image of itself veering around as before, while the other, the real wolf, darted with a burst of speed and jumped, jaws wide and teeth like rows of knives set in a blood-red mouth.

The war mage screamed again as the wolf fell heavily upon it, both bodies thrashing around wildly in the burning sticks and leaves, its clawed feet striking and gouging at the wolf's underside. For a few frantic seconds the two mages were a thrashing blur, then a burst of red flame erupted in their midst like fireworks. The wolf yelped loud in pain and darted away again.

Blood sank thickly down the war mage's chest from where it had been bitten. Thick smoke poured from its horns and its cheeks were blackened as though with soot. But it stood again, teeth bared. The wolf wheeled about, its mirror image turning also to make a figure-eight. From a canter it started its charge, and again the war mage declined to cast. Instead, it moved straight for Eric, and with rough hands it lifted him from the ground and flew.

Eric hardly had time to figure out what was happening before the ground and the woods were suddenly things seen from high above and between his feet. Case and the huge white wolf both looked up as they rapidly dwindled to the size of insects.

The war mage's stink and heat were terrible, almost enough to make him squirm from its grasp despite the certain death a fall would bring. He felt blood from its bitten throat and chest dripping down on him, hot as droplets of boiling water on his neck and upper back.

Soon it descended to a clearing some way west where the woods were thinner, set him down, hobbled to a tree and took bites out of the trunk's bark as easily as if it were crunching into biscuits. Eric rubbed streaked drops of its blood from his collar and raised the gun. 'Take me back to my friend,' he said.

Bark crunched in the war mage's mouth, crumbs spilling from its lips. It patted the air wearily, knocking the gun from his hand and holding up a clawed finger in warning. For many minutes it ignored him and ate bark, until the smoke pouring from its horns gradually thinned to nothing, and they returned to their dirty dull yellow. 'Take me back to my friend,' Eric said.

'You're Shadow.'

'*Stop* fucking saying that. Take me back.' Eric picked up the gun again.

'Two drops in the river,' the war mage said, gesturing incomprehensibly.

'I will shoot you. Take me back now.'

It took Eric by the underarms again and began to fly, its heat now duller. At first he thought it was obeying his wish, but when the treetops were again below his feet, he saw that the huge white wolf ran towards the place they'd just left, and that Case now rode on its back, clutching onto its neck for dear life.

56

They did not fly high enough for a commanding view of the landscape, but the road could soon be seen dissecting the woods, which stretched as far as sight to either side of it. Every so often down in the trees were lone dark shapes standing motionless: Tormentors, *perfectly still*. One was far larger, standing well over the surrounding trees. What's more, that one wasn't very far from the road, over which a wagon train now passed, its passengers oblivious to the deadly peril nearby.

Yet there weren't really enough of the monsters below to explain the vast number of tracks across acres of forest floor . . .

Though his legs dangled over a lethal height, and though its touch repulsed him, Eric never thought the war mage would drop him. He had a feeling the creature felt it had 'rescued' him from the dangerous wolf and, seeing it would lose its fight to the death, had no choice but to flee and carry Eric to safety. He had tried asking what it now intended, or why it felt a need to serve him in the first place, if that *was* indeed its purpose, but its answers were too cryptic to understand.

As they flew into buffeting air, the scrub gave way to rolling fields and remnants of villages with overgrown fields, abandoned wagons and no people in sight. Great blue glass-like domes round as balloons bulged from the earth like massive swollen eyes. To Eric they looked like some kind of covered city, marvellous to behold.

The war mage's grip was tight about his chest, its scraping breath in his ear. Thin threads of magic wound towards the flying mage as though attracted to it. When they passed through denser veins of colour it would put on a burst of speed. The hateful woods were soon gone from sight completely and, as much as he feared for Case still amongst it, this brought no small measure of relief.

Every now and then the war mage set down in a safe clearing below to rest, and ease itself of the heat which accrued in its body from the efforts of flying. Eric wished he knew what to think. *Two drops in the river*, it had said. Had that meant that he and Case followed the same current, the same path, and would end up in the same place? 'Do you take me to Elvury?' Eric asked it. His last attempt to threaten it with the Glock had failed, and now the war mage seemed unconcerned by it.

It cocked its head, animal eyes peering at him, then it seemed to bow. 'A servant,' was all it said. Yet, unless he was mistaken, the next time they took off, they had changed direction, almost as though it had taken his question for instruction and agreed to follow it.

Sleepless hours passed in this fashion — flight, rest, flight — until before long mountains loomed on the horizon.

Both Case and the wolf watched them fly above the line of trees and out of sight, this time headed south-west. The loss of his friend, maybe for real this time, made Case feel so hollow he didn't care, just then, whether or not the wolf meant to rip his throat out.

It didn't *appear* to want that — back by the river it had lowered itself and gestured with its head for him to get on, after all. Now it stood panting to get its breath back, head sunk as though it felt worse than Case did. Christ, how he wanted a drink.

He got off its back and dropped to the ground, wincing as his bad knee flared at the impact. 'Thanks for the lift,' he said. 'Too bad my pack's back there with all the food in it. Hope you know that horned bastard saved our lives. Now what do we do?'

Case had turned away and was kicking at the undergrowth as he spoke, so it came as a surprise when a strained voice answered: 'It saved you? Tell me.'

He wheeled around and saw a sight that made him recoil. The wolf was changing into a man, but was only partly finished. It lay sprawled and shrinking, the beginnings of a face forming from the mess of the wolf's splitting jaws. Its fur had already been shed. With loud cracks the bones broke and changed shape.

It took minutes before the change was complete, and a man crouched in the midst of the shed hair. His age was hard to pick, maybe in the forties, face dark with stubble, lined and creased, hair brown but greying and swept up in two ridges at the sides. He was clad in an overcoat that was green at first but soon shifted colour to match the speckled pattern of the background of trees and undergrowth. Far Gaze watched him and waited impatiently. 'Well? Speak!'

'Sorry, you kind of startled me. I don't often see that kind of thing. Strange world I come from, eh?' Case wearily told him what had happened with the war mage and the Tormentor. Far Gaze held up a palm when he'd heard enough and said, 'We have a long way to travel. I won't trouble you with an account of what I went through to find you. Or of how tired I am. Imagine I simply appeared, for your benefit, a protector, humble, eager to please, with no pains and cares, no wish but to assist.'

Case shrugged. 'It's a deal.'

'You will ride my back. I will be unable to speak to you, and I may have trouble understanding you. If there's anything important to tell me, do it now. This ... process, is less comfortable than it looks.'

'You're about to change back into a wolf?'

Far Gaze didn't bother answering. He lay flat and writhed around in great pain, retching sounds in his throat, foam on his lips. The white fur he'd shed before gathered itself about him again as though drawn by magnet. More sprouted from his neck and face. Case said, 'Can I ask something first? Why did you attack Stranger?'

'Who?' Far Gaze said through gritted teeth which lengthened and moved.

'The woman in the green dress.'

Far Gaze looked at him, grimacing as his bones cracked, extended and reshaped. 'She means ... ill. Whether she ... thinks she ... helps or ... not. She steers us to ... foul futures, your own ... steps leading us all ... down their paths. Why we all ... follow you, only ... the Spirits know. May my ... sight be faulty. Maybe it is. Maybe—' his speech became unintelligible.

Case threw his hands up with frustration. 'You know, it didn't seem like a hard question to me. Where I come from, if you try to bite someone's throat out, you have a reason you can sum up in a few words. Slept with my wife, ripped me off, whatever. You're almost as bad as the guy with horns. *He* was a beat poet and a half, let me tell you. All you magic types crazy, or is it the rest of us? Maybe it sounds to you like *we're* the ones speaking in riddles.'

But Far Gaze said no more, for his jaw fell away and two thick pieces of bone assembled around the gap left there like closing pincers, fur sprouting from them, fangs lengthening. Soon the wolf was back, big as a horse, climbing awkwardly to its feet and lowering its neck again for him to ride.

After a brief internal debate, Case got back on and grabbed its neck tight. The wolf sprang forwards, clumsily at first, as though adjusting to its new form, before picking up speed and bounding through the trees, unmindful of the long groping branches that broke on its flanks.

Case hung on and waited, endured the sting of scraping branches, his eyes shut because every tree trunk looked like it was about to smack them head on. He didn't much care what happened now . . . after parting from Eric so many times and having so many unlikely reunions, he couldn't see luck favouring them yet again.

Nor was he able to see the Invia high above, the survivor of the two who had witnessed his passage from Otherworld, back near the castle. She had seen the disturbances in the air that indicated powerful recent spells, and had come for a closer look. She watched him pass with keen eyes, recognising both him and the charm in his pocket: she had been searching for both.

Neither Case nor Far Gaze saw her swoop after them, maintaining her height for now and waiting for a good moment to approach, her wings beating at air thick with magic.

57

They flew through the night, resting for one long stretch so Eric could sleep, though this was difficult with the war mage rigidly perched nearby, its gleaming yellow cat's eyes flickering about in the darkness, its breath rasping like something about to die. Though it had evidently been as gentle with him as it could be — *a servant*, after all — his chest badly ached from where its arms had gripped him, especially where he'd been stabbed by the groundman's spear, and he was tired of its animal reek.

The night was too complete here for Eric to guess at the kind of terrain below, but they were high up on a hilltop, and had before the light faded been getting ever closer to the mountains. He was so exhausted sleep did briefly drag him like a rough arm under dark dreamless waves.

When a hand shook him awake, he murmured, 'Case?' then screamed shrilly as the war mage's savage, bearded face loomed inches from his own, unblinking, mouth hung open, its foul strange breath overpowering. Then it all came back to him, and they were flying again, day about to break.

As they neared Elvury the war mage gained altitude so it could stay near the thicker threads of shimmering raw magic, which thinned out the closer they got to the city. The less magic air it flew through, the faster its body had been heating; and now Eric cried out, for the mage burned hot against his body. From high up, as they paused to rest on a jutting ledge, Eric saw the large force assembled and waiting in the fields just beyond the mountain pass. There was a swarm of activity down there in the early morning light: voices sounding off, orders being barked, the *chink* of metal on metal — chain mail, and swords being drawn.

Their view of the mountain pass which led to Elvury's gate was not very clear, but there too the ground was alive with activity, only some of it visible, as defenders moved around in their positions along many key points. A war was clearly unfolding, the war none of the Mayors would in their right minds have predicted, nor any general in his right mind have attempted.

But the General below knew things the Mayors did not.

Of course he knew he would soon lose a good many troops, likely half his invading force. And that for economic and political reasons this did not at all displease the Strategists back at the castle. The troops here gathered, though they came from many cities, were for the most part staunch Valour men, and no harm was done in shedding *their* numbers. Meanwhile those unsworn or already accepting Vous as their Spirit — at least professing to — were safe at home or on easy campaigns.

He also knew that — casualties or not — the city *would* be theirs, or at least no longer belong to its current Mayor. For something lurked beneath it the Mayors' Command had not seen coming, and it had already begun its deadly work within the city's gates during the night. The defenders in high places along the mountain pass, waiting to rain death down upon the General's men, would probably just now be getting news of what had begun.

It had started later than intended, of course. The delay had tested everyone's patience, from the poor doomed men who'd slept for a week in these fields, to the distant castle Strategists who were probably still panicking that something had gone fatally wrong after years and years of careful planning.

But at last the General heard horns blowing in the city, the notes which meant *flee, evacuate*. It had begun. By now, if any defenders remained in the high mountain passes, there was a good chance they were the only defenders the city had. There would be, the General was told, roughly a hundred creatures, minus what the city's fleeing military could slay. These, his men — perhaps half the original twelve thousand — would finish off. Then they had a pleasant time of looting and plunder to look forward to ...

The General's main concern now was mutiny as he ordered thousands of men to charge, knowingly, to their probable deaths. Of the twelve thousand gathered, two thousand were here strictly to suppress such an event. Valour men were not noted for cowardice ... nor, however, did they take kindly to treachery, from their commanders or anyone else, hence defectors like Anfen. The General cleared his throat, not without nerves, to give the order to march into the pass.

During the night, pouring from the sewers, from passages below-ground pre-existing *and* those newly forged by groundmen slaves under whips, from the River Misery, which ran in two offshoots under the city's busiest districts, Tormentors came in their hundreds.

If all went well, if the Strategists' estimates were right — and they usually were — by morning, most citizens would have already fled through the southern gates, carrying with them stories of a deadly weapon in castle hands to the cities they escaped to. Not strictly true, but a very useful perception. Those cities would then have hard decisions to make, such as: Align, or be next. This city's wealth, meanwhile, would sit largely abandoned in chests and safes to be pillaged at leisure. And there would be one fewer stronghold for defectors and Aligned country refugees.

The Tormentors rose from belowground into the city's northern quarter. Some were so big that new underground highways had been built just for their passage here from the woods, where they'd been gathered and herded at considerable cost in lives. (The creatures could not easily be predicted and *certainly* not commanded.) At times they tolerated human and animal life nearby, even when it was loud and brash, when fingers were snapped in their faces or when they were prodded with sticks, as experiments had shown. Other times they attacked anything alive, roaming far to seek out prey, using that peculiar magic effect which none yet understood. Their behaviour towards one another seemed to be passive and even co-operative, though not to any observer's view *organised*, as such. But they had never been observed in such numbers and in such close proximity as this. The larger ones were generally the most placid, but always the least predictable. Herding the big ones had not proved possible ... but a handful *had* indeed followed their smaller kindred to the city of their own accord.

This invasion had been a difficult and expensive secret to keep. Very few of those unfortunates mind-controlled and trained to steer Tormentors were left alive in the miles-long tunnels. Many of the creatures remained still and silent in the highways belowground, but enough, easily enough, found their way towards the sounds and vibrations of the city, even as it tossed and turned in its sleep. As they neared the surface, the greatest noise and vibrations came from the northern quarter, and it was there they were drawn. There, in the wide, flat space before the northern gate, and manning the turrets and shelves up along the gate and walls, the city's defenders waited for horn calls in the pass to alert them of the coming enemy.

High on the artificial shelf ringing around and above the city, Anfen tossed uneasily in his bed, trapped in nightmares under Loup's sleeping spell. On his arrival, gazing at the crowds, he had reflected on the presence in the city of spies, usurpers and the castle's Hunters. He hadn't known that operatives had been here for years in greater numbers than anyone feared, chiefly in the city's underground trade routes and their overseeing bureaucracy: smooth-tongued Hunters legally working their way into key positions of the city's governance with a store of gold on hand to bribe, and the skills to murder enemies as needed, all of them taking orders from a distance. The underground highways leading from the woods were not merely for the transport of felled timber — *that* had been guessable enough, to those in the know. But the Strategists had told no one when the invasion would come, or what it would look like.

Nearly two hundred construction workers slept on-site beneath the surface. Tormentors came past their dim lantern-lit bunkers with enough wooden creaking for a ship at sea. Some men woke to screams echoing from deeper down the tunnels, then louder ones from nearby rooms. They found nightmares standing by their beds gazing at them with frozen alien smiles, others passing in great numbers past their doorways. Some thought they themselves still dreamed, even as time lagged and all they knew were razor-sharp points and edges, moving so very slowly.

The Tormentors stalked in their stilted gait past those screaming and fleeing, to the surface's fresher air and better light. Once the last shrieks had been silenced in the bunkers the only sound was the constant *creak creak creak*, magnified many times, as death from beyond World's End climbed at last to the surface and poured out freely onto the streets.

At the city's northern gate, those posted in the many nooks and battlements keeping watch on the mountain pass fancied for a moment or two that the wind bore the sound of screaming. But it was so faint they weren't sure, until those few people out and about at night — vagrants, night-workers, whores and their customers — saw dark, stalking shapes in the gloom, some of them huge.

A bustle of activity began amongst the soldiers. A horn blew, followed by another. Braziers were lit and the place was filled with the orange glow of firelight. All troops were now awake, thousands soon in formation. Orders were shouted. Metal hissed a thousand times as weapons were drawn. Most turned towards the gate, thinking the screams that came from within the city were from artillery fire, missiles catapulted over the city walls and over their own heads — yet, why had no warnings sounded from the mountain pass? No one posted in the high places outside had blown his horn to signal *enemy sighted*.

A clear enough sign came suddenly behind them. A tall shape — surely beyond six man-heights — swept with loping, swinging arms between two buildings. Those who saw it froze for a moment in disbelief before a rain of arrows flew at the lumbering beast. Arrows that struck it skittered off its hide. It stopped and swung its head their way, the enormous mane fanned out behind its head rattling, and stared at them. Another rain of arrows flew and fell; the sound of them glancing off the beast's hide then onto the cobblestones below was like hail on a rooftop.

A whole company rushed over to meet it while it watched them, still motionless. Screams began to sound more frequently from deeper within the city as hundreds of the beasts, smaller than the giant one but almost always bigger than any man, poured towards the waiting soldiers from the shadows with fast jagged strides and turned the area into a churning sea of death.

The huge one ambled over too, as though convinced at last by the screams of fear and pain, and the ring of blades striking hard hides, that it too had a role to play. Arrows from the high wall still glanced off it harmlessly as it reached down into the crowds of men.

58

A hand shook Anfen's shoulder with urgency, rousing him from the deep dreams of his spell-made sleep. If they were supposed to be pleasant dreams, Loup had got the spell wrong, or else the magic was too thin for him here. Anfen had seen nothing but death painted in vivid, sickening colours and marching to horrible music. On waking, his new sword was drawn by old instinct, and he was surprised to see it was Siel by his bed, whose hand usually calmed the instinct to draw his blade when she roused him. 'What's the matter?' he said.

'War has broken,' she replied in a voice of forced calm. 'An emissary came for us. They are evacuating the Mayors, all officialdom, and us. We leave now. No time to pack, they say.'

Anfen was on his feet, slapping his own face to shake off the effects of Loup's spell. His thoughts were sluggish. It was still dark. Out the window there were fires burning below. He could make out part of the city's northern wall at a distance and saw the braziers had been lit. There wasn't much else to see down there, except —

'By all the Spirits! Siel, look at that!'

The huge Tormentor — he recognised it as such at once — strode past the gate. It slowly reached high up the wall and plucked an archer off the shelves up there, while others could be seen leaping to their deaths to avoid its touch. As they watched, it carefully impaled the squirming man it had grabbed on the spike of its left shoulder as though it were placing an ornament on itself. Anfen was sickened to see, in the braziers' light, writhing shapes of other men still alive but similarly impaled on the many long spikes all down the beast's body. Spears and arrows were fired at it from the ground and from the high wall, but it was hard to tell if anything had stuck into it. The beast thumped huge hands against the gate, making it shudder and boom, then ambled away with lurching steps till it was hidden from their view by buildings.

Gazing further across the city, Anfen saw one, two other huge shapes moving about, their outlines lit by fires which had begun to spread through the streets. Horns began to blare as the city wakened from sleep into a nightmare. Anfen was partly awestruck by what he'd seen. 'Valour help us,' he whispered, not even realising he'd said this prayer; having brought such shame to himself with sword in hand and cries to the Spirit on his lips, he'd sworn never to speak Valour's name again.

Siel pulled him from the window, otherwise he might have watched on until it all played out to its end, helpless to look away. 'We must go,' she said.

Anfen came back to himself with a start. 'We're not going with the Mayors. You and the others. Get horses and follow me. We have a new mission.'

He grabbed his things then rushed through the luxury inn with its marble walls, trickling fountains and scented air. Many guests waited in confusion in the lobby, self-important foreign officials among them. He saw one such in the colours of Yinfel, having a heated argument with a girl doing the luggage boy's job, since he'd likely been called away to the gate and handed a bow and arrow to defend the city. Anfen ran over and grabbed the bloated, red-faced man, who reeled back, startled and angered. 'Listen close,' said Anfen. 'A message for your Mayor, Izven. The discussed cargo to be delivered *now*, directly five miles west of the end of the great dividing road. Not a *footstep* beyond. Your Mayor alone to hear these words and hear them soon, or I will hunt you down. The message comes from Anfen of the Mayors' Command.'

He ran outside to the high shelf and forced himself not to look down at the chaos. The first light of day began to turn the sky white. Men with pikes were erecting a barricade at the top of the long ramp down to the city, to keep the Tormentors and refugees away from the city's tall shelf and its precious tunnels out, so the officials could more easily escape. A last group of people escaping the carnage were allowed to flee past before the pikes and spears went up. Those trapped on the ramp wailed and screamed; some passed young children over. The guards took the children and tossed weapons back over the barricade for the rest to defend themselves and defend the ramp.

Anfen ran for the stables, not caring whose horse he was about to steal — the tired scrawny things that had brought them here wouldn't suffice. Siel and Sharfy spotted him and followed, against the heavy flow of people rushing for the secret exits through the caves. Neither of them spoke as Anfen shoved past the protesting stable hands and got up on the finest steed he could find. 'Get yourselves horses,' he ordered.

But Siel had an arrow drawn and a tear sliding down her cheek. At present, the bow pointed at the ground. Anfen looked at her, amazed. 'What is this? Look outside. Tell me what you see.'

'We serve the Mayors' Command,' said Siel, 'not you. Wait for their permission. Whatever happened in the night has surely changed their view of things.'

'There's no time left for their blather. Put your arrow away.'

Siel's arrow rose to point at his chest. He tried to gauge from the look in her eye whether or not she'd shoot him if he rode past her. Probably. So be it. It would count as an honourable death. He flicked the horse's reins.

The stable hands had run back towards the inn to spread word of trouble. Now, a few guards approached along the city's high, curved shelf with weapons drawn.

Sharfy looked from Siel to Anfen to the approaching guards, and he drew the sword he'd bought yesterday from smiths in the Bazaar. It now flashed sideways, knocking Siel's bow off target. The arrow loosed and skidded across the ground. He wrenched the bow from her hands and hurled it into a pile of hay. Soon he too found a quality mount already saddled and climbed up. 'Be safe,' Anfen told Siel, who stood helplessly watching them with tears streaking down her face.

His horse galloped out onto the shelf, rearing as it passed the guards, Sharfy following. They headed against the flow of people for the long ramps down, and found one whose barricade was not yet in place. They began steering through a panicking mass of citizens fleeing for the southern gate. From Elvury, the Wall at World's End would be a week's hurried ride through far safer country than the Aligned north, if they rode like the wind straight down the great dividing road and changed horses at every chance. Which was what Anfen intended.

He hoped that as he rode a way to destroy the Wall would occur to him, for he still had no idea how it could be done.

When Loup heard what had happened, he found a steed of his own and headed after them.

59

'A city,' said the war mage, bowing again as though it were his butler, and pointing a hooked claw at something off in the distance. Though Eric could not see Elvury, he could see smoke pouring into a faintly brightening white sky, empty of magic. He assumed the lack of magic was why the war mage had set him down here, on the ledge of a small cave above the mouth of a mountain pass.

The war mage waited for instructions, cat-yellow eyes studying him carefully. He had no thought for it at all, for below in broad columns soldiers poured from the fields and into the narrow pass with shields held over their heads, boots stomping the ground like a drumbeat. Only after the last row of men had made their way into the tunnel did anything happen: an explosive noise sounded at the entrance, echoing off the sheer cliff faces. A huge column of stone fell out of a groove in the cliff's wall and slammed across the road, making a quick escape back through the pass impossible.

At intervals along the road, smaller columns were by invisible means blown free from the walls with sounds like huge whips cracking to thud down across the path. The invaders scrambled in panic to avoid being crushed, which most of them managed to do. The fallen pillars made their passage slow —

made a charge at the city's gate at the other end of the mile-long pass nearly impossible. Once retreat was cut off, a hail of arrows and stones began to rain down. The shields held overhead made it look as if insects with shells crawled sluggishly along, and sent arrows glancing to the ground with the odd flash of sparks lighting up the pass.

Weighted rope ladders flew up over the roadblocks near the gates, and men scrambled over. Far fewer missiles rained down on them than should have, for many of the pass's defenders had fled their perches and run back to see why horns blared in the city. Two-thirds of the invading force survived their passage through that hellish stretch, to regroup in the space beside the huge gate, safe from attack. None of the rank and file yet knew what awaited them behind the city walls, only that something unnamed would leave Elvury's defences weak by the time they got inside, that their mission was to finish the city off then enjoy a day's plunder before the castle overseers arrived to catalogue the takings.

Back along the 'road of death', as it would be known in tavern lore, thousands of bodies in colours of many Aligned cities were piled in a short space, with no one to collect the wounded or to finish off those dying slowly. At the tunnel's entrance, waiting with the elite unit sent to stamp out any potential rebellion, the General ordered the deaths of those few who'd refused to enter the pass. Some had got away and fled towards the elemental plains, where punishment enough probably awaited them from the wild things there. There had not been many deserters, little more than a hundred in all. The General marvelled at the waste of troops so brave. Vous's feet had trampled this road, and Valour, if he had watched the fight at all, gave no battlefield reprieve.

60

High up as he was, Eric was mercifully too far to see many details in the gruesome picture below. The distant sounds of it, the screams and thuds of heavy rocks toppling, were bad enough. Then had come the huge logs, soaked in flammable oil and tossed down amongst the scrambling bodies, to be lit by fire-tipped arrows.

The war mage hadn't shown much interest in proceedings down there; once or twice it had made rasping speech Eric took to mean it wished for them to leave. 'The city is just over there, isn't it? Is it safe there?'

'*Not* safe,' it answered, surprisingly lucid.

'Are you sure? That army lost a lot of men.'

It clawed the air with its fingers, irritated. 'A ship sails on ... churning waves. A wave crashes into ... churning rocks. Rocks fall on ... churning *ground* ...'

Eric nearly succumbed to the urge to kick it. 'Fuck! I wish you could speak clearer. What do you intend for me, then? To take me to Anfen?'

It looked confused. 'A servant.'

'A servant, great. Know what? I wish you'd change clothes. Is the human skin really needed? It's supposed to look like human skin, to make you feared, right? In fact, *is* that human skin?'

A high-pitched garble sounded in its throat.

'Great. You're wearing human skin. Just great. So is Anfen at the city or not? Let's find him. Take me inside.'

The war mage spat and made a rasping sound of disapproval, but grasped him again and leaped off the ledge. For two seconds they plunged straight down until it veered away from the deathly scene in the pass, making a curved line through the sheer walls for the northern gate. From this short flight, with no visible magic in the air its body was soon almost too heated to bear, its breathing a deathly rattle. Flight in skies thick with magic had heated it up much more slowly.

The huge gate approached. Beyond it plumes of smoke poured into Elvury's skies and horns blew like pained cries. The first invaders to make it through the pass gathered off to the left in an area free from raining arrows and rocks, and waited for others to catch up.

The war mage perched up on a high turret on the gate itself, smoke and stink puffing from its overheated body. The city unveiling beyond was bigger than Eric had anticipated. The far southern gate was too distant to see, even from this high up. Thousands of rooftops and steep roads extended out across ground that dramatically sloped away from the mountains on the right and left of the gate. They'd landed on the highest part of the city's wall, atop of which was a thick platform with room for defenders to take places for shooting below. In both directions were bows, shields, quivers and slings lying discarded. It took a moment for him to realise that what defenders remained did not face the pass, where the invaders still streamed through. They faced back into the city, and from the walls occasional arrows rained down inside it.

Directly below on the city's side was what might have looked like a child's messy room, with toy soldiers scattered around in broken parts, were it not for the litter of organs and blood spread thick on the pavement. Screams and distant sounds like explosions could be heard, and fires raged. There were few survivors moving about.

Still as statues down there — still for the most part — were Tormentors, and suddenly Eric understood: *dead city*; the reason the pit devils had been driven north; and the timing of the troop build-up. There, the reasons stood motionless or stalked around in that jagged, lurching stride, like badly controlled puppets. A mass of spent arrows littered the ground, many of which had hit their targets and bounced away, only the most powerful bows and crossbow bolts piercing the monsters' hides. No foot soldiers remained standing to fight back. In the far distance was the unmistakeable shape of a Tormentor, only it was massive, striding between buildings, then lost from view. 'Holy shit,' Eric said.

'Not safe,' rasped the war mage, clutching at his sleeve, its foul breath like rotting meat. 'You're Shadow.'

In places, the odd Tormentor corpse lay in broken pieces, though each one was massively outnumbered by human bodies. Eric wondered if Anfen's corpse was down there too, and supposed it probably was.

Behind, the arrows and rocks had all but ceased raining down in the pass. There was a bustle of activity on the ground just outside the city, where among the sizeable crowd of invaders who'd survived, battering rams were being prepared for an assault on the gate. The war mage's bird-like feet scratched and tapped impatiently at the ground, as though trying to communicate what its voice had failed to. For the first time, Eric wondered how the locals here would react to the sight of it. He said, 'Stay here. OK? *Don't move.* I have to go speak to one of those archers, but they might think you're an enemy. Understand? I'll be back.'

It cocked its head, but gave no indication of having understood. Eric ran to the nearest huddling shape, some way along
where the top of the wall met the iron gate. A young archer
— fifteen, sixteen at most, with a chubby freckled face and
drooping bottom lip — looked towards him with blank, shell-
shocked eyes. The kid made no motion to use the curved wooden
bow which lay on his lap, one hand limply resting on its string.
Eric kneeled beside him and could smell the kid had pissed
himself in fright. 'I'm a friend,' he said lamely. 'My name's
Eric. Are you OK?'

The kid shrugged without a change of expression.

'What happened here?'

'What does it look like?' the kid said, his voice flat.

'I'm the wrong person to ask. Looks like nothing I've ever
seen before. I'm going to find a man named Anfen. Do you know
of him? He works for the Mayor. Do you know where I'd find
him, or the Mayor?'

The kid shrugged and pointed across where the shelf jutted
from the mountainside, held up by thick pillars and running
like a halo above the city. Perhaps some magic had gone into
its construction, for in many parts it seemed to defy gravity.
Here and there ramps ran down to the city below, but guards
were posted behind barricades closing them off. Rich-looking
buildings were lined along the shelf where the young archer
had pointed, and people were moving there in heavy traffic.
'Why don't you come over there with me?' Eric said. 'They look
safe over there.'

'They'll die soon,' the kid said in that same flat voice and
shrugged. 'Everything will.'

It occurred to Eric that the kid just may have seen colleagues,
mates — even his own father — slain directly below. He crouched
down beside him and put a hand on his shoulder. 'Maybe, but

it's less lonely over there. And wouldn't you like a bite to eat? I sure would.'

The sound of footsteps shuffling behind him. *Oh shit.* The war mage had come. The kid's face broke out of its shocked blankness and his eyes went wide.

'Don't worry, he's with me,' said Eric. To the war mage, *'Don't hurt him!* You don't need to protect me from him, OK? He's a friend.'

'Ah, but,' the war mage rasped, hands moving expansively, face animated, voice fast. 'Once a man approached his mirror not thinking the glass to be *liquid* and in he fell. Drawn sideways he was from a high place such as this into a sea-sized pool of reflection, battered by his own *fists* from the other side of the unshattered *glass*, as per falling rocks into the churning *broth* ...' Its cat-yellow eyes flared wide and it began that swaying dance, side to side on its feet, arms raised high, a growl in its throat. The kid instinctively raised an arrow to the string. *'Certain* fires are not for warmth,' the war mage rasped, a warning finger raised, its voice melding with the growl in its throat. *'Certain* flames don't touch candle wicks but burn them *down.'*

'Settle down, don't attack him!'

'Where *spells* fail are *claws* and *teeth* ...'

Eric felt heat building in the war mage, saw it crouching in the pose it used during its fight with Far Gaze in the woods. A single thread of hair-thin discoloured air wound down from the sky and touched the diamond-shaped tip of its staff.

There wasn't even time to think about it: he took the gun, held it to the war mage's head and pulled the trigger. The Glock's huge noise made Eric almost drop it in shock, made the young archer drop his bow and throw himself sideways, hands over ears. The war mage staggered back a pace or two, its staff clattering to the floor, and its body toppling stiffly over the edge.

Just before it fell, its head revolved very slowly towards Eric, mouth slightly open, eyes wide with what was — he assumed — a look of profoundest surprise.

The body tumbled down. A dozen Tormentors, perhaps drawn by the gunshot, ran towards the city wall and took apart the war mage's body. Eric swallowed, expecting to feel the way he had after shooting the Invia, but somehow he didn't. It felt like he'd just put an animal down, perhaps regrettable but perfectly necessary. There was no more time to reflect, for arrows began to fly from the invaders outside the gate, glancing off the turrets, some landing close to them.

The archer stared at him, not yet recovered from his surprise. Eric put the gun in his pocket. The brief rain of arrows ceased and he chanced a look down. On the wall's other side the invading castle army prepared the battering ram for its assault on the door. Many heads turned upwards seeking whatever had made the gun's noise. 'Come on,' said Eric. 'We have to go. I don't think it'll be safe here much longer.'

'You saved me,' the kid said with no more conviction than someone commenting on the weather. Eric couldn't tell if he was grateful or not.

'I guess so,' he answered. 'Want to do me a favour back? Help me find Anfen or the Mayor.'

The kid nodded and stood, pausing to sling the bow over his shoulder. Eric followed him and tried not to look down on either side. The first battering ram charge boomed out like a massive struck drum, but the iron door didn't tremble. A few more archers were scattered along the high wall, and more could be heard down on lower levels. Eric was shocked that many were as young as or younger than the kid leading him around.

'What was that spell you cast?' the kid paused to ask him. 'What kind of mage are you?'

'Spell? No. It was a weapon. I'm from—' should he tell? '—from Otherworld.'

The kid frowned. 'Where's that?'

'A long, long way away.' For some reason he felt a lump in his throat to say it.

'And the spell was in your weapon?'

'I guess you could say that.'

'Is it the same Anfen who won Valour's Helm?'

'Yes.'

The kid nodded and led him on. There came a bridge which led from the city wall to the thick ledge of a cliff, and from there they came to the artificial shelf ringing the city high above. Soon, though Eric didn't know it, he walked the same path Anfen and the others had walked little more than a day before. Many people stood and helplessly watched the situation below, faces grim or disbelieving, while official-looking groups were led the opposite way, out through the secret passages in the hillsides behind. Eric followed the young archer through the bustling crowd, when suddenly he saw a familiar face among those gazing down at the carnage. 'Siel!' he said. The boy, evidently feeling his task complete and debt repaid, wandered away and was gone from sight in the crowds.

She turned and looked at him with a neutral expression, though her eyes showed she'd been crying. She was not, it seemed, half as surprised to see him as he was to see her. She walked towards him slowly. 'You're back,' she said. 'Have a nice adventure?'

'Hardly. What's wrong? Is Anfen dead?'

She scoffed. 'Shall we send you to check if he's there?' A hand went to the curved blade on her belt and he saw she was shivering with anger. When he got over his surprise, he said, 'Wait! Don't do it. I can explain what happened.'

She inclined her head with a humourless smile as if to say: *I very much look forward to it.* 'And where's the old twit?'

'I don't know. Maybe on his way here with the wolf, Far Gaze.'

She looked with a moment's pause at the war mage's staff in his hand, which he didn't even remember picking up. 'The charm?' she said.

'He still has it.' Eric told his story, the hardest part explaining his motives in following Case, since he'd done it with her own words echoing in his ears. Siel paced back and forth while she listened, tugging on her braids so hard it surely hurt her. The part about Kiown she asked him to repeat word for word, and her eyes shut when she heard it the second time. She said, 'Are you sure?'

'It's all true. Even the part about Nightmare.'

She said nothing, but gestured for him to continue, wiping a fresh tear from her face. When he told her about the war mage, her eyes narrowed and fists clenched. '*They* want you back with Anfen,' she said, incredulous.

'So it'd seem. Case thought the war mage was just nuts, acting on its own, not on orders.'

She scoffed again and paced along the ledge, thinking. People still bustled around them, many now watching the northern gate, at which a steady pounding could be heard from the invaders' battering rams. 'So much you think you know,' she said after a while.

'Of Kiown, you mean?'

Her laugh was bitter. 'And Anfen, of course.'

'What do you mean? You don't think he's in league with—?'

'I don't know,' she said quietly. 'I don't know any more. But I see now why Kiown would fuck anything that moved but not me. I'd learn his secrets.'

They both watched the carnage below for a while without

speaking. 'Why not go riding?' she said at last. 'Let's discover the rest of the surprises. If there are provisions left at our inn, we'll take what we can, but I doubt the important people will have left much behind. No matter. We'll be riding through safer country this time, provided no Invia come for you, Marked one.'

'Where are we headed? Is Anfen even here?'

'He's off to destroy the Wall at World's End,' she said and laughed. She looked down again at the now eerily quiet streets. 'Maybe he's right to try it, whatever the Mayors say. Maybe I shouldn't have tried to stop him. We may soon know. Let's get horses.' She put a hand on his arm. 'And I hope your friend shows up.' It was no well-wishing: *because I intend to slice him up the middle*, her wide dark eyes had said.

61

A human flood poured south: refugees clogged the roads, clutching what possessions they'd been able to carry through the frantic press of escaping bodies through the southern gate. The road was littered here and there with things cast aside as the realities of travel sank in, and a day or two of hauling excess weight proved plenty enough. The inns between Elvury and the closest city, Yinfel, were so stuffed that patrons paid big money to sleep under tables in their pubs, or in their closets. A good number refused to stop moving, certain the Tormentors would pursue them. But no new sightings were heard of.

News of Elvury's doom travelled along the road much faster than the trudge of its refugees, spreading to the other Free Cities, whose forces frantically checked their underground passages and ramped up defences. Tormentors were now widely known of and rumoured to be attacking at the castle's behest. There had indeed been sightings of them in remote places, usually from far away, those who saw them not having known what they saw, those who'd got too close not surviving to report it.

Through these nearly impassable crowds, Siel and Eric set out. That first day he slipped from his mount four times, miraculously escaping broken bones. They were fine steeds, tall and muscled as racing horses. Siel and Eric discovered why the 'important folk' hadn't wished to brave travel on ground-level through the deadly stampede for the southern gate. On one nightmarish street half a dozen Tormentors had gathered to stand around motionless in strange poses, victims littered about their feet. The huge ones had slunk back towards the river as though all following the same impulse and, according to talk, stood motionless along the banks watching people flee, bodies impaled all over them, some still slowly writhing and screaming for help. The Tormentors loose in the city were bad enough; looters, invading soldiers, raging fires and occasional riots had not made things any safer.

The only light moment for Eric and Siel was when they found Loup patiently waiting by the roadside for them with a wide toothless smile and his own plundered horse.

Most on the road, Siel and Eric included, tried not to think about what they'd left behind. They tried to shut out the wailing of refugees unused to war so close at hand and no longer a distant abstraction, unused to being caught in the shadows of a man-god's descending feet. It had all been so quiet for so long, the state of conflict between the Free and Aligned worlds ... tense, but out of sight like an earthquake brewing. The shock on the refugees' sleep-deprived faces said it all, the stagger of their walk as though under new and terrible weight, the disbelief as it sank in: *We're not going home tonight. There is no 'home'.*

Eric felt guilty at his relief on finally passing the grim-faced vanguard and leaving them behind on the road. Siel made no secret of hers. Loup whistled a tune like he hadn't a care in the world.

Meanwhile the General leading the invasion had a far larger 'mop-up' operation on his hands than he had been led to expect.

His men slammed open the city gates at last, lulled by the silence on the other side. He'd expected a few score of the creatures, a hundred at most, not several hundreds of them, all difficult to kill, some huge.

They made a dent in the monsters' numbers before the last of the invading soldiers were killed or fled, enough to make the real mop-up a job at least *possible*. The General had missed something: that while men could be sacrificed, so too could generals who walked on ice that got thinner the closer they walked to the throne of power they served. The Strategists had long ago marked him as 'ambitious', a potential threat, and sought missions suitably deadly to throw him into, so he might have an honourable death for the rank and file's gossip, and be useful as a martyr. That his ambition in reality had extended no further than his achieved rank was neither here nor there.

62

Pushing the horses to their limits and changing them frequently gave Sharfy a sour taste, for he felt horses were friends of men more than servants. Anfen believed that too, but something had changed in him since they'd set out. There was a light in his eye Sharfy didn't much care for, nor did he like the grim silence of their journey, which made every second of it pass so heavily. The road went so much easier and faster with jokes, songs and stories.

Yet he understood what Anfen saw, what the invasion really was: the castle's hand closing its fist around the world at last. If they could take the unconquerable city in one night — years of planning or not, it *looked* like one night's work, and what your enemy *thought* you were capable of mattered as much as what you actually *were* capable of — then, surely, they could take the rest of the Free Cities at their leisure. And would. And the Mayors would begin to ponder whether they should resist the inevitable, or bargain and speed it up, to maintain their own places of power. That seemed, from Sharfy's view, to be written in the lines on Anfen's face.

Sure enough, such were the former First Captain's thoughts. Anfen had been set for a lifetime of war against them. He had not expected his side to win, but nor had he expected to see the war's end while he still lived. In one night he'd learned the final surrender could be only months away. If the Mayors panicked, as they just might, surrender by *tonight* was not impossible ...

But mostly, he pondered how the Wall might be destroyed as the landscape *clip-clopped* by and his body was tossed up and down in the saddle. The great dividing road brought him closer and closer but no ideas came. Few of the confiscated readings had mentioned the Wall. He knew only that it had existed longer than the cities had, longer than humans had. The Wall may have been made by the dragon-youth, or the great Dragon, or by some like force on its other side.

As Otherworld existed on one end of Levaal, it was held there was a world on the Wall's other side. This was claimed by ancient scrolls and artefacts left by the dragon-youth to the first generation of people, along with several other parting gifts of knowledge, all long lost. If Tormentors came from that side, and they weren't some secret creation of the castle's, what other horrors would pour across if Anfen's mission succeeded?

But no. He was well past asking whether or not he should.

They kept trading horses at stables along the way as they upped their pace and put days and leagues behind them. Anfen was merciless. They went past good inns, to Sharfy's growing dismay; he was sick to death of the road and had promised himself a lengthy rest if he made it back alive from their mission in the north. If he broke ranks and stayed at an inn, he had no doubt Anfen would go on without him. Maybe I should let him, Sharfy thought more than once, before realising: I'm not really here to destroy the Wall. Of course not. Stupid! It can't even be done. I'm here to look after *him*. He's coming unstuck like we all thought he might, one day ...

The wall itself could soon be seen, though that didn't mean

they were yet close to it. It stretched as high up as the very roof of the sky, the Wall at its upper parts sky-white so that it blended in and was practically invisible. Lower down, it was a dull glassy blue. On sight of it, the absolute insane *futility* of the mission struck Sharfy as plainly as could be, and he began to wonder about his friend in other ways. Half a dozen disquieting theories came to him: the charm said no such thing, he misheard; Anfen's been mad the whole time, war can do that to a man; the old Otherworlder's disappearance had been planned and staged; Anfen works for the enemy, his whole defection was faked; this is not really Anfen, it is some conjured illusion . . . and more, yet they pressed on, and the mad gleam in the boss's eye never dimmed, nor did the intensity of his silence relent for a moment. Nor did he seem to tire, and only by practically shoving food at his face did Sharfy remind him to eat.

Hour by hour, day by day of the endless *clip clop* of hoofbeats on paved stone. The Wall drew closer. The great dividing road, old as the Wall and splitting the world's vast, reaching east and west realms, carried them mile by mile straight to the middle of World's End.

63

Case had decided his fate long before the opportunity arose to act on his wish. For the meantime, he rode the giant wolf, suddenly feeling light-spirited and free.

For Case, it was a matter of: *how*. A drink would be nice before-hand, one final toast to those good memories, Eric's friendship being one of the latest. Shelly too, how she'd visited him almost every weekend of his sentence with those little surprise gifts. His brother Charles, before they'd parted lives with poisonous words. His old father he'd forgiven, he supposed, but never felt at peace with — no harm in a toast to the man's name. Hell, his first pet dog was worth tipping a cup for. So was the day he was released from gaol, and went to the beach as he'd dreamed of doing, even though it was winter, and just lay in the sand fully clothed, not moving for hours and hours and hours, listening to the waves murmur *freedom*. That was a good day.

His knee sizzled with pain as the wolf bounded along, panting and stinking. Case felt a moment's sympathy for the mage, and for everything else sentenced to physical existence. Out of the trees they came at last, and good riddance to each one of them. And soon the ground sloped upwards, mountains came into view, and the answer was obvious. Just as soon as they were high enough. Right about . . . now.

'Say, feller. Far Gaze, isn't it? They call me Sore Arse. Can we stop a bit? Could use a minute on my feet.'

The wolf was exhausted enough itself from loping uphill. It pulled off the path and found a spot in the shade, lying with its front paws crossed over one another. Far Gaze didn't wish to change back to human form, it seemed. It watched Case with big brown eyes.

Case smiled to put it at ease and sat near the cliff's edge, just thinking for a moment or two. So light of spirit he felt, so free. His body had taken much punishment with all this walking and travel — how nice to ease all that. He stood, stretched, and looked back at the wolf, which raised its head and watched him. Case thought it looked sad. He raised a hand to it in farewell. 'I think you know, don't you? Tell Eric to keep being one of the good guys. Tell him ... shit, I dunno. Tell him I said cheers, and thanks for the scotch.' Case limped towards the edge, performed a cross on his chest, spread his arms, whooped loudly and jumped.

The wolf sighed.

64

It had loomed upon them for nearly a week's riding, and now they came to its base. Anfen stood staring at where the road led straight into it. The country to either side of them was flat and dirt brown, the ground dug and overturned too often over the centuries in search of precious scales for things to grow here now. The Wall loomed so sheer Sharfy almost felt it would topple forwards and crush them.

The stoneflesh giants had become visible a long way back, for they were enormous. Grey as basalt, squat legs and torsos, featureless open-mouthed faces: they could have been statues but for the occasional movement of their flat round heads, surveying the world before them. Their disproportionately long fingers wound like trunks curling into knots of huge misshaped fists. They waited like sentries all along the Wall east and west, enough might in these creatures alone to easily settle *any* dispute among men, should they ever be roused and united to some cause. But the giants did not tolerate each other any more than encroachment on their space by human beings. The giant to the east had turned its head slowly towards where Anfen and Sharfy sat in their saddles on the road. They must have made a curious sight for the ancient guardian; very few people came this close to them, aside from those busy in slave mines far to the east.

'It can be done,' Anfen muttered to himself. 'They would not be here guarding it if it did not have some weakness. It can be done.'

Sharfy didn't want to say it, but: '*How* exactly, boss?'

'We'll see. Five miles west.'

They rode without speaking. The moment was dawning on Anfen, Sharfy sensed, when he would realise it was all pointless, and that he should probably head to one of the cities and report to the first Mayors' Command officer he found. No harm done, of course, apart from a stolen horse probably not even noticed in all the chaos. He'd be better off trying to convince the Mayors again to help him, if this was really likely to change things in the war. Accurate news wouldn't have travelled south any faster than them ... for all they knew, Elvury had been reclaimed by the Mayors. Sooner or later, it would occur to him. Sharfy sure hoped so. Those inns looked like they had comfortable beds, and who cared how good the ale was? It would be nectar fit for a lord after all this riding.

Sharfy hadn't known about the two catapults which waited where Anfen had told Izven to send them. They were already reassembled. Any sign of their city of origin — colours worn by their crew, the runes usually scratched into a panel of their wood — had been removed, but their low-built squarish shape looked to Sharfy's eye like the kind made in Yinfel ... how curious. Not a city known for its war machines; they didn't even use magic-crafting Engineers to enhance their works. One Mayor, then, was in on it, and perhaps *only* one Mayor. Sharfy thought: Anfen may just start a new war into the bargain here, if he's not careful ...

The crews, huge men whose main purpose in life was to lift big stones, saw Anfen approach and began speaking amongst themselves. Sharfy laughed inside at this fine joke. Catapults?

They think catapults will break the Wall? He kept his thoughts from showing and kept waiting for the moment to dawn on Anfen. Maybe he needed a round of launched stones first. Anfen didn't seem inclined to give the order. He sat on the ground with his legs crossed, head in hands. Sharfy told the crew, 'Give it a try. Fire.'

The crew looked at one another. 'Aye, well, yeah, here's the thing we been wondering. Fire at *what*, sir?'

'At what they're pointed at. The *Wall*.'

'Aye, the Wall, sir. Some of us thought that'd be it, only . . .' The crew exchanged looks and Sharfy felt acutely embarrassed. 'Worried about that giant yonder?' said another of the men, pointing at the one to the west, which had turned its head to watch them.

'Plenty of time to see it coming,' said Sharfy, shrugging, though he was, now that they mentioned it, worried about it indeed. 'Holes just behind us to duck into, if it comes. Go on, fire.'

The crewmen shrugged, *food in the belly — s'long as we're paid, we couldn't give a fuck how stupid the orders are —* and pulled taut the creaking twisting ropes which stored energy for the launch. They loaded up the first round of stones into the bucket, lifting them with grunts and heaves. The catapult's arm creaked and moaned as it was pulled back, then it sprang forwards, launching the missile. The heavy stone hit the Wall hard, broke into pieces and fell. The other catapult fired, its cargo hitting the Wall higher up than the first, with the same result.

The crewmen looked to Sharfy. 'Was it to your satisfaction, sir, as much as it was to ours?' said one. The others laughed.

'Keep trying,' said Sharfy, even more embarrassed. They fired again, again, again, until the pile of ammunition had been used up. They had large cudgels for breaking off more stones, if stones could be found, but made no indication of going to seek them.

For a moment, Sharfy thought he saw some sign of damage, but the markings on the Wall were just dabs of powdered stone. It wasn't going to work.

Anfen had sat and watched each flying rock without comment, closing his eyes about halfway through. Sharfy could actually see the ugly moment dawning. It was coming ... three, two, one ...

Anfen laughed. It was not a good thing for Sharfy to hear, for it was loud, uncaring and building to hysteria. He had seen Anfen walk with steady steps into grave danger and out of it, but hysteria was something he'd never thought the former First Captain capable of.

Anfen drew his sword and held it carelessly as he staggered towards the Wall. Sharfy followed him. The catapult crew, panting and sweating, watched him go. 'A sword!' one of them called, while the others laughed. 'Now *that's* a good idea.'

'You soften it up for us,' called another.

At the Wall, Anfen raised his sword and swung it: *chink*. No mark, no crack, nothing. He swung again and again, and beat it with his fists, sometimes laughing, sometimes screaming in rage. Sharfy winced at the senselessness of ruining such a good weapon, newly bought and all, probably one of the last things anyone would buy from an Elvury smith for some time. Panting, exhausted, Anfen sat at last leaning on the Wall and staring ahead.

'Combination of forces,' Anfen murmured, 'that's what he said. It can be done.'

'We should go and talk to the Mayors,' said Sharfy. 'Things've changed. They've lost a city. They'll listen, now. And you have one of them on side already, by the look of things.'

Anfen didn't reply.

'There's an inn not too far. Their ale's good, the crew were saying.' Still no answer. 'Tell you *what*,' Sharfy said, angry now; if he didn't deserve to be agreed with, he could at least be *heard*. '*I'll* go sleep there. Maybe for a week.' He looked nervously at the stoneflesh giant to the west, whose torso had now angled towards them, its interest in them growing. They were probably slow to get going, those ancient guardians, but slower yet to calm down . . .

'If you come to your senses any time in the next few days, come have an ale with me.' Sharfy went to his horse, hopped on and rode away, angling his path for the great dividing road.

Anfen sat there for an hour longer, hoping the giant would come and kill him. The catapult crews had called out to him: 'Sir? Master?' but eventually gave up and began the slow task of dismantling the machines.

The late afternoon gloom set in. Anfen stood, looked at the notched, dented sword. It had come up all right, considering how much he'd laid into the Wall. Suddenly he seemed to see himself for the first time in a long while, and was amazed and dismayed by the sight. An attack of stupidity and it lasted a whole week. What the hell am I doing out here?

He was almost inclined to laugh. Some broken rocks, a dented sword, and all the time he'd ridden down the great dividing road, he'd felt a burning sense that the world's fate hinged solely on *him* . . .

And as he succumbed to laughter, he saw someone else approaching. From her outline against the dimming sky, he knew it was her, but then the glimpse of a green dress was gone. Had she been there at all? 'Hey!' he called to the catapult crewmen. 'Did you see her?'

They traded amused looks. 'Yes, good sir. We see her. Very nice to look at, she is. Would you like us to leave you two alone?'

They roared with laughter. Anfen felt a white-hot flare of anger but he knew the men were right to mock him, however unused to the feeling he was.

He sat back, thinking about Stranger, wondering what she'd say or advise, if she were here. There'd been no sign of her, almost no thought of her since that early morning he'd stumbled out of the underground passage with his arm tired from killing.

A bird cackled its hoarse laughing call, shockingly loud from the bushes to the right of the war machines. The sound startled him, and he looked over only to see a few black feathers gently floating to the ground. Then from behind the scrub emerged a different outline, a limping, hobbling shape, carrying a forked silver staff. That wasn't Stranger.

Anfen got unsteadily to his feet, heart now beating very hard. The figure's limp was pronounced. A long tail of black feathers dragged on the ground behind. It threw back a hood and revealed three thick, heavy horns curving from the sides of its skull, and from the middle, which seemed to weigh down its head.

The Arch Mage turned to the catapults, stopped some way from them, raised both arms high. His body seemed to convulse. A wave of air blew from him, at first just sending pebbles and dust scattering before it swept through the catapults, their crewmen and beyond, blasting all of it into piles of rubble and red streaks in the air. The mess scattered a long way. The silence after the last piece had clattered to rest was one of the most complete he'd ever heard.

The Arch Mage turned slowly to face him. 'Catapults,' he said, a hint of humour in his cultured voice. Anfen stood with his sword poised, knowing it would be useless. How could death be denied him this time? How many times could a man who *wanted* it walk into its jaws and be spat out, when so many who cherished life were eaten away? No matter — he'd go out swinging it, if the enemy came close enough. His mind was very clear and light, suddenly. Here it came, at last. Here it came.

The Arch Mage hobbled closer, the blackened, shrivelled bone-thin leg unbending, but looking fragile enough to break under his weight. Thick gusts of smoke poured from his horns. 'Catapults,' he said with mirth. 'No matter, be heartened. I feel your mission will succeed.'

Ignoring the talk, Anfen held his weapon as though slumped and defeated, watching the Arch Mage hobble closer. The middle horn in his head let off a faint trail of smoke. The square gem in his eye socket, set in skin like cooled wax, spun around, rippling the flesh either side of it. If he was arrogant enough to get within striking range . . . 'Why do you want to talk with me?' said Anfen. 'Why not end it?'

'You are marginally more useful to me alive,' said the voice, mild and rich, pleasant to the ear. 'It may be that you end your own life in grief, or to spite me, but that's of little consequence. The Council of Free Cities knows you set out to do this deed. I made sure of it. They'll soon know you've succeeded, and your stories won't matter to them, whatever you tell them of me and my part. You will be credited for its consequences, not I. Yinfel's part in it will be known too, rest assured. It is already known. The Mayor right now justifies his decisions to the others. Their meeting must sound like a roomful of squabbling hens.'

'You saw the old man and his charm.'

'Of course I did, in the Hall of Windows. I had wished for the Pilgrims both to be with you at this moment, but that shouldn't matter too much. Nor did it matter that the charm and its message failed to reach your Mayors, nor that their decision had no impact on you. I've been fortunate.'

Anfen was counting down the distance, step by step, and was

about to charge, when the Arch Mage — making it seem an afterthought — swiped the air with one hand and and sent his sword cartwheeling sideways till it landed point-first in the ground. He stopped just a few arm spans from Anfen and regarded him with an expression made unreadable by the hideous ugliness of his half-melted face, though the voice softened with regret. 'It's true you've been used. Not all of us can sit on thrones, and enemies don't always do us harm. Know this, for my words are sincere. The conviction you showed, and the intentions you had, were not in themselves *bad* things. Even though by your ignorant measure they have led to a bad result. You have aided the Project, which is a good thing, though you do not think so. May this help shape your coming decision on whether or not you deserve to live or die.'

Anfen could not resist the impulse to rush at that hideous face and strike it. The Arch Mage watched him come, spun on his feet, and suddenly Anfen was careering face-first into the Wall, and struck it hard. The Arch Mage said, apparently to himself, 'Not itself a bad thing, to wish to strike me down. I have insulted your honour, used you as a tool, tarnished your name. All true.' He gazed up at the Wall. 'But for this, your forehead will not get the job done, I fear.'

Anfen crawled to his feet and stood unsteadily. There was a heavy *thud, thud* from away in the distance. The giant had finally decided it did not like the little strangers so close to its Wall, and now it had taken two steps towards them for a closer look. 'There!' said the Arch Mage, nodding again. 'Those, I imagine, have stronger heads than yours. Anfen, you may leave me. I have no use for you here. Go, decide whether you're to live or die. Your horse fled, I fear, when I destroyed the catapults. It will be a long walk for you. An opportunity to ponder things.'

Anfen feigned to walk away with his head slumped forwards,

defeated. He made another lunge, knowing it would be futile, and sure enough, the Arch Mage seemed only to shift his hands in the air, and Anfen found himself flying some distance away, landing heavily on his side.

'A long walk,' repeated the Arch Mage. 'Easier without a broken leg, which is the likely result of another attack on me. Sword in hand or no, your chances of harming me in the slightest are absolutely nil. It could be a painful lesson. The choice is yours. I have work to do.'

65

The Arch Mage peered at the horizon, where he saw something disconcerting: Nightmare was in the sky that way, looking over. And there, further east, another glimmer of light moved closer, which may well have been Wisdom. Until night fell completely, it would be hard to tell if it *was* her, but the power in the sky showed all the disturbances typical of a Great Spirit's presence.

Their presence was heartening in a way, for would they be here if he weren't about to succeed? Indeed, he knew he would; seering was not his field, but this event was a landmark so huge and obvious, even one as relatively blind as *he* had glimpsed it, common in half a dozen wildly varying futures. But how would the Spirits react *afterwards*? Best to get this done ...

The Arch Mage crouched low and began his illusion. It was a difficult one to cast, an original spell of his own make. Had the schools of magic still existed, they would have sung his praises for this creation; who said his only skills were war spells and necromancy? (The ruined schools had paid him *that* much homage, surely, after their temples were brought to ruin before their eyes ...)

He took in power from the air so abundant it was not unlike being back in the castle courtyard, then recited the spell's language. Here was where reality was asked to share what had been a private creation of his mind. The power within and about him slotted into place around the language running across his mind, like a quill across a page, like the very pages he'd carefully composed over years in his chamber. There was that moment of *disconnect* from reality that came with casting a big spell: for an instant — long to him, imperceptible to any observer — he was light as air, suspended from his physical form as though in momentary consultation with the fundamental forces holding all things together, to become for just that split moment a pattern streaked across the wind, which was for a private instant in conversation with the external reality paused around him, invited by the power the spell used, and by its carefully composed language, to *share* his private description; to make its described design — his private reality, made of no more than thought — part of *wider* reality, indifferent to thought, and adopted by whatever fundamental force had created and held aloft all the rest. Reality accepted the spell's design as sound, and agreed the designs and effects were now *real*. Power rushed in. Used-up power *whooshed* out of him like coughed air.

For any mages nearby, the cast spell's visible disturbance of force would be enormous. To say nothing of the burn of it through his body. Already the heat came strong, worse than it had been in practising, thanks to the weaker air (if it were much weaker, though, he would likely split apart like a struck melon). The charged wardens about his neck — rare items to come by, these days — had already absorbed more heat than would have killed him. And while they remained cool to the touch, that little part left over, which his body must endure, was already uncomfortably hot.

Now it began: glassy ripples of obscuring colourlessness puffed and bulged out from his feet, rising bit by bit into a large conical shape and rising like a great pillar of glass into the sky. It expanded and grew, in minutes shifting to adopt a humanoid shape. The colour of it turned basalt-grey.

Practising this spell had sent staff into panic, seeing a giant loose in the courtyard. The distant giant bought the illusion too; it moaned in displeasure as the *new* stoneflesh giant stood insolently close to its own sacred territory. The ground rumbled and shivered as great booming steps brought it over in an awkward swivelling run, legs stiff and unbending. The long misshaped fingers bunching into fists. Off to the east, the next-closest giant also turned to watch. From its mouth too came a warning like thunder at the sight of one giant already in its territory, and another fast approaching.

The Arch Mage backed close to the Wall. The plan had been to somehow lure the giant into a headlong charge. *That* was hoping for too much, it was now clear; the illusion was diffi-cult enough to maintain in relaxed conditions, even with much detail and fine shading sacrificed. The real giant's fist would, he hoped, swing around to pass through the illusory body like smoke, striking the Wall with force of a kind no man or machine in this world had yet at their disposal to employ. How many blows would it take — that was the next question.

So far so good: the real giant, now only metres away, bellowed, confused at the new one's position. Battles for territory were *not* fought close to the Wall; that risked destruction of what they were here to guard! This new giant, it seemed, did not know the rules. The real arm and fist swooped through the air, seeming to move slowly. Through the illusory body it cannoned into the Wall with a blow that made the ground rumble.

The earth shook some more as the other giant off in the east made its charge. The Arch Mage stood calmly in the shaking ground between four moving pillars and remembered what he'd seen in those futures: *it will succeed, it is ordained.* The fists of two enraged stoneflesh giants pounded the same part of the Wall, sometimes battering together within the Arch Mage's illusion.

Great cracks began to appear.

Stoneflesh giants further east and west began turning their heads at the distant racket, and they began to contemplate going over to investigate, for they felt the Wall behind them shiver.

66

Anfen did not watch the Arch Mage's work. He had risen to his feet and headed back towards the road. His body ached and he was deliriously tired, but these were pains he welcomed. It had been a temptation to go and stand in the middle of the giants' affray, be the death honourable or not, but then it had occurred to him precisely where he should go, and what he should do. Unless some peril claimed him on the road on his way there, as it was welcome to.

Behind him, the two enraged giants smashed their great fists through the illusion and into the breaking Wall. The Arch Mage willed them to hurry, knowing that while the Wall's destruction might be ordained, his own surviving the event was a variable. At last a piece of wall suddenly fell away and, the entire structure reacting like a pane of glass, great cracks spread far and wide.

That is enough, the Arch Mage thought, and dropped the illusion, quickly hiding himself with another, far simpler spell. Even this simple spell's heat threatened to tip him over the edge of endurance as he slunk away. Meanwhile the two confused giants now eyed each other off, pausing for just a moment to wonder what had become of the first enemy.

The Wall began to break from vibrations in the ground alone.

When a stray stoneflesh arm fell upon it, more huge pieces fell away, revealing a sky on the other side. The Arch Mage eagerly watched, as his horns poured smoke into the air and his cooking body cooled itself.

Here, he knew, came some uncertain events . . . even, perhaps, some deadly perilous ones for all in Levaal. Every operation bore costs and objectives, and this one had many of both, whatever the unknowns. And for the first time in *human* history, though not for the first time, the far half of Levaal would stand bare to the other.

67

He walked through the night, past nervous villagers who gathered at the great dividing road and stared towards the Wall, where the immense booming sounded like the world itself being pounded to dust. The ground could be felt to shake a long way away.

When the first piece of wall broke off and fell, Anfen felt a rush of wind pass overhead, cold or hot from one instant to the next. Like most, Anfen could not see the glimmering shades of magic in the sky, so he did not see the rush of foreign magic force pouring into Levaal's northern half, and he did not see the native magic pouring *out*. Nor did he see Arch Mage's huge Engineer-built airships parked in the sky some way west, built specially to collect as much of the new force as they could, raw and crude before it mixed with Northern Levaal's airs.

Nor did Anfen care any longer what might or might not happen, to him or the world. He finally understood how little he mattered, which was an enormous relief. All that mattered was the road he now had to walk. It would take some time. Now and then he would fall inert by the roadside, body simply refusing another step. He'd wake, find food, even if it was just a mouthful of leaves and roots, enough to keep him going to the destination he knew he deserved. Most he passed on the great dividing road, seeing the look in his eye, kept out of his way.

With the crowds of locals — some from nearby High Cliffs, some from as far afield as Tanton — Eric, Loup, and Siel watched with disbelief what seemed to be parts of the sky itself breaking off and falling down.

When clouds of foreign magic blew in through the higher gaps, Loup cursed loudly. 'I ain't going near any of *that*!' he cried. 'News to me, whatever it is, but I don't like the look of it at all. I'll be at Faifen, dead air or no. Away from the windows, mind.' He turned his horse, riding it away at a gallop.

Through larger holes, the foreign sky beyond was revealed. As night fell, little could be discerned through it — there were glimpses of hazy red colour, like distant fires, but mostly just the gloom of night. 'He did it,' Siel said for the tenth time, her voice no less disbelieving.

Sharfy, from the window of his inn, said the very same thing. He was quite drunk with ale — had indeed spent a fine evening trading tales with an old High Cliffs veteran in the pub down-stairs — but he knew he saw sights real enough. When a broken piece of wall landed in the inn's yard, smashing down on a wagon parked out front, he quickly packed his things and rode north as fast as he could. He did not know: was this a victory for the Free World, or were they now caught in a vice crushing from north *and* south?

By the roadsides, camps of watchers became a common sight as people stared, mostly in silence, at a dramatically changing horizon.

68

Case saw none of these events. His last sight was to have been the rapidly approaching ground, rising fast as a hand through the air to swat a bug. And this he saw for a second, sure enough — but he had not seen the Invia, who had been following his and Far Gaze's travels for some time, curious and cautious. She had wanted to wait longer yet, for she found the Otherworlder interesting, the shapeshifting mage too, and she wished to know why the old man had been at the centre of so much interest.

When the old man's body was offered to the void, the Invia exclaimed in surprise, then swooped as fast as she could to catch it.

Case just laughed as the Invia bore him skywards, higher and higher with its beating wings. 'Here's good!' he cried, 'drop me here! My God, what a view!'

But of course she wouldn't drop him.

The entire world soon spread out below Case's feet and the wind blew cold, buffeting him. The Invia's grip on him was painfully hard and never seemed like slipping. She did not speak. Where was she taking him? Sightseeing? Why? Why *did* all these creatures and strange magic-using women and man-wolves care about *him*, anyway? It didn't matter! It was all one jump away from being over.

Then he remembered — the charm! Maybe the Invia wanted it back. But why not just take the necklace? Why take him too? He toyed with the idea of dropping it into the sky. Why not? What would it do, kill him? What a shame. He groped in his pocket, but as soon as he pulled it free, the Invia snatched it from his grasp and kept flying up, its long white wings beating the air.

With his eyes on the view below — they had long passed above the clouds, whose shadows crept across the slopes and dips of the landscape — Case did not notice the approaching layer of lightstone bright above his head, dimming with the approach of evening. Only when the Invia took him right to the sky's outer layer did he see it, and marvel at the great curved dome arching across countless acres of sky. But he only got to see it briefly before he was within the sky-roof itself, passing into a crack in the thick layer of lightstone giving way to the dark grey stone above it.

The Invia paused, crouching on a ledge to rest. Above them, the rock funnelled vertically into a gloomy distance, far enough that the light was eventually swallowed. Case was free now to step off and into the deep, long plunge to ground, whether or not the Invia would catch his fall. But suddenly he was intrigued. 'Where are we?' he asked.

She looked at him, weighing the question as though to find if it was worth an answer. Apparently, it was: 'Takkish Iholme.'

'And what's that?'

'The prison of the dragon-youth. A bit higher up and their voices can be heard. If they wish to speak. Mostly, they don't. We are closest to Vyin's prison. He is the youngest, but older than Mountain.'

Case laughed. He still felt light-spirited and free. 'Dragon-youth ... does that mean dragons? Real actual dragons?'

This question was apparently not worth an answer. He tried another. 'Why've you brought me here?'

The Invia weighed his question again then shrugged. 'They asked for you.'

ACKNOWLEDGEMENTS

I'd like to thank Lyn Tranter for her faith in me (not to mention her patience), and Kirsten Tranter, both of whom endured the very first rough draft of this work and provided crucial feedback and encouragement; Stephanie Smith of HarperCollins for taking a chance on me and for her encouragement and patience; Kate O'Donnell, my fantastic editor; Ken for his kindness and advice, without which I'd have imploded long ago; Malcolm Knox and Wenona for their guidance early on; Ali Lavau and Jo Mackay, whom I should have thanked in the previous book's acknowledgements; Carsten from Piper; all the fine folks at HarperCollins and at ABC Books; and thanks to all my friends, family and readers.

Turn the page for a sneak peek
at the second book in the Pendulum Trilogy

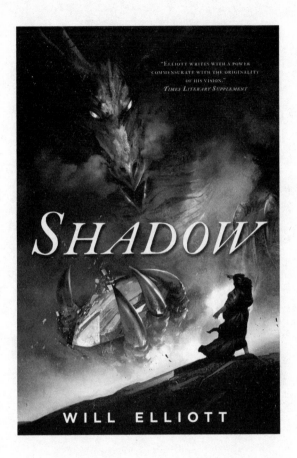

Available February 2015

OUTSIDE OF TIME

1

There are horse hooves thudding on the Great Dividing Road. Their beat is fast, urgent. The world has the soft blurred edges of a dream, the deep purple twilight seeming to filter through water. Fragments of memory like broken possessions float in a dark pool but do not break through to its surface. There is just the beating of hooves: closer, closer it comes.

The man's heart, recently still, now beats in time with that sound. He groans. Warmth flushes through his cold flesh, beat by beat, until it reaches his stiff cold fingers. He cannot remember a thing, not a cursed *thing*: not his name, not how he came to be here in a pool of dried blood. His hand goes to his belly, his hand remembering something his mind does not. Then to his neck.

A light approaches from the south, comes close, swallows him, then heat is washing over him in pulsing waves. Above him is a rider on horseback, who pulls his steed to a halt. It hurts to look at the rider directly. The steed has silver barding which glows jewel-bright. Halted or not, the man can still hear the hoofbeats thudding down. 'Who are you?' he says hoarsely.

A voice, quietly commanding, answers, 'I am Valour. You are reprieved.'

Blooming light flares brightly about the god, filling all the world. The man feels for a long time that he is floating in it, laughing, forgetting everything and knowing only joy until the god speaks again to drag him back to the Great Dividing Road and the pool of dried blood. 'Hear me,' says Valour. 'There shall be no second reprieve, if again you fall. Not for you, nor for any other. I have altered the world itself to return your mortal life. I cannot do so again, lest my creator rise in wrath. Do you understand?'

'I do, my redeemer,' he says though he does not understand. He tries to see the god's face but cannot find its features in the light. He can feel Valour's gaze upon him, cold and warm at once.

'Stand again. You are a warrior, not a servant.'

He staggers to his feet. 'For what purpose do I live, my redeemer?'

'Act as you will: with freedom, till death take you. Take you it shall. But I say this: do not serve the brood. Come what may. Whether I leave this land or remain.'

'But, my redeemer . . . why would you go?' The thought fills him with profound sadness.

'The brood wish to be free, for we Spirits to be gone. The day will come when I must ride to war. I do not know my future.' The light about Valour begins to withdraw.

'Wait! I love you dearly. Stay with me! I do not understand your words, my redeemer.'

'Then hear this. There are two great Dragons, not one. Now they are naked before each other. Ours still sleeps, the far one is awake. They bend their thoughts to war. The Conflict Point is World's End, where stood the Wall. Where the Great Road meets its twin.'

Valour tosses to the ground a chest-panel of plated metal. It lands with hardly a sound. Atop this he drops a sword, sheathed. 'I give you a part of myself,' says Valour, 'so that part of myself remains, if I am sent away. I cannot better aid a mortal man than this. You will take this sword, this armour. If you find a steed, tell it my name and it will serve you. *Do not serve the brood.* For the Pendulum has begun to swing. Hear me? The Pendulum has begun to swing.'

Tears run down the man's face. Then Valour is gone, and the only way he knew it was no dream or fevered vision is the armour and sword lying there for him, and the pools of dried blood. And his heart, beating again.

IN THE SKY

1

'*Asked* for me?' Case laughed. 'Now why the Christ would a bunch of fucking monster dragons or whatever you got up here ask for *me*?'

Evidently this was a question not worth answering, for the Invia ignored it. Her staring eyes were bright as little pools of water in sunlight, though they and her parted lips expressed nothing other than that she watched him. Case wondered if any human emotion stirred beneath. The wind gaily tossed around her snowy hair and ruffled her wings' long soft feathers. She stood on a shelf of air and stared.

Case's feet dangled from the edge of a jutting shelf just above the thick layer of the sky's lightstone. Though it was dimming to usher in night, its brightness was still painful. A long, long way below them the ground waited to thump the life out of him. He was beginning to get impatient for it. He'd flap his arms on the way down, whoop and bray like a jackass. Try not to land on anyone who didn't deserve it, though the odds were slim. He pictured a bunch of people going about their business and a suicidal old man landing among them making a hell of a mess, and he burst out laughing. He tossed his hat into the sky; the wind whisked it out of sight. 'If I jump, you're going to catch me, aren't you?'

Said the Invia, 'Yes. Don't!'

He laughed. 'Why the hell not?'

'It would annoy me.'

'Which would be just tragic. S'cuse me a moment, some things never go out of fashion.' Case scratched his balls with vigour. The Invia unfurled her wings and picked him up with effortless strength. 'Watch what the fuck you're doing!' he snarled as her hands pinched his underarms, already tender from the long flight after she'd plucked him from his would-be plunge to the death.

Her wings beat the air as she carried him higher through a funnel of deep grey stone, away from the lightstone, up to where she had to push him from beneath through a gap hardly big enough. After an uncomfortable crawl the space widened out to a vast cavern of smooth dark walls. Wind came at intervals through a hundred off-shooting holes bored in the cavern's domed roof and walls, singing eerie notes like a huge woodwind instrument being randomly blown. Now and then echoing inhuman cries reached them from deeper within.

Despite himself, Case was intrigued by the sense this vast bare dome was ancient, far older than anything people had built anywhere. Its age pressed down on him so tangibly he could *feel* it. The air was thick with a strange smell. 'Where're your dragons then?' he said.

'Not here! This is the Gate. They never come here. Not much.'

There was a distant thudding sound. The stone underfoot just faintly shivered. The Invia gave a fluttery excited whistle.

'That was *big*, whatever that was,' Case said. He sniffed deeply, trying to place the air's scent. His head began to spin and suddenly he was on his back. His thoughts spun dizzily until they broke down and became colours and shapes floating before his eyes – all the world just coloured shapes, each with its own simple meaning which needed no elaboration. Then there was a pleasant taste he sucked at greedily, something pressing against his lips. Slowly his mind came back together.

The Invia's expressionless eyes peered at him closely while she put her gashed wrist to his mouth, feeding him her blood. 'Are you alive?' she said.

Case wanted to make a smart-arse remark but all that came out was, 'Ehhhh . . .'

'No walkers come here,' she said. A deep piping note played with a blast of cold wind from a nearby tunnel, throwing her hair around. 'The air is very strong here. Walkers are soft as their skin. They don't like it. Foolish walkers.'

There was a burst of movement and the tunnel directly over-head sang its high-blown note. A small flock of Invia poured through, filling the space about the tunnel's mouth. They exchanged fluttery whistles. Each of them shot off in a different direction, one alone pausing to stare down at Case before it flashed away in a blur of white wings and skin and scarlet hair.

The Invia waited for Case to recover from his faint. He was shaken by sudden cravings for half-a-dozen chemicals he'd been hooked on, once upon a time. He'd taught his body in the end to be content with just the booze; it was the best he could do. 'Not sure what hit me there,' he said.

'You're old, for a walker. And sick. Your aura's bad. Faint and sick.'

'Yeah well. You know my idea to fix all that. But you won't let me.' The enormous dome stretched in all directions further than he could see. 'What is this place for anyway? Doesn't look like a gate to me.'

She tapped the grey stone floor with a knuckle. 'Strong skystone. This keeps them here. They cannot break it. Or fit through gaps. They can't even change shape to fit through! It was made for this.'

'Got it,' he said.

'And the gods. *They* make sure it holds. This is how it works.'

'Yes, ma'am.'

'If the gods went away, it might be different.'

'I'll see what I can do.'

She leaned close to him, her bright sparkling eyes going wide. 'Already, Dyan escaped. He's just a Minor, but clever. There could be others, soon. They are trying to find out how. It's hard. Are you ready to fly?'

Case sat up, rubbing his head. Taking this for assent she grabbed him and flew, picking out a gap in the roof from the scores around it. Cold air blasted out in a low note, painfully loud as they plunged through the wide stone maw, the tunnel snaking around but always leading upward. From off-shooting ones to either side came the occasional shriek reminiscent of the Invia's dying wail he'd heard at Faul's place. The sounds' meanings he caught but they made no sense to him, much like catching only one or two words in a long conversation.

After a time the Invia sat him on one of the ledges set in the tunnel's sides, cocked her head and listened. Wind blasted through with a low thrumming note; within the gust a flock of Invia shot past in a blur of white feathers. Case's Invia wrapped her wings around him, shielding him from any accidental collision. Her cool cheek pressed against his; her wings about him imparted strange tenderness, protecting him as an animal protects its young, no human sentiment in the gesture at all. Still he'd have happily stayed in the soft feathered nest all day.

When the flock had passed, she said, 'They heard him speak. Just a word. They have not heard him for a long while! *I* have. They are excited. They should come here more often. Those ones always pester Tsy. He dislikes them.'

Her face showed unusual animation. Not wanting her to remove the tiny house of soft feathers (he stroked them) he said, 'Who spoke?'

'Vyin. He knows you are here. You heard his feet press down, when he leaped from a perch. That was when we were in the Gate. You didn't hear his voice. Walkers can't, unless he lets you.'

She picked him up and on they flew, through an endless labyrinth of stone.

2

In the maze's deepest darkness were what seemed life forms made of strange light, their bodies a twisted glowing core within a blurry nest, their flickering fingers groping blindly at the cavern about them as if seeking flaws or cracks.

There were times the dark was so utterly black Case could grab handfuls of gloom from the air and *feel* it as he squeezed it in his fist. There were passages where the stone creaked and wept with the bitter sadness of someone wishing desperately for the bright world below: for running water, trees, winds, oceans to dive into, glaciers to swat through the waves with a gush of foam and breaking ice, lands to beat into sculpted shapes. But there was only this darkness, the pressing stone walls – the cruellest cage ever made – with no quick and easy mortal death freedom for those here imprisoned. Case almost drowned in the sadness pouring through him, pouring through the very stones. He could not help weeping. Even the Invia wept, her tears splashing down on his head as she brought him higher, deeper and into the sadness, out of his life and into a dream he was sure he'd had long ago.

Then the narrow ways poured into an open space even more vast than the Gate had been. Below them was a kind of ziggurat, a structure of strangely laid slabs of shining black metal with long arms stretching off at different points. The arms spun slowly. More such designs were set into the walls and roof, ugly and incomprehensible things. A city of such buildings stretched back into the dark, though no living beings moved on the smooth barren ground that he could see. A river gouged into the stone floor cast up a long wedge of brilliant light.

The strange smell was overpowering. Again Case's thoughts dissolved to shifting coloured shapes; again the Invia fed him her sweet nourishing blood to bring him back to consciousness. They flew toward a high roof of gleaming stone, carved with runes through which brilliant colour moved and flowed, as though the cavern had a heart and pulse, and these colours were its lifeblood pumping beneath the dark stone skin.

Case threw up.

The Invia descended with a noise of annoyance at the puke on her forearms. 'I should not be here,' she said. 'I would not be, if you could come yourself. Silly walker! You cannot fly.'

She had only just set him down when there was a sense of something large rushing toward them, a mouth opening wide enough for Case to walk inside, pearl-white teeth so close Case would have (if he'd had time) been certain meant to eat him.

Instead, the Invia gave a surprised squawk as the jaws closed upon her. The thing – whatever it was – rushed away with her so fast it was gone in the ink-thick gloom before he'd turned around to check he'd actually seen what he thought he'd seen.

'Hello?' he said.

A high-pitched wail bloomed through the cavern from the direction she'd gone, its echo slow to fade. Something further away called in answer, but the sound was not made by an Invia. Then silence fell.

For want of better ideas, Case walked to the bank of that glowing river, which seemed filled not with water but with liquid light. Despite its brilliance the light did not penetrate the cavern far or deeply. The footing was bad and Case could not see what he slipped and staggered on – it felt powdery. Bits and pieces like beach shells kicked from his feet and clattered musically together. In parts the floor was ankle-deep with them. Shells? He knelt, felt one, and found it was actually a scale, its colour hard to make out this far from the river's light. The scale was similar but not as big as those Kiown and Sharfy had made such a big deal of. He fished around in the powdery litter for a whole one, compared it with the memory of those Eric had shown him. Smaller, he judged, and thinner.

About Case loomed the odd tall structures he'd seen from high up, twisting and writhing like living alien things. He had to rub his eyes, for it seemed the nearest structure was solid as metal yet behaving like liquid, fluidly changing shape and remoulding itself.

He pegged a scale at it. As though by magnetic force, the spinning scale was drawn to the structure's wall, struck it then glanced away with a *chink!* The moving structure froze motionless, so suddenly it imparted a sense of vertigo that made him stagger. There fell heavily on Case a sense of being observed.

' he called. 'Any chance of a beer?'

The structure burst into motion again with greater speed. He looked away, dizzy.

It was then that a voice seemed to vibrate through Case's body: *You stare at things I have made. But you do not understand them.*

The glimmering light-play over the roof snuffed itself out. He felt something approach, something huge. A swirl of darkness blacker than the rest gathered itself up before him and assumed a massive shape. Close by there was a thundering *boom, boom*: the noise of very heavy pillars being dropped. Case felt and heard the ground groaning under the weight of something enormous. Two points high above gleamed and sparkled down at him in twin bursts of unclasped light.

Case could only laugh in awe. Around the two lights – eyes, he understood, though they seemed like pieces of a star – was a huge head, reared back on an enormously long, arching neck, between huge, spreading, pinioned wings. *Look away*, the voice ordered.

Case looked away.

The voice seemed to come not from the dragon's head, but from the ground at Case's feet, vibrating through his whole body. It said, *I have not been beheld by your kind before. I find I do not wish to be. To have you here brings me not rage, as I'd feared it might. It brings a sadness I had not expected.*

I try now to speak in a voice like yours, so you can hear me. It is difficult to express so little. To express much more would drown your mind with my thought and nothing left of yours.

Case laughed again. He had never been so small in all his life and the feeling was somehow liberating. Why fear? This enormous monster was really no larger than familiar old death! 'Are you *the* Dragon?' he said. 'The one they all talk about?'

I am Vyin, the eighth of its young. At your feet is a gift I crafted. It was not made for you. Do not touch it yet. Look at it.

On the ground something flashed among the piles of broken and powdered scale. It was a necklace, gleaming and beautiful. *The others do not know my thoughts, or of your being here. With effort and cunning I hide you from them. I hide this gift also, though they will learn of it in time, and they will rage. It may be that they make gifts of their own, to be this gift's kin, and rival. They may try. If so, they have less than the lifespan of a man to do what I have done with care over many lifetimes of men. A thousand eventualities I saw. In the crafting I prepared for each. Their efforts will be rushed. Do not touch it yet. Watch me.*

One of the dragon's feet shifted forward, swept away a mound of crushed scale and revealed smooth stone beneath, which creaked and groaned as its foot pressed down. Scales rippled, tendons pulled taut as clawed toes bigger than Case clenched, breaking off a piece of the floor. The great beast's paw turned upward. On it lay a slab of stone the size of a car. Vyin's claws wrapped around it.

This, and all things, are made of the same stuff, only in different amounts and arrangements. Watch. Vyin crushed the slab, the cracking noise of it like firing guns; crushed it so thoroughly only fine dust remained when the dragon's paw opened again. A faintly blown breath puffed the dust into the air where it hung in a glimmering cloud. The dragon's paw brushed through it. *I can shape from this raw material many better things, things of more use than the stone it was before. Do you understand me?*

Case felt dizzy. 'No. No, sir, I don't.'

The dragon's huge head bent closer to him; faint hints of light flickered across its rippling scales. *You too are made of this* *t* said, *though each of your kind is arranged uniquely. Things*